I0629680

James Harrington's

Magnifica

The Last Enchanter

ISBN: 978-0615827681
First Printing, June 2013
Revised Printing, February 2017
Cover Art by Tina Pankievich
Editing by Meghan Harrington

This is a work of fiction. Names, characters, businesses, places, events and incidents are either the products of the author's imagination or used in a fictitious manner.

This book is dedicated to my loving wife and son, without whom, this would never have been written.

"I don't know about this, sister. Are you sure?"

"Yes Roselyn, their story needs to be told."

"I doubt many will believe us."

"I know that, but we owe our friends as much. If it wasn't for them, our world might not exist anymore."

"Ariel … I hope you are right…"

"Let's begin."

Chapter I

"Toby, get up! You're going to be late for class!"

Toby's eyes shot open and he sat up quickly without thinking. A loud thud and blunt pain almost instantly flowed through his head as it impacted on the top bunk, "Ow, f...!"

He slammed his fist against the bed frame before glaring at the person who had roused him. His roommate stood at the door pointing a stubby finger at the clock on his wall, "Come on man, it's 8:45! You know how Professor Arias reacts to tardiness."

Toby shook his head as he fixed his dark brown hair, "Gishan you're a dwarf, don't you have a stone somewhere to bang?"

The stubby teen crossed his arms, "Oh funny! Because all dwarves are miners, right? At least we live more than a measly hundred years."

"All right, all right, I'm up. Happy?"

"What would you do if you didn't have me around?"

"Find a less annoying roommate!"

Once the pain went away, Toby stood up and looked around. His dorm room was a mess. Clothes and empty beer bottles littered the floor, the posters were falling off the wall, and the beds looked like they hadn't been made in months.

Toby could have cleaned things, but he was used to it being this way. *It's not a mess, it's controlled chaos.*

At least that's what he told himself as he quickly grabbed a shirt off the floor, threw it on over the wrinkled jeans he had been sleeping in. Nearly dressed, he grabbed a pair of sandals and slid them on his feet.

"Really," Gishan scoffed, "sandals in February?"

Toby looked up at his roommate as he strapped them around his ankles, "How warm has it been out recently, 60 degrees?"

"Still too cold for me…"

Once Toby was ready, he grabbed his books and joined Gishan at the door. He easily towered over the dwarf by at least 2 feet, "Okay I'm ready, let's go."

"I think it might be time for a laundry run." Gishan sighed as he scratched his chin stubble.

"Too much trouble besides, weren't we just at your parent's house?"

"Yeah," Gishan chuckled as he turned to the door, "well… we could always do it ourselves?"

Looking at the piles of laundry that were almost completely covering their floor, Toby had a sudden change of heart. He hated having his roommate's mother help him with laundry, but the pile had grown to the point where their small washers wouldn't do the job. Plus he knew his uncle would never help him out with it. "Fine… Why don't you give your mother a call and see if they would like a visit this weekend."

"Thought you'd see it my way. Come on, we're going to be late."

Toby followed his roommate out the door and down the hallway. Unlike their room, the hall was almost sterile with beautiful carvings of heroic figures on the walls and newly polished hard wood floors.

The building was quite old as was evidenced by the musty smell and the old style steam heaters that lined the hallway. Most of the residents had lost count of how many times the clanking and hissing of those heaters had kept them awake.

Toby had been known to spend hours inspecting the carvings on the walls trying to determine who they were of, but there was no time for that now. The two friends raced down the hall, flew down the front staircase, and found themselves in the main courtyard.

It was another unusually warm day at Arcanus College in North Boston. The sun shined down over last remaining piles of snow from a pre-Christmas storm. It had been the only snow they'd seen that year.

Various students, both dwarven and human made their way to various engagements and classes across campus. Everyone was dressed as though it were spring weather. Most had on jeans and t-shirts, but still kept jackets with them just in case.

The main building was almost a quarter of a mile across campus, though it seemed longer than that to Toby. By the time they reached their classroom, the door was already closed. They were late.

Gishan shrugged, "Well we could just chalk this up as a sick day?"

"No way," Toby replied, "today we're learning about the second war of the Alliance. It's the big one, and I don't want to miss it."

"Fine," Gishan replied, knowing that there was no point in arguing, "but I never got what you loved so much about these fairy tales. They happened thousands of years ago. Hell, we don't even know how much of these stories really happened and how much is mythology. Why did we even take this class? What does a 'Survey of Pre-Western Civ.' have to do with either of our majors?"

"It's one of the last core requirements I need to graduate. You can go back if you want, but I'm going in."

"Whatever dude, right behind you…"

The two of them slowly opened the heavy wooden door in an attempt to sneak in unnoticed. They proceeded into a lecture hall with over a hundred students in attendance and tried to find open chairs in the back of the auditorium. Their plan failed however, when a gruff voice from behind made them jump, "Ah Gishan Nemog and Tobias Arrigan, so glad you could make it."

Shit...

Shit!

The two friends turned to see that Professor Arias had been watching them the entire time. The man towered over the two boys with his arms crossed under his black robes. His white hair was indicative of dealing with students like Gishan and Toby a little too long, "That's what now? Three times you've been late to class? We haven't even been in session two weeks!"

"Sorry Prof," Gishan replied, "we um…"

"Were up drinking rock salt vodka all night." Arias interrupted, finishing his sentence. "That's pretty much all I've heard you talk about. If you lay off that dwarven swill, you might actually make it to class on time."

Soft chuckling could be heard around the room as the professor turned back to the board, "That'll be a five page paper, typed, single-space, due on Friday for the two of you. I want you to examine the significance of the Second Alliance War with emphasis on the Ulium Plague."

"The Elven plague." Toby whispered to Gishan as they sat down.

"I know!" The dwarf spat back. "Believe it or not, I do pay attention."

The professor glared at them both, "Glad to hear it. Now if you two don't mind, I have a class to teach."

Toby nodded, "Sorry professor, it won't happen again."

Professor Arias rolled his eyes as he turned to his board, not believing a word of anything they said, "All right open you books to…"

"Excuse me…" A faint voice chimed in from the back of the room. "I'm very sorry I'm late."

The whole class turned to see who had spoken this time. The professor's eyes followed the voice to the back of the room. Standing at the door was a young woman with fair skin, bright hazel eyes, and long blonde hair. Her bangs were partially braided and tied around the back of her head to keep her them out of her eyes.

Toby's eyes widened as he saw her standing behind him. Her slender body and beautiful face made it difficult for him to turn away. She was fairly tall, somewhere around 5'7 or 5'8, he guessed. Then he noticed something extremely irregular. As she brushed her hair back, revealing her ear, he noticed that it was slanted slightly back and was ended in a sharp point at the top. This was no human female.

He quickly turned back to face forward. *No way...*

An air of disgust came over the room as Professor Arias looked at her with scornful eyes, "Ah this does seem to be the day for tardiness... Well, who are you?"

The girl spoke with a light accent that wouldn't have been recognizable to most, but Toby picked up on it right away, "My name is Lia'na of the White Water Clan. I just transferred to Arcanus this spring and signed up on the last day of open registration."

She walked down the aisle to the professor and handed him a piece of paper. He took the sheet and only half-glanced at it, "Oh very well… Looks like I'm going to have to have a few words with the people at registration… take a seat Leena."

"Lia'na, sir... it's pronounced..."

"Very well." The professor interrupted. "Take a seat so we can get started."

"Lien ni, Professor."

She turned to look for an open seat and spotted one near the back of the room. The moment she sat down, the students around her moved away or turned their desks so that she couldn't see their faces. She looked down at her books and looked like she was trying to pretend she didn't notice.

Toby couldn't believe his eyes, "Are you seeing this, Gishan, an elf, here at Arcanus."

Gishan snorted, "Not many of those sharpys left. Wonder what brought her out of the woods?"

"No idea."

"Something wrong?" Toby asked, seeing the disgusted look on Gishan's face.

"Elves and dwarves have never gotten along. Let's just leave it at that."

"Whatever. I thought elves had their own colleges."

"Well she's here now. Just keep her eyes off me. I've heard they can bewitch you."

"Oh relax Gishan, I don't think she's going to come anywhere near you. Where do you get this stuff?"

Gishan didn't reply, opting to eye Lia'na for a few moments before turning back to Professor Arias as the lecture began. Toby was mystified by Lia'na's appearance. Even though she dressed like any normal girl in their early twenties, her fashion sense was quite elegant and what most people had come to expect from an elf-girl. She wore a white blouse that had short sleeves, a square neck, and seemed to drape down over her stomach like a dress. Her black jeans had odd, stiched-on, designs going up the legs that seemed to shimmer in the sunlight.

After a few moments, Lia'na looked up at Toby and returned his gaze. He quickly turned his attention back to the front of the room, hoping Lia'na hadn't seen him staring at her. *Shit.*

She smiled and went back to straightening out her books as class continued, looking up every so often to see if she could catch him staring again.

II

Professor Arias was a brilliant lecturer, who clearly knew his stuff. Not only that, but he seemed to enjoy teaching. Still there was only so much history Gishan could take in one sitting. He could feel his stubby legs ache as the class dragged on. More than anything, he wanted to be outside doing something. He fidgeted around as Toby hung on every word the professor spoke.

Professor Arias finished the first part of his lecture dealing with how the First Alliance War had begun. He then moved on to the Elven history segment, "Now who can tell me what caused the Ulium disease that contributed to the downfall of the Elven clans and the endangerment of the species?"

A few hands went up, including both Toby's and Lia'na's. Arias ignored Lia'na's hand and turned to Toby, "Mr. Arrigan splendid, let's see if you've been studying."

"Sir, according to what the ancient texts, provided by the dwarves, tell us is that during the Second Alliance War, a group of elves sacrificed themselves to destroy the Lux Mundi."

"Very good, and what is the Lux Mundi?"

Toby thought carefully about what he had read online a few nights earlier. His textbook had disappeared under a pile of his clothes, so he held out hope the Wikipedia's information was accurate. "The translation is 'Earth's Light.' It's believed to have been a large monolith made of solid diamond."

"You might want to look more into your studies, Mr. Arrigan. The actual translation is 'Light of the World.' You were close, but not quite there. That would get you a B in my class, unacceptable."

Toby rolled his eyes while Arias turned back to his board and drew a picture of a massive diamond. As he worked, Toby began mocking the professor's words and hand gestures. He wasn't certain, but he thought he'd heard a giggle come from Lia'na's direction as the professor continued, "However, the rest of your information is correct. This monolith was said to be an unusual orange-colored diamond and is believed to have not been from this world."

Toby sat back and soaked up everything the professor said like a child listening to a bedtime story, "Legend tells us that a huge meteor fell from the sky soon after the formation of the Alliance and slammed into the summit of Mount Vesuvius. A group of dwarves that had been mining in that area saw the impact and proceeded to investigate. Upon finding the meteor crash site, they discovered the Lux Mundi and, thinking that it was a gift from the Gods, built a shrine around it. This shrine stood for many thousands of years, through uncountable wars."

Another student raised his hand and was immediately called on, while once again Lia'na was ignored, "Professor, can you talk about the correlation between wizardry and the Lux Mundi."

"I'd be happy to. Based on the latest scientific analysis of the Vesuvius crater, researchers have theorized that the meteor came from our asteroid belt. They believe that billions of years of direct exposure to the sun contributed to the unusual radioactive properties that the diamond possessed. The radiation mutated the cells of many humans and dwarves, giving people the ability to cast magic and thus wizardry was born… or so the theory says."

Arias took in a deep breath as though he was bracing himself to give them bad news, "During the Second Alliance War, many enchanters vied for power in the Alliance, believing themselves to be the rightful rulers. After a continual stalemate, the Elven clans sought to end the fighting and believed that the only way to do it was to stop the enchanters. In their minds, magic was the direct cause of the war. They broke rank with the Alliance and marched to the summit of Vesuvius. There they conducted a sacrificial ritual and destroyed the Lux Mundi."

Lia'na felt glaring eyes being levied against her like a cold breeze passing over her skin. She huddled her shoulders together and attempted to ignore it as the professor continued his lecture, "Whatever they did caused a catastrophic eruption which covered the land around Mt. Vesuvius, including some scattered cities. The few elves that made it off the mountain were stricken with an illness that no one had encountered before. Slowly over several millennia, the disease began to fester amongst the Elven people. Herbs and medicines helped slow the disease to a crawl, but eventually the illness would claim every elf."

He looked at Lia'na as the next part of his lecture began, "However part of the fallout of World War 2 was the discovery of the existence of elven tribes. Some had been captured by the Nazis, and out of fear, were placed into camps. Following the war, other clans came out of hiding, asking for help with the Ulium. The dwarves returned to the surface after sensing the tectonic shifts resulting from our atomic bomb attacks on Japan. Fortunately for the elves, we had made significant scientific and medical advancements during the war. Funding from the new United Nations was allocated to finding a cure, and as you all know by the fact that one of them is now a classmate of yours, they were successful. Elven infants began to be inoculated during the mid-1960s."

A dwarven student on the other side of the room sneered, "Should have just let them die!"

Toby looked over at the boy and then at Lia'na. He turned in time to see a tear fall from her eye as she spoke up, "Excuse me, Professor, but your information is incorrect."

Oh dear God... Toby thought to himself as every eye in the place focused on the young elf-girl.

Arias was a very prideful person who did not like to be challenged, especially by a new student, but he beckoned to her to stand. Lia'na obeyed his gesture and once she was on her feet, the professor addressed her in a condescending tone, "Well then please educate us with the correct information."

Lia'na nodded, "I apologize for the outburst professor, but elves have never believed that magic was evil. Our people believed that the diamond was creating the abominations that plagued our land. That, and the constant factionalist wars, started by enchanters attempting to gain control of the alliance, was slaughtering innocents by the millions. My people are a peaceful race; we wanted an end to the blood-letting and saw the destruction of that sacred diamond as the only answer."

Scattered laughter could be heard around the room. Even Professor Arias had to cover his mouth to hide a smirk. Lia'na stood in silence, facing down the scornful stares of her classmates.

Arias quickly regained his composure and cleared his throat, "Leena, what you are referring to are myths and legends that were passed down by Elven elders in an attempt to quell the hatred of your people. There is no evidence that such creatures existed at that time. What we do know is that your ancestors' actions are what destroyed the Alliance. Following the destruction of the Lux Mundi at around 60,000 B.C., the dwarves withdrew from the Alliance and burrowed deep underground while you elves hid deep in the rainforests, jungles, and remote areas of the world, leaving mankind to fend for itself. The loss of magic and the vacuum of power caused multiple wars and endless strife. As a result, almost all records of man's scientific and engineering achievements from then were lost to myth and legend and their cities were reduced to rubble."

Professor Arias pulled down a map and displayed it to the class. Toby recognized it as a map of Northeast Africa and the Middle East in the Iraqi area. Arias continued speaking as he pointed at it, "Mankind literally had to start over without any help. After the collapse of the Alliance, it appears that people split up into small tribes and nomadic colonies based solely on their geographical locations. The ancient language was altered and slurred, becoming several different languages. For thousands of years, the elves and dwarves became part of the myths surrounding the Alliance, having cut themselves off from humanity. It is theorized that some Norsemen may have had brief contact with elves as they explored their homeland. This would account for much of the Norse mythos we now have. Over time, human settlements took to warring amongst each other, having no central government. We were left to bring this world back into order, and for thousands of years, we did just that."

Professor Arias turned and pointed at the map, "Until discoveries of the ancient Alliance cities covered by volcanic ash at the base of Mount Vesuvius, deep underneath the Pompeii ruins, it was believed that the Mesopotamian Empires such as the Akkadian and the Babylonian were the earliest central empires on Earth. What we know now is that they were merely the first empires created exclusively by man. The Alliance had existed several thousands of years prior. What was so tragic about this is that while the Empires were a massive step forward for man, in every measurable sense, they were easily three thousand years less advanced than the Alliance. So unfortunately, that is the legacy left to us by the elves."

Lia'na remained standing, expressionless. Gishan shook his head, "Is she just going to stand there taking that abuse? Why doesn't she just sit down?"

Toby watched her for a few moments, she had a stoic look on her face, but her eyes looked sad. After a few moments of watching her, he couldn't stand it anymore. He stood up without a word to Gishan and spoke, "But Professor, wasn't there recently an archeological find in Romania which indicated that creatures such as the griffon and Cyclops may have existed at some point?"

Arias rolled his eyes, "Yes, yes, I have heard similar stories. However those fossils are believed to have been from millions of years before the wars. If these creatures existed during the age of the Alliance, then there should be more surviving evidence besides myths and legends. Does that mean they didn't exist? Not at all, but until we find evidence of them living around the time period in question, I'm afraid all we have to go on is the history in our books. So let's not give into wild ideas."

"Okay." Toby replied as he returned to his seat, ignoring Gishan's suspicious stare. He looked over at Lia'na who also had finally sat back down. She flashed Toby an appreciative smile before turning her attention back to Professor Arias.

As the professor finished his speech, he looked at his watch and smiled, "Well it looks like that's all we have time for today. Tonight, read chapter's 3 and 4 in your books, on Wednesday we'll be talking about the beginning of the Mesopotamian civilizations. Have a good rest of the day."

The students got up and filed out. Gishan was the first one out the door, followed closely by Toby. Lia'na saw them leave and quickly grabbed her books to try to follow them. As she stood up, another student's arm impacted against hers, sending everything flying out of her hands.

The student called back to her, "Go back to the forest, sharpy!"

Lia'na shot up and flashed him an angry look before kneeling down to pick up her books. By the time she had everything together, the classroom was empty. She stood up and headed to the door.

Outside, there was a large crowd that was difficult for Lia'na to navigate through. She wasn't used to such huge gatherings as she had spent only the occasional weekends in the city and the rest of her time with a clan of twenty. She had lost sight of Toby and decided to speak to him before the next class.

On the other side of the crowd, Toby stood with a group of guys talking about their plans that night, "Anyone going to McAlister's later? I hear they got a new keg of Sam Adam's dwarven ale."

Gishan shook his head, "Arias is a prick, but he's right. We've been drinking way too much lately. I even get hangovers on nights I don't drink now!"

"How does that even work?"

"No idea, but I'm laying off tonight."

"Fine… -Anyone else?"

His friends all gave him apologetic looks, indicating that they didn't feel like doing anything on a Monday night. This annoyed Toby, "See, this is why I hate Mondays. Sundays and Mondays man, they suck ass! Nothing stays open late, and no one wants to go out."

Another dwarf in the group shrugged as he stepped away, "It's too early to be thinking of booze anyway, I'm heading to the dining hall, I didn't get breakfast this morning. Let's hope brunch is still being served."

Toby smiled and shook his head, "Like your fat ass would miss another jelly doughnut?"

"Go screw." He replied in a simultaneously annoyed and amused tone. "Your not eating breakfast is what causes you to sleep for so long. Have a few good hardy meals. That'll get you to class on time."

"Really," Gishan chuckled, "and here I thought it was the all night bingefests."

The entire group laughed as they began parting ways. Gishan turned to Toby as the last few people walked away, "I still can't believe the nerve of that sharpy. Standing up and challenging Arias like that is one way to get reamed out."

Toby nodded, "Sadly, I agree, his arrogance is infamous, but the fact that she's an elf probably didn't help things either."

"Right... Well I've got geology at 10, so I'm out."

"A dwarf in a geology class. It doesn't get much more stereotypical than that."

"Yeah, yeah, much like a human who doesn't know when to shut up. See you tonight."

Toby didn't have another class on Mondays so he decided to head to the pool and get some exercise. As he moved away from the crowd, something shiny caught his eye. The reflected sunlight was as blinding as a spotlight being shined directly into his eyes at a concert. As his vision compensated for this, he turned to see what was causing it.

To Toby's surprise, it was Lia'na's hair shimmering in the sunlight as she walked. The young elf approached a group of girls that were standing around chatting. The moment they saw her, the girls quickly dispersed.

Lia'na frowned as she watched them walk away with scornful looks. She was about to give up socializing and walk back to her dorm for yet another day in seclusion when she noticed Toby looking in her direction. Her features perked up and the same smile he'd seen in class appeared on her face.

Oh God, she's coming this way... He thought to himself, *what do I say to her? I've never talked to an elf before.*

Toby's heart beat a little faster with every step she took. He knew that he had to get control before she said anything or he'd wind up looking like an idiot. *Come on Toby snap out of it, she's right in front of you.*

"Um… hi there. Enoi Mae. Tobias, isn't it?"

Toby immediately snapped out of it, "Oh um... yeah, Tobias Arrigan, but everyone calls me Toby. Your name's Leana, right?"

"You're close. It's pronounced Liah nah, emphasis on the 'ia' instead of the 'ana.'"

"My bad."

"It's okay. It's nice to meet you. I just wanted to say lien ni for your help with the professor earlier. It was getting a little embarrassing."

"I... I'm sorry, I don't speak Elvish. Lien ni?"

"It means thank you. I was taught English and Elvish at the same time so I often mix words."

"Ah that makes sense. I actually like it, I have no idea what you're saying, but it sounds cute."

Lia'na's grin widened on the right side of her mouth, "Cute huh? Well not a lot of people would have stood up for someone like me."

"Like you?" Toby replied, feigning a confused tone.

Lia'na's eyes narrowed as she ran a finger over the tip of her ear, "Don't play dense, it really doesn't suit you."

"Well to be honest, it was really painful to watch. Professor Arias is a brilliant man, but he's a complete ass. It's no secret he doesn't like being challenged. You'd do best to just sit there, smile, and nod if you hope to ever pass his class. If not, he'll make your life hell."

"I see... well lien ni for the warning."

"Hey Toby," a voice called from behind, "what are you doing with that sharpy? Come on man, you heading to the gym?"

Toby closed his eyes and sighed before calling back, "Give me a minute, Tom."

When he opened his eyes again, Lia'na had a hurt look on her face. He sighed, "I'm sorry about that."

"Don't worry about it." Lia'na replied, shaking her head. "I'm used to it by now."

"Look, I..."

"I have to go. Lien ni... Thank you again. See you around."

Without letting him say another word, she quickly walked away. Toby squeezed his fist as he turned to his friend, "Damn it Tom!"

"What? She's a sharpy, Toby. What are you doing hanging around with the likes of her anyway? Are you trying to kill your rep, or do you just not even care?"

Toby put his hand on his friend's arm as they headed for the gym, "I don't understand the hatred everyone has for elves anymore. I get what happened on Vesuvius, but that happened thousands of years ago, do we really need to still hate them over it? She had nothing to do with it."

"It's not just the war." Tom replied, brushing the red hair out of his face. "They've been disease-ridden for years and they don't seem to react well to interspecies mingling. In fact, I've heard it often ends violently. Whatever hate is being tossed their way, they've more than earned."

"Well... maybe, but you can't really blame them for that. There's only what like 900 of them left? I guess a small amount of xenophobia should be expected from a species so desperate to save itself."

Tom thought about it for a moment and nodded, "Yeah I guess, but she's still not someone you want to be seen with. Come on man, if they want to stick to themselves, let them hump away in the woods."

"Thanks for that mental image." Toby replied, rolling his eyes. "Since when do I care what other people think? She's cute, she seems nice, albeit out of place, but who cares? Elf, dwarf, or human, should it really matter? Don't forget, they live longer thus stay young longer."

"Whatever dude. You want to kill your rep by going after that elf-girl, I'm not going to stop you. Come on, let's get to the pool before the next set of classes gets out and it gets crowded.

III

The lower temperature of the pool water was soothing as it caressed Toby's skin. A nice couple laps after class was always something he'd enjoyed. Part of him still missed the good old days of the swim team in high school. It wasn't the same without the competition, but he still savored it.

After his tenth lap, Toby climbed out of the water before his skin began to wrinkle. He grabbed a towel from the cart at the entrance and headed to the locker room to change. He threw on his shirt and pants and collected his belongings from the metal cage before heading for the door.

Once he was outside, Toby made his way across the courtyard, trying to decide where to go. There was a bronze monument that stood in front of him in the middle of the walkway. As he looked over the statue of some guy who had probably been dead for hundreds of years, his phone beeped and vibrated, signaling that someone was trying to get in touch with him.

Toby reached into his pocket and pulled out his android. He swiped his finger across the screen and waited for his home menu to come up. The screen flashed and it showed the time being 12:03pm. The mail icon also appeared on his task menu. He tapped the button to see that Gishan and the rest of his crew were meeting for lunch. He didn't feel like hanging out, so he texted back that he would not be joining them and instead went back to his room.

The dorm was still in complete disarray, but he didn't care. After moving a small pile of clothes, he lay down on his bunk and grabbed the TV remote. Channel 5 news popped up on the screen, but Toby could have cared less. It was little more than white noise to him as he found one of his textbooks and began flipping through the pages. As he searched for where he'd left off, a picture fell out on to the floor.

Toby watched the photo hit the ground, picked it up, and looked at it briefly. It was an old, faded, picture that displayed a man not much older than he was, wearing aviator sunglasses and a black leather jacket. The man was seated on a motorcycle, looking off into the sky.

Toby recognized his father and lay back for a few minutes looking at the bike he was sitting on before deciding that he needed to get off campus. Toby had never met his father as according to his uncle, the man had died before he was born. Lucky for Toby, the father he never knew had left him a very special gift that made his life much easier. He got up, walked out of his room, made his way out of the dorm, and headed to a small storage facility up the street.

*

After a brief ten minute walk, Toby arrived at the gate with his key. He gave the gate keeper a nod as he walked down the first row of orange doors until he reached number 148. The key fit the lock and released the latch. There was a low grinding noise as the metal door slid up and light poured into the dark room.

In the center rested a tarp draped over something big. Toby pulled the tarp back to reveal the bike from the photo. He smiled as the sun gleamed off of the old 1960 Harley Davidson.

Toby ran his hand over the blue and white finish on the bike's chassis. He spent two years restoring this bike after it had been sitting in the shed for almost fifteen years. He mounted the bike, started the engine and revved it to hear it purr. The engine sounded like diesel truck as it exited the storage unit.

The bike took Toby to his favorite cruising spot. After about 20 minutes travel, Revere beach came into view. He brought his old bike as close to the beach as he could and then turned north on Revere Beach Boulevard. It was still way too early in the year and not nearly warm enough out for beach goers, so the road was all but deserted. Cruising up and down the boulevard near the beach was when Toby felt the most alive. The engine of the bike roared, letting anyone nearby know to clear the way.

As the bike picked up speed, Toby's eyes suddenly began to go dark. Strange images of a man with a sword in his hand, fighting an odd creature that Toby hadn't seen before, appeared in his mind. There was a sudden bolt of lightning and a flash.

A loud horn snapped Toby back to reality. There was a car in his path and no time to get out of the way. Toby was certain he was dead and began to think about being airborne like a stunt rider. He expected to be dead any minute, but the honking horn began to dissipate and the wind in his face felt strange. When he opened his eyes, he realized that he had somehow flown over the car that he was about to hit. His bike's tires screeched as they struck the pavement again.

Toby brought the bike to an immediate halt, nearly flipping himself over the handlebars, and looked at the car fading into the distance. *What just happened?*

Toby parked the bike in the nearest spot. He looked at the tires and suspensions, and then looked down the street at where he had almost been hit. There was no incline, no bump, nothing that could have explained why his bike had suddenly gone airborne. The tires on his bike were also perfectly intact.

After meticulously inspecting his bike for any damage, Toby decided that this was one mystery he wasn't going to be able to solve. He gave up and spent the next few hours walking along the beach. He enjoyed the cool breeze passing over his skin and was soothed by the sound of the waves breaking on the shore. As the sun was getting close to the horizon, a chilly breeze began to pick up. He decided that it was time to get going.

The bike was waiting for Toby as the sky began to get dark. He hopped on and started the engine. Within seconds, the bike was heading back to Arcanus.

Toby wanted to get his bike back before the storage unit guards left as he wasn't fond of walking around there in the dark. As he travelled, the sky turned from blue to orange and the clouds slowly darkened to purple. He watched the buildings pass by as the sky got darker and lights came on in the buildings.

Finally, the storage facility came into view. Toby turned in and brought the bike to a stop just outside the unit he had left open. A dwarf walked by and nodded, "Nice bike!"

"Thanks!"

Toby killed the engine and walked the old Harley into the unit, covered it over, and closed the steel door. Toby still reeked of gasoline from the restored engine, but he didn't care. The sun was nearly gone as he made his way back to campus.

IV

Toby crossed the courtyard, heading back to his room. As he reached the door to his building, he heard something in the distance. He couldn't quite reconcile what the noise was, but it definitely sounded like someone had cried out momentarily. He stood there in the dead silence for a few moments straining his ears for any follow up.

After scanning the area with his eyes and ears, he dismissed the noise as his mind playing tricks on him. The door slowly creaked open and he was about to step inside when he heard the noise again. This time, there was no doubt in his mind, someone needed help.

The door slammed shut as Toby let go and stepped back out into the night. He quickly ran in the direction of the sound. The courtyard blew by as he picked up his pace. He heard the sound again from the side of one of the lecture halls. The voice sounded oddly familiar to him, but he couldn't put his finger on it. He rounded the corner quickly and, without enough time to react, ran into a guy wearing all black. The two of them fell to the ground dazed for a moment.

Toby shook off the impact and stood up. The other boy had already gotten to his feet, "Hey, what the hell are you doing? Can't you watch where you're going?"

Toby nodded, "Sorry, I didn't... wait... Tom? What's going on man…?"

Toby's words trailed off when he noticed two more guys, one dwarf, and one tall human standing behind the Thomas in the shadows. Toby recognized them from his class, "Michael, what are you doing out here this late? I didn't think you lived on campus."

As though giving him an answer, Toby heard a low whimper in the darkness. The voice was unmistakably female and he was certain that it was one he'd heard before,

"What the hell is going on here Tom? What are you guys doing?"

Michael stepped in front of Tom and turned back to the group, "I'll take care of this guys, just give me a moment."

Tom lowered her eyes and backed away as Michael confronted Toby, "This doesn't concern you, Toby. Walk away and no one gets hurt. I'm not going to say it again."

The weak voice appeared in the darkness again, "Tobias, piele help me!"

"Elvish…?" Suddenly, Toby knew who it was.

Angry, he glared at Michael. "I'll ask you one more time, what the fuck is going on here?"

"Nothing you need to be concerned with." Michael replied. "We're just teaching this worthless sharpy a lesson."

"For what? What did she do to deserve this type of schooling? –Tom, what the hell? What would your family think if they heard about this?"

Tom backed up into the darkness and looked the other way as Michael sneered, "For leaving the woods where she belongs, and thinking she could just come here and fit in."

Toby couldn't believe what he was hearing, "This is so wrong... No, you guys are done. She's coming with me right now."

Michael and the dwarf chuckled, as the dwarf spoke up, "Why do you care so much? She's a tree-humper."

"No, she's a fucking living being, a person who feels things and has the same rights we do! Now I'll give you one last chance. Get the hell out of my way."

Toby tried to push by without starting anything, but Michael grabbed his arm, "What are you going to do if we don't?"

Toby brought his other arm around, balled a fist, and let it impact in Michael's stomach. Michael wheezed as all the air instantly escaped his lungs. As he released Toby's arm, a second fist impacted on Michael's nose.

The dwarf took a step forward as though he was about to come to Michael's aid, but Tom held him back, "I wouldn't try it, Toby will kick your ass in seconds."

Michael fell to his knees as blood poured out of his nostrils. He looked up at Toby, "You broke my nose you asshole!"

"If you're smart, you'll let that be your only injury tonight." Toby replied. "If you're smart."

Michael looked back into the darkness and then up at Toby, "She's not worth it… but you are. Watch your back."

"Whatever, Mike. Maybe next time you'll think twice about crossing my path. It's a bad move if you plan on breathing much."

Michael struggled back to his feet and nodded to his friends, "We'll let him have the sharpy. Come on, I need to do something about my nose."

Not another word was spoken as the three of them ran off. Toby shook his head as he straightened himself up, "Animals…"

His attention returned to the darkness as the faint sound of sobbing began again. As the darkness cleared out of his pupils, his eyesight confirmed the voice was who he thought it was, "Lia'na… Are you all right?"

Lia'na was lying against the brick wall. The skin on her arms was cut and bleeding, her cheek looked like it was ready to swell up, her nose was bleeding, and her hair was a mess. The top of her blouse was torn open and missing three buttons. It no longer covered the black bra or the gemmed necklace she was wearing underneath.

"I wasn't trying to cause trouble, honest. I just wanted something to eat," she replied, "that's all."

"I believe you." Toby said in a comforting tone. "What happened?"

Lia'na covered her face with her free hand, "They wouldn't let me go to the dining hall. They said I wasn't fit to eat with the other students. When I tried to get past them, they hit me and dragged me out here. I fought back, but they just hit me harder."

"Bastards... I never thought anyone I knew would be capable of this. Indifference is mean enough, but this is brutality."

Toby could see the tears from her eyes falling down her cheeks and knew she needed to move, "Are you hurt bad, can you walk?"

As Lia'na struggled to stand up, Toby tried to take her arm, but she pulled away, "Piele, don't touch me... I... just don't."

"As long as you're okay to walk, not a problem."

She managed to stand up okay, but the moment she put weight on her left foot sharp pain shot through her leg. She yelped and began to fall. Toby reacted quickly enough to catch her before she hit the ground, "I don't think so. It looks like you could have a twisted ankle or maybe a sprain."

Lia'na looked at him with fear in her eyes. Toby saw it and spoke in as comforting a tone as he could, "Lia'na, I'm not going to hurt you. I promise, but you're not going to get far on your own. You need to trust me."

Everything inside Lia'na screamed at her to just hide and not tell anyone, including Toby where she was. She wanted to get away from both prying and sympathetic eyes, but her foot ached every time she put weight on it. She couldn't get away on her own and what was stopping those thugs or others like them from coming back if she sent Toby away? It was obvious that she had no other choice but to trust him.

"All right." She replied taking his hand.

Lia'na tried to take a step using Toby for support so that she didn't put as much weight on her foot, but it still was not enough and she nearly fell again. Toby shook his head, "You're going to need more help than just my hand."

No longer having any choice but to rely on her rescuer, Lia'na closed her eyes and sucked down a deep breath, "Tobias, piele just get me out of here. Take me somewhere safe."

Toby nodded and got under her left arm, "All right, let's get you to the campus clinic."

"No!" She replied. "No… just get me out of here. I don't want to file a report, I just want to hide, piele."

"Are you sure? The authorities should know about this, and you should get checked out."

"Given how people have reacted to me since the day I left the reservation, I doubt they'd do much. Tobias, I don't think I'm that badly hurt, piele just take me somewhere I can hide out."

Toby sighed, but agreed, "All right… where do you live? We can go back there."

"No… Piele… I don't… um…"

"All right," Toby cut in to spare her any more of a struggle, "we'll go to my place."

"I don't want to go there either." She said in a low voice.

Toby did the best he could not to get annoyed, but he had run out of places to take her, "Lia'na, I don't know where else you want to go. Is there a friend or family member you want me to call?"

"No…"

"Not a single friend who could look after you?"

"You've seen how I've been treated since I first showed up on campus. Right now, you're the closest thing I have to a friend."

"What about family?"

"I..." Lia'na thought for a moment. Her clan elder would want to know what happened, but did she really want to admit it was a mistake to attend human college?

Finally, Lia'na looked up at Toby, "No, no one I want to call."

At this point, Toby had no other ideas and didn't know what to do. He didn't want to put more pressure on her, but they couldn't stay where they were, "Okay, then what do you want to do?"

"Um..." Lia'na couldn't decide. She knew she couldn't get away on her own, and she was afraid that if Toby brought her back to her room, he'd leave her there. She didn't want to be alone, but at the same time, she didn't want to be seen. Her mind was in a million places at once, and it was impossible for her to sort everything out in her current condition. Tears flowed down her cheeks faster than before. Her mind was still in panic mode and she was unable to think clearly.

Toby picked up on her anxiety and didn't push her anymore, "Take your time. I'm not going to leave you here."

Lia'na sighed. She didn't know what to do. Going back to her room wasn't what she wanted, going back to this boy's room probably wasn't a good idea, and going to the clinic was completely out of the question.

Toby could see that she was in pain and decided to offer his suggestion to speed up her decision, "Okay look, since you obviously don't want to be alone, why don't we go back to my place for a little while. You don't have to stay long. You can just get cleaned up, and decide what you want to do. That way you're not in a dark alley trying to decide. How does that sound?"

Lia'na sucked in a labored breath and nodded, "Okay..."

She wasn't sure what to make of this decision, but she wasn't going to make it across campus on her ankle. It was in bad shape and she couldn't put any weight on it. She leaned into Toby as they began to walk, slowly and carefully to prevent her from falling.

Much to Lia'na's relief, very few people were walking across campus at this point and things were pretty quiet. The pair struggled across the walkway until they got to the building where Toby was staying. It took them twice as long because Toby had to mind both his and her footing. He didn't want to go to fast and risk her falling over.

When they finally reached the door, he pulled on the handle to open it and guided Lia'na inside. The hallway to his room seemed like it was a lot longer than normal. It was well-lit but deserted as the two of them proceeded forward.

They were almost to Toby's room when two other students, friends of Toby's, rounded the corner. They eyed Toby suspiciously as they started down the hall in the opposite direction. Not sure what to make of what they saw.

Toby wasn't sure if they were looking at him for Lia'na's condition, or if it was because he was with an elf. He glared at them, "John, Matteus, not a word!"

The two boys shrugged and continued walking like nothing happened. They disappeared around a corner, knowing that Toby had meant what he said. As soon as the other two students were out of sight, Toby and Lia'na continued walking until they arrived at Toby's room.

Gishan was lying on his bunk enjoying another night of vegetating after a large meal when the door suddenly swung open. It impacted against the wall so hard that the room shook. This startled the dwarf who shot up out of bed, "God damn, fucking moron, what on Earth…"

His eyes focused before he could finish the sentence, "Toby, what the hell are you doing? Why is she here?"

Toby carried Lia'na into the room and set her down on his bunk without looking up at Gishan, "Look, I know what you're going to say, but she got jumped outside. She took a beating dude, pretty bad too. What else could I do?"

Gishan hopped off of his bunk and examined Lia'na's face. He didn't particularly care for elves. It was a fact that he made no secret of, but things like this, elf, human, or dwarf, were unacceptable even to him, "Who did this?"

"That bastard, Michael." Toby growled.

"Michael, Arias's class? He was always a prick, but I never thought he'd pull something like this."

"He wasn't alone either. There were two other guys, a dwarf that's in our class and... Tom..."

Gishan's jaw dropped open in disbelief, "No way, we both know Tom. He can be a tough guy sometimes, but I couldn't see him abusing a girl like this."

"Believe it. He looked like a dear in headlights when I showed up."

Gishan looked at Lia'na again as she lay on the bed. For the first time in his life, he was actually feeling sympathy for an elf, "Does she need anything? –You want me to grab something?"

Lia'na kept quiet as Toby shook his head, "I think she'll be okay, she just needs a place to hide out and rest for now."

"In that case, I'll bunk out so you guys have the room. – I hope you feel better."

Lia'na forced a small smile, "Lien ni, I'm sorry to put you out…"

Gishan shrugged, "Don't worry about it. Just don't make it a habit."

Without another word, he grabbed a bag and headed for the door, "I got my cell if you need anything. Hit me up."

Toby nodded, "Will do. Thanks partner, I appreciate it."
"You owe me."

Toby smiled and turned back to Lia'na, who was holding her white blouse closed with her right hand and keeping herself balanced with the other. She rested her back against the bedpost as Toby sat down next to her. He noticed that she was trying to guard herself and quickly turned to his drawer, pulling out his last clean shirt.

When Toby held the black t-shirt out to Lia'na, she looked at him oddly and shook her head. He smiled and spoke to her in a calm tone, "Go ahead, and put it on. I promise it's clean. It's better than trying to hold your shirt closed."

Lia'na hesitantly took it from Toby and fitted it over her head. It was at least two times her normal size. Once it was on, she fidgeted with the torn blouse she was wearing and pulled it out from under Toby's shirt. She hesitantly handed it to him as she inched her way further back.

Toby looked at the blouse and shook his head. In addition to missing buttons, it was ripped in three places, "I don't think you'll be wearing this again."

Lia'na didn't say a word. She didn't even bother looking at the shirt. Instead she pulled her knees up, rested her arms over them, and hid her face. Toby knew she would need time, and probably some space, but he needed to make sure that she was physically okay first, "Can I take a look at your leg?"

No response.

"Lia'na, can I look at your leg?"

Again, no response came.

"All right Lia'na, I know you're scared, but your leg could be badly injured. May I please take a look at it? I'm not going to hurt you. Once I'm done, I'll leave you alone, I promise."

Lia'na quietly moved her left leg to the edge of the bed, letting Toby know he could look. He smiled as he put his hands around her ankle, "Thank you, I promise I'll be careful."

He unstrapped the sandal she was wearing and rolled up the bottom of her jeans so he could see her ankle. It looked like a bruise was forming and it was beginning to swell, "I need to make sure it's not broken. I'm just going to check the ankle. This may ache a little, but let me know if it hurts badly."

"Do what you have to."

Toby nodded, relieved that she was actually talking to him, and caressed the ankle bone to make sure it was still in place. As he pushed against it, she flinched, but otherwise didn't move. He continued rubbing the ankle gently, "Does it hurt when I do this?"

"No."

Toby moved down her leg a little bit more and began to rub again, "How about here?"

She paused for a moment and peaked up from her arms, "That actually feels nice."

Toby continued caressing around her ankle for a few moments as Lia'na's skin broke out in goose bumps. She still wasn't entirely comfortable with Toby touching her. After what happened, a guy touching her skin made it crawl. Her mind was conflicted; part of her was still on the defensive and wanted to pull away, but the other part knew that this boy was one of the good ones and was only trying to help.

As Toby worked, Lia'na slowly became less and less apprehensive about his touch. The way he caressed her ankle with such tenderness, calmed her down. Toby was about to move on to another part of her leg when she spoke up again, "Don't stop..."

"No problem, tell me if I hurt you."

Lia'na watched Toby as he ran his fingers over her ankle, trying to make the pain go away. It felt good at first, but then his fingers ran over something still causing her to let out a faint yelp.

Toby stopped and looked up at her for a moment, "Sorry."

"It's okay. It felt good until you pressed there."

Toby gently pressed on the bone next to the bruise. It appeared to still be in place and solid. Convinced that it wasn't broken, Toby gently placed her leg back on his bed, "It's going to be okay, but you should probably ice it or it may swell."

He quickly got to his feet and headed for the door, "I'll be right back. I'm going to get you an ice pack."

For a second time Lia'na didn't move, but Toby swore that he heard her ask him to hurry back in a faint whisper. He quickly opened his door and ran to the common area down the hall. It was little more than a galley style kitchen taking up part of the hallway. It had a small stove, a microwave, and everything needed for a student to cook if they didn't feel like heading to the cafe. However students were to provide their own food. Ground coffee had been left out for them, but little else.

A white box with a red cross on it was bolted to the wall on the opposite side. Toby pulled it open and grabbed two ice packs, some disinfectant, and cotton swabs. Before heading back to the room, he remembered that she hadn't eaten anything. He pulled his android from his pocket, and hit speed dial #5.

The phone rang for a moment and a voice with a thick Italian accent picked up, "Rucci's, can I help you?"

"Yes, I'd like to place a delivery order?"

"Not a problem, that's dorm one at Arcanus College?"

Toby loved new technology, and now that these places automatically saved phone numbers with their addresses, it made things easier, "Correct."

"All right, what can I get you?"

Toby thought for a moment. He didn't know what Lia'na's eating habits were. Did elves even eat meat? They lived in the woods for the most part so they could be vegetarian. From what he had read they were light eaters, so he decided it was best to order a few things, "I'd like a steak bomb sub with peppers, onions, and cheese, a supreme Italian, and a Caesar wrap, hold the chicken. All large, please."

Toby could hear the man typing away on a computer for a moment before he came back on the line, "Okay, any sauce on the Italian and bomb?"

Toby nodded, assuming that he'd most likely wind up eating the steak bomb, "Peppercorn on the bomb and light Italian on the other one."

"All right, that's $25.40 and it'll be about twenty minutes, okay?"

"Perfect. Thank you."

"Have a good night."

Now that there was food on the way, Toby headed back to his room. Lia'na had barely moved and he could still hear her crying. He felt his heart sink from the sound. Here was an innocent girl whose only crime was having pointed ears. It wasn't right and it wasn't fair. Toby knew he couldn't erase what happened, but he could try to help her get through it.

Before going anywhere near her, he went into his bathroom, grabbed a clean cloth and wet it with warm water. He then turned back, closed the door to the bathroom behind him, and sat down next to Lia'na, "Do you want me to look at those cuts on your arms?"

Lia'na sighed and raised her head. Her eyes were bloodshot and soaked with tears. Toby cracked the one-time-use ice packs he had brought back and placed one on her leg. Once it was set, he handed her the other one, "Put that on your cheek."

Lia'na took the pack from Toby and did as she was told. While she tended to her face, Toby used the cloth to clean her arms and then dabbed some disinfectant on the cuts. None of them were really that bad and he was sure they'd heal up in a day or two, but better safe than sorry. He finished up cleaning her cuts and offered her the cloth, "Do you want to use this on your face?"

Lia'na took the cloth from him and wiped her cheeks and forehead. She then dabbed her eyes until they were dry. Doing so proved to be a waste of her time as more tears appeared to replace them.

Toby shook his head, "I wish I'd gotten there sooner."

Lia'na refused to look Toby in the eye as she spoke, "The elders warned me that this would happen. They told me I wouldn't be accepted because I'm an elf. They said people would abuse me."

Toby bit his upper lip, knowing that he'd be hard pressed now to try to challenge such a viewpoint, "I wish I could say something to make you feel better... but to be honest, I never thought something like this would happen. Those guys were always smug jerks, but this is a new low."

"Why? Why do they hate me so much? What did I do?"

"You didn't do anything. It's because you're an elf."

"I get that, I know what racism is."

"Sorry. It's just the history your people have, it still angers some. It's unfortunate, but you're guilty by association only."

Lia'na lowered her eyes, "It's not fair. I've worked so hard to get this far. This is the reason I transferred schools in the first place."

A sudden knock made Lia'na jump. Toby looked over his shoulder at the door, "Who is it?"

"Rucci's delivery, I have your order."

Lia'na's eyes perked up a little, "You ordered food?"

Toby nodded as he got up and went to the door. On the other side was a young man dressed in yellow and black. He smiled as Toby came into view, "Good evening, that'll be $25.40."

Toby handed him $35 and took the brown paper bag that he was holding. The man was about to reach into his change purse but Toby just shook his head, "Keep it."

The man's eyes widened, "Well thank you very much! You have a good night now."

"You too."

He turned back to Lia'na, who was now staring at him oddly, "What is this?"

"Well you didn't make it to the café. So I assumed you were still hungry. I put in an order at the sub shop down the street."

"You didn't need to do that."

"Where would I be if I only did the things I had to do?"

Lia'na was about to say something when her stomach made a low growling noise. She chuckled softly, "Well my stomach thanks you."

Toby opened the paper bag, "I didn't know what to get, so I grabbed a few things."

"I'm not picky."

"All right, well..." Toby looked through the bag as he spoke, "we've got a steak bomb with peppercorn, a supreme Italian, and a caesar vegetarian. Take your pick."

Lia'na's eyes lightened up a little more, "I'd like the steak, piele."

"Really?" Toby asked in disbelief.

"Yes, really. Why do you look so surprised? That steak bomb sounds really good."

"Well... I don't know, I guess I got it into my head that elves ate lighter than that."

"Sometimes we do, but we're not strictly vegan or anything, not all of us. We enjoy good food as much as humans or dwarves."

"Spoken like someone who's never eaten a dwarven five course meal."

"I mean, if you got that for yourself, I won't take it from you."

"No not at all. I'm not even that hungry."

"Are you sure? I do like steak but..."

Before she could finish her sentence, Toby reached into the bag, pulled out the package that was labeled 'steak,' and handed it to her, "All right, it's yours."

She took the sandwich and opened the packing, "Okay, wow... these are huge!"

"Rucci's makes them big, but they're great for the price, and you won't find a better one around here."

Lia'na shrugged and tried it. The steak was perfectly cooked and the peppercorn gave it an extra kick. She took one more look at the sandwich and began to devour it.

Toby watched her wolf the food down, "Easy, it's not going anywhere, and I don't want to have you choking on me."

She ate quickly, stopping only to breathe. As she reached the middle where the sub had been cut, her stomach began to ache. "This is too much. I seriously can't eat another bite."

"I told you."

Lia'na wrapped the rest of the sandwich up and grabbed one of the brown napkins which had been in the bag, "It was really good though, Lien ni."

"You're welcome, though you eat like you haven't had anything in days."

"How much do I owe you for this?"

"You don't. Don't worry about it."

"Are you sure? I've already been an inconvenience..."

"I'm sure. After everything that happened tonight, just take it easy."

Lia'na lay back in the bunk, finally able to calm down, "Lien ni."

"No problem. If you decide you want to go back to your room, let me know. Don't feel like you have to though, you are welcome to stay here as long as you need."

Lia'na looked out the window into the darkness. Much to her own surprise, she was actually considering staying put. *What is wrong with me? I should just go back to my room and get some sleep, but I don't think I'm up for walking that far, and it wouldn't be right to ask him to carry me. After everything that's happened, am I really going to let myself be this vulnerable?*

Lia'na was still on edge, but it was more a fear of being alone than it was being around Toby. Something inside told her that she could trust him. After weighing out her options, she finally made up her mind, "Well... I really hate to be an inconvenience and it's a little embarrassing to ask but..."

Toby nodded, "Go ahead."

"Would you mind if I spent the night? I still don't feel safe going back."

"That's fine. You can stay here as long as you need."

Toby was relieved that she wasn't keeping him at arm's length anymore. Lia'na made herself comfortable and cradled his pillow, "Are you sure you don't mind...? I mean we just met so I can imagine what you think of me for this, but I'm... I mean... um..."

"I don't think any less of you. It's not like we're sleeping together or anything like that. So what are you worried about?"

"I... I guess nothing." Lia'na replied as she closed her eyes. "Lien ni."

Toby threw one of his blankets on the top bunk and climbed up. He lay down and flicked on the TV. There was some kids show on the first channel he went to. Obviously he had no interest in it and moved on to the next one. There wasn't really much of anything on, which was normal for a Monday night. Plus this would normally be the night that Gishan hit one of his adult networks.

Lia'na lay in bed trying to come to terms with what had happened. Elves were barely tolerated outside of their reservations, but she had no idea that anyone would blatantly hate her. How could this have happened? She was attacked by three guys who would have done God only knows what if Toby hadn't shown up. The only thing she was guilty of was being hungry. Now here she was sleeping in a human's bed, in his room.

Though Lia'na was growing more confident that Toby wasn't going to hurt her, the moment she closed her eyes chills ran down her spine. It didn't seem like she was going to get any sleep that night at all. She was just too scared and the problem was that she didn't even know what was scaring her.

On the top bunk, Toby sighed and shut the TV off. He didn't feel comfortable in complete silence and turned his MP3 player on. He kept it low as he wasn't sure whether or not Lia'na was sleeping, but it was loud enough to help him settle in.

The music turned out to be just what Lia'na needed. Her nerves finally began to calm down as the music slowly lulled her off to sleep. Her shaking slowed and her cuts didn't hurt as much anymore.

As Toby turned off the light, he noticed the sound of steady breathing beneath him. It wasn't erratic like she was crying and it didn't sound like she was struggling at all. It was a big relief to hear that Lia'na had finally calmed down enough to go to sleep.

*

Toby woke up around 8 the next morning. He was adamant that he would not be late for any of his classes today, so he kept his bag packed on the table next to the bed. He jumped out of the bunk and noticed that Lia'na was gone. The bed had been made for the first time since he moved in, and there was a folded piece of paper sitting on the pillow.

Toby picked it up and unfolded it. Inside was a brief letter in very pretty handwriting;

> "Tobias,
>
> Lien ni so much for everything last night. I will never forget what you did for me. Even when I wasn't so trusting of you, you were patient and caring. I don't think you know how much it meant to me. Any girl would be lucky to have a friend like you. Tell your roommate that I'm sorry for inconveniencing him. I got an early start, so I'm going to head back to my room to clean up and hopefully start the day. I'd be worried that someone would question how beat up I look, but everyone seems to look the other way when I approach, so it shouldn't be a problem. Don't worry about my ankle, it feels much better. I'll drop off your shirt later. One last time, Lien ni for everything. You've earned my trust, as well as my friendship."

The letter was signed, "Nira arsha, Lia'na."

Toby didn't speak Elvish, but he assumed that it meant 'Your friend, Lia'na.' *Glad I could help,* Toby thought to himself as he folded the letter back up. *Wonder if I'll ever see her again...*

Toby kept his eyes out all across campus for any sign of Lia'na, but she never made an appearance. Wednesday finally rolled around and it was back to 'A Survey of Pre-Western Civ.' with Professor Arias. Much to Gishan's surprise, Toby was the first one out of bed and was showered and shaved before his roommate was even roused. When he finally woke up and saw Toby, he shook his head, "What's with you man? All of a sudden you're mister responsible?"

"You think I want to get another paper, or worse?"

"Justify it all you want, we both know why you want to get there so early."

Toby shrugged, "Yeah I don't know about her, she disappeared before I woke up and I haven't seen her since."

"Probably went back to her own kind. Good riddance."

Toby glared at the young dwarf, "That's not cool man. I know she's an elf, but what has she done to make you hate her?"

"Uh... Well nothing really."

Gishan frowned, "Maybe you're right... maybe. She did seem like a nice person. A couple millennia of prejudices are hard to wash away, but I guess I'll need to start working on it if elves are going to be going to school with us. I just hope they give us better treatment than they did back in the good old days."

"Lead by example. It's a different time, so you never know."

"Yeah, yeah, spare me the boy scout routine. You meet one pretty elf-girl and now you're ready to become some kind of an equal rights activist. You take being whipped to a whole new level. Heck you barely even know the girl!"

"I wouldn't go that far, but I do think they deserve better than the treatment that Lia'na's been getting."

"Dude come on, no one deserves what she got."

"Right... All right well come on, Gishan let's go."

Gishan got up, got dressed, and followed Toby out of the dorm. They hoofed it across campus just like they did two days ago. This time however, they arrived at the lecture hall on time.

Gishan sat in his normal chair at the back of the room, but Toby remained standing as he looked for Lia'na. There were easily a hundred students in this hall, but Toby had good eyes and was certain that she was nowhere to be found. His heart sank in his chest as he let out a deep sigh.

Gishan frowned, "I knew it. Sit down Toby. We still have a few minutes before class starts."

As Toby turned to find his chair, he saw Michael and his two friends staring at him, "Well look who it is boys!"

Michael walked up to Toby, followed by the dwarf. Tom was nowhere to be found. Michael's nose had a small bandage holding it in place, "How's the sharpy, Toby? Did you two have fun the other night?"

Gishan stood up, sensing trouble, "Michael, why don't you find someone else to bother before something bad happens to you?"

"Caused by you Gishan? Please..."

Toby stepped between them and glared at Michael, "You really hurt Lia'na, you know. She was too afraid to even go back to her own room!"

"Who cares?" Michael said. "Like I said, she's a sharpy who should have stayed in her own land. Maybe now she will."

Michael smiled malicously as he continued, "Although I got to admit, she was kind of hot. I would say you owe me one for setting you up to be the hero, and I still plan to collect for the bloody nose you gave me."

Toby clenched his jaw as he felt his anger begin to boil over inside him. "What were you planning on doing to her had I not shown up?"

When Michael didn't answer, Toby shoved him hard, "Answer me, you son of a bitch!"

Michael stumbled backwards a few steps. In an effort to save face, he quickly recovered and responded by shoving Toby back into the wall. Several nearby students jumped to their feet. Some backed away while others got ready for a brawl.

Gishan moved in between and grabbed them both, "Hey, hey, cool it, both of you!"

The lone dwarf was not strong enough to stop two raging freight trains from colliding. Several other students surrounded Michael and Toby and prevented them from getting anywhere near each other. Toby fought to get at Michael, determined to punch him out. He fought hard against the crowd, but it was obvious that he wasn't getting through.

Toby's world went red and a sensation came over him that he could not explain. The tension inside Toby became so intense that he was ready to explode. As his rage broke through the surface, he yelled out, "Get back!"

Toby's voice sounded almost demonic as it echoed throughout the hall. To everyone's horror, the moment he thrust his arms out, the other students were pushed away by an unseen force.

Gishan took a nervous step back, "Toby..."

Toby's eyes had turned milky white and his hands were glowing red. He was breathing heavily and sweat began to bead on his forehead. When Toby saw his hands, he gasped, "What is this?"

As he calmed down, his hands stopped glowing. His breathing began to slow as he noticed the whole room was staring at him.

Toby ignored them, glared at Michael, and pointed at him in an accusing way, causing the other students to take another step back, "I don't care what you think of elves, of me, or of anyone else. I don't care about what they did to make you feel that way about them. All I know is if I ever find out you laid another finger on that one, it's your ass, got it?"

Michael didn't get a chance to respond. The air was broken by the raspy sound of Professor Arias' voice, "What's going on here?"

Michael's eyes never left Toby's, "Nothing professor, nothing at all."

Arias looked at him for a moment and then turned to Toby, "What about you, Mr. Arrigan?"

Toby nodded, "Like he said professor, nothing. Could you excuse me from class today? I'm suddenly not feeling all that well."

Arias looked at Toby suspiciously for a moment. The professor studied his eyes and concluded that he was telling the truth, "I still need that paper from you on Friday, but for now, you're free to go. I hope you feel better. I'll have Gishan drop off notes for you later."

"Thank you Professor."

He left Gishan and the other students behind in class, not knowing what to think. Gishan wanted to chase after him, but Toby raised his hand and shook his head as he disappeared down the hall. *This is bad...*

**

Across campus, at that very moment, Lia'na was laying in her bed staring at the ceiling. Yet another day was about to blow by without her making any contact with the outside world and she was perfectly fine with that. After everything that had happened, she wasn't sure if she even wanted to stay on the campus or admit defeat and go home. Though one student had been kind to her, most did their best to make her feel unwelcome around them.

A sudden chill shot down her spine, her skin broke out in bumps, and she sat straight up. Her eyes were wide as she threw her window open and looked across campus. Her sight focused on the main auditorium where the class she had skipped was taking place. A gasp escaped her lips as a wave of energy overtook her. The skin on her arms tingled and she trembled as she inhaled deeply.

Lia'na couldn't shake the feeling that something bad had just taken place, when it suddenly hit her; Toby and the guys who had attacked her were all in that class. Another chill ran down her spine, "Tobias... oh no..."

She jumped out of bed and changed into sweat pants and a t-shirt. Once she was presentable, she grabbed a thin jacket, ran out of her room, down the hallway, down a flight of stairs, and out the door. The moment the cool spring air touched her skin and ears, she froze in place. Her head cocked to the side and she closed her eyes.

After a few moments of listening to the wind, Lia'na gasped, "Tobias... this can't be..."

**

Toby stormed back to his room, barely able to keep the flood of emotions at bay. His mind was filled with questions, while his heart was pounding in both confusion and rage. What had just happened, how did he push those students away, and most importantly, what was it about that elf-girl that pushed him to this?

The dorm came into view, but Toby didn't want to go there, he thought about getting on his bike and going for a ride, but with his heart racing and head spinning, he didn't feel safe doing that either. He didn't know what to do; all of his friends were in class and he had nowhere left to go. He leaned up against a wall and put his right hand up to his forehead. *What's going on? I'm coming apart here.*

Toby felt his world begin to spin around him. He was about to fall over when he heard someone grabbed his arm and called to him, "Tobias, are you okay?"

His head turned to see Lia'na standing over him. Her face was still bruised, but it looked like the rest of her injuries were healing. She grabbed his other arm to help him stay on his feet. "Ta Diesu, you look like you're going to get sick."

"I am."

"Tobias… I felt something a few minutes ago. It was like a cold burst of energy blew through my window and struck me."

"Is there a point to this?"

Lia'na nodded, "I'm getting to it. The energy came from the auditorium. Weren't you there, what happened?"

Lia'na saw Toby lean forward and thought he was about to fall over so she put a hand on his chest. At that moment, she felt his heart racing, "Okay, let's get you inside before you collapse."

Toby nodded and pushed himself off the wall. The two of them walked across campus back to Toby's dorm. The door flew open as they walked in and proceeded down the hallway to his room. They were about half way down the hall when Matteus came out of his room having just woken up.

"What happened to you, Toby? Spending time with that sharpy wind up getting you the Ulium?"

Toby stopped dead in his tracks and glared at Matteus. Once again, his eyes turned to a milky white and began to glow. He raised his fist so that Matteus could see it. Matteus backed up slightly as it began to glow red.

Toby clenched his jaw and growled at his friend, "Back off!"

Matteus nodded and stepped backwards into his room, "Whatever you say Toby."

Lia'na's eyes never left Toby as she coaxed him towards his room. His eyes quickly returned to normal and his fist stopped glowing, "What's happening here?"

"We'll talk about it once we're in your room safe from prying eyes, come on." Lia'na said.

She pushed Toby into his room, stepped in behind him, and closed the door. Toby watched her franticly fasten the deadbolt and then turn to face him. There was a look of extreme concern in her eyes, "Now I want answers, what happened? Why was there a sudden burst of energy coming from class, are you all right?"

"That's none of your business." Toby replied as lay down on his bed, looking away from her.

Lia'na grabbed his shoulder, "Don't be like that, I know something happened in that room. Was it because of me?"

While Toby was relieved that she was actually talking to him, she couldn't have chosen a worse time. He didn't want anyone near him because he had no idea what was going on. If there was even the slightest chance that he could lose control again and end up hurting her, then she needed to be as far away from him as possible.

"Just because I helped you the other night, doesn't mean that you now have the right to butt into my life. Feel free to use the door."

He hated saying it, but it was for her own good.

Lia'na's chest felt like a knife had just pierced through her heart. It wasn't easy for her to trust or talk to anyone at this point, but here she was trying and this is what she got. "How long have you been able to use magic?"

Toby turned back to face her and glared into her eyes, "I said you can leave, now please get out!"

Lia'na straightened herself up to prevent tears from falling, "Fine!"

She unbolted the door and walked out of the room, letting it slam behind her. Once she was alone, she closed her eyes as tears began to fall. She realized that she may have pushed too hard, but she still felt hurt by his words. Why would he act like that? What would cause a guy who was so sweet to her mere hours ago get like this? It didn't matter now anyway. She was finished.

Lia'na could put up with a lot, but not being treated that way under any circumstance. She stormed off and headed back to her room. Maybe it was time to consider just packing up and going home.

Toby tossed and turned for a few minutes. He felt awful about being so harsh, but he still felt that she had no business prying into his personal life. *Who does she think she is, demanding answers like that?* He thought to himself, *you save a girl once and she suddenly thinks you owe her explanations for what or who you are?*

It took Toby a moment to calm down, but once he did, he began to think more clearly. *Still, she was only trying to help. That was nice of her, even if it was a little pushy, but what did she mean about using magic? What does she think I am, a magician? Well... that actually would explain a few things.*

Finally, Toby came to the conclusion that while he was right, he had also been needlessly rude. *If she'll speak to me, I'll apologize.*

At that moment, Gishan came through the door, "Dude, are you all right?"

"I'm better than I was, why?"

"Why, why?" Gishan scoffed. "Um, let's see man, you went berserk in class, you nearly kicked the shit out of Michael, and then you somehow sent students flying... The fuck?"

He shook his head, looking at Toby, "…and then I just saw your little sharpy running away from here with tears in her eyes."

Toby sighed, closed his eyes, and lay back on his bed, "Ugh… shit…"

"We've been friends a long time Toby. Heck, you've practically lived at my house these past few years. You can tell me, what's going on?"

"I wish I knew Gishan, I'd tell you if I did…"

He turned and peered out the window, "…but I think the only person who could tell me, is the one I just royally pissed off."

VI

Toby took a brief nap after talking to Gishan. In his dreams all he could think about was fire and darkness. As the moments passed, the fire intensified and was then replaced by a bright light that extinguished the flame instantaneously. Toby's eyes shot open and he gasped for air. He sat up and wiped his forehead which was now covered in sweat.

After a few minutes of fighting through a haze, Toby decided that he'd had enough. He got up and went into the bathroom. Gishan smirked from his bunk, "Finally going to shower?"

"How many days have you gone without one in the past?" Toby fired back as he closed the door behind him.

He locked the door before stripping down, turning the shower on hot, and then getting in. The heat from the water and steam cleansed his skin as he scrubbed in some of his body wash. He then ran some shampoo through his hair and rinsed it out.

Once he was clean, Toby turned the shower handle to the right, causing the water to get cold. The sudden shift in water temperature sent chills down his spine, but he adjusted quickly. As the steam cleared and the cool water poured down his back, he began to feel reinvigorated, as though the cold water had recharged his batteries. He continued to turn to the handle, making it colder and colder.

When his skin couldn't take it anymore, Toby turned the water off and stepped out of the small stall that was their shower. He dried off and walked out of the bathroom. Gishan looked up as the door opened, but quickly wished he hadn't, "Oh God… Toby… Come on man! Friggin take some clothes with you when you go to shower!"

Toby shrugged as he put on new underwear, "Oh relax, you've been in a gym locker room before."

"Yeah and why do you think I don't work out much?"

"Because you're a lazy slob?"

"Okay, that too, but I still don't need to see your... business!"

"Closet case." Toby said as he pulled on a pair of jeans and threw a shirt on over his head.

Once he was dressed, Toby brushed his thick hair back and slid his feet into his shoes. Gishan looked at him oddly, "You going out to start more trouble?"

"More than you know."

Gishan rolled his eyes, "Just don't get yourself arrested. I'm not bailing your ass out... again."

"No worries. Thanks for that again, by the way."

"It was either that or let you get raped in jail. I'm starting to think that the latter might have been the better option."

Toby laughed as he walked out of their room into the hallway, "Catch you later."

"Yeah, yeah, whatever."

Toby headed outside and began to run across campus to one of the other dormitories. He had no idea where Lia'na was staying, but if there was ever a good place to start, the Leslie House was it. It was an all-girl's dorm and the best place to start looking.

Leslie House was unlike any of the other dorms on campus. Most of them were large concrete or brick buildings, but this one was a brown house that looked like it had been converted to be used as a residence. It seemed to suit the female students who wanted some privacy.

Toby stood outside for a second, not sure where to start looking. Then he saw two girls coming out of the house with books in their hands. As they stepped on to the paved walk-way, Toby approached them, "Excuse me?"

They both stopped and looked at him. The shorter of the two, an Asian girl, spoke up, "Hi."

"Do you know where I can find a girl named Lia'na?" Toby asked.

The girl twisted her lips, thinking. It seemed like she'd heard that name before, but couldn't put her finger on it. Finally, she brushed a few strands of her brown-highlighted black hair out of her face, "The name doesn't ring a bell. Does she live in this house?"

"I don't know, but you'd know her if you saw her, she's…"

Toby paused for a moment, bracing himself for a disgusted reaction, "…she's an elf."

His words caused the girl's eyes to perk up, "Oh her! Yes she lives here. I didn't know her name, but she's wicked nice. Yeah look on the second floor, I think she's in room 204."

"Thank you very much!"

"No problem." The girl replied as she turned and walked away with her friend.

Toby walked up the stairs and into the house. He passed by the common area where a few girls gave him odd looks, but he ignored them and continued on. Leslie house was completely different from his dorm. It had a more homely look. The walls were painted white, the smell of food that didn't reek like bad cheese or noodles floated in the air, and the floors were clean.

Oh man… He thought to himself, *talk about hostile territory.*

Toby was determined to spend as little time there as possible. He hurried up the stairs and down the hall. Finally, he reached room 204 and knocked on the door. At first, there was no response. He was about to walk away when he heard the latch being unhooked and the door creak opening.

Lia'na appeared in front of him. Her face quickly twisted into a scowl and she crossed her arms, "Well, what do you want?"

Toby looked nervously into her dagger eyes and breathed in deeply, "I… came to say I'm sorry."

"For what, accusing me of being nosy, or yelling at me when I was trying to help you?"

"I…" Toby thought about his words carefully before responding. His first impulse was to apologize for the second part as he still didn't think he was wrong, but if there was one lesson life had given him, it was that when a girl is giving you dagger eyes, diplomacy is the best course, "Both, I guess. You caught me off guard, when I was already a little disturbed. I didn't know how to react and I just wanted to be alone. After what happened in class, I was afraid I'd hurt anyone who got too close, so I was desperate to get away from everyone, including you."

Lia'na studied his face for a moment before rolling her eyes and opening the door wider, "Come in, sit down."

Toby promptly followed her through the door. The room was barely a closet with only enough room for a bed and one desk. There was no private bathroom like there was in his dorm, and only one window. The room was painted all white, which seemed a poor choice for any college dorm room, especially when posters were added to the walls. Toby often theorized that college dorms and apartment complexes did this so that they could charge for damages, but that was just his unsubstantiated paranoia.

Lia'na leaned against her bed and brushed a strand of hair behind her pointed left ear, "So what do you want to talk about?"

"I… uh…" Toby stuttered for a moment, trying to find the right words, "I was wondering if you manage to get off campus much?"

"A little, I have bike. I can go to the store, but not much further than that."

"Would you like to go somewhere?"

"Where did you have in mind?"

"Somewhere nice, a place I go when I need to clear my head."

Lia'na didn't know what to think about this. She was still mad at him, but he did save her from God-only-knows-what just the other night. Still it was a lot to go with a guy to destinations unknown after what she'd been through. She was about to turn him down when she realized that after everything, she at least owed him a chance to redeem himself, "All right… sure let's go."

Lia'na grabbed a thin windbreaker off of the back of her chair as Toby stood up. She let Toby lead her out of the dorm while brushing the rest of her hair behind her pointed ears, "Where are we going?"

"Just trust me."

A million thoughts were rushing through Lia'na's mind. She admittedly didn't know this boy very well, but she wasn't afraid of him. Why would he put himself at risk to save her only to turn around and hurt her himself? It made no sense, so she put the thought out of her head and decided to give him a chance. *Don't put him in the same boat as the other guys. For now, just see what happens.*

Lia'na followed him beyond the campus limits and around the next block until they arrived at the storage unit. Her eyes narrowed as they walked through the gate and down one of the isles, "Is there something here you want to show me or something?"

"We can't get out of here without proper transportation."

"That a fact…?" Lia'na asked, getting a little suspicious. "You're starting to sketch me out a little here Tobias."

"Will you please relax?"

"No I will not." Lia'na replied sternly. "I just followed a boy I barely know off campus to some secluded storage facility with no rhyme or reason. That goes against everything we're told in orientation about keeping safe! You're really starting to make me nervous now, will you piele…"

Her voice trailed off when he opened his storage unit and pulled back the tarp, revealing his motorcycle. Lia'na's eyes widened. It was the most beautiful bike she'd ever seen, "Ai iesau… a Harley-Davidson FLH Duo Glide!"

Toby looked up in surprise, "You know bikes?"

"A little. A guy from my clan was absolutely obsessed with them."

"Boyfriend?"

"No!" Lia'na said with a smirk. "More like a brother, but I haven't seen him in a long time. He went off to the Rocky Mountain Clan out west to marry a girl he met."

She went over the bike as though trying to grade it, "Where did you get this? Is this a custom built or original?"

"It was my father's." Toby said in a boastful tone. "I spent a few years restoring it. The engine is all original, but a few rusted parts needed to be taken off and the finish needed to be redone."

"Well these old ladies don't have the same power as the modern equivalent, but I'll take leather and steel over vinyl and Plexiglas any day."

After a few minutes, she peeled her eyes off the bike and looked up, "This is really cool."

"Thank you."

Lia'na quickly realized what was happening, "Wait, we're going to take it out? You expect me to ride with you on this?"

"Yup." Toby replied casually.

"Tobias I… I don't know about this. Is it safe?"

"What don't tell me that this is your first time out on one?"

"Um, yeah, it's not like my clan had access to a lot of this stuff. The only bike I ever saw was a lot more modern than this and it was a lot bigger."

"Don't worry. I won't let you get hurt."

Lia'na hesitated as she looked the bike over. Toby had installed a two-person seat with support so someone could lean back and hold on to a bar behind them, if they so desired. She slowly shook her head while deciding, but finally sighed, "Okay, I trust you. I just hope I don't live to regret it."

"Good." Toby replied with a smile as he handed her a helmet.

She snapped it in place over her head, but it didn't cover her ears very well. Obviously, it wasn't made for an elf. He then also handed her a pair of sunglasses before putting his own pair on. She looked at him oddly, "No helmet for you?"

"Nah, it just makes you a better looking corpse if anything happens."

"Oh that's reassuring!" Lia'na yelled.

Toby laughed as he revved the engine. Lia'na leaned back and grabbed on to the bar behind her. The engine roared as they slowly rolled out of the unit. Lia'na felt it jerk forward and began to panic, "Tobias, I think I've changed my mind, I don't want to…"

The bike suddenly jolted forward again and they were off before she could finish her sentence. A loud scream escaped her lips as she held on for dear life. Toby chuckled under his breath as he listened to her. Lia'na's heart was beating so hard that she was sure it would burst out of her chest. She leaned forward, closed her eyes, and grabbed on to Toby's jacket. She then buried her face in his back, petrified that she'd fall off.

After a few minutes of almost having a panic attack, Lia'na calmed down enough to open her eyes and look around. To her surprise, it was actually an exhilarating to watch the scenery blow past them. She finally loosened up and opened her eyes even wider.

Once they cleared the tall buildings and turned onto the main street, in the distance, she could see the massive Hancock Tower high above the other buildings in Boston. It was an awesome sight. Much to her amazement, she was actually enjoying this. A wide smile briefly appeared on her lips as the world blew by.

VII

The bike rode on for about 20 minutes until Lia'na saw a white sign which read 'Entering Revere EST 1871.' Before long, she noticed another sign. This one was for the VFW parkway. They soon turned on to Beach Street.

Lia'na could smell the sea breeze as the ocean appeared between the buildings in the distance. Once Beach Street ended, Toby veered left onto Revere Beach Boulevard and slightly picked up speed. The engine roar as the wind blew by.

The view was spectacular. Lia'na's eyes darted in every direction. She'd never really been to the ocean before as her people dwelled inland, "Ta Diesu, this is incredible!"

Toby smiled and yelled back to her, "I thought you'd like it."

"You thought correctly, ta arsha. Lien ni for bringing me here."

"Ta arsha? So we're friends again?"

Lia'na rolled her eyes and nodded, "Yes, I forgive you."

"Good."

He slowed down a little as they approached Carey Circle. Just as before, the area was almost completely deserted with the exception of a few joggers. He pulled into the circle and parked his bike right at the beach. The tide was coming in and so the waves were slowly crawling up the shore.

An excited Lia'na jumped off the back of the bike, pulled her helmet off, and ran up to the wall to see the ocean. Toby turned his bike off, pulled off his leather jacket, and followed her. She turned to look at him as he leaned down next to her, "I've never been to the beach before."

"Really, never?"

"We never left the reservation much growing up. It's part of the reason I wanted to go to school away from the other elves. I wanted to see the world."

"I can understand that."

Lia'na remained quiet for a few moments before turning back to Toby, "Do you come here often?"

"Yeah, you really don't want to stick around here too late, but during the day, it's a pretty nice place. Riding up and down Revere Boulevard helps me clear my head."

"I can definitely see why."

After about ten minutes of staring at the ocean and sucking in deep breaths of the sea breeze, she turned around and leaned against the wall, "So you've successfully abducted me, and taken me to a far-off destination away from prying eyes. You've got me all to yourself now, do you want to talk?"

"Yes… I think I need to."

With his hands firmly planted on the concrete, Toby turned around and pulled himself up so he was sitting on the wall. His eyes focused on the brown condo building behind him, "How did you know?"

"About the disturbance in your class?"

"Yeah, you weren't there."

"No… but the aura was so strong, it was hard not to notice. I could feel it like a blast of cold wind."

"How?"

"My people are sensitive to all things in nature. Magic draws its power from life, death, and the elements. When you used your magic, you drew the heat out of the air and let it empower you."

"Magic… So what, I can pull a rabbit out of my ass?"

Lia'na rolled her eyes, "You're not buying any of this, are you?"

"No. The Lux Mundi was destroyed years ago and the rumors of it giving people the ability to use magic are a mix of truth and legend."

"All legend is based in-part on a reality. In this case, it's no mere bedtime story."

Lia'na sat next to him and looked into his eyes, "Have you ever wished for something to happen and it became reality? When you experience intense emotion, does the world around you seem to be affected?"

That seemed to catch Toby off guard, "Occasionally, but it's never been this strong. Usually I let it go like it was a coincidence."

"I knew this day would eventually come. It was only a matter of time before I met a sensitive."

"A sensitive? What does that mean?"

"You have the gift of the enchanters. Your unrefined powers are quickly manifesting."

"I don't understand, how did this happen?"

Lia'na shrugged, "In the old days, being a sensitive was a rare gift. Only one in a several thousand had the abilities, and of those thousands, only a handful ever realized their powers."

"But how is that possible? The Lux Mundi was destroyed millennia ago."

"Not quite…" Lia'na whispered. "Not all of it."

"What do you mean?"

Lia'na closed her eyes and unzipped the windbreaker she was wearing. She then unbuttoned the collar of her shirt and pulled it apart to reveal the necklace that he'd seen the other night. It was gold with an odd looking medallion that encased an orange stone in the middle. Toby's eyes widened, "Are you telling me…"

"Yes, my ancestors were the ones who destroyed the diamond. When it shattered, one piece was recovered before the rest plunged into a volcano. It was fashioned into jewelry and passed down through the generations. It contains only a fraction of the power the original diamond had, but it is enough to affect a sensitive."

"So you're the reason this keeps happening?"

"Well not entirely." Lia'na replied. "My shard only enhances what's already there. Nothing can force you to use your powers. An instant burst of strong emotion can cause it."

"Strong emotion... yeah that sounds about right."

"Tobias, tell me honestly, what happened?"

"Only if you call me Toby like the rest of my friends."

"Okay fine. Ta arsha, Toby."

Toby smiled and sucked in a deep breath, "Okay well I was worried when I didn't see you in class. Given what happened, I was afraid you were either too scared or that you had left school, or worse."

"I was scared." Lia'na admitted. "I can't explain it, after what happened, I just wanted to hide. I didn't want to see anyone. I guess part of me still feels that way."

"I don't blame you for that." Toby said as he put his hand on her shoulder.

His touch made her flinch a little. Realizing that he may have just crossed over the line, he pulled away, "Sorry."

"No don't be. It's not your fault. Quite the opposite... I mean…"

"You don't have to say it."

"Yes I do." She replied as her lips quivered. "If I don't, it'll just eat away at me forever and I will not spend my entire life being a victim."

She sucked in another deep breath as tears formed in her eyes, "The second time they hit me was after they tore my shirt. I put up a fight and one of them smacked me with the back of his hand. I'm positive that they would have raped me had you not shown up."

Tears began to flow down her cheeks and she fought against quivering lips, "I wanted to tell you, because I wanted you to know how much I appreciate what you did."

Toby rubbed her arm trying to calm her down, "It's okay, and I know that. Michael admitted as much in class. That's why I got so mad. I felt my blood boil and it felt like something exploded inside of me."

Lia'na wiped her eyes and struggled to regain her composure, "That sounds about right, at least from what I've read. What a mess. Ta arsha, I'm starting to think it would have been better had I just stayed on the reservation."

"You can't be blamed for just living your life. I don't even want to hear any more of it."

"Lien ni, for that." She said quietly. "Could I ask you…?"

Her voice trailed off for a moment allowing an uncomfortable silence to take over. Toby sat back and looked into her eyes, "Yes?"

"Tell me about your family." Lia'na replied. "Enchanter powers are passed down through heredity. Someone in your blood line must have had the same powers."

"Hell if I know. My father died before I was born, according to my uncle. My mother raised me until I was three years old. I only have a few scattered images of her in my mind. It's not much. I was too young when she died."

An apologetic look appeared on her face, "I'm sorry."

"It's okay. It happened. There wasn't anything I could do about it. Though... I sometimes wonder how different my life would have been had they survived, but it's not like it's something that depresses me anymore. I barely knew them and I have a good life."

"So who raised you?"

"My uncle Jacob did until I was old enough to fend for myself."

"Fend for yourself? You mean he gave you the boot?"

Toby laughed, "Of course not. He's a good guy, but he didn't ask to raise me. I kind of got thrown in his lap. When I got old enough to understand my situation, I figured out that my uncle had given up a lot to care for me. I didn't want to be a burden, so at 18, I packed my things and told him I was going out on my own. He didn't like the idea at all, but I was adamant. He kept my room up, but I only rarely used it."

"But how did you live? An 18 year old out on his own, that's a tough life."

"Yes... Fortunately my parents set everything up in their will. The old family house was sold off, but I got every penny of it. That plus they had a considerable stock portfolio that had been maintained, and a decent savings. It was enough to put me through college and sustain me for about six or seven years until I got my act together."

"So where do you live when you're not at school?"

"I actually have a permanent residence on campus and I spend a lot of time at my roommate's house. They kind of took me in, but always feel like a burden, so I've been shopping around for a condo for myself or something."

"I couldn't imagine what that's like." Lia'na admitted. "I was raised by my entire clan in New Hampshire."

"That must be nice, but you've got to understand a little. I mean how many of your kind are left?"

"Not many at all. I don't have an exact count, but I know it's less than a thousand. It can be a little hard to grasp that I'm a member of an endangered species."

Toby turned himself around so that he was facing the ocean. They sat in silence for a moment before an idea popped into Toby's head. He pulled his shoes and socks off, and rolled up his pant legs. Then, before Lia'na could figure out what was going on, he began to run towards the water.

Lia'na looked at him oddly, "What are you doing?"

Toby stopped just as the cold water began to caress his toes, "Come on!"

"No way, it's too cold!"

"Aw come on, it'll be fine."

Lia'na sighed as she stripped off her windbreaker and placed it on top of Toby's jacket. She then rolled up her own pants and pulled off her sandals. Once everything was secure, she jumped over the sea wall and ran down the beach after him.

Toby began to run again once she was within a few feet. Water splashed up all around them as they ran through the surf. Lia'na chased him down the beach. The more she ran, the more her legs got soaked. As she got close enough to grab him, something caught her foot, causing her to stumble. Toby reacted in time to stop her from falling into the surf. He grabbed her by the waist and held her until she regained her balance.

Lia'na placed her right hand on Toby's shoulder to balance herself and looked up into his eyes. She was mystified by what resembled a pair of blue sapphires. Toby didn't let go as time slowed to a halt. The water that had splashed up around them slowed until the small drops hung motionless in the air.

Lia'na smiled nervously as she grabbed on to his arms. She could feel her heart race and began to tremble. Despite her best effort to hide it, Toby noticed, "What's wrong?"

"Nothing's wrong, why?"

"You're trembling."

"The water's cold." Lia'na said as she looked down at her feet.

Toby smiled, "Bullshit."

"Will you just shut up and hold me, instead of analyzing everything to death?"

Toby chuckled as he pulled her close. As their bodies pressed against each other, the diamond around Lia'na's neck began to glow dimly. Toby felt his heart seize up as she rested her head over it. He fought to fill his lungs with air as it felt like his chest was going to collapse. At that moment, a large column of wind swirled around them, sucking water into the air. As the column climbed over their heads, it shimmered from the sunlight passing through it.

Toby looked up in amazement. What he was seeing was physically impossible, but here it was. He looked at Lia'na, "Is this a dream?"

Lia'na shook her head, "It's as real as you want it to be."

"How are you doing this?"

"I'm not doing anything. You are."

"How?"

"Isn't it obvious? Strong emotions push an enchanter's power to the surface."

Toby turned back and focused on Lia'na. She returned his gaze, "Go ahead, reach out with your mind, you can control it."

Toby closed his eyes and lifted his arms off of Lia'na. The water intensified and the column grew taller. At the top, Toby made it plume and spray out like a fountain. Lia'na smiled as she watched him work. Toby was only able to keep focus for a few moments. His breathing became labored and the water column collapsed.

The water crashed down around them drenching their pants. Toby sighed as his eyes opened and he lowered his arms. He felt dizzy and almost fell forward, but Lia'na was there to keep him from falling into the water. Their faces passed within an inch of each other as his chin came to rest on her shoulder.

It took him a moment to shake off the sudden drain of energy, but when he came to and pulled back slightly, his face stopped in front of hers. They stared into each other's eyes for a few moments.

Lia'na's eyes were big and easy to read. They were full of life, but he could also see sadness. She had been through a lot, but somehow managed to grin and bear it. He pushed closer to her until their lips touched, barely giving a thought to the consequences.

Lia'na was in a momentary state of shock as they kissed, but as her heart skipped a beat, she closed her eyes and pressed back. Her left hand found the back of his neck and gripped him tightly.

Their lips remained locked for a few moments before she finally released him and he pulled back. Her heart was racing and her lungs felt like all the air had just been forcefully sucked out of them. She looked up at Toby and smiled nervously, "Iesau, that was…"

She bit her lower lip hard as she turned away from him. Toby looked at her confused, "What is it?"

"No… nothing."

She glanced around quickly as she faced the shore, "Iesau look at us; we're soaked. We should probably head back before it gets any colder out. We don't want to catch our death here."

"Um… okay."

The two of them walked out of the surf, back to the sea wall without saying a word. Toby caught Lia'na glancing over at him a few times, but she refused to look him in the eyes. It was an awkward walk back to Carey Circle. Neither one spoke even after reaching the sea wall.

Once they got their jackets back on, and sat on the bike, Toby looked back at Lia'na, "Look, I'm sorry if I made you uncomfortable. We can pretend that didn't happen if you want."

"You didn't Toby I…" Lia'na nervously stammered as she tried to find the right words.

She didn't want to offend Toby or say anything else she might regret, "You didn't, but I don't want to talk about this here. Can we please, just go?"

Toby shrugged, "Fair enough."

The bike roared as Toby hit the ignition. This time, Lia'na was more relaxed about riding on the Harley and leaned back against the hand rest. The bike sped off back to storage unit.

VIII

The trip home was not a long one, but it gave Toby enough time to go crazy from repeating what happened at the beach in his mind. It didn't help that his legs were freezing or that Lia'na was completely silent. No matter how many times he went over it in his head, he came to the same inescapable conclusion; he should not have kissed her. *What were you thinking Toby? She's an elf, you're a human. You have any idea what you're getting into?*

At that moment, his logical side kicked in; *Yeah right... since when do I care what other people think? If the 'right' in society is what Michael was planning on doing, then I don't think that's where I want to be. Maybe kissing her was wrong, but I wasn't going to know that if I didn't try..*

Finally, Toby could take anymore, balled a fist and hit the gauge in front of him on the bike. His sudden outburst made Lia'na jump, "Are you okay?"

"Yeah I'm fine, don't mind me."

Nice job dude, Toby thought to himself. *She probably thinks you're nuts now!*

Lia'na's mind wasn't doing much better as the sudden collision of emotions had her re-examining her decisions. *Maybe I shouldn't have gone with him to the beach. If only I could explain why I was out of it... he probably thinks he went too far. He is nice, and I do like him... but my clan wouldn't approve of this... but when have they ever approved of anything I've done? I hate keeping this from him, but he'd probably turn his back on me if I told him...*

Moments later, they arrived back at the storage unit. Toby hopped off his bike, grabbed some cleaner, and quickly wiped down the finish to prevent any rust from forming on it. Once he was done, he covered the bike over and locked up the unit. He then turned back to Lia'na, who was beginning to shiver, "Ready?"

"Yes." She replied, anxious to get behind closed doors.

The two of them walked quickly and got back to campus in half the time. Toby fully expected Lia'na to turn and head back to her own dorm, but to his surprise, she stayed on his heels. Their legs felt as though they would fall off from the cold.

They arrived at his dorm and went inside. Toby reached into his pocket and grabbed his key. He was about to unlock it, when he realized that Gishan was probably on the other side. Toby sucked in a deep breath. *God only knows what he's going to think this time.*

Toby inserted the key, turned it, and opened the door. Much to his relief, the room was empty. On his bed was a poorly written note;

> *"Toby,*
>
> *Bunking out for the night man. Yes, it is exactly what you probably think it is. I'll fill you in on all the details tomorrow... whether you want to hear them or not.*
>
> *-Gishan"*

"Oh good lord!" Toby exclaimed, rolling his eyes.

"What is it?" Lia'na asked.

"Well the good news is I've got the room to myself tonight... The bad news is I'm going to be losing my appetite for a week after I hear about the night Gishan had."

"Um, I'm sorry? How long have you two known each other?"

"Since High School. We both lived in Natick before we came here."

"Natick? I've heard it's a pretty nice area."

"Yeah it is. I loved living there."

Toby could see that Lia'na was still shivering, so he turned up the heat and closed the door behind her. He then walked over to his closet and pulled out his only clean bath robe, "Here, you can wear this if you want to take off those wet pants."

She looked at the robe and shrugged, "Okay…"

"Don't worry, I'm going to hit the shower real quick. You can change while I'm in there."

"Lien ni."

Toby grabbed a dry pair of pants and underwear from his drawer and turned to the bathroom, "I'll be right back."

Lia'na nodded as he closed the door behind himself. Once he was alone, he stripped off his damp jeans and tossed them over the shower curtain. He then pulled off his shirt and placed it on the towel rack. The hot water sprayed from the shower head as he turned the handle and jumped in. His legs began to sting a little due to the intense temperature change, but the pain quickly went away as the blood flow picked up.

Steam surrounded him and his skin began turning a dark pink. After a few minutes, he decided that he'd had enough and turned off the water. He quickly dried off, got dressed, and exited the bathroom.

Lia'na was waiting for him, wearing his robe. He noticed that she was still shivering, "Are you okay?"

"Yes. I'm sorry, elves don't handle being cold and wet so well."

"You can take a hot shower if you want."

"Are you sure?"

"Yeah go ahead."

Lia'na looked at the goose bumps forming on her legs, "I guess I don't have much choice. Lien ni."

She stood up, grabbed her jeans and the towel, and walked into the bathroom, closing the door behind herself.

Toby called to her from the other side, "I'm out here if you need anything."

"Lien ni."

She locked the door and pressed her back against it. *What am I doing,* she thought to herself, *I barely know this boy. What would my clan say? After what happened, I should be more guarded than this.*

Lia'na realized that maybe she wasn't being fair. *He did save me when I needed it the most. He didn't have to, and he never asked for anything in return, but do I really want to let my guard down this much and risk hurting him? I just don't know...*

When Lia'na had finally made up her mind, she stripped out of his robe and hung it on a hook behind the door. Then she unbuttoned the blouse that she was wearing and stripped off her bra. To her annoyance, the bottom of her shirt had also gotten wet. Finally she pulled off the bikini briefs that she had been wearing and turned on the shower. The heat warmed her pale skin as she stepped under the water.

The spray of the shower caressed her body and made her feel a lot better. She stopped shivering and breathed in deeply. The humid air soothed her lungs and allowed her to breathe more easily.

After a few minutes of savoring the heat, she turned off the water and let herself drip dry before grabbing the towel. She wrapped herself in it and tied the ends together on her side.

Lia'na brushed her wet hair back behind the points of her ears, making sure that her braids were still intact. She then grabbed her bra, ran the straps over her arms and hooked it together. Finally, she pulled on her bikini bottoms and wrapped herself tightly in Toby's robe.

When she was finally decent, Lia'na decided to rejoin Toby in his room. *I'm out of my mind, I'm out of my mind, I'm out of my mind,* she kept repeating to herself as she reached for the handle and opened the door.

Toby was sitting on his bunk trying to find something on TV when she appeared. The moment he saw her, he promptly stood up, "Feeling better?"

Lia'na nodded, "Much better, lien ni."

"You're welcome... I uh... heated up the subs from last night. I thought you'd want to eat."

Poor boy, she thought to herself. *He's trying so hard to behave himself and here I am nearly naked under his robe, not helping things. It's like dangling a piece of raw meat in front of a hungry dog.* "I appreciate it, I actually am pretty hungry."

He held a small tray up to her with two sandwiches on it, "Take whichever one you want."

"Lien ni, but can you do me a favor?"

"What's that?"

"Calm down." She said in a soothing voice. "You're acting all wired, like you're hooked up to a car battery. I'm sure you've seen girls in less than this."

"Well... yeah... I don't mean to seem standoffish. It's just... after what happened to you... for you to be here now..."

"Takes a considerable amount of trust. That's true, but you more than earned my trust that night."

"Good to know." Toby replied as Lia'na took the other half of the steak bomb.

Toby didn't eat much. He had a lot on his mind and instead just watched Lia'na as she ate half of the steak sub. After she finished, Toby finally spoke up, "I need to know more about these powers. No one's had these abilities in thousands of years and even then they were all myth and legend. So what should I do now? Are these powers dangerous?"

Lia'na shrugged, "That depends. They certainly can be."

"How?"

"Well you saw what you did when your emotions boiled to the surface. Your powers are only going to get stronger. So eventually, if you get mad enough, you could accidentally launch a fireball at someone."

"What? So I could actually hurt someone?"

A deep sigh escaped his lips, "Great... now what am I supposed to do, lock myself away?"

"No, of course not. I'll help you."

"How? What are you going to be my master or something?"

Lia'na laughed as she tried to explain, "I wouldn't go that far. I don't know how to use magic, but traditionally elves are required to learn the mental disciplines from a young age. It's why we're able to focus on tasks so easily. I can teach you how to do it, which should help stop you from blowing anyone up."

"So I'll be able to cast spells or something?"

Lia'na shook her head, "Like I said, I'm no enchanter, and I don't know how to cast spells. Unfortunately that's a long lost art."

"So I'll be able to control it, but not use it?"

"Pretty much. I'd be happy to get in touch with my clan elders to see if they have any recommendations, but none of them ever thought that they'd meet an enchanter in their lifetimes."

Toby wasn't happy. He stared down at his hands and shook his head. Lia'na put her hand on his shoulder to comfort him, "I know this is tough to swallow, but you can still live a normal life. I'm willing to help if you want."

Toby raised his head and looked at Lia'na. Her hazel eyes were slightly bigger than his and were quite beautiful as they shimmered in the setting sun. Looking at her, his problems suddenly didn't seem so bad, "All right, but before I accept your help, you have to do something for me."

"And what's that?" Lia'na asked as she eyed him suspiciously.

"Tell me about yourself. I've told you what I know about my family, but I don't know much about you."

The right side of Lia'na's mouth sharpened into a smile, "Fair enough, where do I begin?"

She thought for a few moments about her clan's history before continuing, "Well I'm a part of the White Water Clan. My people always favored the woodland areas near rapid rivers to build our homes, which have traditionally been tree houses. It was actually a big adjustment for me to sleep in a room that wasn't high up off the ground."

"How come?"

"It's just different. When you're high up in the trees, the air is thinner and you don't really hear anything on the ground. Mostly I'd sleep to a gentle breeze or maybe the sound of an owl or hawk nearby. Cars and things scampering on the ground are not sounds we're used to."

"I can imagine, but why rapid rivers?"

Lia'na shrugged, "Our people felt connected to them in some ways. The water served as a test of endurance for our warrior cast, and provided us a quick getaway from danger. The sound of the surging water also made it difficult for invaders to be able to hear where our people were hiding."

"Well I guess that makes sense, but what about your parents?"

Lia'na lowered her eyes, "They were the last victims of the Ulium, born a few years before a cure had been discovered."

Toby let out a brief sigh, "I didn't mean to pry."

"No, it's okay. You were curious, and I asked you about your parents, so it's only fair."

Toby wasn't sure if he should press for any more information. He wanted to know more, but he didn't want to bring up any more sour memories. Fortunately, she continued her story without being asked, "My clan raised me together. I stayed with various people until I could contribute. Once I was old enough, they wanted me to travel to the Netherlands to attend school with the main concentration of my people."

Finally Toby had an opening; he had wondered why she decided to come to a small, albeit reputable school like Arcanus. He had a slight feeling of trepidation as the words left his lips, "Why didn't you?"

"Everyone thought I should have, but I secretly applied for a government scholarship and was awarded a free ride to leave the reservation."

Lia'na's smile became more devious as she continued, "You should have seen the look on my clan elder's face when I told her what I was doing."

"Nice, but that doesn't answer my question."

"Why? Well to be honest, my people became xenophobic after the Ulium vaccine was discovered. Our species was dying out, not only from the Ulium, but from interspecies mating. Elven half-bloods were quickly outnumbering purebloods. The high elders felt that there shouldn't be any further mating between humans, dwarves, and elves. In an effort to preserve our race, anyone who was 50% elf or less was exiled from the lands set aside for us."

Lia'na twisted her lips as an annoyed look appeared on her face, "I didn't agree with their decision and I still don't. It was a group of human doctors which saved us from extinction. To close ourselves off from the world once we got what we wanted was incredibly selfish. So I defied them and said I was coming here to learn and grow. I came here to become a healer."

"Pre-med?" Toby asked as his eyes lit up. "Me too, do you have a specialty?"

"Elven anatomy and physiology. I may not agree with their views, but I do still want to help my people. What about you?"

"Genetics. I've always been interested in how breeding between species is even possible."

"That's a good one. Especially since our races supposedly evolved in different ways."

**

The two continued talking late into the evening. After what seemed like an eternity, Toby decided to try making another move. They were already sitting close to each other, so all Toby had to do was close the few inches between them. He could have measured the distance between them with his finger and thumb, but it felt like miles as he moved towards her. Either she didn't notice or didn't care, because she didn't try to back away or get defensive.

Toby waited for an opening, which finally came when Lia'na quieted down, "Toby… I really want to thank you again for everything. You've made me feel welcome like I'm not wasting my time here. I…"

That was his cue. Toby didn't waste another second and moved in. Their lips connected and he pressed them even tighter.

Once again, Lia'na was caught off guard. *What is it about this boy? Why is he interested in me, in an elf? Most*

of his kind look down on my people, why is he different?
The questions passed through her mind for a few minutes
before she focused on the most important one. *Why do I
even care? I like him, he likes me, that should be enough.*

At first, Toby wasn't sure if she'd reciprocate or smack
him. Much to his relief, Toby felt additional pressure on his
lips as she pushed hers into him. Toby ran his right hand up
her arm and pressed it against her back. They were both
using opposite hands to hold themselves up on the bunk, so
Lia'na raised her left hand and placed it on his back.

Their hearts raced as they held each other for too short
a time. Finally the moment Lia'na dreaded arrived when
their lips parted. Lia'na let air escape her still puckered
mouth. Her eyes didn't leave his as she bit down on her
lower lip.

Toby looked at her oddly, "What?"

"What does this mean?"

"I don't really know. What do you want it to mean?"

"Toby I…" Lia'na hesitated. More than anything she
wanted to unburden herself to Toby, but there were some
things that she knew that he wouldn't understand. "I want
this… I really do, but you have to understand. I'm elven,
there's a lot of baggage that comes with me."

"I don't think there is a person alive who doesn't have
baggage. I'm honestly not thinking that far ahead. What I
am thinking is that you're an intelligent, beautiful, person
who is still able to smile even after going through something
no one should ever have to. That's someone I'd like to get to
know and I don't care if you're an elf, human, or dwarf."

"You're really sweet," Lia'na said as her cheeks began
to turn red, "oblivious, but sweet."

Lia'na peered into his eyes, trying hard to read them.
She knew that it would be easier if she just turned him down

and went on her way, but seeing his sincerity, she couldn't say no, "All right, well if you're sure, then let's just see where this goes and leave it at that for now."

"Sounds good." Toby replied, clearly happy with her answer.

Lia'na leaned into him as the last rays of sunlight disappeared from the dorm window. Toby put his arm around her and gently squeezed. She closed her eyes as his warmth soothed any concerns she still had, "I guess I'm not going anywhere again tonight."

Toby looked down at her as she relaxed, "I can take the top bunk if you want."

"Eventually, but let me have this moment."

"No problem."

IX

Toby was awakened by the sound of an annoying chirp coming from his dresser. Much to his surprise, he was propped up against the bedpost in a seated position. Lia'na was lying on his knee fast asleep. His eyes widened, *oh shit... way to go dude, you just got her to open up to you. Now things are going to be awkward!*

Toby was careful not to wake her as he moved her head to his pillow. She stirred a little as Toby shut his alarm off. Realizing that he had to get to class, Toby grabbed a new shirt and changed out of the one he was wearing.

Lia'na opened one eye slightly and watched as he took his shirt off. He was in fine shape, not overly muscular, but not skin and bones either. Once he had another shirt on, she opened her eyes, "Enoi mae."

Toby jumped at the sound of her voice. Part of him was hoping that he'd get out of there before she woke up, but that didn't happen, "Um... Good morning?"

Lia'na slowly sat up, keeping one hand on the robe's opening, "You have class?"

"Yeah from 8-11, then I'm done for the day."

He slowly turned to face her once he'd straightened himself out, "Do you want to get lunch after?"

"Sure, sounds good."

Toby twisted his lips as he was hesitant to say anything else, but finally decided that dancing around things would get him nowhere with Lia'na, "Are you going to stay here, or go back to your room?"

Lia'na thought for a moment and decided to have a little fun with her newfound love interest, "Do you want me to stay here?"

She smiled as Toby went pale. *Too easy...* Lia'na stay on his bed, blinking her eyes at him.

"It's up to you."

Lia'na felt a twinge of irritation. *Oh now you're going to play the same game? No fun!*

She crossed her arms as she spoke, "Would you like it if I was still here when you got back?"

This is getting me nowhere, Toby thought, *and being open with her is what got me this far. Just tell her!*

Toby sucked in a deep breath, "It'd be nice."

Lia'na's smile widened and lay back slightly, "Then I'll wait here."

Toby sighed in relief as he grabbed his backpack and opened the door, "I'll see you after class."

Lia'na nodded as he closed the door. He made sure it was locked before he leaned against the adjacent wall for a moment. *Yes!*

*

Class took a lot longer than Toby expected. He found himself unable to focus in cultural biology, and nearly sent his frog sample flying across the room in Anatomy and Physiology. All he could think about was Lia'na and the events that brought them together.

It was incredibly frustrating. Toby was in class while the cutest girl he'd ever seen was waiting for him back in his dorm. He then thought of something he probably should have remembered before asking Lia'na to stay; *Gishan... oh no... I better hope he doesn't get back there before I do.*

Toby put the potential disaster out of his head while the professor gave her lecture. She spoke about the uses of medicine and ethical practices. Toby understood he needed this class for his major, but didn't get why it had to be so dry.

An hour went by as Toby stared blankly at the front of the room. It felt like he was being lectured, and not like a professor would do, more like a parent. It seemed like an eternity, but once she was finally finished, a strong sense of relief poured over him. He packed up his bag before running out of the classroom.

Toby cursed his luck when he realized that his final class had let out ten minutes late. Not knowing if Gishan was on his way back yet, he quickly darted across campus. As his dorm came into view, Michael suddenly obstructed his path and stopped him dead in his tracks, "Hey Toby."

Toby smiled deviously, "Hey Mikey, how's the nose?"

"Oh it's fine now, thanks for asking." Michael replied, feigning appreciation. "So how are you and the sharpy getting along? Has she let you in yet?"

"Shut up!"

Michael stepped back with a fake look of shock on his face, "Oooh so you couldn't get into her pants huh?"

"Get out of my way you prick." Toby replied as he brushed past.

"Fine, whatever, just know I'm watching you, and the sweet little sharpy."

Toby stopped dead in his tracks and turned around, "That a threat? She's an elf, and her name is Lia'na. Unless you want something more permanent than a busted beak, I'd watch yourself. I'm not afraid of you."

"Then you have nothing to worry about. See you around Toby."

As he turned his back on Michael, Toby fought the inclination to bust up his nose again. He put the confrontation out of his mind and kept walking. He knew that Michael wouldn't let it end there, but there was nothing he could do at that moment and getting into a fight would likely expose him to more manifestations of his power.

*

Meanwhile, in the dorms, Gishan was still glowing from the previous night's activities. He couldn't wait to tell Toby all about it. With the room key in hand, Gishan unlocked his door.

As he slowly pushed it open, he heard movement on the other side. *Toby must have gotten out early,* he thought to himself. However, when he pushed the door open, what waited on the other side was the last thing he expected.

Gishan found himself standing in his doorway with the elf-girl that he had met earlier looking back at him with a startled expression, "Gishan!"

Gishan's eyes narrowed, "Lia'na? What on Earth are you doing here? Wait... oh don't tell me..."

Lia'na struggled to reply, "Gishan, I... I thought..."

At that moment, Toby appeared behind the dwarf, "Hey Gishan, have a good night?"

"Yes... as did you apparently." Gishan replied with an unimpressed stare.

Lia'na frowned and crossed her arms, "If he did, it's not in the way you think."

"Uh huh..."

Toby knew that this meeting would soon be inevitable, but he was hoping it would be a lot smoother, "I asked her to stay."

Gishan rubbed his forehead, "Really man? So you and the sharpy?"

Toby was about to say something when Lia'na shot to her feet and glared at Gishan, "I don't appreciate that. I'm a person, and my name is Lia'na. We're not 'sharpys'any more than you're shorties. We're elves."

Gishan straightened up, realizing his error, "I... fuck, I'm sorry. It's a phrase I hear all the time, and since we don't see elves very often, I guess I'd forgotten it was kinda a racist term. Still that's no excuse."

"Apology accepted." Lia'na replied.

"I guess I shouldn't be surprised." Gishan said as he turned to Toby. "The one elf on campus and you're after her."

"After me?"

"Are you kidding? He's been talking about you for days. It actually got kind of annoying...."

Toby rolled his eyes and sighed, "You have a problem with it?"

"I guess not. I'm back from a human's room myself so... yeah."

"Good enough." Toby replied with a smile as he turned back to Lia'na. "Lunch?"

"Sure," Lia'na said, looking at her stomach, "but can we stop by my place first so I can change?"

"Not a problem. –Coming Gishan?"

"Nah, I think I need some time to recharge the batteries." Gishan repied as he closed the door behind them. "You kids have fun."

Lia'na led Toby out of his dorm. They walked together across the campus back to her room. They entered Leslie House a few moments later and Lia'na led him up the stairs to her room. She unlocked her door and turned to Toby, "Just a minute."

Toby nodded as she went in and closed the door. He heard some rustling and drawers opening and closing as he waited. At first it wasn't a big deal. He knew she was changing for lunch and had been in the same set of clothes since the day before, but after twenty minutes or so, it started getting a little tiresome.

When the door finally opened, Lia'na stood on the other side with her hair fixed, her makeup done, and she was wearing clean clothes. She had changed into a white top with floral designs near the hems, black slacks, and a beige knit shawl. Toby looked her over as she stepped out of the room. She was still trying to brush her hair behind her pointed ears, "Do I look okay?"

"Beautiful. You do know we're just going to lunch and not out to a fancy meal in Boston, right?"

Lia'na crossed her arms and pouted, "Oh so you ask me out, kiss me, and now that I've said yes, you're not going to treat me like a princess?"

Okay, now she's just messing with me... again.

Toby laughed, "Tell you what, if we survive to the weekend, I'll take you to any restaurant in Boston you want."

Still wanting to play with Toby a little bit, she frowned, "You have me at a disadvantage, sir. I admit I don't know Boston as well as I should."

"No problem, I know it very well. I'll find us a really nice one to try."

"It's a deal."

They left Leslie House and headed back out to the main campus. Lia'na's eyes darted back and forth looking for any sign of trouble. She felt safe with Toby, but didn't want to see him get into another fight.

As they entered cafe, Toby noticed his friend Tom standing at the entryway. When she saw Tom, Lia'na cringed. Despite biting her lips closed, she was unable to hide her feelings from Toby. He looked at Lia'na oddly as her pace slowed. He quickly took a small step in front of her as his eyes caught Tom.

Part of her didn't want to even see the guy. Seeing him sparked a memory that caused the bruise on her cheek to burn. The other part was ready to go into attack mode. As her face burned, she grabbed Toby's hand and held on tight, though she wasn't sure if she took Toby's hand to let him defend her, or prevent her from doing anything violent.

As they approached the hall, Tom looked at them nervously. Toby stopped and let go of Lia'na, "I'm taking her to get some food, got a problem with that?"

Tom shook his head, "Toby how long are we going to be like this?"

"I don't befriend rapists."

"What?" Tom asked as he glared at Lia'na. "I don't know what she told you, but I didn't do anything like that. Michael was the one who hit her!"

Toby looked back at Lia'na. His eyes asked her if what Tom was saying was true. She nodded in the affirmative, so he turned back to Tom, "Maybe not, but you wouldn't let her get food, you helped him gang up on her, and you didn't do a damn thing to stop him from beating on her."

"Look, I didn't know he was going to do that. I thought he was just going to scare her. Had I known..."

"You wouldn't have done a damn thing. That makes you just as guilty. You stood by when he hit her, and you stood by when he ripped her shirt open, didn't you?"

Tom's lower jaw quivered, "I... um..."

"That's what I thought. I have nothing else to say to you. I'll give you the same courtesy I gave Mike. Stay away, far away from me and I'll do the same with you."

Toby was about to step away when he remembered one last thing, "Oh, and if I find out you so much as darkened Lia'na's doorstep even a little, you're dead. Got it?"

Tom nodded as he looked at them both, "Yeah Toby, I get it... look, I'm sorry."

Lia'na gave him a slight nod, but wouldn't look him in the eye. She clenched her jaw and kept it shut. She'd always been someone who could turn the other cheek, but what would have happened to her if Toby hadn't shown up was more than she would be able to forgive. She just didn't have it in her.

Tom turned around and walked away without another word, "Enjoy your lunch."

Once he was out of earshot, Lia'na exhaled, "Was he a friend of yours?"

Toby nodded, "I knew him for a long time. We used to go to the gym together and hung around the same crowd."

"So I cost you a friend.... I didn't know."

Toby stopped in his tracks and turned to her, "Fuck him, I don't befriend people who pull shit like that. He acts all righteous like he's a good guy most of the time, but when push came to shove, he was a different person. I can't believe he would stand by and allow a woman to be assaulted."

Toby put his hand on her cheek and turned her head so her eyes met his, "This was not your fault. Tom chose his side and I chose mine. It happens sometimes. It sucks, but when our friends turn out to be something other than what we thought they were, this type of thing happens."

Lia'na nodded, "I guess you're right. Come on, let's go eat."

Toby turned and walked through the doorway with Lia'na close behind him. Toby grabbed a chicken sandwich off of the deli tray and waited for Lia'na to grab hers. He then pulled out some money and stood with her in the checkout line.

Once they got to the register, Toby handed the cashier a couple of dollar bills, and pointed to Lia'na's tray, "Hers also."

The cashier nodded and added her order to the total. Lia'na smiled, "You don't need to keep doing that. I have my own money, you know."

"I know, but I did."

Lia'na rolled her eyes, "Fine, but I got the next one."

"Maybe."

Lia'na sighed, "Do you plan to always be this frustrating?"

"As often as I can be. It's just what I do."

"Nice... This will be an interesting relationship."

X

Toby spent the next few months delegating his time between class and Lia'na. His friends were hesitant to accept her at first, but as time passed and they got used to her, she became one of them. Nothing really ever came of Michael's threats other than an occasional crude gesture from a distance. Tom quickly hid away from the spotlight and didn't participate in any further activities with the group.

It took Gishan some time to get used to the reality of Toby's abilities. It was hard to believe that Toby was a magic wielder, but after the outburst in class, it made sense. Despite Toby's fears, Gishan kept it quiet.

Lia'na enjoyed the frequent trips to Revere Beach with Toby. It was during this time that she began to teach him how to focus his mind. Though, she often wondered what would happen if he had the chance to reach his full potential. Just how powerful was he? Were his powers elemental, white, or black? At this point there was no way to be certain.

As their relationship became public knowledge, life changed for Toby on campus. Most of his friends stuck with him, but he had become a social pariah with others. In his biology classes, Toby's relationship was used as an example when the professors talked about interspecies breeding. It got really awkward some days.

Toby decided that it had become time for him to make a big push to move off campus. He contacted the real estate agent he'd been working with to put in an offer on a nice place he'd seen. He quickly calculated what he could afford and placed an offer that would allow him to buy the condo while still having enough money to sustain himself until he finished college and got a full time job.

The offer was submitted and came back accepted a few days later. Before Toby knew it, he had bought a small condo in Saugus. It was ample for him being as close to Revere as he could afford. The sellers were anxious to get out of ther condo and passed papers very quickly. Once that was done, he immediately began moving his things in.

As the days got warmer and more people frequented Revere, Lia'na and Toby weren't able to train at the beach as much, but they still enjoyed spending time there every chance they got. Lia'na loved running through the surf, feeling the sand between her toes, or even just walking along the shore with Toby.

Toby realized that summer was around the corner and he dreaded it. Lia'na's Elven reserve was in New Hampshire just outside of Milan, which was far from Saugus or Arcanus. The distance wouldn't be too bad as he was living just north of Revere, but he'd gotten used to seeing her every day.

Lia'na felt the same sense of dread. She'd grown attached to Toby as the months went by and wasn't ready to put their relationship on the back burner for the summer. She considered her options and knew that she had to return to her clan at some point, so she called her reservation in an attempt to make plans.

*

May came quicker than either of them wanted it to. Lia'na was still working out the details, but she was determined to make her plan happen. One night as the two of them relaxed together in Toby's bunk, she rolled on her side and looked up at him, "How did your anatomy exam go?"

"Not bad, I think I did all right," Toby replied, "but why does it always seem like the multiple choice questions have multiple right answers?"

"That's good, at least you got through it. You were worried about that one for weeks."

"Yeah well, Professor Edwards isn't the easiest grader."

"Yeah I bet." Lia'na said in a low voice.

Toby looked at her as she stared off into space, "Are you okay? You look like there's something on your mind."

Lia'na lowered her eyes, "Toby, can I ask you something?"

"Uh oh, what's up?"

Lia'na was extremely nervous. After everything she had gone through just convincing her clan that College with humans was a good idea. Now she was planning on taking another step over the line and God only knew where that would land her, "Toby, how long are we going to dance around this?"

Toby sat up slightly and turned to face her, "What are you talking about?"

"Summer's almost here, we have another week, and then I'm leaving."

Toby sighed as he lay back on his pillow, "Yeah I know, I've been trying not to think about it."

"Well we need to. What are we going to do?"

"I can come visit you whenever you want. I mean, I was going to see if I could get a job for the summer, but I'm sure I can get some days off. You could come down and stay at my new place."

"I still can't believe you bought a condo. How much money did your parents leave you?"

"Enough to get by. Plus I've been adding to it over the years and never really spent anything I didn't have to."

"Well, that's smart I guess," she admitted, "and now you have a permanent home."

"Exactly, no more mooching off of my roommate's family. They've been great, but my time was going to come sooner or later."

Lia'na still thought he was crazy to buy the place, but she understood why he wanted to. Still, she needed to redirect the conversation back to their summer plans, "I don't know about coming down, Toby. I don't really have a car. I take buses back and forth."

"Well then I can come see you. It's no big deal."

There was a detectable level of hesitation in Lia'na's voice as she spoke, "I… have a better idea, if you're interested."

"I'm listening."

"I spoke to my clan elder. I told her about what you did for me and she'd like to meet you. My clan is extending you an invitation to come stay with us for a while."

"At the Elven Reservation? I didn't think they'd welcome an outsider. I've heard about them going so far as protesting hikers on their land."

Lia'na bit her lip hard, "Well, because of how you helped me, they decided to make a special exception. You want to know more about my people? Now's your chance."

"Cool." Toby replied happily. "In that case, I'll pack a few bags and go with you."

"Really?" Lia'na said in a partially excited tone.

"It's one of the advantages of being on my own; I can do whatever I want for the most part."

*

As the next week went by, Toby finished up his exams and got ready for what he was sure would be an interesting experience. He didn't know what to expect from the elves. He had never even seen more than one or two at a time. This could easily be a culture shock. It didn't help that his mind was loading up with questions; would they welcome him, would they like him, and most importantly, would they approve of him dating one of their own?

The day finally came when the two of them began making their way to New Hampshire. They hopped a bus that took them to the Orange Line. When the train pulled into Downtown Crossing, they switched to the Red Line and went to the terminal at South Station in Boston.

Toby and Lia'na grabbed their bags and headed up the paved staircase from the subway terminal to the main station. Though she had seen it before, Lia'na was still amazed as she passed through the glass doors. The inside of the station was all marble and granite. She stopped for a moment with her eyes wide, looking around.

Toby smiled and took her hand as she watched people walk by, "It's incredible what you humans have built here."

"Not just humans, the dwarves supplied a lot of this stone for us, from what I heard."

Lia'na's head kept darting back and forth as they passed a news stand and an ATM kiosk. At the other end of the main station a bookstore, train station, and several eateries stood, surrounded by travelers.

Outside at the terminal, a large coach bus was waiting for them at the stop. Toby took Lia'na's hand as they sat next to each other three rows up from the back of the bus. There was a loud hiss and the door closed.

Toby watched the bus terminal disappear from view and turned back to Lia'na, "So… anything I should know before I meet your family?"

Lia'na had a nervous look in her eyes as she responded, "Yes, they're a very traditional people; they don't like a lot of new technology. So if you're going to use any electronic devices, do so in private. That includes your phone. Keep it on vibrate, and don't answer it at gatherings in the presence of the elder. Speaking of which, when it comes to the elder, don't speak unless spoken to. Finally…"

Lia'na's voice trailed off and her lips quivered. Toby's eyes narrowed, "What is it?"

"Piele don't get mad at me for this."

Toby rolled his eyes, "I hate it when you do this. Usually you say that when you know it's something that will make me mad."

"Exactly... Piele?"

"Fine, what is it?"

"Piele don't mention anything… about us."

Toby glared at her, "You haven't told them?"

"No. Try to understand it's complicated. You think the kids on campus didn't take news of us very well… It's worse with them. Piele, I promise I'll make it up to you."

"They need to know." Toby said in an angry tone.

"I know that, and I promise I'll tell them, just piele let me do it on my own terms."

"Fine, but you could have told me this before I agreed to go with you."

"Don't be like that. We're going to have fun and I will tell them while we're there, I promise."

"All right." Toby replied, clearly not convinced.

The bus passed over a large bridge and the sound of wind hit the side of the bus as the two of them watched the city pass by. Toby spent some time thinking about what Lia'na told him about her family and wanted to ask her about them, "Lia'na, how old is this elder?"

"She's in her mid-forties. Why do you ask?"

"Mid-forties is old enough to be an elder?"

Now Lia'na understood where Toby was going with his question, "She was among the first elves in my clan to receive the vaccination. Most that were older than her have long since died of the Ulium. The only ones left are the High Elders and most of them are very sick as well."

"I see."

*

The trip took about three hours. Toby watched as the busy industrial areas began to give way to the large trees of New Hampshire's forests. Before he knew it, the bus was pulling into the station where they would be getting off. It slowed to a halt and let out a low hiss as the doors opened.

Lia'na took Toby by the hand and led him off the bus. Once they were on solid ground, Toby grabbed their bags and turned to see where they were going. Lia'na moved towards the parking lot.

There was a small group of people standing at the other end of the terminal, waiting. They were unmistakably Elven. This was no doubt their ride to the reservation. Toby sucked in a deep breath and followed closely behind Lia'na.

Suddenly, Lia'na's eyes lit up when she saw an older woman standing in the group, "Masarabi!"

The woman smiled and spread her arms as Lia'na took off running towards her, "Eluvi, Lia'na, lineas habi."

Lia'na wrapped her arms around the woman, "Eluvi, Masarabi!"

Then she turned back to Toby, "Elder, this is Tobias Arrigan, the one I told you about."

Masarabi looked Toby over for a moment and nodded, "Eluvi, Toby. Lineas to our home."

Toby thought back to some of the Elvish Lia'na used, "Eluvi, Masarabi, lien ni."

Lia'na smiled as a surprised look came over the elder's face, "You honor me, young man, with the proper use of our language."

"It was the least I could do for someone who has opened their home to me, but unfortunately that's all the Elvish I know."

"It's never wise to use up all your tricks at one time." The elder chuckled.

"Sage advice."

Lia'na turned and spoke to the other two elves that had come with Masarabi. They walked to the van that was waiting for them in the nearby parking lot. The van was an old maroon dodge ram with three rows of seats. It was dented on the outside, but the interior looked brand new.

Lia'na sat next to Toby while the elder took the seat in front of them. As the old van started up, the elder brushed her silver-lined hair back and turned to the side so that she could see Toby, "So, Lia'na tells me that you were of some assistance to her a few months ago on campus?"

"Well, it wasn't anything major, just a couple of punks. I did what I hope anyone would do in the same situation."

"I fear that hope might have been misplaced. Still, you have my unending gratitude for keeping her safe."

Toby looked over at Lia'na, "It was my pleasure. I made a friend out of it, so it was more than worth it."

The elder nodded as she turned to the other side, "Lia'na, I trust that this experience has given you a little more insight into your choice, and you are ready to come home?"

The elder's question caught Lia'na off guard, "Masarabi... no, I stand by my decision. I'm not giving up on my scholarship, or how I wish to live. Toby should be more than enough proof that not every kaylra is as you say."

"Indeed? I would have thought you'd finally seen the world for what it is. Do you think this young man wants to be burdened with continuously coming to your rescue?"

Toby was about to speak up when Lia'na raised her hand to silence him, "Masarabi, can we speak of this later on, in private?"

"As you wish."

Toby looked at Lia'na with a confused expression. The moment their eyes met, she turned away in anger. *We're goung to have fun huh? Off to a great start...*

The rest of the ride was silent and awkward. Toby didn't know what to make of any of this. He understood that her family didn't want her going to school with humans and it made sense why. However, he also understood her need to gain important experiences and to not be restrained by overbearing parent figures. It was a conundrum and both sides had a point that made sense.

Toby's thoughts were interrupted as the van came to a halt. The doors opened and everyone jumped out. Toby got out behind Lia'na and surveyed the reservation. It was all well-kept woodland lands with beautiful flower gardens and the sound of raging water from the rapids behind it.

Toby closed his eyes and breathed in deeply. The flowers had been organized in a way so that their colors were paired up to form an interesting pattern on the ground. They were fed by moisture coming off the water.

The sound of the water and the smell of the fresh air, filled him with a sense of serenity, "This is beautiful, we don't have places like this in the city."

Lia'na smiled, "I knew you'd like it."

The elder strolled ahead of them, "You are most kind, Tobias. Our people work hard to keep this place."

The elder clapped her hands together and instantly, two more elves landed next to them. Toby didn't even see them hiding in the trees and was startled by their sudden appearance. He looked up and scanned the trees to see if there were any more of them.

Lia'na laughed, "You can look for hours, and you won't see them. The sentries are trained to be masters of blending into their environment."

The elder turned to face her sentries, "Take Tobias's and Lia'na's things to their accommodations."

Toby let go of his bags, allowing the sentries to take them. The sentries had dark hair and what looked like war paint on their faces. They were dressed in old-style tunics and cloth pants. As Toby handed off his last bag, the sentry closest to him nodded, "You are welcome in our home. We hope you find it peaceful."

Toby smiled, "I'm sure I will."

Lia'na took his hand, "Come on. Let me show you the rapids."

As she was about to lead Toby away, she turned back to the elder, "Dinner at the same time?"

The elder nodded, "As always."

As Lia'na led him away, Toby looked back to see that the sentries had disappeared again, "Those sentries... that's kind of spooky."

"They are trained to be stealthy and deadly. You don't want to get on their bad side."

She led Toby over to water where they watched the mist flow off the white rapids as it crashed by. Toby put his arms over her shoulders. Before he could pull her close to him, Lia'na ducked out shaking her head, "Toby piele, not here. We don't know whose watching. If they see us..."

Toby nodded, "Sorry."

"Not your fault. Come, let me show you the rest."

There were torch poles all along the shore that were lit at night to keep the river illuminated. Lia'na led Toby to a small pool that was fed by the rapids. The torches were much lower to the ground all around it, and flat stone slabs lined the opening.

Toby inspected the pool to see what it was. A small gust blew the steam from the water into his face, "A hot spring?"

Lia'na nodded, "We can't explain why it's here, but it's a nice way to unwind at the end of the day. We can come back here later."

"Glad I brought swimming shorts."

Next Lia'na showed him where they lived. Each house was elevated at least ten feet off the ground and built into the tree they were attached to. Toby was led up a long, winding staircase to his room. All of his things had been left there for him.

Much to Toby's amazement, they had electricity that appeared to be generated by solar panels on the roofs of each house. Even more impressive was the fact that they had running water and showers in these houses. Lia'na backed out of the room, "Well, rest up, get yourself settled, and I'll see you for dinner."

She pointed across the walkway, "I'm in the next room if you need anything."

Before she turned away, Toby remembered something he wanted to ask her, "Lia'na, quick question."

She paused and looked at him, "Yes?"

"What's a kaylra?"

"You are. It's the Elvish word for human."

Toby nodded as she closed the door behind him. He turned back and looked at his room. Everything was made of wood for the most part, the bed, the tables, everything. Before he could unpack his bags, his door flew open and he felt a hand grab his shoulder.

Toby was whirled around to see Lia'na smiling at him. She closed the door and pressed him against the wall, "This is for being so understanding."

She kissed him deeply and held him in place as he rested his hand on the small of her back. When she let go, she was breathing slightly heavier. Her eyes didn't leave Toby's as she backed out the door biting her lip, "Dinner in an hour. It's in the main hall below us. See you then."

"I'll be there."

He laid himself out on the queen sized bed in the middle of the room. *What are you doing here Toby?*

Something isn't right. Why hasn't she told the elder about us? Is she embarrassed to be in a mixed relationship? No, that's not like her, there has to be something else...

Toby cleared his mind and got changed into some nicer clothes. He straightened up a button-down dress shirt and put one some nice khakis on. He wasn't sure if any of this was really needed, but he decided that first impressions were important, so he went to work.

A knock came at his door as he finished up. He opened the door to see Lia'na standing behind it. His eyes went wide when he saw her. She was wearing silky white robes that almost looked like they glowed. Her hair was done up in braids with intricate wooden charms holding them in place, and a gem draped down the center of her forehead. He also noticed she wasn't wearing any makeup.

"Wow. You look amazing."

"Lienes." She replied with a blushing look. "You too."

She held her right hand out to Toby. He took it and held on as they walked down the flight of stairs to one of the central buildings between the trees. Inside stood a large table with plates of food completely covering the surface. One by one, the elves of the clan filed in. They all stood at their chairs, waiting for the elder. Toby followed Lia'na's movements as she stood close by to make sure that he didn't make a fool of himself.

The elder finally entered the room and stood at the head of the table, "Eluvi mana."

"Good evening." Lia'na whispered into Toby's ear.

Toby nodded as the elder continued, "We have a guest with us today. Miastre Tobias Arrigan. He is a friend of our sister Lia'na, who saved her from harm during her time away from us."

A polite applause came from the room as Toby gave a slight bow. The elder took her seat and raised her arms, "You may all be seated, let dinner commence."

They sat down and began to eat. As Toby added some bread to his plate, the elder spoke up, "So Tobias, tell us what you study at this college of yours."

Toby cleared his throat, "Well I'm a pre-med student with a focus on inter-racial genetics."

"Ah…" The elder replied. At first, Toby didn't know if she knew what that meant, but then she leaned forward and spoke again, "So you study half-breed children?"

"Exactly. I've always been intrigued by how two different species of sentient beings, with different traits and DNA, could procreate. You'd think they'd be incompatible. It's like trying to mate a dog with a cat, it just wouldn't work, but the children always seem to come out strong. Mixed breeds always seem healthier, livelier, and are less susceptible to illnesses than purebloods."

Toby looked around the room at the elves eating their food, "No offense, of course."

"None taken, it is a fascinating phenomenon. However I didn't think that there were many hybrid children between elves and humans left out there, after the Ulium was cured."

Toby nodded, "That's true, but there are still enough to do case studies on. We also have donated embryos that have been preserved and computer modeled DNA sequences."

The elder sat back, "I see, very interesting indeed."

Lia'na quietly smirked as she knew that her elder had no idea what DNA sequences or embryos were. Toby ate his meal quickly and spent the rest of the time talking to the other elves around him. They were understandably curious about Toby, and his story.

As time passed and the sun began to disappear behind the trees, the elder raised her hands, "Well, it is getting late. Let us adjourn from dinner."

Everyone stood up and cleaned off their plates. Toby brought his over to the sink where an elf on kitchen duty took it and cleaned everything. Then Lia'na guided Toby out of the hall and back to his small bedroom. She stood by the door looking into his eyes for a few minutes, "I'm going to turn in, it's been a long day and I'm tired. You should too; you have quite an adventure ahead of you."

Toby smiled, "I can't wait."

Lia'na had a small grin on her face as she threw herself into his arms. As soon as she was close enough, she pressed her lips against his and held on for a few moments, savoring the feeling. When they finally released each other, Lia'na took a few steps backwards in an almost seductive manner, "That's payment for not letting you touch me earlier."

Toby nodded and he exhaled, "Worth it."

"I'm glad. Have a good night."

As the door closed behind her, Toby fell backwards onto his bed. The hand-knitted blankets and sheets were incredibly soft as they caressed his skin. *What a day,* he thought to himself. *This will be an interesting summer.*

XI

Over the next few weeks, Lia'na showed him as much as she could, and what she couldn't, the sentries did. Her clan was small, with only 20 elves, but this was the norm, given how diminished their numbers were.

It wasn't long before Toby felt like he completely fit in. Part of him wasn't looking forward to leaving at the end of the summer. The sentries taught him how to blend into his surroundings, hunt for food, and one day in mid July, even challenged him to a river rapids boat race. The head sentry, Auro, was particularly adamant that he join them, "Come on Tobias. Let's see if you can master the wild waters!"

Lia'na completely objected to is, "Toby, if you've never been on the rapids before, you could drown!"

Not wanting to disappoint his hosts, Toby felt that he had to partake as though it were a rite of passage. So without thinking, he jumped into the boat and turned to the sentries, sitting in their own, "You ready?"

Both boats were untied and began flowing down river. Several elves watched from the shoreline as Toby realized he'd been had. The boat jerked around a few times and before Toby could react, it flipped over. He found himself clinging to the keel as the boat picked up speed.

Lia'na ran along the shore screaming out to the sentries, "Auro, if he drowns, you'll be next!"

Toby's boat jerked around as it continued to pick up speed. Meanwhile Auro and the other sentry had to keep making corrections to keep their boat going directly into the flow. Toby grabbed on and straddled the bottom of the boat like it was a surf board. The wind whipped through his wet, matted, hair as he held on tight.

To everyone's shock, Toby's boat crossed the finish line first. The elves cheered as Toby grasped a fallen branch and pulled himself out of the water. The sentries' boat came to shore nearby. The moment it touched land, the two sentries jumped out and made their way to the crowd.

Lia'na gave them a devious look, "Some sportsmen you are! You just got beat by a guy with a half-sunk boat!"

Auro chuckled, "It was a loss worth taking."

Everyone cheered for Toby as he dried off while tending to his wrecked nerves. Lia'na helped him up as the sentries patted him on his back. Toby was waterlogged, but he was happy. Lia'na had been worried about him and it appeared that he'd earned the sentries' respect. He went to bed with a feeling of accomplishment as he closed his eyes.

*

The feeling was shattered the next morning by the sound of a blaring horn. He ran to the window to see three black cars and a brand new van pulling up. A second group of elves had come to meet with their brethren. Instead of being welcomed, Toby almost immediately became an inconvenience and was asked not to join them at dinner. Even Lia'na disappeared for hours at a time.

These new elves were not like the ones he'd been visiting with. When Toby tried to talk to them and ask them about their clan, they walked away, ignored him, or acted hostile.

One day while was exploring with Auro, the one sentry that still spoke to him, Toby ran into one of the elves from the other clan. He stopped for a moment, hoping that since they weren't near the tree house, he could get in a word about their clan, "Excuse me, I..."

The elf turned around and without any warning, hit Toby in the stomach. Auro placed his hand on his belt, ready to draw a dagger if the elf tried anything else while his friend recovered.

Toby wheezed before regaining his composure, "Hey, asshole!"

Lia'na saw the commotion and came running. She got to them just in time to prevent Toby from attacking the unexpected guest of her clan, "Hey, Toby, no! He's not worth it, trust me on this one."

Toby hissed through his teeth, "What the hell is his problem?"

"Calm down. Piele, I'll see to it that the elder deals with him."

Her voice calmed Toby down and he turned away. Without another word, he headed for his room, leaving Lia'na and Auro standing there. She'd barely talked to him in days, and now he had very little to do other than hide in his room, which seemed to be what the clan wanted.

As the weekend neared, Toby was fed up. *Screw this... even Lia'na doesn't seem to want me here anymore.*

He began to pack his bags, feeling that he was no longer welcome. He'd give it another day or two, but if things didn't change, he was going to ask to be taken back to the bus station. He knew that it would probably hurt Lia'na's feelings, but he doubted she'd even notice he was gone.

Toby's thoughts were interrupted when he heard harsh voices below the floor of his room. Toby left his room, made his way down the stairs, and stopped outside the main hall. He carefully positioned himself right next to the door in order to listen in without being seen.

One of the voices was Lia'na's. She was unmistakably angry as she spoke to the elder, "How could you blind side me like this? He's crude, conceited, and I don't want anything to do with him! I'm supposed to have at least another year!"

The elder struggled to calm her down, "I don't like this any more than you do, but this choice was made when you were born."

"Your choice, Masarabi, not mine. I won't go through with it!"

The elder sighed, "Obviously your time with the humans has clouded your mind. I was afraid this might happen. Have you forgotten the plight of our people? Have you forgotten the fact that we are dying out?"

"Dying out for the same reason we now hide in our trees. We refused to accept help from others until it was almost too late. Now we're making the same mistake all over again."

"Yes, that is true, but I can't change the mistakes of the past. Believe me if I could do such a thing, I would have long ago, but what's done is done. So we all have to accept our roles, including you."

"No." Lia'na shouted. "I won't let you use me as breeding stock. You're not forcing me to mate for the sake of saving our race. How could you put this all on my shoulders?"

Toby gasped and almost fell backwards. He couldn't believe what he'd just heard. *What?*

The elder lowered her eyes, "It is out of my hands. Your betrothed is here and he demands to see you."

"I won't. He won't touch me."

"Because of the human boy, Tobias?" Masarabi asked in an accusing tone.

Lia'na lowered her eyes, "I..."

Masarabi's accusing stare pierced Lia'na's heart, "I'm not blind and I'm not stupid. I see how you to act together and I know what he is to you. When you first wrote to me about him, I had a feeling something like this was going on."

"Is that why you invited him up here?"

"Yes. I knew you would go out and have fun, but I didn't think that you'd be so reckless as to have a relationship with one of them behind our backs. Are you willing to sacrifice the welfare of your people for a fling with a kaylra?"

"Of course not, but I haven't had a 'fling' with him. He's never even made a move to try. His intentions have been honorable since I met him. I would not throw away our welfare for some fling, as you called it. That's not what this is about!"

"Then what is it?"

Lia'na put a hand to her head as it began to pound, "The freedom to choose. I want to be able to make my own decisions. That's why I left in the first place. It's what's right, and I will not mate with Aritem."

"At least talk to him child. Listen to what he has to say, and maybe you can work something out with him."

Lia'na was beyond frustrated. She was ready to burst into tears and punch something. Defeated, she closed her eyes and turned away from the elder, "Fine."

Toby felt his face get red hot as his chest suddenly felt like it was being squeezed. He now felt that he should have just stayed in Boston and focused on moving his things into the new condo, or spent time with Gishan's family. Instead he was an unwelcomed guest in a land of reclusive creatures, and the elf-girl he was dating apparently had an arrangement with someone else. Before he flipped out, Toby went back to his room and punched the wall. His fist hurt and began to bleed, but he didn't care.

Toby threw himself on his bed and struggled to breathe normally. He was beyond frustration and anger. Neither of those feelings could compare to what came next. Realizing that the woman he had spent so much time with was set to spend her life with someone else. It was somewhere between a feeling of jealousy and loss. They had only dated for a little over five months, but the connection was there and they both knew it.

No matter what he did, Toby was unable to get comfortable. The rage and feeling of betrayal, coupled with the sucking void in his chest was making it impossible. No matter how many times he rolled over.

A tingling sensation entered his hands. He looked down to see that they were glowing white. *Oh dear God, not again.*

The tingling was spreading as his power began to overflow. Toby knew he had to get out of there before anything happened. *I can't breathe here... I... I have to get out!*

The door to Toby's room flew open, and he charged down the flight of stairs. Once he was on the ground, he stormed over to the rapid water and sat against a nearby stone. His heart raced as he felt his blood begin to boil. His hands began to shake even worse and the violent water began to die down.

Toby realized what was going on and tried to channel his anger, but this time, it didn't work. Instead, Toby instinctively curled his hands like he was holding a bat and raised them above his head. They pulsed as he moved.

The water plumed as he raised his arms. A pillar of water formed out of the plume and began to grow. As the moments passed, Toby could feel himself becoming more and more powerful. His hands began to shake and his eyes rolled over white.

To stop his hands from shaking, Toby balled them into fists and clenched his jaw. He was hoping that unleashing his power this way would prevent him from hurting anyone later and threw all of his energy into it. Finally, he lowered his arms and released the pillar. As the water came crashing down, He noticed that his hands were glowing even brighter, and that glow was beginning to spread to the rest of his body. *No... it's not working!*

The light pulsated off of Toby's skin, and little ghostly forms appeared out of the mist in the water. They were as beautiful as they were mystical and they danced around him in the air. The scene somehow managed to calm him down a little.

Toby had no idea what was going on, but he didn't care. His legs gave out on him and he collapsed against the rock. As the light dimmed, he could feel his whole body go limp and within moments, his world went black. His body slumped over the stone as he passed out.

*

The next day, Lia'na's mind was going a mile a minute. Toby wasn't in his room, and her suitor was demanding to meet with her. She could have cared less about Aritem and wanted to go find Toby, but the other clan had guards posted on the tree to make sure she didn't try anything. She couldn't believe that the elder would drop this on her now, especially when she still had another year of school left.

At this point, Masarabi's motives didn't matter. Aritem was there, and he wasn't going to take 'no' for an answer. Her worries about Toby would have to wait. She was being forced to meet with this thug that she had been set up with on the day of her birth.

In the main hall, Lia'na stood in the traditional robes of her people as the elder smiled at her, "He'll be along any moment now. You look lovely."

Lia'na shook her head, "I'm here at your request. Once he's said his peace, I'm leaving."

Just as she finished, the door swung open and in came a muscular elf with long black hair and a half-goatee on his chin. He looked over Lia'na carefully, "So you're Lia'na."

"You're Aritem."

"Good, now we can settle our business."

"What business do you have with me?" Lia'na asked in a stoic tone.

"Marriage. You and I are betrothed and were supposed to be married on your 18th birthday, but you petitioned for a postponement which you were granted to go to school, despite my objections."

"I still have another year. I'm not finished yet."

Aritem shook his head, "I don't want to hear it. You're just trying to postpone the inevitable. I know about what's been going on with that kaylra. That's going to end, now."

"I am not your slave. That is not your choice to make!"

"Nor is it yours. You know the laws of our people. Since you have been obstructing our traditions, I have declared Fou'tar. The High Elder Council has approved it, and you are bound to the law."

Tears appeared in Lia'na's eyes, "I don't care about your laws. Nor do I have any feelings for you. I refuse to take part in this."

Aritem felt the anger well up inside him. Before he knew what was happening, Lia'na was on her back. Her left eye was closed, and her cheek was turning red. Masarabi looked at him in shock as she ran to Lia'na's side.

Aritem took a step back and was about to apologize, but he quickly stiffened up again, "I... I expect you to be present tomorrow at the Fou'tar acceptance meeting. If you're not, I will come find you. You may not like this now, but you will learn to love and honor me. Forget about this college nonsense and accept your place."

Lia'na looked up at him with hate in her eyes, "I will never..."

"We'll see." Aritem replied as he turned and left the room.

Masarabi knelt down next to her to try to help. As Lia'na fought to get up, the elder elf held her arm to balance her. "Are you okay?"

Lia'na tore herself out of the elder's grasp once she was on her feet. "You sent for him."

Lia'na's voice was almost a growl. "You saw Toby as a threat and sent for Aritem before anything could happen, didn't you?"

Masarabi nodded and let out a deep sigh, "Yes… I did what I thought was right, Lia'na… I'm truly sorry…"

"For what? You got what you wanted. The rebellious girl is being silenced. You've condemned me to this… You've caged me."

When Masarabi tried to speak in protest, Lia'na turned away, refusing to listen, "Where is Toby… I need him, now!"

"I don't think that is such a good idea. If Aritem were to see you…"

"I don't care what you think," Lia'na screamed as she turned back to face the elder elf with her fists clenched, "and I don't care about Aritem. Where is Toby?"

"I don't know. No one has seen him since yesterday."

Lia'na glared at Masarabi and took a threatening step towards her, "What did you do to him? Where did you send him? Did you scare him off or force him to leave?"

"I didn't do anything to him." The elder elf replied defensively as she stepped back and raised her arms, expecting an attack. "I haven't even spoken to him in a few days."

"You're lying! Since that… mate you chose for me arrived, Toby has been treated like an inconvenience. You didn't even want me spending time with him. Instead you had me off running errands!"

"I thought it was for the best. Look at it from my point of view; you're an elf, he's a human. What good would come of that, a watered down bloodline and children that no one would accept?"

"Watered-down?" Lia'na repeated, struggling to comprehend what the woman who had helped raise her said, while at the same time, cope with her own outrage. "How dare you…"

"Lia'na, listen…"

"No, you listen, and listen good Masarabi!" Lia'na shouted, unwilling to let the elder speak. "Looking at the difference between Toby and Aritem, I'd say any half-blood children would be raised a much higher caliber than pureblood elves would ever be. If Toby and I were to ever get that far, those children would be respectable, contributing members of society. Worthy of a lot more credit than you would ever give them. You've ruined my life! You... y... you..."

Lia'na couldn't get the word out. Despite all of her rage, she still couldn't say what was truly in her mind. Masarabi covered her mouth with her hand, unable to respond to such an accusation.

They stood in silence until a voice from behind them mercifully broke the air, "Masarabi, I apologize for the interruption."

"No apology necessary, sentry. What is it?"

The sentry stood at attention as he gave his report, "We've found Mr. Arrigan. He's been sitting down by the river, near the hot springs. We don't know how long he's been there, and he's not responding to anyone."

Lia'na blew past the sentry and ran down the stairs. Her bare feet crushed fallen leaves and blades of grass as she ran to the water's edge. She was completely unprepared for what she was about to see.

It took Lia'na a moment to spot Toby sitting against a large rock. His face looked disheveled as though he hadn't slept in days. Lia'na walked cautiously towards him and knelt down at his side, unsure what to expect, "Toby?"

At first Toby didn't react and continued to stare blankly at the river. Lia'na grabbed his shoulder and shook him, "Toby!"

Finally, Toby came back to reality. His peacefuly trance stemming from the drain of his powers began to disappear. He looked up annoyed, "What do you want?"

Lia'na was taken aback by his tone, "I... I've been worried about you, and I didn't know where you were."

Toby exhaled softly, "I'm surprised you even noticed that I was missing."

"I'm so sorry Toby. I didn't know all of this was going to happen, and I didn't think Masarabi would let you be treated so poorly. She's been keeping me away from you as much as possible."

Toby turned further away, preventing Lia'na from seeing his face. She put her hand on his cheek to try to get him to look at her, but he refused to budge, "That can't be what's really bothering you. You wouldn't get this bent out of shape. What is it, talk to me."

"I know... I know about Aritem... the bastard who punched me... I know about how you are betrothed to him. I know how he's here asking for you."

Lia'na's eyes narrowed, "Who told you?"

"I overheard your argument with the elder last night. You don't think that might have been a pretty valuable piece of information to give me before I made a complete fool of myself?"

"Toby... you didn't. I tried to warn you. You have to understand... because of the Ulium, only one in five Elven children is female. From the moment we leave the womb, we are betrothed to a companion. We have no say in the matter. Believe me, I've done everything I can to avoid it. You didn't make a fool of yourself, it's not like that."

"Then what is it? First you don't tell anyone about us, and then you don't tell me about this! You told me you had baggage, but this is a lot different than what most people would consider baggage. How can I trust you, when it seems like all I am to you is a dirty little secret?"

Lia'na curled up her legs and hid her face, "Is that all you think you are to me, a dirty secret?"

"That's how it feels some times."

Lia'na shot to her feet, "Then you can't trust me, not at all…"

Toby glared at her, ready to tell her off when he noticed a red mark on her cheek, "What happened to you?"

It took him a second, but he realized that he'd seen a similar mark on her face before, "Wait… did someone hit you?"

Lia'na turned away, covering the mark, "What do you care? You're just my dirty little secret."

Toby let out an annoyed sigh as he tried to talk her down, "Lia'na!"

Lia'na ran off into the trees without another word, doing the best she could to keep her eyes hidden. She ran up to her room and slammed the door. It was so loud that Toby swore he'd heard it over the rushing water.

Finally alone again, Toby stared off into space. Letting Lia'na have it like that cut him deeply, but it had to be said. Whatever happened now was out of his hands. *How could she lead me on like this? Why not just tell me from day one?*

His thoughts were cut short as a throaty voice broke the silence, "Oh the tangled web of youth and the harsh sting of a young heart being broken. I do sometimes miss those days."

Toby snapped out of it and looked up to see Masarabi, "Elder, what can I do for you?"

"I was hoping to speak to you." The elder replied. "May I sit?"

"Of course."

The elder secured her robe and sat on the grass, "We have been neglectful of our honored guest. For that, I apologize. Our friends from the north can be demanding."

Toby didn't respond and looked back out on the river. The elder took a deep breath, "You care a lot for Lia'na, don't you?"

"Look, elder, I…"

"You do. No no, don't deny it. I've seen the way you look at her and I've seen how her eyes light up at the very mention of your name."

That caught Toby's attention, "Maybe, but what does it matter now?"

"It matters a great deal to her."

Now Toby was through biting his tongue, "I've had enough of this… I want to go back to the bus terminal. I want to go home. Regardless of my feelings, I wasn't looking to get involved in a love triangle."

"Of course, I'll have a sentry take you to the terminal as soon as you're ready. You can make your way home from there, but I need to ask you something first."

"And what's that?"

The elder studied his features for a moment before speaking, "Do you love her?"

The hair on the back of Toby's neck stood up as his head turned to face the elder elf, "What?"

"Do you love her?"

Her question caught Toby off guard. What could he say? He'd only known her for five months, but they had spent most of that time together and had nearly become inseparable.

Toby closed his eyes, "She's unlike anyone else I've ever met. Even the worst day seems a lot better when she's around. Yeah… I love her… very much."

"Very good." The elder replied happily. "Very good... then you may be the very person I was hoping you would be.."

Toby lowered his eyes as the elder reached under her robes. A small package covered in cloth appeared in her hand. Toby eyed it for a moment, "What is that?"

Masarabi ignored the question as she spoke, "Listen to me very carefully, sometimes people make decisions with the best intentions, but don't consider the consequences. I wish I had realized it sooner, but what's good for the majority isn't necessarily what's right."

"Elder, what are you saying?"

"You've shown respect for our laws and traditions during your stay. Aritem has called for the Fou'tar in response to Lia'na's avoidance of his betrothal rights."

"Yeah and what can I do about it?"

The elder held out the package to Toby, "You only have one chance, tomorrow at 10am. Once the clans ratify the Fou'tar, then regardless of Lia'na's objections, she will be honor bound to him for life. She'll have to marry him. Terrible things happen to those who don't obey it. As an elder, there is nothing I can do. Under our law, an elder's word is beyond questioning, thus I am forbidden from making a challenge. An outsider however, should have no issue doing it."

The elder stood up and turned away from him, "I'll have a sentry standing by. When you are ready to leave, let them know and they'll take you away from here. Until then, the room you've been staying in is yours."

"That guy gave her the mark on her cheek, didn't he?"

She took another step and turned back, "10 a.m. tomorrow, I hope you're the hero she thinks you are."

Toby carefully opened the package. Inside was an old book with a green cover and gold writing. Thankfully, it was in English instead of Elvish."

"What am I supposed to do with this?" Toby asked as he looked back up.

To his surprise, Masarabi was gone. Toby scratched his head, extremely confused. *What's going on? Did the elder just try to convince me to break up the... whatever this is?*

Toby opened the book again and looked at the title page. It read, 'Elven Clan Law and Code of Conduct.' He immediately slammed the book shut, looked around, and ran back to his room as fast as he could to avoid being seen. Once he was behind closed doors, he began flipping through the pages. There had to be something in Elven law that could prevent this insane ritual.

Toby still felt a sharp pain in his heart for telling Lia'na off. He wasn't wrong, but knowing now what he did, he could understand why she didn't want to tell anyone. Part of him wanted to go apologize, but he knew that time was against him.

Toby was determined to find some way to help her. Maybe if he could set her free, things might smooth over. If not, at least he'd saved her from a metaphorical prison. The pages began to blur as he quickly flipped through them.

Finally, Toby stopped on page 155. There was a small passage underlined. As he read the code, he raised his fist in triumph, "Ah hah, yes!"

XII

The next morning, the two clans gathered in the hall. Chairs had been reorganized so that the local clan elder, and the visiting one, would be able to sit together. Aritem was dressed in a black and white tunic as was expected of him for when the unmarried betrothed met in the same room.

Loud gasps erupted amongst the clans as Lia'na walked in defiantly wearing a red dress instead of the white robes that she had been given. Aritem smirked at her pointless protest. He stood next to his betrothed in front of the elders and waited for them to speak.

The visiting clan elder, Nartem, who also happened to be Aritem's father, sat on the left and spoke first, "Aritem, you have made the claim of Fou'tar. Your betrothed has been derelict in her responsibilities."

Aritem nodded, as Masarabi took a deep breath, "Lia'na, were you made aware of the marital request?"

"Yes…"

"And yet you refused to respond, and worse, began a relationship with a kaylra?" Nartem asked, questioning her in a threatening tone.

Lia'na snorted and turned her head so Aritem couldn't see her face, "That is none of your business."

"I see." The elder replied triumphantly. "Well then, it would appear that we have met our burden of proof, both with your testimony, as well as the evidence gathered by Elder Masarabi."

Lia'na turned her back to Aritem's father as he continued, "I move that she be ordered to remove herself from the human institution, and submit to the claim of Fou'tar as is my son's right under Elven law!"

There was a brief silence as Lia'na turned and looked pleadingly at her own elder, "Masarabi, piele…"

Nartem shook his head as Lia'na's elder refused to respond, "Masarabi is bound by the law, as are you. Unless you have anything to add to the proceedings, we will proceed immediately with the Fou'tar and bind you to Aritem for life."

"Like hell!" An angry, but familiar, voice thundered from behind. "I come here in objection to these proceedings."

A wide-eyed Lia'na turned to see Toby storm into the room, once again dressed in the best clothes he had. As the room broke out in loud gasps, Aritem's father stood up, "What is the meaning of this?"

Toby stepped between Lia'na and Aritem. He placed his hand in hers, and glared at Aritem's father, "Linoi e torbius chlu!"

The elves looked at each other bewildered as this outsider issued a formal challenge to the rite of betrothal. "You have no right." Aritem scoffed. "You're not even Elven! Leave now, if you value your life."

Toby smiled and held out the green book, "I don't think so. Read your own laws, it specifically says anyone of non-elder status can issue a challenge, anyone, including me."

Toby then turned back to the elders, "You know what I'm saying is true."

The two elders looked at each other for a moment. When they turned back, Aritem's father lowered his eyes while Masarabi spoke, "Master Tobias Arrigan, time and again you have shown respect for Elven law. You honor us with your adherence to it."

The elder turned to Aritem's father. The man had a disgusted look on his face, as everyone waited for him to react. No one knew what to expect.

After a brief silence, the Aritem's father let out a sigh, "Oh very well... Lia'na, will you allow this... human to make a challenge on your behalf?"

Lia'na was in shock. Part of her couldn't believe that Toby was doing this after everything he'd said, but the other part of her couldn't believe that she was surprised, "I... "

She looked over at Toby, who made a slight gesture with his hand for her to say something. Once her mind caught up with reality, she nodded, "Yes, whole-heartedly I do!"

"What a surprise." Nartem replied sarcastically as he turned back to Toby. "All right Tobias, you have the floor. What is the basis for your challenge to the Fou'tar?"

"There are two parts to it." Toby replied as Lia'na squeezed his hand. "First, the maiden has entered these proceedings against her will. According to your laws, that is grounds for a challenge."

"Not anymore." Aritem's father replied aggressively as he stood up. "Once our numbers dropped to under a thousand, that law was changed by the High Elders. It is no longer a valid defense under Elven law."

"I figured as much. Which is why I have a far more egregious charge; Aritem is unfit!"

Aritem clenched a fist by his side as his father's brow furrowed, "What charge do you bring against my son?"

"Assault. I have it on good authority that Aritem struck his betrothed. Your law clearly states that this sort of offense more than meets the requirement for challenging the Fou'tar."

Shouts of anger and disbelief echoed through the hall as both sides were clearly riled up by the accusation. The sentries, whom had been Lia'na's friends, drew knives from their belts and made threatening gestures towards their guests. Almost immediately, the visiting clan responded in kind.

Masarabi shot up out of her seat and raised her hand as she shouted at them, "Mirie!"

The groups immediately put their weapons away, bowed to the elders, and returned to their seats. Though they had quieted down, angry looks continued to shoot about the room. A fight could have erupted again in a split second.

Toby turned to Aritem, "You're going to pay for hurting her, just so you know."

Lia'na was smiling for the first time in days as Nartem's face turned red, "You better have proof in some form, young man. God help you if you don't."

Toby put his hand on Lia'na's cheek and turned her face to the side, "Note the mark on her cheek, one that may soon become a bruise!"

"A bruise?" Aritem's father scoffed. "People get bruises all the time, are you really going to use that as your main source of proof?"

"No, elder." Toby replied as he smiled and pointed to Masarabi. "I have all the proof you need; the word of an elder, which is beyond contestation according to your law."

He quickly turned to Masarabi, "Madam Elder, please speak."

Masarabi gave Toby a look of gratitude as she stood up, "The kaylra speaks the truth. I was in the room when it happened. Aritem struck her with the back of his hand across her cheek."

The yelling started up again as Masarabi sat back down. Aritem's father slammed his fist on the table to quiet everyone. As he waited, he gave his son a disgusted look. He knew of his son's temper, and until now had been able to see past it.

As an Elven elder, Nartem was against spousal abuse in any form. It was an extremely dishonorable action. That said, Aritem was still his son, and he knew he still had to help the boy.

When everyone finally settled down, he spoke, "As is my responsibility under our law... I submit that Tobias has met his burden of proof to my satisfaction. Therefore, the objection is upheld. However, Aritem does have a second option, the ring."

Toby's eyes narrowed, "The ring?"

Lia'na spoke up from the side as a fearful expression came over her features, "It's a duel. You, as the challenger, act as my knight. You will be required to engage Aritem in combat. Should you refuse, your objection will be cast aside and I will immediately be honor bound to him."

Aritem smiled, "And I'm placing the challenge. Tomorrow afternoon."

His father nodded, "As the challenger, you may choose the mode of combat."

"No holds barred. This will be fun."

Masarabi looked at Toby, "This is your only chance to back down. There is much danger ahead if you accept the challenge, but you know the consequences of withdrawal. You must make the choice, do you accept the challenge?"

Toby looked at Lia'na. She shook her head with a worried look, "No, you can't do this. It's not a fight to the death, but people have died in the ring. I don't want that happening, especially not on my account."

Toby shrugged as he turned back to the elders, "I accept the challenge!"

"What," Lia'na screamed, "no!"

Aritem laughed, "Too late, the challenge has been accepted. Tomorrow, you are mine. 3pm do not be late."

Aritem stormed out of the hall. Others filed out behind him, some of whom still argued amongst each other. It was so volatile, that Toby half expected a fight to break out once they got outside. Aritem's father turned to Masarabi "I'm not finished here. I have no doubt you had a part in this."

"Believe what you want." She replied. "Our laws are clear."

Nartem sneered, "Torae doth! You won't be able to hide behind them for long, especially when my son wins tomorrow."

The elder watched as he walked away. Lia'na turned to Toby and pushed his shoulder hard so that he was facing her, "Fool, Aritem is a warrior from his clan. You don't stand a chance!"

"No faith." Toby replied. "I do have some tricks up my sleeve."

Masarabi approached them from behind the table, "Nevertheless, you are outmatched. I fear that tricks will not save you. I'll have my sentries give you as much mentoring as they can. Meet them downstairs in a few minutes."

Toby nodded as she left the room. Lia'na looked up at Toby, "Why... why did you come back? I thought you hated me?"

"I'm mad at you for hiding this from me," Toby admitted, "but I don't hate you."

Lia'na lowered her eyes and buried her face in his chest, "I don't care if you win or lose tomorrow. Just piele don't get yourself killed. I would not be able to live with myself if you died for me."

Toby smiled, "Don't worry. I plan on doing as little dying as possible."

She grabbed him, threw her arms around him, and squeezed tight, "Toby…"

Toby held her for a few minutes before prying out of her grip, "It looks like I have work to do."

Lia'na watched him walk outside and down the stairs. Once he was out of earshot, she droped to her knees and whispered in his direction, "Te arshana ni... I love you."

As Toby reached the bottom of the stairs, he was met by the two sentries that he had been exploring with. They stood on either side of him with watchful eyes. Toby smiled at the one on his right, "Hey Auro…"

Auro looked at him with so little emotion, he could have passed as a statue, "Tilek and I have been asked to prepare you for your duel tomorrow."

Toby nodded, "Let's do it."

The two sentries took Toby out into the woods. They made their way to the small clearing where Toby was to be trained. As he set up, the sentries disappeared from behind him. He realized quickly that he was alone and went on the defensive.

Before Toby could react, Tilek descended from the trees right on top of him, knocking him to the ground, "Clear your mind, and listen to the trees! You can't be worried about what's going on around you, or the prize at the end of your fight. You focus on those things, you will lose."

The elf did a back flip off of him and disappeared into the trees again. A second later, Auro appeared behind him, striking him with a staff. Toby fell to the ground, his back was throbbing from the hit. Determined not to be defeated so easily, he got back to his feet and faced the elf.

Auro smiled, "You are weak, and you won't be able to save Lia'na at this rate. Focus your mind, and shut out everything else. You need to focus on your attacker!"

Toby tried again and again as the two elves dances around him in and out of view. Their taunting was beginning to annoy him. Hours passed and Toby was getting banged up pretty bad.

Finally, the sentries decided they'd had enough. Auro shook his head, "This is your last chance. You're not focused. You're too worried about what will happen to Lia'na. If you cannot parry at least one attack, I fear you may be beyond hope. One last time, keep your focus on the moment. Listen only to what you need to hear, and you have a chance."

"I understand, let's do this."

As the sentries disappeared into the trees one more time, Toby closed his eyes and focused his mind. At first he didn't hear anything. He continued to strain his ears in every direction. There was a sound of wind passing through the branches, creating a sort of white noise, but that's not what he was looking for. In the distance, a dear was grazing on a little grass. Again, not what he was searching for.

After an eternity of silence, Toby heard the sound of wind breaking around a flying object and the sound of feet impacting on tree trunks. This was it, he quickly jumped into the air, using what martial arts training he'd picked up when he was younger, and performed a spin kick.

Toby's aim was dead on, his foot impacted on the sentry's stomach. Auro fell to the ground wheezing. Toby stood over him, "I did it!"

The elf looked up at him, "You haven't won, you forgot something…"

At that moment, the other sentry attacked from behind. Toby raised his fist and connected with the other elf's face. He fell to the ground, dazed.

Auro smiled, "Good, now we've got a real fight."

The three of them engaged in martial arts, attempting to best each other. They used staffs, knives, and anything they could find in the wilderness. The sentries tried two more times to attack from the trees, but after Toby cart wheeled out of the way, it was obvious that their special moves were no longer an advantage.

After a good 40 minutes of vicious combat, of stalemate fighting, and of thrusting and parrying, all three of them had exposed each other's weaknesses. Toby had a staff pointed at his throat and another on his ribs. The elves smiled, thinking that they had won, when Toby directed their attention to their own bodies with his eyes. Toby had capitalized on them both leaving themselves vulnerable. He had a knife to Auro's throat, and a staff against Tilek's temple.

Tilek lowered his weapon and stepped back, "A draw…"

"You're ready." Auro said smiling. "Good job, you should be able to give Aritem a run for his money tomorrow. Remember what we told you about focusing. For now though, your body must need rest. Go back to camp and relax, you have earned it."

Toby nodded and bowed in the traditional martial arts form, "Thank you both."

They both watched as Toby limped off towards the houses. Tilek turned, "$50 says he gets crushed tomorrow?"

"$100 says he doesn't." Auro replied.

"How can you be so sure?"

"Aritem is fighting for his own greed, but Toby, he's fighting for something more. He fights for what's right. I'd place a bet on him any day of the week."

**

Stiff, Toby struggled to climb the stairs and get to his room. When he opened the heavy wooden door, he saw a piece of paper sitting on his bed. He lay down on the bunk and unfolded it. Inside was Lia'na's easily recognizable handwriting,

> "Ta arshana,
>   Piele meet me at the hot spring tonight. 8pm sharp. Piele don't be late. I've arranged for some alone time for us. It's very important to me that you be there.
>   -Lia'na"

Toby scratched his head as he looked at the letter. She'd never called him 'ta arshana' before. It was always ta arsha. He knew that 'ta' meant 'my' but didn't recognize the rest. He had a vague idea of what it could be, but decided to dismiss it. He wasn't going to put her on the spot like the elder had put him.

Toby looked at his watch, it was only 6pm. He had some time and desperately needed to take a nap. Not a single muscle in his body had been spared the grueling workout, and his bruises began to pulse. He set his alarm for 7:30 and passed out. As he slept, he returned to his dream world where he could see white lights around him and a dark sphere which was instantly shattered by the lights.

Inside was Lia'na, covered in blood. She wasn't moving and her eyes were closed. Her wrists had ropes tied around them, but they weren't connected to anything.

Toby's eyes shot open as he breathed deeply. His watch alarm was going off and it was 7:31. He stared at it for a moment before switching it off and trying to relax his nerves. *God... what is that... could that be Lia'na's fate if I lose?*

Toby eventually got up and changed into a swimsuit, hoping that the hot water would sooth his bumps and bruises. He then grabbed a towel, and slid on a pair of sandals that he'd found under the bed. His feet ached as he headed down to the water.

The sound of the rapids grew louder as Toby neared the torch lights. He walked along the path for a few moments until he arrived at the hot spring. It was still early and the sun had not quite set. The sky was a beautiful orange and purple with a slowly dimming half circle of light getting smaller on the horizon. Toby released the air from his lungs and closed his eyes.

The mist from the rapids mixed with the steam from the hot spring and created a soothing mist that seemed the swirl around Toby. The combination of warm and cold temperatures envigorated his soul as he stood silently.

"Relaxing, isn't it?" A low voice asked.

Toby opened his eyes and turned to see Lia'na standing behind him as the sky darkened. She wore a black hooded cloak that kept her shrouded in the darkness. It was as though she was trying to stay hidden.

Even with Lia'na's eyes shaded, Toby could detect an air of discomfort in the way she moved, "Lia'na what's wrong?"

Lia'na pulled the hood back and looked into his eyes. Her hair was tied behind her pointed ears, held in place by elaborate braids. She had a small white flower with bright green petals nestled behind her right ear and looked like she was ready for prom or a wedding. The view was blemished only by the bruise on her cheek, "Toby, I want you to leave, now. Get off the reservation and never come back."

"What?" Toby asked surprised. Her words shot him through the heart as he looked her over in confusion. "Why, what's wrong?"

Lia'na lowered her eyes, "I'm not going to let you fight tomorrow. It's too much to ask. I'd rather lose you forever than watch you get pulled apart!"

"You really don't have any faith in me do you?" Toby asked in an accusing voice.

"I have all the faith in the world in you, but Toby Aritem was born and raised a hunter and a warrior. He's been fighting since he could stand. I believe you'll go out there with everything you've got... but so will he. Toby, he will kill you."

"I know how to fight too, Lia'na. I've been taking martial arts for years. How could I live with myself if I didn't try?"

"Toby, I'm not worth it. There is no need for you to risk..."

"I don't want to hear this!" Toby yelled, cutting her off. "You may not think you're worth it, well that's your opinion, but I do. So no, I'm not leaving, not until I make sure you're safe from that asshole."

"Then I'll go with you." Lia'na replied with a hint of desperation in her voice. "Anywhere you want to go, I will follow you. We'll leave the reservation tonight."

"And do what? I doubt Aritem would just let you go that easily. Lord knows, I wouldn't. I'm sure he'll come after you."

"So?"

"Is that how you want to live? Constantly looking over your shoulder? If he does find us, no Elven law will protect you."

"Toby..."

"Exactly, so enough of this. I'm facing down Aritem tomorrow. You may think it's not worth it, but I couldn't stand the thought of you having to give everything up. So what's say you follow me to the hot spring?"

Before Lia'na could say anything in protest, Toby stripped off his shirt and sandals, and tested the water with his toe. It was hot, but well within tolerance. He waded in slowly and settled against one of the stone slabs. The pain throughout his body slowly disappeared as he soaked. He exhaled, put his head back, and closed his eyes as everything relaxed. It was completely tranquil.

Lia'na untied the cloak and let it fall off her shoulders, giving Toby a chance to see what she was wearing underneath when he opened his eyes. Standing in front of the burning torches, she looked like a medieval princess with white and green robes that had flowers embroidered into the cotton. The robes draped down to the bottom of her thighs, leaving her legs bare.

Toby's eyes moved upward as he looked at her, "Lia'na, you look beautiful."

"Lien ni… these robes were what I was supposed to wear to the Fou'tar. I remember seeing other elf-girls dressed the same way when I was little. I couldn't wait to try my own on."

Lia'na chuckled at the thought, "I'd been dazzled by stories of times long before the betrothal laws. If only I'd know."

"Why are you wearing them now?"

"According to the ancient tradition, back before Elven girls were forced to marry, we wore these only for the person we…" Her voice trailed off before she could finish the sentence. It was hard for her to look at him as she spoke, "Toby, you have been ta arsha for months now. You have done so much for me without even being asked to."

"It wasn't anything big."

"Yes it was," Lia'na insisted, "to the point where you even managed to impress my elder. That's saying a lot… but what's more important, you've impressed me."

"It was more than worth it. Look where we are now."

"Yes, look," Lia'na said as her smile disappeared, "you're facing down Aritem tomorrow and, as you pointed out, I'm not worthy of trust."

"Lia'na, I didn't mean that."

"Yes you did, and you were right. I have kept too much from you. Things I never should have. It would have been easier had I just told you what was going on from the beginning."

Lia'na looked down at the water for a moment, "Toby, my relationship with you was never fake or a fling. It means more to me than I think you realize. You mean more… and I never had any intention of marrying that… monster."

Toby swam closer so he was able to see the hazel in her eyes, "I believe you."

"I'm glad, but that doesn't excuse my behavior. I put you through so much… too much for most people."

She kicked off her sandals and stepped onto one of the stone slabs to soak her feet, "Yet after all that, you're still here. You're still fighting for me...You know... the elder told me what you said to her."

"What was that?"

Her big hazel eyes sparkled from the light of the torches surrounding the pool, "Ni arshana tae."

Toby had no idea what she had just said, "Lia'na, I don't speak Elvish."

"I know. Toby, did you read the rules of the challenge?"

"I didn't get that far, why?"

Lia'na walked daintily on slabs as the hot water caressed her feet. When she stood in front of Toby's clothes, she smiled, "According to the law, as you are my knight, if you win, the betrothal rights fall to you. From there, you can take me or free me."

Toby rolled his eyes, "These laws are nuts! Do you get any say?"

"Yes. I can ask for another challenger if I don't approve of your victory."

"That's it? It's a wonder any woman sticks around in your clans. This is pretty much slavery."

"That's one way of looking at it, but our laws and traditions are different from those you're accustomed to. Humans number in the billions, dwarves are probably similar in numbers... but us elves only number in the hundreds. Our laws were created to help our people survive."

Speaking those words made Lia'na clench her fist, "But they are out of date and unfair, I agree. If they were more balanced and gave women equal standing in these betrothal ceremonies then maybe it wouldn't be that bad. However, that's just not the case. I'm actually amazed they didn't fix the laws to prevent outsiders from issuing a challenge."

"Perhaps they didn't think one would be so bold?"

"Maybe…" Lia'na agreed, "but rest assured, that's one mistake they won't make twice. That will be on the books before you know it."

"Glad I got mine in when I did then."

"You're risking your life," Lia'na said lowly, "and instead of thinking of the reward, you're more concerned with my feelings."

"That's what I do, I want you to be happy and free to make your own choices. So if I win tomorrow, I'll free you from these archaic laws. You'll be able to do whatever you want."

Lia'na's smile widened, "Then tomorrow, you can set me free and see if I come back, but tonight… I'm yours."

Toby looked at her oddly, "What are you talking about?"

Lia'na didn't reply, instead she pulled at her robes and allowed them to fall to the ground, leaving her completely naked with the exception of her diamond shard. Toby's eyes widened as he looked at her slender body. He had been caught off guard and was speechless.

Lia'na stood silently for a moment, allowing him to take it all in. She bit her lower lip as Toby's eyes traced over her form. She could feel her skin tingle as his eyes passed over every curve. It was as though a goddess had just appeared to him. Euphoria overtook her as she watched him admire her figure, making her feel more attractive than ever.

As the cool air touched her bare skin, Lia'na quickly jumped into the water and slid under the surface. A second later, she came up right in front of him. Toby felt her body press against his. Her silky skin felt incredible as it touched his in the steaming water. She looked deep into his eyes, "Hold me… the way you did that first time at the beach."

Toby began to feel his heart race as he placed his hands on her back, it was uncontrollable. As he looked down at her resting her head on his chest, he felt numb. She was perfect, her body only had a slight tan, her wet blonde hair shimmered in the fire and she had an incredible figure.

Lia'na relaxed and savored her time with him, "Toby... Ta arshana, I owe you so much."

"Ta arshana? What does that mean?"

"My love."

At that moment, Toby felt his skin begin to pulse. The golden glow that he had experienced the day before began to illuminate his skin. Lia'na opened her eyes when she felt the vibrations.

As Toby's skin pulsed, little sparkles of light appeared around them. These sparkles looked like spectral comets dancing in the moonlight. Each one of them resembled fiber optic lights as they changed color.

Lia'na was amazed by what she was seeing. She raised her right hand out of the water and allowed one of the sparkles to land, "I don't believe it..."

"What?"

"Toby, these are spirit embers. They flock to the powers of an enchanter who wields spirit energy."

Toby was getting confused, "What does all this mean?"

Lia'na allowed the ember to fly off of her hand and watched disappeared into the mist, "Each enchanter is attuned to one form of magic or another. Red, blue, and green are elemental colors. Red for fire, blue for water, and green for nature, but then there are also light and dark enchanters."

Toby was anxious for her to get to the point, "And?"

"Well... light enchanters are said to be the ones who are in God's favor. They have been blessed from birth. They draw upon life energy to cast spells of healing and unleash holy wrath on their enemies, but they also have limited access to the color spells as well. Dark enchanters are the opposite, they sacrifice their own life energy for power. They become powerful quicker than any other class, but that comes with a price; it eventually kills them."

Lia'na looked into his eyes, "I'm relieved to see that you're an enchanter of light. Had you been dark, I would have been very worried. Light's far more powerful in the long run anyway."

She moved in closer to Toby again as the embers lit the water and filled the sky more than the dimming torches could. Her arms rested on his shoulders while his found her hips. They held each other tightly in the warm water for as long as they could. Their lips pressed together once more while the embers began circling around them.

As Lia'na held on to him, she noticed that her skin was also beginning to glow. She gasped as an intense feeling of pleasure overtook her senses. Her skin eventually became an aura as bright as Toby's.

The water was warm, but Lia'na began to break out in goose bumps as she felt Toby's fingernails pass gently over her hips, stopping at her thighs and then going back the other way. She let out a deep sigh as a chill passed down her spine. Her eyes closed as she rested her head on his chest.

Lia'na was completely exposed and had given up the last of her defenses, but she no longer cared. The feeling was so intense that nothing else seemed to matter.She fought back against it one last time to try to convince Toby to leave, "Toby... please?"

Toby looked down at her, surprised by her using the English version of the word 'please,' "What?"

"Don't do this... Take me away from this place. Take me anywhere, I don't care, just don't make me watch you face Aritem tomorrow."

"You know if I were to agree to that, you'd probably never be able to come back."

"No, maybe not... but that choice was taken from me long ago. Its a heavy price... but I don't want to spend my life huddled in the corner of the home of an abusive husband, in constant fear. If those are the choices, I'll take exile."

"I know you would." Toby replied. "But you love your clan, the whole reason you're studying medicine is to help them."

Lia'na didn't move, "I know that... but at this point, I don't care. I just don't want to see you get killed!"

"I won't. I don't plan on dying tomorrow. Can't you just trust me? I'm fighting for you, to help you. You've trusted me in all else, why can't you now?"

Lia'na was blindsided by his words, he was right, and she knew it, "Okay Toby, you win, but I don't care who comes out on top tomorrow, as long as you walk off the field alive. That's all I care about."

"Fair enough." Toby replied as he held her close, savoring the feeling of the warm water as it passed over their bodies.

Once their skin began to prune, the time had come to get out of the water. The glow disappeared from Toby's body and the embers slowly faded away into the night. Neither of them wanted to see such a perfect moment end, but they couldn't stay in the water. It was getting late, and they both had a big day tomorrow. Destiny was not going to wait for anyone.

As Toby got dressed, Lia'na looked at the rapids, "Can I borrow your shirt?"

Toby had the shirt on over his head already, but when she asked for it, he pulled it back off and gave it to her. She quickly put it on, allowed it to drape down to her thighs, and grabbed her betrothal robes. Instead of putting them back on, she held them over one of the torches until they caught fire.

"What are you doing?" Toby asked.

Lia'na waited while the robes burned and then threw the remains into the rapids, "After tomorrow, I won't need them. Those are the clothes of a slave and I'm no one's slave."

Toby smiled nervously, "Right."

"I have faith in you, ta arshana... I should have all along."

"I'll try not to disappoint you."

"As if you ever could."

As the torches began to fade, Lia'na and Toby made their way back to the tree houses. No other elves appeared to be out and about this late in the evening. The whole area looked deserted as they climbed the wooden stairs.

When they reached Toby's room, to his surprise, she didn't turn to go back to her own. Instead, as he opened the door, she looked at him sweetly, "Toby, I don't want to be alone tonight. Do you mind?"

"I never did before. The bed has extra pillows so you should be comfortable."

Lia'na slid into the bed next to him under the warm blankets. Once Toby got comfortable, he felt a sudden pressure on his chest. Apparently, Lia'na had decided to use Toby as her pillow. She closed her eyes and exhaled, "Toby, whatever happens tomorrow... Te arshana ni..."

He smiled as he pushed against his pillow "I love you too."

Though Toby appeared relaxed, his body was a mass of quivering nerves. He looked down at Lia'na as she rested on his chest. She looked content as she drifted off to sleep.

Toby took some comfort in knowing that she was safe. No one could hurt her as long as she remained with him, but even as he watched her sleep, he couldn't shake the images of her in the water with Aritem or in bed with him in the same way as she was at that moment. It left a sickening feeling in his stomach, and he found himself unable to sleep. The wonderful memories they had created mere minutes ago were now tainted by this fear.

Toby gripped the mattress with his hand and exhaled slowly to try to relieve the tension. No matter how much he tried to clear his mind, he was unable to shake these feelings. *God help us...*

XIII

The next morning came too quickly. Toby had barely gotten enough sleep to function. As the sun came up, Lia'na squinted, "No... no not yet, I don't want it to be morning."

Her rustling caused Toby to stir, "Ugh... I don't think we have much of a say in that."

"No we don't..." She replied as she climbed on top of him, "Is it too cliché to call last night magical?"

"Maybe a little."

Without another word, Lia'na bent her shoulders back so she could lean in and kiss him. Toby ran his hands up under his borrowed shirt and caressed her back. Their bodies still felt incredibly warm from the night before as they lay together, but Toby's fingers still managed to give Lia'na chills from the sensation.

Lia'na began to kiss Toby's neck as his fingernails traced up her back. In response to his touch, she quickly ripped the shirt off, allowing him to go further. His right hand continued over her shoulder and down her chest. His hand then gently caressed her left breast, which was firm but very smooth. His touch caused her to breathe more heavily than before.

Lia'na responded by moving away from his neck and kissing him firmly on the lips. Toby gathered what little composure he had left and gently pushed Lia'na back so he could look into her eyes, "Are you sure about this?"

A gentle whisper was the only response he received, "Te arshana ni."

She slowly pushed herself further down under she felt a slight pressure against womanhood. She pushed a little harder until it parted, allowing Toby inside of her. All around her thighs felt like they were about to explode as she dropped onto his chest, "Why can't this moment last forever."

*

Hours passed and neither one of them left Toby's room. Their small bubble of paradise shattered as Toby's alarm sounded 3pm. Both of them perked up and realized that the time had come.

Toby got up and got dressed, "Stay here, I'll be back after the fight."

"No way." Lia'na replied as she put Toby's old shirt back on. "I have to be there. I'm responsible for getting you into this, and I can't just sit idle by. It's my right by law to be there."

There was no way of making her listen as she ran out of Toby's room and went to her own to throw on some decent clothes. From the bottom of the wooded steps, Aritem's thundering voice could be heard as he called out, "Tobias, get your weakling kaylra ass down here and meet your fate!"

A few moments went by as a crowd of elves formed around him. He called out again, "Tobias!"

"Looking for me?" A voice in a mocking tone came from behind.

Aritem smiled and turned to see Toby standing behind him. He scoffed at Toby's smug demeanor, "It's not too late to back down, you know? What makes her so special, she's just a sharpy to your people anyway?"

Toby picked up one of the staves that had been left against the tree nearby, "That you even have to ask that question is proof enough that you don't deserve her."

Aritem sneered, "Fine then. Are you ready?"

"Lead the way."

The group proceeded to the clearing where the battle was to take place. The two clan elders were already there. It was a large commotion as Toby and Aritem stepped out into the middle of the field.

Masarabi stood up, "This battle is a test of strength, of righteousness, and of determination. It shall be fought until one is unable to stand, dies, or concedes. The one that remains is the one that is favored by fate to take the maiden for themselves."

Toby began breathing heavily as he watched his massive opponent twirl his staff like a ninja sword. *Oh man Toby, how did you get yourself into this...?*

Toby looked over to the sidelines to see his pointy-eared love looking on with worry. *Ah yes, that's how. Well guys have done dumber things than this to get a girl... I guess.*

Masarabi raised her hand, "Let the dual commence!"

The two fighters began walking opposite each other in a circle. Aritem smiled maliciously, "Ready to meet your end?"

"Only if you can actually fight an armed man. So far all we've seen you do is beat on a defenseless woman half your size! "

Aritem roared and charged at Toby with his staff. Toby dodged out of the way and swung his own at Aritem, hoping to connect with his spine. Luck wasn't with Toby as it seemed Aritem was prepared for this. When Toby's staff came down, it impacted against Aritem's. The elf had managed to swing the staff around quick enough to protect his back.

Toby pulled away and held his staff in both hands defensively. Aritem came at him and slammed the staves together. Toby could hear his begin to splinter under the blow. He knocked Aritem away using all the strength he had. Once Aritem was back enough, Toby performed a spin kick and knocked the staff out of Aritem's hand.

Aritem's weapon went flying, leaving him with his bare hands. This didn't seem to be a problem for the elf though, he raised his fists and went on the attack. Toby raised his staff to block Aritem, but that impact of his fist caused Toby's staff to splinter. Toby threw the broken wood pole away and deflected Aritem's attacks with his own fists.

Toby was quick, but Aritem had more power. He knocked Toby's hand out of the way and struck a devastating blow on Toby's cheek. Blood spattered from Toby's nose as he backed away.

The beating was relentless and Toby was unable to block all of his shots. The hits he took damaged his left eye so that it could no longer open, his nose was gushing, and his cheek was swollen.

Toby clenched his jaw, unwilling to go down. He swung his fist so that the back of his knuckles impacted on Aritem's nose. There was a loud cracking sound as blood spewed from the elf's face.

The White Water Clan cheered as Toby momentarily had the upper hand. Aritem rubbed his nose with his hand, "Very good... been a while since I've seen my own blood."

He dashed at Toby, hoping to score a deathblow, but Toby dodged out of the way and jumped on his back. Hoping to end the fight quickly, He wrapped his arms around Aritem's neck and squuezed as hard as he could.

Toby's hopes were dashed as the massive elf yanked him off and threw him to the ground. Toby covered his face as multiple fists came down on him, seemingly all at once. Aritem was lightning fast.

Lia'na couldn't stand watching this and turned to the elder, "Masarabi, please stop this! It's barbaric!"

"I can't," she replied, "our laws are clear, this is his choice."

Lia'na thought for a moment before responding, "What if I consent to marry Aritem?"

The elder looked at her sharply, "Is that what you want?"

"No one has ever really cared what I want, Masarabi! The only person that ever has, ta arshana, is being killed! I can't watch this. It's too much."

Masarabi sighed, "There is nothing I can do. If you want the fight to end, he needs to give up."

Lia'na nodded and frantically turned back to her love, "Toby, listen to me!"

He glanced over for a brief second, signaling that he'd heard her. She shook her head, "I can't stand this anymore! Concede!"

"No!" Toby yelled back, ducking in time to avoid another blow to the face.

Aritem's miss gave him an opening. Toby open palm chopped him between his ribs. The shock gave Toby enough time to perform an uppercut.

Unfortunately, the attack wasn't strong enough to take Aritem off his feet. It only dazed him momentarily. All it did was give Toby enough time to get back to his feet. He attempted a spin kick, but Aritem recovered in enough time to catch his foot. Three of Toby's best attacks thus far had done nothing, but he was not giving up.

Toby unleashed a vicious string of fist attacks. It was all he had learned from his days studying martial arts, but Aritem seemed to have a counter for everything he did. It was very quickly apparent to Toby that he was very easily outmatched. Aritem grabbed Toby by the neck and slammed him into the ground again.

To make sure Toby couldn't get back up, Aritem picked up the splintered piece of Toby's staff and stabbed it into Toby's leg. Toby cried out as the sharp pain entered his knee. Aritem pulled the bloody staff back and held it over his head, ready to deliver a killing blow to his chest.

Lia'na turned to Masarabi a second time, "He's down and he can't get up. It's over!"

Masarabi raised her hand, but Aritem's father cut her off, "Be silent, it'll be over momentarily!"

Lia'na shook her head, "He's incapacitated! This is against our laws!"

No one appeared to be listening to her, so she turned back to Toby, "Use your magic! Find the power within yourself! Do it before he kills you!"

Toby was about to respond when he took another blow to the face. That was it. His head hit the ground and his vision blurred.

Tears flowed down Lia'na's cheeks as she watched the one she loved being pummeled. In her mind, that final blow was her own fault and she knew what she had to do. *I'm sorry...*

Before anyone could react, Lia'na dodged around Masarabi and the group that stood with her, and dashed out onto the field.

"Child, no!" Masarabi cried.

It was too late. Lia'na was too far away to be grabbed. She ran at Toby as Aritem was about to deliver a punch so powerful, it would no doubt have been a killing blow. She had only seconds to spare.

Aritem stood over Toby with a gleeful look in his eyes. *This is it.* Toby thought to himself as he fought to stay conscious. *I didn't think I'd go out like this.*

He closed his eyes and waited for the impact that would end his life, but it never came. In its place, Toby felt a slight pressure on his side and the soft caress of a gentle hand on his face. Someone was lying on top of him.

"No!" A familiar voice cried out.

"Get out of the way, Lia'na!" Aritem snarled. "This challenge is not over!"

"The challenge is over!" Lia'na shot back. "Toby is incapacitated. He can't defend himself any more. By our laws, once he is down and cannot get up, the fight ends. These are our laws and to violate them is a punishable by exile!"

"He's still conscious. He needs to concede."

"As my knight, I concede on his behalf. It is my right!"

Aritem shook his head and tried to grab her in order to pull her off, but another hand grabbed his, "No, mirie!"

Aritem looked down to see that his arm was being held by Masarabi, "That is enough, you've won and as such the Fou'tar will be honored."

Masarabi looked down helplessly at Lia'na, "She is now honor bound to you."

Toby spat out blood and looked up at the group, "No, I do not concede!"

"Quiet!" Lia'na said harshly. "That's no longer your choice."

Toby was about to say something else when his eyes began to blur. He'd taken too many hits to the head and passed out.

*

Pain shot through Toby's arms as he woke up. His eyes opened to discover that the scenery had changed. His wounds had been tended to and he had been placed in the bed that he and Lia'na had occupied the night previously.

In a fit of rage, Toby fought the blankets back and tried to stand. Pain shot through his right knee, causing it to collapse out from under him, "God damn it…!"

The door flew open as Toby cursed and Auro appeared on the other side, "My friend, you should be in bed."

"Where is she?" Toby demanded.

"Already gone."

"What? You let her go?" Toby shouted.

"I had no choice, our laws are clear and she submitted to the will of Fou'tar in order to save your life!"

Toby felt as though his insides were about to explode. He focused that energy into his hands. He was about to strike Auro when the energy backfired and hit Toby's wounds.

Auro took a step back as he watched, "My friend, your hands... what are you doing?"

Toby's hands glowed as the injuries quickly healed up and the pain went away. He then looked up at Auro menacingly, "Apparently I can heal myself. Now tell me where the fuck she is!"

"You... you're an enchanter?"

"Where is she?"Toby demanded.

Auro nervously placed his hand on the knife hanging from his belt, "I'm under orders... I can't tell you."

"Who's orders?"

Toby could see Auro's eyes begin to water as he looked on, "... Lia'na's."

Toby showed Auro his glowing fist, "I could kill you... or pummel in the information out of you."

"If you are truly an enchanter, I believe you, but will you? Do you think that's what she would want for you?"

Toby pushed Auro out of the way and raced down to the base of the tree. His eyes darted around the woods. No one was around. All he noticed was the old van that the elves used was opened and his bags were in the back. He clenched his fist as his anger built up again, "Masarabi!"

No response.

"Masarabi!"

His voice echoed throughout the woods. He couldn't be sure, but it almost seemed like the trees shuddered in reaction to the thunder of his voice. He waited a few moments as his voice echoed before shouting again, "Masarabi!"

"No need to shout!" A terse voice replied. "Keep your voice down before you attract unwanted attention."

Toby turned to see Masarabi's scornful face glaring at him. He returned it with far more malice, "How could you... You let that punk take her?"

Auro stood next to her, "Be careful elder, he's an enchanter."

Masarabi looked at Toby as his hands continued to glow a burning red, "So it is true... I didn't want to believe it when Lia'na told me... –Tobias, I had to."

"He'll abuse her! He already has!"

"I know that..."

"And you let him take her? You help rasie her!"

The elder glared at Toby, "Do not presume to lecture me on my relationship with her. I understand how you feel, but I am bound by Elven law. If I had gone against it, Nartem and his ilk would have filed a protest with the High Elders... they would have taken my clan from me and put it under Nartem's rule. I couldn't allow that."

Toby was through listening, "Where the fuck did she go?"

"I can't tell you that."

Toby felt his blood boil. His hands shook, "I will burn every tree here to the ground if you don't tell me where she is."

"No you won't." Masarabi replied in an almost sympathetic tone.

"You sure of that?"

"Yes."

"How?"

"Because you're not Aritem. You're not that evil and unlike him, you care about what Lia'na wants and how she feels."

"What does that mean?"

"She doesn't want you to come after her."

"How do you know?" Toby demanded.

Masarabi sighed, "Lia'na made us all promise not to tell you. If you trespass on Elven land, we're well within our rights to punish you in accordance with our laws… and this is Aritem's clan we're talking about. Likely they would kill you if you're caught."

Toby let out a defeated sigh as he lowered his hands, "The fuck am I supposed to do? Just let her go?"

"If you love her and honor her, then yes. She surrendered herself to save you. Even if you go after her now, she would refuse to go with you. She knows her place."

Toby didn't trust Masarabi. If he told her that he was planning to go after Lia'na, likely she'd warn the Northern Clan that he was coming. He sighed and lowered his eyes, "I want to leave, now!"

"I figured as much." Masarabi responded. "Your bags have been packed and I have asked Auro to see you to the bus station."

In other words… to make sure I go home. Toby thought.

"This is for the best. Once you get home, forget her and forget everything you saw here. Live your life. This was never the right thing for either of you."

Toby pretended not to notice as Auro stepped towards the van. He pointed an accusing finger at Masarabi, "You are going to burn in Hell for what you've done."

Masarabi nodded, "I know… but hopefully this will help redeem me a little."

Masarabi stepped forward and held out a small package that looked like a rectanglar box. It was about 8x10 and was a few inches thick. Whatever it was, was wrapped in very old leather. He looked at it and back at her, "What is this garbage?"

Masarabi flashed a perturbed look at him, "This 'garbage' as you call it is one of the sacred relics of my people. It is one of the last surviving enchanter's tomes from the Alliance. Ordinarily, I'd never let a human have something so precious... or dangerous, but I feel we owe you this much."

"So what good is this going to do me?"

Masarabi shrugged, "It contains instructions on how to perform and control powerful enchantments... should you ever need them."

"Why would I?"

Masarabi turned and headed for the treehouse, "I can say no more. Farewall, enchanter, may you live an honorable life."

Toby wanted to say more to her, but what good would it do? Clearly in her mind, everything that happened was meant to happen and there was nothing anyone could do to change it. *Fuck this...*

He turned and headed for the van, "All right Auro, you all clearly want me off your land. So get me out of here before something bad happens."

Auro nodded and jumped in the driver's seat next to Toby, "As you wish."

The van started with a clanking roar and slowly took off down the dirt path.

Within minutes they were back on the road. Toby said nothing to Auro the entire trip. What was the point? He'd already threatened the elf's life. He wasn't going to tell him anything more now. Clearly his promise to Lia'na was more important to him than her saftey. All he could do was sit staring out the window.

XIV

The bus ride home was uneventful. Toby spent the entire time on his phone trying to figure out where the Northern Clan was. *North of New Hampshire? That limits our options to Maine, Canada, and Alaska.*

To his frustration, Toby's search turned up almost nothing. He was able to locate documentation of an elven compound in Canada, but was unable to locate its address. He was becoming more and more anxious. Not helping matters was the amount of pain that he was still in. The healing enchantment he'd performed was superficial at best and his injuries were still plaguing him. As the pain got worse, his left eye closed and was hard to reopen, but he was determined to find the answers he needed.

*

Three hours later, Toby waved his key fob over the sensor on the door of his condo, causing the indicator light to change from red to green as it unlocked. Toby's new condo was three doors down the shared balcony on the 4th floor, numbered 485.

Toby looked over the condo; the walls were all tan with a brick fireplace as the focal point. The living room and hallways all had hardwood flooring. Perhaps most impressive was the large balcony with a beautiful view of Boston.

The place was a mess in boxes that he still hadn't cleaned up. Packing paper lined the sides of the door from when he'd unpacked various items. He sighed as he pulled his cell phone out of his pocket and dialed Gishan's number.

Almost immediately after dialing the number, a gruff voice appeared, "Yo!"

"Gishan, I'm home."

"What?" Gishan replied in a surprised tone. "So soon? Dude, I thought you was spending the whole summer up there! Everything okay?"

"No... she's gone."

"You two break up?"

"No."

"Well what the fuck, man. What happened?"

"Are you busy?"

"Am I ever?"

"Get over here when you can and I'll explain it to you."

"I'm getting in the car, explain now."

"Fine... apparently elves have this sort of mating ritual where they're paired with a mate from birth."

"And she didn't tell you this?" Gishan asked.

"No... not until he showed up."

"The fuck? She never seemed like... you know, that type of bitch."

Toby shook his head, despite Gishan not being able to see it. "I don't think she planned on going through with it."

"Oh yeah? So what happened?"

"He tried to force it, but she didn't want to... I tried..."

"You fought him didn't you?"

"Yeah."

"Got your ass kicked, didn't you?"

"... Yup."

"Got kicked off their land?"

"Yeah."

"And she had to stay with him?"

"Pretty much. I got knocked out and by the time I woke up, they were already gone."

"Where?"

"Somewhere in Canada. I don't know..."

"What the fuck you doing home then, you obviously want this girl. Go fucking get her!"

"I can't! I don't know where she is!"

"Huh?"

"There's no address in Canada for the elven sanctuary and I'm still pretty hurt."

"How bad could it be?"

"He stabbed me in the leg with a broken poll."

"Shit... you been to a hospital?"

"Long story."

"That's a no."

Toby's temper began to flare again, "Look that's not important right now! This guy is going to beat her into submission if we don't find her quick!"

"Right, I'm on my way. Do you need anything?"

"Just your help."

"All right then."

**

Toby and Gishan spent the next 48 hours trying to get some information either from witnesses who had claimed to have been to the sanctuary online, or through more official channels. They were getting nowhere and it was getting to Toby, who was already on edge.

Gishan wasn't doing any better as he paced Toby's living room after turning on the TV, "Look, I've already been on hold for ten minutes. I'm trying to get some information on the elven sanctuary."

"..."

"Because someone I know went looking for it and hasn't been seen in days. I need to go find them!"

"..."

"No, I don't... no... Do not put me back on hold, don't you dare... don't..."

Gishan lowered the phone, "Motherf..."

"No luck with the embassy?"

"No."

Toby put his head back on the couch, nursing a headache, "Ugh... tomorrow we'll just take what information we have and go looking."

"You all right man?" Gishan asked. "You look like you're gonna get sick. You haven't really slept since I been here."

"I'll sleep when I'm dead."

"May happen sooner than later, keep this up."

Gishan grabbed the remote and flicked through the channels, looking for something to take their mind off of their troubles while Toby sat back listening to the heavy rain pelt the building. He pressed the 'next' button fiercely before settling on an evening news station. Though it gave them a slight distraction, the news was nothing more than the same thing they saw every day; another update on the problems in the Middle East, politics, and awful local events unfolding.

Toby was about to tell Gishan to shut it off when a light knock came at the door. It was so faint, he had barely heard it over the heavy rain. He turned and looked behind him at the door, "Did you hear that?"

"What?"

"I think someone's at the door."

"I didn't hear anything."

Toby started getting up, but Gishan jumped out of his chair before Toby could, "Stay put, man. I'll check and see who it is."

Toby sat back and closed his eyes. He breathed in deeply and pictured that night with Lia'na. He thought about everything that had happened; The fun, the pleasure, the enchanted glow of the torches, the warmth of the water, and the smoothness of Lia'na's body pressed against his. Then remembered the horrible imagery from the dream he'd suffered that night. Tears entered his eyes as the horror overtook him. *That's likely exactly what's happening... How could I let it? She must hate me now.*

"Toby man..."

His silent trance was broken by the nervous tone of Gishan's voice. He opened his eyes and stared straight ahead, "What."

"You better come here, quick."

Toby sighed as he stood up and limped over to the door, "What is it man, seriously I was just starting to rela..."

He suddenly forgot what he was saying as Gishan stepped out of the way. His good eye widened momentarily, "Lia'na..."

The young elf was a shell of herself. She had no rain coat and she was still wearing the same clothes that she'd had on the same clothes that she'd been wearing the last time he'd seen her. Her hair and clothes were filthy, she was soaked, and looked like she hadn't slept in days.

Gishan stepped back and turned for the kitchen, "I'll... leave you two alone. –Toby, I'm in the kitchen man, you need me, you call."

"Got it."

Toby stepped closer to the door and leaned on the frame, taking the weight off of his bad knee. Lia'na smiled, trying to offset the look of shame on her face, "Hey..."

Toby gazed at her without any detectible emotion, though inside, he was happy to see her, "Hey."

Lia'na nodded as though acknowledging some unspoken accusation Toby had levied against her, "Toby... I came here to say that I'm sorry."

"Look, Lia'na..."

"No." Lia'na replied, putting her hand up to Toby's mouth, but not quite touching it. "Please, hear me out before you say anything."

Toby nodded, allowing her to continue, "You were right. I... should have told you everything from the begining. Maybe we could have come up with a plan, but I didn't. I made my choice and I have to suffer with it."

Tears welled in her eyes as she looked over the bruises on Toby's face, "Seeing you like this is beyond torture. I never wanted you to get hurt. I never meant for it to happen."

She bit her lip and lowered her eyes as she shifted in place, "I love you. I mean that..."

Toby shook his head, "Lia'na, I can't be hearing this. You made your choice, you're with him now. I..."

"No... I'm not."

"What?"

"I told you, I had absolutely no intention of ever mating with that horrible elf. I don't care what my people say. Aritem wanted me to be a submissive house wife. That's not me. The moment the car stopped at a light, I got out and darted into the woods. They came after me, but the training I did with Auro helped me hide in the trees until they gave up and headed back to their car."

Toby watched her as she moved uncomfortably under his gaze, "I can't go home... violating the Fou'tar is an automatic expulsion from any and all clan territory. I'm in exile for the rest of my life."

She took a step closer and finally found the strength to look Toby in the eye, "I'm sorry... and I do love you. That's all I wanted to say. I screwed up royally, and I'll understand if you slam the door in my face. If you want me to leave... I will and I promise you'll never have to deal with me again. I've made my choices. Now I have to live the life I've chosen... and I am ready and willing to spend it pleading for your forgiveness if that's what you really want."

Tears began to flow down her cheeks as her voice began to crack, "But I'm kind of hoping that you'll cut me a break... Just this once, please?"

Toby sighed as he slouched back slightly, "You know I don't blame you for any of this."

"You should."

"I don't... and I love you too."

Lia'na sobbed softly, likely grateful that the rain masked her tears, "How ironic... it would have actually hurt less if you'd slammed the door in my face."

"Stop that."

She looked up at him, "So what now?"

"First, get inside out of the rain before you catch cold."

Lia'na cautiously stepped through the doorway into the living room. She slid her sandals off and did the best she could to dry her feet. Her eyes scanned the condo carefully, as though sensing that someone was about to jump out at her.

Toby closed the door and limped into the bedroom, grabbed his bathrobe, and went back out to the living room. He handed it to her and beckoned to the bathroom, "Go hang your clothes on the shower rod and change into this."

"Lien ni..."

Toby waited outside the door as Gishan appeared from the kitchen, "So she's back?"

"Seems like it."

"You know they're going to come looking for her."

"Maybe..."

"So?"

Toby shrugged, "I don't think they can legally take her. She told me that she has dual citizenship between her clans and the U.S. If they try, I'm not sure our government would be too happy."

"I dunno man, that's some serious gray area."

"Well I'll cross that bridge in due time."

"Right."

Gishan looked like he had something else to say, but didn't want to volunteer it. Toby rolled his eyes, "What...?"

"I was just thinking man... do you really want this again? I mean... after everything she put you through?"

"It wasn't her fault."

"You sure of that? She kept quite a lot from you."

"I know that, trust me we had this fight."

"All right dude, it's your life and all, I just don't want to see you getting hurt again."

"Not the first time I've had a relationship go sour, you know?"

"No, but it is the first time you've cared about one this much. You're in a much more delicate situation now."

Toby leaned his head back and sighed, "Dude spare me the brotherly bullshit. I'm okay... sort of, and I know what I'm getting into."

"All right, man."

Behind the door, Toby could hear Lia'na continuing to cry as she slowly stripped out of her clothes. He felt bad, knowing that while his wounds were physical, the ones she was dealing with were far deeper. She'd lost her family and her home in one day and then came begging forgiveness from a spurned boyfriend who could have slammed the door in her face. It couldn't have been easy.

His heart sank and he stepped back, waiting for her to finish up. His head began to spin from dizziness, making lean against the wall again. He breathed deeply for a few moments, attempting to regain his balance, hoping that she wouldn't see it.

His hope was dashed when Lia'na reappeared at the doorway. Her eyes were still wet and completely bloodshot, the braid in her hair was a lost cause that would have to be redone and her nose was bright red like she had a cold.

Lia'na's heart was completely broken by her own making, but she knew that she had bigger problems at that moment. Toby looked terrible and was leaning against the wall like he was about to fall over. She quickly grabbed him and got under his arm, "Ta arshana, come on, let's sit you down."

"I'm okay."

"No you're not. You're bruised all over and I don't know how your leg cleared up so quick, but it looks like it still hurts."

Toby collapsed on the couch as Lia'na leaned over him and looked into his eyes, "I'm really worried... you may have a concussion. Maybe we should get you to a hospital."

"No... I'm okay."

"How can you possibly be certain?"

Toby raised his hands, let them glow and placed them on his head, "I did a little training during the brief times I was supposed to be sleeping. I wanted to come rescue you and knew I had to heal up. I think I can do this..."

"Ta arshana?"

Toby closed his eyes and focused, making his hands glow brightly. Lia'na gasped and stepped backwards as she watched him, "How...?"

Toby closed his eyes and allowed the glow from his hands to enter his head. His skull glowed for a brief moment before the light died down and returned to normal. He opened his eyes as his skin returned to its normal hue and he regained his composure, "I had already figured out how to heal. It was just a question of making the enchantment more powerful."

Lia'na sighed as Gishan came back in the room. He exchanged glances with Lia'na for a moment before coming around the couch and facing Toby directly, "Hey man, it looks like my job is done here. You gonna be okay?"

"Yeah man, thanks for everything."

"No worries, you'd do the same for me if it was someone I cared deeply for."

A warm feeling entered her heart and for a moment, she allowed her lips a partial smile. It was short-lived, however, when Gishan looked back at her. It was cold and angry, almost like the first time that he'd seen her.

In her mind, Lia'na felt as though she deserved his scorn for what she'd put Toby through. She lowered her eyes in acceptance as Gishan spoke, "You are so lucky to have him, just so you know."

Lia'na nodded, "Trust me, I know... I won't forget."

"That's my best friend there, my brother, as far as I'm concerned. Don't mistreat him again, got it?"

"Come on buddy, lay off!" Toby said in a slightly irritated tone.

"No..." Lia'na said as she turned to him. "He's right. – Gishan, I have never nor would ever willingly put him in harms way."

Looking directly into Toby's eyes, she spoke with a level of assuredness that even seemed to convince Gishan, "Nor will I ever again let him be hurt if I can prevent it."

"All right then." Gishan replied. "I'm out."

"See ya man." Toby said as Gishan grabbed his keys on the table and headed out the door.

Lia'na looked Toby's face over as her eyes once again welled up, "I'm sorry Toby... I'm so sorry."

"Shh." Toby replied. "It's over now, you're safe and that's all that matters."

"But your face..."

"Will heal, all of the bruises and cuts will heal."

He touched Lia'na's chin, "Enough, okay?"

"Okay..."

"Look, just promise me one thing."

"Anything."

"No more secrets. If there's anything I need to know, I want you to tell me right away."

"Never again... if I think of anything, I'll tell you. As far as you're concerned, I'm an open book."

"Good."

They sat silently for a few moments before Toby leaned in towards her. Lia'na knew what he wanted, closed her eyes, and gently leaned in and kissed him. Her whole body shook as she threw her arms around him and gave him a gentle squeeze.

As Toby pulled away to take a breath, Lia'na curled up on the couch, facing the TV and rested her head on his knee. She let out a deep sigh, causing Toby to look down at her with a concerned expression, "You okay?"

"No."

"What's wrong now?"

Lia'na closed her eyes, "I've violated the Fou'tar... In one more day I'll be branded an outcast, unwelcome on any Elven land."

"Not even the other clans will let you in?"

"No." Lia'na adamantly replied. "Once you're disgraced by one, none of the others will give you a second look. As far as they're concerned, I'm unclean."

She placed her hand on Toby's knee as she continued, "I don't know what I'm going to do now. I'm all alone."

"It's a big world out there, plenty of opportunities and adventures to be had. Didn't you tell me that you had a free ride through college?"

"Yes, but that doesn't cover summer classes or room and board during the intercessions. I can't just live on campus all the time; I don't know how I'd afford it."

Toby's mind was struggling to come up with suggestions. There was one on his mind that he really wanted to offer, but again, they hadn't been going out that long and he wasn't certain it was appropriate, "Well... I mean you can get a job and get a place off campus, like I did."

"Yeah… If I can find a job, but the apartment would need to be close to the campus or to the T. Otherwise I'd never be able to get around, not having a car and all."

Toby could see that this option was extremely complicated and had failed to quell her fears. Could she even find a job? Even part time ones were getting scarce. What could he do? Even he was having trouble finding a job. For the most part, he had worked freelance on computers, but that was on an as-needed basis, and he only did it for spending money so he wouldn't cut into his savings.

He had nearly run out of ideas, only one was left, "Well you have another option…"

"Oh yeah, what's that?"

"You could…" he shuddered nervously as the idea forced its way past his lips, "what I mean is, I have the condo… it's small, but it has two bedrooms, and you could…"

"Move in with you?" Lia'na asked in surprise. "Really, you wouldn't mind?"

"Not at all. I trust you, and we have gotten close. It seems like it may be our best option."

"Our best option." Lia'na repeated. "Toby, are you sure? This is your first real home we're talking about."

"I'm sure. I already know what it's like to live on my own, so don't worry about that."

"I… I just don't know."

"Well I mean… It doesn't have to be permanent." Toby said in a convincing tone. "You could come and stay until you find a place of your own. If it means that much to you, you can always take the other bedroom. That way we could be like roommates. So it won't be too intimate."

"That's… actually quite reasonable."

Lia'na turned over and looked up at Toby. Her eyes began to dry and for the first time in a while, it looked like she was going to calm down, "Toby, te arshana ni, if you're sure you're okay with it, I'll live with you, at least for now."

"For now?"

Lia'na smiled snidely, "Let's just see where it goes before you start getting any ideas, okay?"

"Well... yeah. We both still have a year of college ahead of us and then probably grad school. I can't predict the future... All that matters to me in this moment is that you're okay. I want you to be happy and safe."

"I want that for you too."

"I know."

Lia'na turned back to the TV, "I think I still have some money in the account that Masarabi set up for me... I'm going to take out what I can... I'm going to need to get some clothes and some other things I'll need."

"You don't have anything?"

"Besides the clothes I left here... no. The rest are up in New Hampshire or in the dorm. I can't get them until the fall."

"All right, we'll go out tomorrow and grab some things."

"You really are my knight in shining armor," Lia'na said softly, "aren't you?"

"I try." Toby replied. "Oh that reminds me..."

Lia'na watched as Toby grabbed the book Masarabi gave him off of the table, "Your elder gave this to me before giving me the boot. Do you know what it is? It's in some weird language that I can't read. She said it was a tome of some kind?"

Lia'na sat up and let Toby place it on his lap. The cover was heavily worn vellum, with metal clasps opposite the spine, and a symbol of a crystal on the cover. She gasped upon looking at it, "In Tome de Magnifica... So the legends were true… It's one of the last enchanter tomes in existence."

"You've heard of it?"

"We read about this book, but we were told it was pure myth and that most likely it didn't exist at all. History has long since forgotten it."

"Then how did the elves have it?"

"I don't know. The elves have passed artifacts down from generation to generation."

She touched the fragmentum medalion she wore, "Including this... though I was told that it wasn't even real."

Toby smirked as he looked at his right hand, "Well obviously it is."

"And so is this..." Lia'na said, looking at the book.

She looked closely at the language in the book. It was written in ancient hyroglyphs that were ornate and written in verticle lines, "This... this must be the language of the Alliance."

Toby released a sigh that was so potent in annoyance, the hair stood up on the back of Lia'na's neck, "Great, how does Masarabi expect me to use this?"

Lia'na smiled as she looked at the pages, "It's several thousands of years old, what did you expect that it would be written in American English?"

"Well no, but there can't be a person alive who knows how to read it."

"Maybe there is."

"Who," Toby asked, "Masarabi?"

"I doubt it, but I remember a teaching from when I was younger. An enchanter can ask a tome to reveal its secrets."

"What? So what am I supposed to do, talk to it? Is it going to answer me?"

Suddenly the book flipped three pages. Toby looked down startled, "I didn't even feel any wind."

"There wasn't any." Lia'na insisted with a nervous grin. "Ask the book, Toby."

Carefully, Toby picked the book up by its spine. *So now I'm talking to books?* He looked at it for a moment, thinking that this was crazy, "I need answers... Can you help me?"

The book began to vibrate, causing Toby to drop it on the bed. They both backed away slightly as the pages flipped on their own until the book closed. It sat still for a few moments before shaking and then flipping open again. Toby looked down at the page in front of him. To his shock, the text in the book was now in English.

Lia'na smirked, "I guess you have your answer."

Toby began to read through the pages, "The book talks about the Lux Mundi and how its powers came to exist. There's a passage in here about the physical makeup of the diamond. It also talks about a curse that would befall anyone who attempted to destroy it."

"The Ulium." Lia'na said glumly.

"Yeah, it also expressly forbids the use of this book by any dark enchanters."

Toby continued to flip through the pages for over an hour as it became darker outside. Toby stayed up for another few hours before Lia'na grabbed his arm, "I hate to ask, but I'm really tired... can we get some sleep?"

Toby nodded, closed the book and put it on the coffee table next to him. He got up and walked over to the doorway leading to his bedroom. He turned back when he noticed that Lia'na hadn't followed him, "Coming?"

Lia'na looked up at him from the couch, "Really?"

"Yeah, why not?"

"I... I don't know... I didn't think..."

Toby came back out and put his hand on her cheek, "Has anything changed?"

"I don't know. I feel like I've done so much damage. I don't really know what to think."

Toby sighed, "Lia'na, we've already been through this. We had that fight, we dealt with the situation, and we got by it. Now you're here... and I'm beyond relieved."

"Really?"

Toby nodded, "I haven't slept since I got home. I was so afraid of what was happening to you. I was trying to figure out where the elven sanctuary in Canada was so I could come get you."

Lia'na looked into his eyes, "I'm sorry I worried you, but I meant it when I said that I'd never allow myself to be mated to him. Te arshana ni and there is so much more I want to do and experience."

"I know that. So lets get started, shall we?"

"Sounds good."

Lia'na smiled, got up, and followed him into the bedroom. Toby yanked off his jeans and got under the covers while Lia'na shed the robe he'd given her and slid in next to him. As soon as Toby stopped moving, she turned on her side and curled up next to him.

The touch of her skin against his arm became a comforting mechanism that helped slowly lull him to sleep. As his eyes closed, he felt Lia'na's head move closer to his ear, "Toby...?"

"Mmm?"

"Te arshana ni."

"I love you too."

After a few moments of silence, Toby released his breath, "Maybe keeping the Magnifica isn't good idea. That book might be better off locked up and kept secret."

Lia'na was about to respond when they heard light gust of wind outside their window and what sounded like a whisper. Toby's eyes shot open and he sat up, looking at the window. They were both slightly alarmed by what they'd heard and the hair stood up on the back of Toby's neck. He felt as though something was watching them.

When no further sound came, he lay back down and relaxed. Lia'na watched him carefully to make he didn't make his injuries worse. "Toby... Normally, I'd agree with you. From a young age, taught to fear and respect books that deal in magic and the supernatural.They can't be taken lightly. What is contained in them could be turned into horrible weapons."

Lia'na was nervous that the price for knowledge might be too high, but she knew that Toby wanted to learn more about his gifts. He was the last of his kind, so no one could help him truly master them, but this book might have some answers. "Unfortunately... I don't think that's an option. I've taught you everything I've been instructed on, but to learn how to truly control your powers, you need a master enchanter."

"And none exist..."

"Toby, I'll be here with you." Lia'na insisted. "We've come this far together, if the answers you need are on these pages, then we've got to find them."

"So what should I do then?"

"I don't know. Just be careful, not everything that is done can be undone. This book may provide you with answers and abilities, but I've heard horrible stories about what happens when people mettle with powers that they don't fully understand."

Toby yawned as his head turned to Lia'na, "Well we've got a lot to figure out... and we're not going to figure it out right now. So let's get some sleep."

Lia'na smiled, "All right. Good night, ta arshana."

"Goodnight."

Lia'na lay in Toby's arms and was slowly lulled off to sleep as Toby gently caressed her body. He started at the tip of her left ear and made his way down her shoulder, and continued to her hip and thigh. It wasn't long before Toby also fell asleep.

A few seconds went by as Toby rested, but his peace was cut short by a large boom. His eyes snapped open and to his horror, he was no longer in his condo. Rain began to pour down on him, soaking his body, and the t-shirt and jeans he was now wearing. Toby ran to a nearby railing where he discovered that he was on a large cargo ship. The name on the side read *Luca Ricci.*

This can't be real, Toby thought to himself, *what am I doing here?*

He turned and looked as crewmen ran past him screaming. *What's going on here…? Lia'na, where are you?*

Toby grabbed another man as he ran past, "What's going on here? Have you seen a young elf onboard?"

The man shook his head in a panic, "Esegui, demoni … demoni!"

"Demoni?" Toby repeated as he turned to the back of ship. That's when he saw three dark ghostly figures flying towards the ship while two others had already landed. Two of the ghosts slammed into the ship's super structure while the third hit the bridge. The entire aft tower burst into flames.

Now Toby understood, "Demons!"

Thunder and lightning crashed down around the ship as two more men ran past. One of them grabbed Toby and yelled at him with a thick Italian accent, "To the boats, signore, hurry!"

Toby quickly followed the men as one of the ghosts gave chase. They arrived at the front of the ship, only to be cut off from the bow by two more ghosts. Having nowhere left to run, one of the men dropped to his knees and began praying. Toby heard the heavy breathing of the ghost closing from behind.

As the creature approached, Toby turned to face it. The creature materialized so that its top half took the form of a cloaked human. Only its lower face could be seen under the dark, misty, robe. When it saw Toby, it stopped in its tracks and hovered around him for a moment. The creature seemed almost bewildered to see him. It began to hiss and uttered a low growl, "Tobias…"

His eyes snapped open and he found himself back in bed. The thunder and lightning outside continued, but he was home in reality. Still in a state of shock, Toby shot straight up and put a hand on his chest. He was covered in sweat and gasping for air.

Lia'na was roused by the sound of his labored breathing and turned over to see what was going on. When she saw Toby panting and completely soaked in sweat, she sat up in a panic, "Ta Diesu! Toby… Toby, are you okay? What is it? What happened?"

She got beside Toby, and grabbed his right arm. With a firm grasp on him, she then reached around his back and grabbed his left. She became even more worried when she felt his body trembling uncontrollably, "Come on Toby, talk to me, what's wrong?"

Toby couldn't respond to her as his lungs were still struggling to take in air. Lia'na didn't know what to do, rubbing his arms wasn't solving anything, so she got on her knees behind him and placed her hands on his back to try rubbing right over his lungs.

Toby felt Lia'na's gentle touch and it helped him breathe normally again. Lia'na then quickly moved herself around Toby and rested on her knees again in front of him. She wrapped her arms around him, and kissed his neck. Her tenderness successfully calmed him down.

As Toby stopped shaking, Lia'na moved back a little and placed her hands on his cheeks, "Can you speak now?"

Toby nodded, "Yes… I'm okay."

"You had me worried, I thought you were suffocating. What happened?"

"Something…" Toby replied as he sucked in a deep breath, "something evil is coming this way. I saw it… it was on the *Luca Ricci.*"

"The *Luca Ricci,* what is that, a ship?"

"I was there. It was in a storm. Then…"

"Then, what?"

Toby inhaled another deep breath as he spoke, "It was attacked. They didn't stand a chance."

"In a storm? I've never heard of anyone attacking a ship in turbulent water."

"No. It was attacked by ghosts!"

Lia'na shifted the pressure off her knees and sat next to him with a worried look, "Ghosts? What'd they look like?"

Toby closed his eyes, fighting to remember, "Just flowing black rags with human faces. One of them recognized me and called me by name."

Lia'na hugged him and rested her head on his arm, "It was probably just a dream."

"No. I've had night terrors before, but they didn't scare me like this. This was a full color dream. I felt everything, the fire from the ship, the wetness of the rain, the coldness of the wind, and the terror of the men onboard. I swear to you, something happened."

"I believe you, ta arshana, but right now you need to rest. Lay down with me, and when we get up tomorrow, we'll look into it. Remember the name of that ship."

"I can't sleep."

"Then don't. Just hold on to me."

Toby slowly laid back in bed and put his arms around Lia'na's body. He placed his hands on her chest and stomach as his head pressed on the pillow. Lia'na smiled contently, "Te arshana ni. It will be all right, I promise."

Toby breathed more steadily now and closed his eyes as he pressed himself against her, "I hope you're right."

XV

Lia'na was woken up the next morning to see Toby staring at the ceiling, "Enoi mae, did you sleep at all last night ta arshana?"

"Good morning. No…"

Lia'na turned over so she faced him, "It was really that bad?"

"Yeah… I can't shake what I saw… something bad happened yesterday. I just know it."

Lia'na yawned as she sat up, "I believe you, give me your phone."

Toby grabbed his jeans off of the floor and pulled the phone out of his pocket. He quickly switched it on and handed it to her, "What do you need?"

She took the phone and opened the browser. Google came up, allowing her to run a quick search. She frowned, "I don't see anything on here about a wreck being reported or a ship gone missing."

Toby looked at the display, "Search for the *Luca Ricci*."

She typed in the name and hit search. A Wikipedia site came up describing a large cargo ship, "Well the *Luca Ricci* is a fairly new dry cargo ship, commissioned in Italy. I can't find anything on who operates it, but apparently it's on its way here with some valuable cargo."

"Any idea what that cargo is?"

"Nope."

Toby laid back and sighed, "That ship will never make it here."

"So what do you think we should do about it?"

"I don't know."

Lia'na nodded, "Well I doubt that there's anything we can do right now. Let's get up, get straightened out, and get some food. You were covered in sweat last night. You really need a shower."

"But the ship?"

"There hasn't been any reports of issues with it."

Toby grabbed her by the arm, "Lia'na, it was attacked!"

"I believe you ta arshana, but what can we do about it? Who would we call?"

"The Coast Guard?"

"And what would we tell them? That you dreamed the ship was in trouble and because of that, you believe that it was attacked? What do you think will come of that?"

Toby let out another sigh. She was right, no one would believe them. They likely wouldn't bother checking, and if they did and discovered that something had gone wrong, he'd most likely have a swat team at his door, "All right. You've got a point."

"I want to help, Toby. If you want me to try to reach out to someone, I will but..."

"No, it's fine. You're right."

Lia'na's stomach growled as she stood up. She smiled sheepishly as Toby stared at her, "Sorry... I haven't eaten in a few days."

"Okay I'll get you some breakfast."

Toby got up and headed to the kitchen, only to have Lia'na jump in front of him, "Shower first, then food."

"Ugh... fine!"

Toby stood looking down at his dark outline in the sheets. Lia'na made the bed as Toby grabbed a towel, "You coming?"

Lia'na's eyes narrowed and she smiled, "I was beginning to wonder if you were even going to ask."

She followed him into the bathroom and waited while he got undressed and followed him in the shadow. The water was warm and soothing as it poured over their bodies.

Lia'na turned around, closed her eyes, and put her face under the shower head. As the water poured down her cheeks, she felt a slight sensation on her head.

Lia'na opened her eyes to see what was going on and noticed some white foam sliding down her shoulder. Toby's hands ran through her hair and caressed her scalp. She closed her eyes and leaned backwards as he worked. His hands ran over her scalp and then down through her hair. The feeling of his hands against the back of her ears was electrifying. Her ears had always been sensitive as most elves' were. His touch caused her to exhale deeply and lean back even further.

Once Toby was done, Lia'na turned around and let the water rinse her head, "Iesau, I've never had a guy even offer wash my hair before."

Toby paused for a moment, "How many guys have you been in the shower with?"

"One or two."

Lia'na noticed that Toby had an odd look on his face as she looked him in the eyes, "What, is that a problem?"

"Well no, it's just…"

"You thought I was a sheltered little forest elf? Wait, are you jealous?"

Toby narrowed his eyes as he looked at her, "What, no!"

"Ta Diesu! You are! You're jealous!"

Toby leaned back against the wall with an annoyed look on his face. Lia'na leaned in, arched her neck, and looked up at him, "Ta arshana, you are too cute!"

Toby rolled his eyes as she teased him. After a few minutes of torture, Lia'na pulled him off the wall and wrapped her arms around him, "Let me put your jealousy to rest. I may have been a naive little elf-girl, but I've been going to college outside the reservation for three years now. I've stayed with other clans, as well as in dorms. I've done some crazy things, but I've never mated with anyone else. You are the only one, you."

The look of annoyance slowly disappeared as she peered into his eyes, "Feel better now that you know that you're the only one who's ever gotten everything?"

"Yeah, yeah, I guess."

"Good, now turn around."

Toby promptly obeyed as she rubbed his back down with soap. Once they were completely clean, Toby turned the shower off, got out, and picked up the two towels that he had left folded on the sink. He handed one to Lia'na before wiping himself down with the other.

Toby finished quickly and watched Lia'na as she ran the towel down her body. She smiled when she noticed him watching, "Enjoying the view?"

"Always."

When she was done, she wrapped herself in the towel. She was about to turn around when she felt Toby's arms on her shoulders. They came together and rested on her stomach. Lia'na closed her eyes and leaned back into Toby. She ran her own hands up his arms as he held her, "Te arshana ni."

"I love you too. I'm happy you're here."

"Me too... I'm just so... releaved."

"Oh?"

"Yeah, I can't explain how, but I always knew that something like this could happen. Now that it has, it's like a dark cloud has finally disappeared."

They savored the moment for as long as they could when a knock at the door broke the serenity. Lia'na's ears perked up, "Get dressed, let me check..."

She held the towel and went to the door. Being as quiet as she could, she took a look through the small peep hole. She squinted to get a good look at who was there.

Toby threw on a black shirt and jeans. His eyes scanned the floor for a pair of sox when he heard a faint cry come from the living room. He jumped over the bed and ran to the doorway.

Lia'na was standing with her back pressed against the door. Her skin was pale and her eyes wide. When she saw Toby, she put her right index finger to her mouth, signalling him to be quiet.

"It's Auro." She mouthed, not making a sound.

Toby's eyes narrowed. How could the elves have figured out where he lived? He quietly stepped into the kitchen and grabbed a steak knife as a second, louder, knock came at the door.

He stepped forward with the knife behind his back, "Bedroom."

Lia'na nodded without saying a word, tiptoed over to the bedroom and shut the door.

Toby waited until she was out of sight and then opened the front door with the knife behind him. Auro stood on the other side and smiled as the sunlight flooded the dark apartment, "My friend, good morning."

Toby acted surprised. His eyes narrowed as he looked at the elf, "Auro...? I didn't think I'd ever see you again. What are you doing here?"

Auro frowned, "Sorry to just drop by... I found your address online and was told to check in. The Northern Clan returned to our land... apparently Lia'na escaped from their convoy."

"Escaped? You make it sound like she was a prisoner."

Auro nodded, "You know full well that I share your opinion of what was happening to her."

"All right... but what brings you here?"

"I think you know."

Toby's eyes narrowed, "Tell me."

"Do you know where she is?" Auro asked suspiciously.

"No."

"Really?"

"I just said no."

"So she hasn't tried to contact you...?"

Toby sighed, "Look, I got the shit kicked out of me by one of your guys. I lost my girlfriend, and I've been sitting here for days in pain. Now you're coming here accusing me?"

"I apologize..."

"Let me ask you, Auro, what if I said yes? What if I said she was here? What would you do?"

"They told me to bring her back... at all costs."

Toby nodded, "In other words, even if you have to come through me. Wonderful."

Auro's eyes wandered past Toby into his condo and fixated on a pair of elven sandles that were behind the couch, "I see..."

Toby followed his gaze and realized that Lia'na's sandles were in view. He quickly stepped into Auro's view, clenching the knife behind his back. *Shit!*

Auro nodded, "Hmm... well okay. If you haven't seen her, you haven't seen her. One sec."

Toby waited to see what he was about to do. Auro grabbed his cellphone, pressed 'send,' and held it close to his ear, "Yeah its Auro."

"..."

" No, she's not here."

"..."

"Yeah I'm sure. I checked the place out.I can't find any evidence that she is, or ever was here."

"..."

"No she would have been here by now."

"..."

"All right, I'm on my way back."

Toby loosened his grip on the knife. He was still suspicious of Auro, but he was slightly more relaxed, "So what now?"

"Well she's got till the end of the day. If she doesn't return, the Northern Clan has already filed the Fou'tar violation with the High Elves. She'll be labeled an exile and unable to return to our lands."

"That stinks."

"Maybe... or maybe she's better off."

Auro reached next to the door and picked up a green cloth sack that he'd place next to the entrance, "Here."

"What's this?" Toby asked.

"It's all the stuff that Lia'na left in her room in the tree house. All of the clothes she brought home and a few pieces of decor."

Toby looked at him oddly, "So what do you want me to do with it?"

"Keep it. I have a feeling you'll find a use for it." Auro said with a wink. "Besides, I'm sure she'd rather you have it."

"... All right, if you're sure."

"Thanks."

Auro stood at the door silently for a few more moments. The silence was uncomfortable for the both of them and Toby was reaching his limit, "Was there anything else you needed?"

Auro shook his head, "You know... I spent a lot of time with Lia'na. She was like a little sister to me. I taught her a lot of the things that I was taught as a sentry. I really enjoyed those times. I just wish I could tell her that... and that I'll always look back on them fondly."

"I'm... sure she knows that."

"I hope so." Auro replied, keeping his gaze.

After another moment of silent, Auro turned and looked at his van, "Well... I'd better get going. I've got a long ride ahead of me. Where ever Lia'na is... I hope she's found what she was looking for. Sorry to bother you."

"No problem. Me too."

Auro stepped away from the doorway and headed back to the old van. Toby watched him suspiciously until the driver's side door was closed and he was driving away. He wasn't certain about what had happened, but something told him that they were safe.

He turned to see Lia'na standing in the doorway to the bedroom with tears in her eyes, "Did I do the right thing?"

"What do you mean?"

"Was I being selfish? I left the clan that raised me, I violated our laws by dating a human, I backed out of my betrothal, and I let you risk your life for my freedom. I'm starting to feel like I'm the most selfish b..."

"Enough!" Toby interrupted. "Did you do the right thing? I can't answer that for you. I know you did what you thought was right. You did what you had to do, what anyone who wanted her freedom badly enough would have done, and even if you were being a little selfish, so what? This is America; you have the right to decide what you want for yourself. Freedom of choice isn't asking a lot."

Lia'na lowered her head and feigned a smile, "Lien ni... ta arshana. It's just hard knowing who I didn't even get a chance to say goodbye to."

"Well I mean if you want to go back..."

"No!" Lia'na shouted. "Trust me, I don't. Life isn't always fair and it's something I have to learn to live with. Going back is nothing but pain and sorrow. It may have been where I grew up... but now... It's a prison that I don't want to go back to."

"Okay."

She staired at the door for another moment as Toby turned to the kitchen to get her some food, "Goodbye..."

XVI

Lia'na finished up her pancakes and sat on the couch, staring at Toby's phone as the loading screen froze up. She closed the web browser and tried again. The same thing happened the second time. She lowered the phone and put her head back, "Ugh... I hate these things."

"Is that why you don't own one?" Toby asked as she turned on the TV.

"Partially, but also once you start using one, your life becomes almost dependent on them. Think about it, you sacrifice your sense of direction to navigation apps that tell you where to go. Everything about your life is laid out in plain sight for all to see, whether you like it or not."

"You sound like one of those anti-technology activists."

Lia'na smiled, "I'm not. I just don't see the need to own one. I still use a laptop, I know how to drive a car, though I need to get a license, and I enjoy everyday innovations. One of those naturalists wouldn't do any of those things."

"I guess not."

She rested her head on the back of the couch, "So this is home... I can't say I ever thought I'd call Massachusetts home. I always thought I'd live on the reservation."

"Your home is with me now for as long as you want it."

"Lien ni."

She thought about it for a moment, "It'll be nice waking up next to you every day and I love that you have access to the roof. The view up there is incredible."

Lia'na took in a deep breath as she looked around the sparsely furnished condo, "I forgot how wonderful your home is. That's an incredible view of the city."

"Don't you mean our home?" Toby asked. "You live here too."

Lia'na turned and looked at him. A faint smile appeared on her face, "Yes... our home. I live here now too, don't I? Sorry, it's still sinking in."

Toby nodded as she walked back over to him and wrapped her arms around his shoulders, "Lien ni for making me feel so welcome."

"Don't mention it."

Lia'na nodded and handed him the phone. At that moment, Toby noticed she was rubbing her arms as she looked around. Her breathing was slightly labored and she was becoming fidgety, "Toby um... I think I'm going to go up to the roof for a little while. I'll take your laptop and look up the *Luca Ricci.* If I find anything new, I'll let you know."

"Are you okay?" Toby asked, concerned.

"I'm fine, I just need some air."

"All right."

Without another word, she picked his laptop up off the counter and disappeared, leaving Toby to finish cleaning up. He grabbed her bag and began to unpack her clothes. Thankfully, he'd had already moved his dressers in and had ample space for their clothes. Though he had no idea he'd be moving in her things as well. At most, he thought he'd be keeping a few sets of her clothes for when she spent the night.

On the roof, Lia'na set Toby's laptop down on a small bench and did a search for the *Luca Ricci.* She took a minute before clicking on the information, savoring the cool air and the view of the now-distant city.

Though it was miles away, Lia'na could hear the distant sound of thousands of cars on the road. To her, it sounded like a constant gust of wind passing by her ears. It would be something to get used, but at least it was a relaxing sound.

Lia'na closed her eyes and pictured the tops of the trees in her forest. The sound from high up on one of the branches was similar, but much closer to a gentle whisper. The thought of those high up trees began to make her heart ache. She was certain that if she asked Toby, he'd take her somewhere with tall trees that she could climb, but it wouldn't be the same. The view would be different, as would the sounds and the smell.

Realizing that she was now going to have to get used to living a different lifestyle in a place that was completely foreign to what she was used to, Lia'na buried her face in her hands and began to cry. *It's not fair,* she thought to herself, *was freedom so much to ask? My only crime was being born a girl.*

In her heart, she was truly happy to be there with Toby, and she knew that they would have fun together. Before that could happen though, she would need to cope with the change of scenery and learn to live with the fact that she could never go home or see her family again.

A loud beep from the computer's speaker made her jump. She wiped her eyes and looked down to see that she had a pop up on the screen saying the computer was running a virus check. She closed the window to bring the search engine back up. When she clicked on her search results, what lit up the screen was shocking. Several articles came up reporting on a disaster. She quickly knelt down and began reading.

Lia'na became so immersed that she didn't notice the hand descending on her shoulder. The sensation of Toby's warm touch made her yelp in fright. Toby smiled, "Sorry, I didn't mean to scare you."

"It's all right. I was actually just about to come and get you. You're not going to believe this… actually you might."

"What did you find?"

She looked up at Toby with fear in her eyes, "You were right."

"What?"

"That ship was attacked, last night. She was found heavily damaged and adrift on the coast."

Toby went pale, "No..."

"There's more."

"What'd you find?"

Lia'na returned to looking over her data, "Well it looks like information about the cargo she was carrying."

Toby's eyes narrowed, "And?"

"That's what scares me. They were transporting artifacts. An American archeologist, John Tyran, had apparently obtained rights to dig on Mt. Vesuvius. He claims to have found something of monumental importance that proves his theories correct. It's apparently something that could change our understanding of Alliance history."

"Maybe he found relics?"

"The ship was outfitted for transporting radioactive material. What Alliance artifact would be radioactive?"

Toby took a step back, "You don't think that fool located the remains of the Lux Mundi?"

Lia'na looked at him blankly, "The article doesn't say. Apparently the ship's contents have been deemed classified. I sincerely hope not...most of my people paid the ultimate price to destroy it."

Her words brought Toby back down, "I know…"

After staring at the computer screen for a few minutes, Lia'na finally spoke up, "The blood strewn about the ship is confirmed to be that of the crew. Whatever killed them didn't leave much for anyone to find. The damage is pretty extensive. It looks like the ship is being declared a total loss and will be broken down once she's towed in... Oh God..."

"What?"

Lia'na looked up at Toby with a fearful expression, "Her holds were completely empty."

Chills flew down Toby's spine, "Now whoever attacked that ship may have the pieces of the Lux Mundi... the most powerful artifact in history... and they know who I am."

"We don't know that for certain." Lia'na insisted. "All we know is he found something near Mount Vesuvius. People have been digging artifacts out of that mountain for years. There could be another explanation."

"Really?" Toby asked in an unconvinced tone.

"It's not impossible."

She quickly turned back to the keyboard and brought up Google, "Let me run a search on this John Tyran guy."

Toby nodded as she typed his name in below the colored letters spelling 'Google.' Instantly several articles and biographical information came up on John Tyran. Lia'na read quickly as Toby looked on, "Let's see... he's 45 years old and is considered one of the leading experts on the ancient Alliance. He was part of the team that discovered the first remains of the ancient city north of Persia, and..."

"What is it?"

She turned and looked Toby for a moment before reading the rest, "Using what scientific data we have on the activity of Mt. Vesuvius, John Tyran believes that he can locate the remains of the long lost Lux Mundi. He believes them to be buried very deep on the southern side of the Mountain."

Toby sighed as he knelt down next to her, "He was looking for it..."

Lia'na nodded, "It appears he had a theory as to the remains' exact location. That's where all the articles end."

Toby looked at the screen with her, "There's nothing else?"

"Nope. It's like all of this guy's work stopped at this point about a year ago."

"He found it. There is no other explanation."

Lia'na didn't want to admit it, but the evidence was there, "It looks like it…"

Though they had finally solved the mystery of his dream, a lot still didn't add up. Toby needed more answers than what he had, "I don't understand, why would it come here? Why not keep it in Italy?"

Lia'na clasped the shard that hung around her neck, "The Lux Mundi was an artifact of intense power, but also infamy. Perhaps Italy didn't want it on their soil, maybe they didn't know, or maybe they thought it'd be safer here. I have no idea."

She closed her eyes as her mind was taken over by intense fear, "The fools… they dug up something that should have remained buried. This could have a high price tag."

"Is the Lux Mundi as dangerous as the elves believe?"

"I don't know, but my people still tell stories of how anything that was exposed to the diamond for too long was bent and twisted into horrible creatures. When I was younger, I thought they were just campfire ghost stories. I had no idea that they might actually be true. Actually now that I think about that, it makes those campfire stories a lot more frightening."

Toby stood up, "And you now wear a part of it around your neck…"

She clasped the medallion in her hand and turned the gem over a few times, "It has never harmed its wearer. I assumed that the power this shard holds is infinitesimal compared to what the whole diamond can do."

"I think you should destroy it." Toby replied in an adamant tone. "Who knows what it could be doing to you and most of the people who had it before you were already infected."

"No one knows I have it other than my clan. It's all I have of them and it's been passed down through generations of my family. I've already been forced to give up so much. I don't want to give up any more."

Toby rubbed his forehead, "I don't agree with this. You're putting yourself in terrible danger."

"I seriously doubt that. You're talking about ifs, maybes, and ancient legends. I'll admit that the stories gave me pause when I first put it on, but no one who has worn this gem has ever suffered any detrimental effects. It's harmless, I swear."

"Harmless, unless the person who slaughtered the crew of *Luca Ricci* comes looking for it. If they're looking to rebuild the Lux Mundi, no doubt they'll want all the pieces."

Toby knelt down next to her, and peered into her eyes, "I know I've figured out how to use magic, but I still haven't mastered it, and I seriously doubt that there is anything in the Magnifica about fighting ghosts."

The thought of those ghosts coming after them made Lia'na's blood run cold, "Ta Diesu... that's true. They could come looking for it, but they don't know where it is or who has it."

"They found the other pieces... and they were able to haunt me. Is that relic really worth your life?"

"No, of course not. It's just hard for me. This is the only thing that I have of my family, of my clan. It's hard to think about parting with it."

"Lia'na, I know it's tough and I wouldn't try to force you to do it. The decision has to be yours, as you said, the necklace belongs to you."

She turned away from him and looked at the shard, "Okay Toby... you win. I'll do anything for you, after what you've done for me, you've earned it. If you feel that strongly about it, I'll destroy the fragmentum. I just wish there was another way."

"It's for the best. How do we do that?"

"I don't know, but there has to be a way."

"How did your people do it before?"

"Self-sacrifice. Elves sacrificed their life blood to bring it down."

"That doesn't make any sense. Human blood makes it stronger, but elf blood destroys it?"

"It makes perfect sense. Why do you think there's no record of an Elven enchanter?"

Toby shrugged as she continued, "We are sensitive to nature and the supernatural, but we can neither control, nor wield it. Our bodies don't absorb the energy of the diamond, they cancel it out, or so I'm taught."

Toby started to be able to make sense out of this, "So Elven blood will break the diamond down."

"Yes… but don't forget, doing so is what caused the Ulium. It's not a good idea to try again. Even though there is a vaccine, it won't save someone who is already sick. My ancestors were unable to destroy the diamond. Their blood just shattered it."

"All right... We'll hang on to it for safe keeping until we can figure out how to destroy it. Did you find any other info online?"

"No… nothing. No one has claimed responsibility for the attack and there is no evidence pointing to any group."

At that moment, Toby remembered something from his book, "Come down stairs."

Lia'na got up and followed Toby back down to the condo. They sat at the kitchen counter as Toby pulled out the Magnifica. He quickly flipped through the pages until he came across one passage regarding the use of enchanters in ceremonies conducted by a group called the Fillis de Lux.

"Heretics…"Lia'na hissed when she heard the name.

"You've heard of them?"

"Yeah, they were an ancient cult focused on worshipping the Lux Mundi. They viewed it as a direct link to their God. I don't even want to get into the details of the hedonistic ceremonies they performed to gain more power."

"Do you remember what you said about dark enchanters sacrificing their life energy to gain more power?"

"Yes and I know where you're going with this. Sacrificing the life force of others to gain more power worked pretty well according to history. It's something they weren't above doing."

Toby closed the book and looked out the window towards the city, "Is it possible that the Fillis de Lux still exists?"

"It's not impossible, but if they do, I'd be willing to bet that they're the ones who stole the diamond's remains."

"And they'll try to find a way to restore them."

Lia'na stood up, "If that's the case, then they'll need an enchanter of considerable power."

Toby began to feel sick as he thought about what that meant, "But... you said that there aren't any others."

"There aren't..."

"So what are we going to do?"

"We need to find a way to hide your powers. I can try to help you with that, but I need to learn more about your family line. I need to know just how potent magic is in your blood. Would anyone be able to give us more info on your parents and perhaps your grandparents?"

"My Uncle Jake. After I went to college, he bought a place in Brookline near Longwood Ave. He should be able to help us."

"Can we call him?"

"Yeah." Toby said as he pulled out his phone and tapped on his uncle's number.

The phone rang several times before going to voicemail. Toby tried again and again it went to voicemail, "He must not be home, I'll try again in a little bit."

Toby dropped on to the couch in front of the TV, "I don't like this."

"I know, ta arshana," Lia'na said sympathetically, "but we'll talk to your uncle and figure this all out. Try to take your mind off of it."

"I don't know that I can."

"Then let me help you." Lia'na said in almost a whisper.

"How?"

She smiled and got on top of him, straddling his waist. Her knees bent and her back arched as she began kissing Toby's neck. Slowly she made her way to his face, kissing his forehead before pressing her lips against his, "Te arshana ni…"

XVII

Toby tried to contact his uncle continuously over the next few days. Each time all he got was the voicemail. A week passed and still no word. Toby was beginning to get restless and worried about the man who had raised him. Lia'na would often get dizzy watching him pace back and forth around the condo before demanding that he sit down.

"Maybe he's out of town?"

"I don't know... He has been known to disappear for weeks at a time, but he usually at least leaves some contact info."

"What's the most he's ever disappeared?"

"A month or two?"

"So... maybe that's what's going on?"

While trying to contact his uncle, Toby also had to focus on getting both he and Lia'na settled into the condo. Thankfully, it didn't take long for Toby to get everything he needed to move in. He furnished the rest of his home from a second-hand store with some fancy antiqued furniture.

Lia'na added a more welcoming touch to the place by bringing home plants and Elven décor. Toby was more than happy to let her decorate the bare walls, though he wasn't sure where she was getting the displays. No store sold that sort of artwork, at least none that he knew of.

There was a bit of a stir around the condo association about the idea of an elf living amongst them. Though no one would come right out and say it, there were a few people who were uncomfortable with the idea. However, the association was also aware that there was nothing they could do about it without breaching several anti-discrimination laws. Rather than cause trouble, they accepted Lia'na's presence. The worst Lia'na and Toby ever encountered was a few whispers behind their backs.

Even with free reign to decorate the condo as she saw fit, Toby noticed that Lia'na was still very melancholy. Any time he questioned her about it she would deny that there was problem, which only made things worse. He didn't want to make her uncomfortable, so he never pressed her too much on it, but it still felt like he had taken a fish out of water and she was slowly suffocating.

Toby had kept the book of Elven law and tried to find something, anything, that could overturn her exile, but the laws were absolute. Every law, clause, passage, and line had been carefully crafted to prevent someone from being able to jump through a loophole. She could never return and there was nothing he could do about it.

Early that Saturday morning, Toby was up cleaning from the previous night's meal when he heard footsteps behind him. He never had a chance to turn and see who it was. A pair of arms wrapped around his chest and a face leaned into his back. He smiled as he rubbed the hands now holding him in place, "Good morning."

"Enoi Mae, ta arshana, you're up early." The voice replied.

Toby nodded, "We made a mess last night, and I'm just trying to get everything in order."

When Lia'na released Toby, he turned to face her and gave her a brief kiss. She was dressed in Toby's white Boston Red Sox jersey as she often did when she went to bed. It was massive on her, draping down passed her knees so that it was impossible to tell if she had put underwear back on or not. Big Papi's number 34 completely covered her back.

Toby had bought her pajamas, but she seemed to prefer his shirts. Her hair was still braided, but otherwise unkempt. He smiled as he looked at her, "The Tumble Inn Diner is right down the street if you want to get some breakfast."

"I'm not really hungry. Do you want me to make you something?"

"Nah. I was just seeing if you were hungry. I'm good."

Lia'na chuckled softly, "Well... since neither of us is hungry... I think I'm going to get dressed and go up to the roof for a little while."

"Again?" Toby asked in an annoyed tone. "You spend an awful lot of time up there, more than you spend in the condo I think."

Lia'na looked away as she slowly walked back to the bedroom, "It's very tranquil. I see the city around me for several miles, but it still feels like I'm on the branch of a tall tree in the forest."

"Are you really okay?"

"Yes, I just need some air, that's all. I won't be long, I promise."

Lia'na disappeared through the door, heading to the roof. Toby finished cleaning their living room table and dropped down on the leather sofa once he was finished. He didn't think Lia'na was lying to him, at least not intentionally. She clearly didn't want to worry him with her problems. He knew she wasn't happy, but what could he do?

The walls were covered with an eclectic combination of sports memorabilia, Boston knick-knacks, and Elven art. He'd given her permission to redecorate as she saw fit so she'd be comfortable, but it wasn't working.

Ideas flew through Toby's mind as he tried to think of something. *I could take her hiking, or to a park, but that would only fix things for that day, and I doubt people would approve of her climbing trees in a public park.*

Toby knew that he needed to confront her about it. He couldn't deal with his other problems until he knew that she was okay, but if she was already uncomfortable, pushing her away even more was not going to solve anything. Still, perhaps if he talked it out with her, they could figure out a way to make her more comfortable.

Toby couldn't remain silent anymore. He pushed himself off the sofa and headed for the roof. The exit way to the roof was little more than a well-insulated steal door. It was a good thing too because the moment he pushed the door open, he was hit with a blast of cold air.

The condo association had turned the roof of the building into a nice patio. Only the top floors had direct access to it, but anyone who wanted to go there could head up the back way. The ground was mostly granite walkways that were trying to give off the illusion of a garden path, but it wasn't working for Lia'na.

The condo association had wanted to turn the roof into a garden and immediately jumped at the chance to have Lia'na do some planting when she offered. For her, it would be a nice diversion when she wasn't in class.

Lia'na was leaning on the railing on the opposite side of the city view, looking north into the hills. She didn't react as Toby approached, but when he placed his hands on her arms, she leaned back into him, resting her head on his chest, "Hello there."

"Hi."

"What are you doing up here?"

"I came to see how you were doing. I can leave you alone if you want."

"No it's okay, I was just watching..."

Toby squinted as he looked off into the distance, "Watching what?"

Lia'na smiled as she turned around, "I guess I don't really know, just whatever happens to pass by my eyes."

Toby frowned as he looked at her, "You're not happy here, admit it."

"Toby I... I grew up in the woods. I'm used to open spaces and climbing trees. The dorm life on campus was hard enough, but that was a temporary thing and I always knew I could come and go if I needed to."

"I'm not forcing you to stay inside." Toby said defensively. "If you want to go somewhere, you know you can. Just let me know you're going."

"I know that, Toby. I never said you were forcing me to stay here, and believe me, if I wanted to go somewhere bad enough, you wouldn't be able to stop me anyways. You've been very sweet offering to take me out places where I could feel more at home, but it was just different back during the spring. If I wanted to leave and go home to the woods, I could. Now..."

She looked at him in the eyes and placed a hand on his cheek to keep him from looking away, "I am happy to be here with you, I swear. I just need time to adjust to my new surroundings. Going from the forest to a cityscape with different sights, sounds, and smells is a bit of an adjustment to someone who is sensitive to such things."

The left side of Toby's mouth turned downward again. Lia'na saw it and gave him a kiss, "Toby, I promise I'll be okay, just give me time."

Toby placed his hand over hers, "All right. I'll give you your space."

"Thank you for understanding."

Toby nodded as he headed back downstairs. He flopped down on the couch and tried dialing his uncle's number. Once again, no one picked up. He waited about ten minutes and tried again, still nothing. Toby gave up and tossed his phone on the couch. Lia'na came down from the roof in time to see his phone go airborne, "Still no word from your uncle?"

"No. I'd hate to just show up at his home without calling."

"Maybe it's time to consider it. He does live alone, does anyone check on him?"

"Maybe… and no, no one does."

At that moment, there was a knock on Toby's door. He got off of the couch and looked though the peep hole. Seeing no one on the other side, he cautiously opened it, "Gishan!"

Gishan appeared on the other side with a woman standing next to him. Her skin had a dark tan, but her hair was a light brown. This was probably the woman he had been bragging about.

Gishan smiled, "Toby, where have you been? Lia'na shows up and you go silent. I know you're moving into your own pad, but we still like to hear from you once in a while. My mother was getting worried!"

"You mother was?" Toby replied with a sinister smile.

Gishan rolled his eyes, "Fine, you're going to make me say it. I was worried."

"You could have just called."

"So could you. I will when you will."

"All right..." Toby conceded. "Please come in."

Gishan stepped through the door and saw Lia'na standing off to the side, smiling nervously. Gishan's eyes narrowed, "Hey Lia'na."

She nodded, "Hi."

Toby looked at the young woman standing at the door, "Are you planning on introducing me to your friend here Gishan, or what?"

"Shit, I'm sorry."

He quickly turned to the woman, "Toby, this is Giselle de la Fuente."

Toby smiled, "How's it going? I'm Tobias Arrigan."

She shook his hand and nodded, "I've been told so much about you. Thank you for taking the awkwardness out of this. It didn't look like Gishan was ever going to do it."

Toby laughed as he beckoned Lia'na forward, "This is Lia'na of the White Water Clan."

"Formerly of the White Water Clan, Toby. –It's nice to meet you."

Giselle looked at Lia'na's ears, "You're an elf? Gishan didn't tell me that."

"Afraid so."

"Sorry, it's just... I've never seen an elf before. Not too many travel down south."

"Where are you from?"

"Texas." Giselle replied proudly.

"Yeah definitely not. Elves don't do well in intense heat."

Giselle looked at Lia'na and Toby standing together, "So I didn't think elves dated humans anymore."

Lia'na's smile disappeared, "It's... frowned upon, I think by both sides, but it's not forbidden."

"Wow, so you two are regular trail blazers."

Lia'na shrugged, "I guess."

"Please don't think I'm racist or anything. I've just never seen it before, but who am I to judge, I'm in a mixed relationship too."

Gishan smiled and nodded as Toby looked at him, "Is this the same woman you told me about?"

"Oh yeah." Gishan said with a smug look.

Giselle turned her attention back to Lia'na, "So formerly of the White Water Clan? There's gotta be a story there."

"Some other time, maybe." Lia'na said quietly. "I'm sorry, but we just got done living it. The shock is still settling in."

"Yeah probably best." Gishan agreed. "These two have been through Hell. –Speaking of which, Toby you guys want to get out? We were in the area, heading into Boston and thought we'd ask."

"Well we were going to go check in on my uncle." Toby replied. "We haven't heard from him and he hasn't answered the phone."

"You think something might have happened to him?"

"Maybe, he could just be on another one of his month-long vanishing acts, but I need to be sure. If you don't mind stopping off there first, yeah we'll go."

"Why not? I haven't seen Uncle Jake in a while, be nice to say hi."

Giselle turned to Toby, "So where does your uncle live?"

"He's got a nice place in Brookline." Toby replied.

As Toby thought about heading into Boston, he realized that he was nowhere near ready, "Listen, if you guys don't mind, the TV remote is on the couch. Lia'na and I haven't showered yet. Just give us a few minutes."

Gishan nodded, "Take your time."

Lia'na and Toby headed to the shower while their guests sat down. They closed their bedroom door, stripped out of their night clothes, and quickly got in the shower. The hot water relieved any remaining drowsiness as it cleansed their skin.

After the shower, Toby threw on a black t-shirt, some cargos, and a white dress shirt that he left unbuttoned. Lia'na grabbed her favorite top. It looked like a miniature dress that came down to her waist. She paired the shirt with some denim shorts that only covered a small portion of her legs. Finally presentable, Toby and Lia'na were ready to rejoin their friends.

Lia'na opened the door a crack and looked out. She giggled as she turned to Toby and pointed. Out on the couch, Giselle was practically on top of Gishan as their lips pressed together. Toby smacked his forehead, "Great, I have a pair of rabbits in my place."

Lia'na had to resist bursting out laughing as she grabbed a hair brush and began to straighten the tangled mess on her head. Toby opened the door and made sure it creaked to give his friends enough time to straighten up. The sound made Giselle dive back to her seat as Toby opened the door fully.

Lia'na followed Toby out of the bedroom still struggling with her hair. The brush accidentally nicked part of the braid that she had tied around the back of her head, causing it to fall out, "Damn it, I just redid this last night!"

Giselle stood up quickly, "May I? I used to braid my sisters' hair."

"Sure, lienes."

Lia'na sat next to Giselle as she undid the remaining braid in Lia'na's hair. She had an odd look on her face as Giselle pulled the braids differently than what Lia'na was used to. Once she was done, she tied both sides together on the back of Lia'na's head, took the brush, and straightened the extra few inches so it blended in with the rest.

When Giselle lowered the brush she turned Lia'na around to make sure it was straight, "Okay, go take a look."

"Okay." Lia'na replied as she went into the bathroom and used both her hand mirror, as well as the vanity to inspect Giselle's work. The braid was much smaller, done in a fashion that definitely wasn't Elven. She braided four strands instead of just three. They were tightly wound, but they looked nice.

She came back out and looked at Toby, "What do you think?"

"I like it."

"Me too. –Lien ni, Giselle… thank you, it's different, but it looks much better."

"It should hold better too."

Gishan stood up and walked over next to Toby, "Well if we're all done with the girly stuff, your concerns and my stomach aren't going to satisfy themselves."

"You're right." Toby replied. "We should go."

Lia'na grabbed her hand bag, "Are we heading for the train?"

"No way." Gishan said with a chuckle. "I've recently come into possession of a better mode of transportation."

"Do I even want to know?" Toby asked.

Giselle smirked as they headed outside. Sitting in the parking lot was a green 4-door Jeep wrangler. The roof and trim were all black, and the fenders had been chromed.

Toby shook his head, "Good God dude, compensating much?"

"Definitely not!" Giselle replied with an evil grin.

"Thanks," Toby replied sarcastically, "TMI!"

Lia'na's cheeks turned red as she and Toby climbed into the back. Gishan hopped into the elevated driver's seat and turned the key in the ignition. The engine roared to life as the gauges turned. He tapped the wheel smiling, "See Toby? Much better than the T, and more comfy than your bike."

"Hey, I like that bike!" Lia'na shot back. "It's how Toby whisked me away that first time."

That caught Giselle's interest, "What kind of bike?"

Toby looked at her boastfully, "It's a restored 1960 Harley FLH Duo Glide."

"It's pretty awesome looking." Lia'na chimed in. "You should see it."

"Nice" Giselle replied, "My father had a '68 BMW series R60. Not as classic as yours, but such a smooth ride."

Toby nodded, "I've seen those, all black with a silver trim, they're pretty sweet."

Giselle sat back in her seat and faced forward, "So how long have you two known each other?"

Toby was about to reply when Gishan cut in, "They met around the same time we did. Toby saved her from a few campus thugs."

"Let me guess," Giselle replied in an annoyed voice, "hassling you for being an elf?"

"Putting it mildly."

"Racist bastards, people never learn."

"Is that why you're dating a dwarf?" Gishan asked with a grin.

"Uh no?" Giselle replied. "Dwarves are worse, I'm dating you because the sex is good."

Toby smacked his forehead while Lia'na looked out the window with an uncomfortable grin and a slight blush. After letting his hand slide down his face, Toby spoke up, "You must have pretty low standards."

Gishan narrowed his eyes, "She does, but they're still higher than Lia'na's obviously."

"Hey!" Lia'na shouted as she looked at Gishan via the rear view mirror.

The group laughed as they hit Route 1 south, heading for Brookline. Gishan's jeep sounded like it was going to warp as it picked up speed. The trip only took about 20 minutes before the city came into full view.

As they entered the more industrial areas, Lia'na covered her ears and clenched her jaw. Toby noticed that she was struggling and rubbed her arm, "Hey, you okay?"

"Just give me a sec." she replied, wincing in pain.

Giselle looked back at them, "What's going on."

"It's the city." Lia'na replied. "My ears aren't used to this commotion. It's a little overwhelming."

Toby watched her with a hint of confusion, "But I thought you'd been here before?"

"Once or twice," she admitted, "but not often enough for my senses to be acclimated to this."

"Do I need to pull over?" Gishan asked.

"No, I'm fine... it just takes me a minute to adjust."

Within a few minutes, Lia'na unclenched her jaw and let go of her ears, "Okay, it's less offensive now. I'll be fine."

"Are you sure?" Toby asked with a high level of concern.

"Yes. It just takes a moment for my hearing to adjust to the sound. Elven ears have a keen ability to tone down loud noises."

"So do humans. It's called going deaf."

Lia'na rolled her eyes, "Oh stop, elves don't have that problem. Our ears are designed to prevent that from happening."

"Whatever," Toby said, not fully convinced.

Lia'na sighed, "You worry too much. Really I'm fine, let's just enjoy the day."

Soon the Jeep pulled past Coolidge Corner and turned onto Winchester Street. There were large brick and stone condos on either side of the street. Gishan hated the idea of parking in that neighborhood because the town was relentless with ticketing and towing people who parked incorrectly.

Carefully, Gishan pulled up to side walk, put the jeep in park and got out to inspect his parking job. There was no sign indicating that they couldn't park there, so once Gishan was satisfied, he turned back to the driver's seat and pulled the key out of the ignition, "All right, we're good, everyone out."

Toby got out and walked over to Lia'na, who was already on the sidewalk, "How are you handling the noise?"

"I'm okay now." She replied. "I think I'm getting more used to it."

"Why does the noise hurt you so much?" Giselle asked.

"An elf's hearing is about twice as good as a human's."

"Gotcha." Giselle said as they looked at the buildings. "So which one?"

Toby beckoned the group to follow, "This way, it's about a block down."

"Why didn't we park closer?" Giselle asked.

"Because it's all residential parking further down," Gishan replied, "and I don't feel like getting towed."

As the group headed down the next block, Toby noticed a nervous look on Lia'na's face, "What's wrong?"

"Does your uncle know about... us?" Lia'na asked.

"Yeah I told him about you."

"Yeah but does he know that I'm an elf?"

"No, I never really got a chance to tell him. When we check in, he usually says like three words to me and hangs up. I tried, but I never got an opening."

"So he doesn't know..."

"Hey I tried. It's not like I was hiding it. We just barely talk and he hangs up before I can get into any real detail. He's always busy doing something and has never been the sentimental type."

"At least you tried... but what will he think?"

"I doubt he'll care. I've never seen him really have any problems with elves. Don't worry about it unless it comes up."

"It shouldn't." Gishan cut in. "Uncle Jake's always been a cool guy."

"All right." Lia'na hesitantly agreed.

As they group approached the door to his uncle's building, Toby noticed that something was amiss. There were two Boston Police Department squad cars out in front of his uncle's house, and officers were standing near the door. Toby and Lia'na ran to the building as Gishan and Giselle followed close behind.

Toby came to a stop in front of the porch and walked up to one of the police officers. The man was wearing a dark navy blue uniform, and had a short crew cut, "Excuse me, officer, is everything all right here? Did something happen?"

The officer turned to Toby with a gruff look on his face, "There was a break-in here, we got a call on it this late last night when the neighbor noticed that the door had been busted. "

He looked over the group with narrow eyes, "Do you folks live here?"

"No." Toby replied. "We're here to see my uncle."

"Who is your uncle?"

"Jacob Arrigan."

The officer looked him over for a moment, "Do you have some ID?"

Toby pulled out his driver's license and handed it to the officer. The policeman looked at it for a moment and handed it back to him, "Young man, your uncle's home is the one that was broken into."

Lia'na put a hand over her mouth as Gishan gasped. Toby was ready to panic, "Is he all right?"

"We don't know. He's not in there. All we found were some droplets of blood that may or may not be your uncle. When's the last time you talked to him?"

"It's been a while. I've been trying to get in touch with him, but he never answers his phone."

The policeman pulled out a piece of notebook paper and began taking down what Toby was saying. He finished writing and looked at Toby, "Do you know anything else that might help us find him? Any places he may frequent, or a friend he may have gone to?"

Toby shook his head, "No, he's a bit of a loner and I stopped living with him a few years ago."

The officer thought for a moment and pulled out some pictures, "Do you recognize these symbols?"

The pictures the police officer showed them were circles with odd writing and symbols drawn in them, they appeared to be painted in red. Toby recognized the walls they were painted on, but it was Lia'na who stepped forward, "I do."

She looked at each of them closely, "They're occultist symbols."

"What, like wiccans?" The officer asked.

"No, these were used by cults that existed long before the wiccans. They used these symbols when they performed rituals."

"How do you know that?" Giselle asked.

"I was taught about the ancient arts from childhood." Lia'na replied. "It's required learning for all Elven children as a way to preserve our heritage."

The officer listened carefully to Lia'na as he wrote the information down. Toby peered inside through a window. What little he could see was a mess. Chairs were overturned and broken glass covered the floor. As Lia'na finished talking, Toby turned to the officer, "Can we go in?"

"Absolutely not." The officer replied. "This is still a crime scene. We can't let anyone in until we're finished."

Toby looked at Lia'na with worried eyes. The officer saw that they were concerned and flipped his pad over, "Why don't you four give me your names and phone numbers in case we need any more information. I'll also give you a call if we hear anything."

They each gave the officer their information before turning back towards Gishan's jeep. Toby was going pale, "I need to find him. He's pretty much the only blood I have left!"

"Okay." Lia'na agreed. "Where shall we go look? Do you have any idea?"

"No, like I told the police officer, I don't know where he'd go or what he'd be doing!"

"Piele calm down, ta arshana, I'm trying to help you."

Toby sighed, "I know... I'm sorry. I guess there really isn't anything we can do."

"Just keep your phone nearby just in case the police call." Lia'na replied.

"Your elf here is right, man." Gishan said. "You can't do anything for now."

"So what are we going to do?" Toby asked.

Gishan felt his stomach rumble, "Well I don't know about you, but I've never seen an Italian meal that didn't relieve all pains, at least temporarily."

Toby looked at him angrily, "How can you think of food at a time like this?"

"Hey man, I'm worried about Uncle Jake too!" Gishan shot back, "but we have no idea where to look for him. Best we can do is stay nearby in case the police call us. There's no reason we can't get a little nourishment, you know?"

Lia'na nodded, "That does sound good. I've never really had Italian."

"What?" Gishan asked in shock.

Lia'na shrugged sheepishly, "Well I've had Italian subs and pizza, but nothing else really."

Gishan's jaw was nearly on the ground, "So you've never had a steaming bowl of spaghetti and meat balls, or ravioli, or tortellini, or stuffed shells?"

Lia'na smiled and shook her head. At that moment, Gishan put his foot down, "That's it. It's Italian time. I know this awesome little bistro on Newbury Street. We're going!"

Toby sighed, knowing that he wasn't going to win this one, "Fine..."

Gishan led them back to the jeep, refusing to let go of the fact that Toby's elf girlfriend had never eaten Italian. They got into the jeep and pulled off Winchester Street heading down Beacon Street to Commonwealth Ave.

It was a short trip, but it stretched on for Toby as his mind raced. He didn't feel like being in an enclosed space with Gishan, who was uncomfortably fixated on the fact that Lia'na had never eaten Italian. He had to watch as the poor elf-girl was sitting next to him with her hand on her stomach while Gishan relentlessly listed off the different menu options.

It took forever to find a parking space, but after three passes, they found one right in the middle of everything. It was an awesome find. They could get to any of the shops or restaurants within a few minutes from where they were.

This was a day of firsts for Lia'na. She had never been to Newbury Street before and was wide eyed as they walked past the beautifully-built brown stone buildings with old world turreted windows. Sure she'd been in Boston a few times, but that was usually either at one of the museums or the Commons, "Ta Diesu, this is actually pretty nice. I'd heard about Newbury Street before when some of the girls in my dorm talked about shopping here, but never got the chance to come."

Toby got out of the jeep and helped Lia'na down, "Someday I'll take you over to Quincy Market and the water front. It's a lot of fun during the summer. They also have outdoor restaurants and different street performer shows going on all day."

"I'd like that. That'd be a nice date location."

Gishan turned off the jeep, hopped out, and was joined by Giselle on the sidewalk. They made their way down the street. On either side were high-end stores, mostly offering various designer clothing. A shirt caught Giselle's eye and she turned to Gishan, "Could we go in for a moment?"

Gishan rolled his eyes, "Ugh, fine... but make it quick!"

"Come on, Lia'na." Giselle beckoned.

"Eh... thanks, but that store doesn't look like my style... or price range." Lia'na replied.

Giselle shrugged and took Gishan by the hand, "Suit yourself."

Lia'na stood on the sidewalk a few feet away from Toby as she surveyed the surroundings. People eyed Lia'na as they walked by. Toby swore he heard the words 'tree humper' and 'sharpy' from one or two passers by. He could feel the anger building up inside.

A second later, Lia'na jolted forward and fell to her knees as a man brushed by, "Move it, sharpy."

Toby moved fast and grabbed him before he could get away, "You want to try that on me asshole?"

Toby's other hand was balled into a fist, ready to strike when Lia'na glared at him, "Toby no, let him go. Don't cause trouble. You'll just get yourself arrested."

The man fought out of Toby's grip and ran away, "Enjoy your fungal infection, elf-lover."

"No, really," Toby called out, "come back here and say that to my face."

Lia'na frowned, "Toby..."

The man picked up his pace as he ran down the street. Toby called after him, "Don't run, I didn't hear you clearly, seriously, come back here and repeat that!"

"Toby!" Lia'na yelled as she got back to her feet. "You've made your point."

Gishan and Giselle came running out of the store as Toby took Lia'na's hand, "Are you okay?"

"Yes," she replied, "he just pushed me down, I've had worse."

"Where'd the fuck take off to?" Gishan asked.

Lia'na pointed down the street. "He's long gone. Don't worry about it."

"You really have a good temperance, you know that?" Giselle observed.

"Getting pushed down isn't the worst I've ever dealt with."

"I know," Toby admitted, remembering the day he met her, "but that doesn't make it any less wrong."

Lia'na shrugged, "I'm used to it. People always have to have something to hate. There is nothing we can do to change that, so there is no point in losing any sleep over it. Just stay close to me."

"All right." Toby replied.

The group continued down Newbury Steet to the little Italian restaurant on the corner. There was almost no indoor restaurant other than a few tables. Everything was outside behind a rot iron gate.

The tables and chairs were all metal, painted black to match the gate. They had umbrellas in the middle and candles next to them. The waiters and hosts were dressed in black with white aprons, making the restaurant look very upscale in appearance.

The hostess smiled as she eyed the eclectic group in front of her. It wasn't every day that they had two humans, an elf, and a dwarf getting a table together. She collected four menus and guided the group to a corner table where they sat down.

Much to Toby's annoyance, Gishan started up again, "Now if you're really hungry, you want to go with either the chicken parm or the veal marsala. Stay away from the chicken marsala, it's a little too dry for my taste. The scampi is all right if you like seafood, but the alfredo sauce is much better."

Lia'na listened intently as Giselle leaned over and whispered to Toby, "How long do you think she can go on listening to him like this?"

"I'm not placing a wager on that one." Toby replied. "Lia'na has patience like no one else I've ever met. Even if she's not interested in the subject matter, she'll sit there listening intently for hours."

"That's actually kind of sweet." Giselle admitted. "Having someone who will listen to you go on a tirade for hours and not blow you off. It must be nice."

The group looked over the menus quickly as they decided what they wanted. Lia'na was a little more confident about selecting a dish now that she had been schooled on fine Italian cuisine. When the waiter came around to take their order, Gishan went first. The waiter took down what they wanted one at a time until he got to Lia'na. She took one more look at the menu and chose, "I'll have the Seafood Alfredo with the lemon glaze."

Gishan nodded, "Oh, good choice!"

"Thank you." Lia'na replied with a smile.

Toby scratched the back of his neck as he looked around. Gishan decided to start up another conversation, "So how's the magic training going?"

Toby glared at Gishan with an angry look. Giselle smiled, "Yeah, Gishan, keep that down."

Lia'na looked across the table at Giselle, "You know?"

"Yeah Gishan told me about it." Giselle replied. "Don't worry. I know how to keep secrets, unlike your friend."

Toby sighed, "Well… it's going okay. We've found a book that's helped me learn to wield spells, and Lia'na has helped me control my emotions."

"So can you cast anything?" Gishan asked.

"Yeah." Toby replied. "Mostly healing spells, but I have been able to conjure up a few tricks using plants and such."

Giselle looked across the table at Lia'na, "So how do you help him train? You're not an enchanter too, are you?"

Lia'na put down the piece of garlic bread she'd decided to munch on, "No, elves have never been enchanters, but to keep with tradition, we are taught how to resist magic. I just taught him what I know."

"Ah interesting…"

XVIII

Their food arrived promptly. Lia'na's eyes went wide as she swallowed the first bite. The rich flavor of the Alfredo sauce with a hint of lemon was an all-new sensation.

As wonderful as the new experience was, it was mired by the fact that Toby appeared conflicted. She watched as he kept one eye on his phone and constantly looked over his shoulder. She would have given almost anything to assure Toby that his uncle was okay, but even she had her doubts.

The group ate and enjoyed the atmosphere for another hour or so before they decided it was time to head out. Gishan and Toby split the bill as they got up to leave. They began discussing what they were going to do next.

The moment that they got up from their table, the group heard a shrill scream from down the street. There was a loud boom and debris went flying everywhere. Car alarms went off and people scattered any way they could.

Toby grabbed Lia'na's hand as he tried to figure out what had happened. He peered down the street, trying see through the gray smoke. Suddenly, three dark entities flew towards them.

Toby went wide eyed, "No... It's the black ghosts I told you about from my dream."

"Ta Diesu," Lia'na exclaimed, "they're real…"

Two more entities appeared behind Toby, blocking any chance that the four of them had of getting away. Toby built up his emotions, he thought back to what happened to Lia'na on the day that they'd met. He thought about Michael's face, and the fact that his uncle was missing. Anger built up inside of him as he attempted to use his powers. Nothing happened.

Lia'na saw what he was trying to do and shook her head, "You're an enchanter of light, not darkness. Anger and sadness won't trigger your powers."

Toby looked at her oddly, "It did before…"

"Did it," she asked, "or did you have another image in your mind?"

Toby thought back and realized that she was right, though on the surface he was angry, the only thought he had in his mind after the fight was a picture of Lia'na when they were in the hot spring together and the fear of losing her to that brute. They were feelings of love and concern, not rage and jealousy. Toby began to picture the happy times that they had shared and felt a deep serenity overtake him. At that moment his hands began to glow white.

As the ghosts approached, Toby thrust his hands forward, unleashing white spirit beams that knocked the first ghost out of the sky. The black rags tightened and took the form of a man clad in all black. He quickly jumped into the air and transformed back into a ghost.

Three of them shot towards Toby like rockets. He waived his hand from left to right, creating a magical wall, and then thrust his hand forward, sending the wall shooting towards the ghosts. They darted upward to avoid being struck and pulled away.

At first, Toby was able to successfully defend his friends, but the lead spirit quickly landed in front of him, took human form, and waved his hand, "Enough!"

Toby recognized the voice, but could not make out his face under the cloak he wore. Toby once again unleashed a blast of white light, but this time the man in black thrust his own hand forward and blocked the attack. He then clenched his fist and made a tugging motion.

Instantly, Toby's attack ceased. He looked at his hand and tried again, but the magic would not obey him. Having no other options, Toby stood in front of Lia'na as Gishan pushed Giselle next to her and put up is fists, protecting their flank, "I got your back, Toby."

Toby nodded as he glared at the man coming towards him, "Who are you, what do you want?"

The man smiled, "Ah Tobias, I'd know that face anywhere… You should know that I am the man that changed the course of your life forever."

"How?" Toby demanded.

"I knew your father. Let's just leave it at that for now."

"Who are you?" Toby asked in little more than whisper. He couldn't escape the notion he somehow knew this man.

The cloaked man seemed all too happy to answer him, "You may call me Alistair, High Priest of the Fillis de Lux."

Alistair pulled his hood back, revealing an elderly looking man with a white beard and long white hair that was done back in a ponytail. However, despite his obvious age, this man stood tall at 6'6, and was as upright and alert as Toby.

"No way…" Lia'na replied, "Elven texts speak of a dark enchanter known as Alistair, who was a high priest of the Fillis de Lux, but that was thousands of years ago! Are you seriously trying to make us believe that you are him?"

The man laughed, "And what if I am, is that so impossible to believe?"

Toby watched his every move as he stepped closer, "Stay back!"

The man spread his arms, revealing himself to be unarmed, "Relax my friend. I'm not here to hurt you. We've come for an object I happen to know you have in your possession."

"What would that be?" Toby demanded.

"You have a piece of the Lux Mundi."

Lia'na placed her hand over the shard on her necklace, "Never… I know what you're planning. You want to restore the Lux Mundi."

"Would that be such a bad thing?" Alistair demanded. "Look around you. The world is run by greedy squabbling politicians who, since they came to power, have only looked out for their own best interests. Restoring the Lux Mundi will aid us in toppling these governments and seizing control in the chaos, forming a central hierarchy and bringing order to this chaotic world."

Lia'na shook her head, "Order under the Fillis de Lux. Somehow I doubt that you are any less corruptible. History has shown us time and time again what happens when one person or group of people hold all power. It never ends well. The world is no longer right for the Lux Mundi. Magic has been all but forgotten, and the supernatural is dismissed as myth and fairytale."

"I don't care what you believe. You are nothing more than a filthy sharpy."

Giselle stormed up next to Toby, brandishing a gun, "FBI, freeze!"

Gishan looked up in shock for a moment as she nodded to Toby, "If he tries anything you can't handle, give the word and I'll blow his ass away."

Toby nodded as Alistair turned back to him, ignoring Giselle completely, "Make her give it to me and you can live out your days in peace with your little Elven whore."

Lia'na didn't give Toby a chance to answer, "I can't let you do this. The Lux Mundi is too easily used by evil. I won't allow you to rebuild it!"

"Then you will die, and I will take the shard from your corpse."

The other black ghosts swarmed around them as Alistair unleashed another dark attack. Toby felt his powers return and blocked the attack with his own light beam. Though he was completely focused, Toby could see that he could not hold out against Alistair. His beam weakened and was slowly driven back. He was completely outmatched and didn't know how long he could fend off Alistair's attack.

Giselle squeezed the trigger and fired off three rounds at Alistair. The shots seemed to bounce right off of him as though there was some sort of invisible wall in the way. Giselle took a step back and turned her gun on the ghosts coming at them.

Lia'na saw her friends struggling to fight against these dark creatures. In a desperate attempt to quickly end the fight, she grabbed a steak knife off of a nearby table, ripped the shard off her neck and clenched it in her palm. Toby realized what she was doing and cried out, "Lia'na, no!"

Ignoring Toby, Lia'na ran the blade across her hand next to the shard. She yelped and dropped the knife as blood dripped from her palm. She dropped to her knees as pain shot through her arm.

Gishan got down on his knee next to her, "Hey what are you doing? You okay?"

Lia'na nodded, "I'm fine... help them."

Alistair saw what had happened and screamed as his attack ceased, "Do you realize what you've done? You bitch!"

Alistair extended his other arm and unleashed a second dark beam similar to Toby's light attack. Toby's beam weakened as Alistair sneered, "Die!"

Toby raised his arm to block the attack. To everyone's surprise, the black beam instantaneously broke against a white force field just in front of Toby. Alistair saw that there was no way to get to Lia'na and ceased his assault.

As the battle ended, the other ghosts turned around and headed back to wherever they had come from. Giselle kept her gun pointed upwards as Toby stared Alistair down. The old man looked past them to Lia'na, "You are a fool. Destroying your shard may reduce the Lux Mundi's power, but it will still be enough to accomplish our goals."

"It's a start." Lia'na shot back, fighting through intense pain.

Alistair looked at Toby with disgust, "Your father would be very displeased with you, first to find out you're with a filthy elf, and then you hindered his goals of true power."

"What happened to my father?" Toby asked.

"Well since you've now become an obstacle in my mission, I suppose I should tell you."

"Out with it!"

"He became one of us." Alistair replied gleefully. "He was my friend. When we took him from your family's home, it caused quite a stir. He was as resistant as you are now, but he eventually joined us."

Toby took a step back, "No... It's not true. My father wasn't that type of man, it's impossible!"

"You know nothing about your father, only what your mother told you and believe me, she didn't know much. Your father had the same desire you do. He also sought to learn about his power and gain strength from it. He became my most treasured apprentice, but his powers were limited, there was only so much he could do. I will say this though; through it all he did miss you, your beautiful mother, and that 1960s Harley."

Toby felt an intense sinking feeling in his heart. He didn't want to believe a word of this, but knew very little about his old man, apparently even less than he thought he did. Alistair could be lying, but Toby had never been that lucky. His head throbbed and he dreaded asking any more questions, but knew that he wouldn't be able to rest if he didn't know the truth, "What happened to him?"

"His desire to be more than he was consumed him. In the end, he was willing to do almost anything to gain more power. Anything... even if it meant the cost of his own life. He merged himself with the shards of the Lux Mundi that I had already recovered. He thought it would give him the power that he desired. His body was absorbed and the creator only knows what happened to him after that..."

"You trained him, and then you drove him to madness."

Alistair shrugged, "I guess you could look at it that way, but that was never my intention. He was young and stubborn, but he was my friend."

Toby lowered his eyes. His mind couldn't process all of this information. His father was one of the bad guys? That went against everything his mother told him. At that moment, Toby felt a serious sinking feeling in his heart. If his father fell prey to that kind of ambition what was to stop him from following the same path? His powers were unstable, what could they drive him to do?

Alistair stepped forward and spread his arms, "Join me Toby, I can feel your power. It emanates off of you as brightly as the sun and with your help, we can complete the last step of the joining and the Lux Mundi will be complete. Think of it, no more corruption, no more chaos, and no more war. Once we have the power of the Lux Mundi on our side, we will topple nations and bring order to the world."

"Order... " Toby said in a low voice, "under you?"

"And why not? I have existed since before recorded history and I shall live well past its end. Join me, and I will teach you everything you wish to know."

"No!" A shrill voice cried out from behind. "Toby, don't be tempted by him, you are not your father. Your destiny isn't predetermined. You are better than that, don't believe it."

"I never knew my father." Toby said in a low voice. "It's been hard living without him."

Alistair held a caring hand out to Toby, "I know it has, but you don't have to live under a shroud of ignorance any longer. Come with me, I have the answers you need.

Together, we may even be able to find a way to extract him from the diamond."

Toby's eyes went wide, "He's still alive?"

Alistair nodded, "His spirit lives on in the reformed part of the diamond I've collected. If we can restore the rest of it, even without the elf's shard, we may be able to extract him."

"You're lying!" Lia' na said in an accusing tone.

"Me, lie?" Alistair replied in an amused tone. "Never, the truth is far more advantageous."

Lia'na saw the look of confusion on Toby's face. His mind was racing and she knew that Alistair's offer was tempting, "Toby, piele don't listen to him. The Lux Mundi is evil. It's what destroyed my people and plunged the Earth into years of war. If it's not destroyed, history will repeat itself."

"And if it is, my father will die!" Toby yelled.

Behind them, police sirens could be heard in the distance. Alistair looked back for a moment, "It seems company is coming."

He quickly turned back to Toby, "You don't have to answer me now. Think about it, but don't take too long."

As the sirens grew louder, Alistair snapped his fingers, causing himself, and the ghosts to disappear. Toby stepped forward, his head still full of questions, "Wait, Alistair!"

Alistair ignored him and vanished in a puff of smoke. The threat was seemingly gone, so Toby ran to Lia'na's side. His heart froze when he saw the blood dripping from her hand, "Are you okay?"

Lia'na held up her hand, revealing a small pool of blood and the shard slowly changing color from orange to black. There was a low humming noise as the diamond began to disintegrate and turned to dust. The remains rested on Lia'na's hand and swirled up her arm. Toby quickly wiped them off. He then focused his energy and tried to heal her wound. As his energy impacted on the cut, it forced his hand back, "I can't do it…"

Lia'na nodded, "It's okay, you tried."

"But why, I was able to heal myself before, why can't I do it with you now?"

Lia'na shrugged, "Maybe it has to do with the shard, or maybe you're distracted. Don't worry about it. I'm okay."

Toby took off his collared shirt and wrapped her cut tightly. Lia'na's breathing slowed and she winced as Toby worked. Gishan heard the police sirens getting closer, "I think it's probably best if we clear out before the police get here."

Toby nodded, "Not a bad idea, we should get Lia'na to a hospital anyway."

The group piled into Gishan's jeep and sped off towards the nearest hospital.

*

Ten minutes later, Lia'na was brought into the ER at the Brigham and Women's Hospital. Toby, Gishan, and Giselle stayed with her. Lia'na forced as big a smile as she could, "I'm okay Toby. You can relax. It doesn't hurt as bad as it did."

Toby shook his head, "The pain is not what I'm worried about…"

At that moment, Gishan couldn't hold back his anger anymore and turned to Giselle, "Agent de la Fuente is it? When the hell were you planning on telling me?"

Giselle sighed, "Not that this is the time or the place for this, but I suppose I do owe you an explanation."

Both Toby and Lia'na also turned to listen in as Giselle sucked down a deep breath, "Okay… I'm an undercover agent with the FBI. I was assigned to Arcanus and took on the persona of a student. My job was to first successfully blend in and then find the elf that carried the last shard of the Lux Mundi."

Toby's eyes narrowed, "What did the FBI want with Lia'na?"

"Nothing, we just wanted to observe her to see if she had unlocked its power, and if you had, confiscate it."

"But why?" Lia'na asked.

"The rest of the Lux Mundi had just been located and was on its way to the US." Giselle replied. "We were planning on confiscating your shard the moment the crystal arrived here for study. We couldn't risk it being dangerous."

"So the US Government wanted the whole thing?" Toby asked. "That sounds safe."

Giselle nodded, "Unlike Alistair, we had no plans to use it."

"So you used me? You had a little fun while doing your job?" Gishan asked.

Giselle shook her head, "Look, it's not like that, I needed a cover, but when I met you... things changed."

"Stow it." Gishan replied. "I've heard this movie crap before. Is your name really Giselle?"

Giselle nodded, "Yes... but my last name isn't de la Fuente. It's Cortez. Look, I can't make you believe that I'm telling you the truth, but I can tell you that since I met you, I was careful to keep you and my mission separate. I didn't even know your roommate was dating Lia'na until later. If you don't want to believe that, I'll leave."

Gishan thought about it for a moment, "Nah... stick around, you helped save our asses today. I'll figure out what to do with you later."

Giselle smiled and nodded, satisfied with Gishan's decision. Toby shook his head as he turned to Lia'na, "If that's not love, I don't know what is."

At that moment, an ambulance rolled up. Two EMTs got out and rolled out a stretcher. They ran it inside as quick as they could.

Toby overheard their yelling, "He was found in an alley, bleeding out. He has no identification on him."

Toby looked closely at the man's face, he couldn't see much as the EMTs were in the way, but the moment one of them moved, he could see it clearly. His eyes went wide, "Uncle Jake!"

Toby stood up and ran towards the stretcher. Lia'na got up with him and walked as fast as she could to stay with him. Giselle and Gishan followed closely behind as well. One of the EMTs looked at Toby, "Sir, do you know this man?"

Toby nodded, "He's my uncle. His name is Jacob Arrigan."

The EMT turned to the admitting nurse. She came out from behind the desk, "Do you have some ID?"

Toby pulled out his wallet and showed her his driver's license. The nurse nodded, "All right go ahead in with him."

Toby followed the stretcher in with Lia'na close behind. The nurse was about to stop her, when Toby turned around, "She's with me."

The nurse nodded, "Fine, but no one else."

Toby nodded to Gishan, who turned back to his seat with Giselle. Lia'na followed Toby down the hall until they got to a small waiting area. The first EMT that had spoken to Toby originally turned to him, "You'll need to wait here. He's going into emergency surgery."

Toby nodded and took to pacing back and forth around the chairs. Lia'na sat down cradling her hand, "I'm sure he'll be okay."

"I hope so… He may not have been the best parent in the world, but damn if he didn't try hard. I wouldn't be where I am now if it weren't for him."

"I can't wait to meet him. He sounds almost as wonderful as his nephew."

*

An hour went by while Toby paced the floor. Lia'na still hadn't been called in to have her hand looked at because of the high volume of intakes the hospital was dealing with, but the nurses did come by to take her information, give her some medicine for the pain.

"Who would do this?" Toby asked. "Why would they do this?"

Lia'na sat back and closed her eyes, "I think you know who…"

"Alistair… I agree… but that doesn't answer the why."

"It might." She said as a sigh escaped her lips.

Toby looked at her oddly, "Are you okay, you look pale."

"I'm fine, it just hurts. Don't worry about me, ta arshana. Focus on your uncle."

Finally the surgeon who had been working on Jacob came out. He wore a protective cap on his head, but the mask over his mouth had been pulled down. He wrapped his white lab coat around the blue scrubs, straightened his glasses, and walked over to Toby rubbing his hands. "Mr. Arrigan?"

Toby turned to the doctor as Lia'na stood up next to him, "How's my uncle, is everything okay?"

"Your uncle lost a lot of blood, and I mean a lot of blood. It's a miracle he made it here alive. Whoever attacked him, cut him in ways that would make him slowly bleed to death. We've given him blood transfusions and stitched him up as best we could, but…"

Toby felt his heart seize as the surgeon spoke, "… the damage is too extensive. His wounds just aren't closing. We can't do anything more for him."

Toby rubbed his forehead. He began shaking and breathing heavily. Lia'na comforted him with her good hand as best she could. He had a lump in his throat and fought to speak, "Is he awake?"

The surgeon nodded, "Yes, and you don't have long. I think you should go right in."

"Thanks doc, I know you tried. " Toby said as he and Lia'na raced into the room where Jacob was resting.

Toby breathed in deeply as he entered the room, "I can save him... I have to save him."

Jacob had his bed slightly elevated so he could see what was going on. He was conscious and aware, but his sight was fading as Toby ran in, "Uncle Jake!"

Jacob turned his head slowly, "Toby... my boy, how are you? Sorry I haven't called in a while."

"You were busy uncle." Toby said, fighting back tears. "I always understood, you know that."

"I should have been better... I should have known better."

"Stop it uncle! You did the best you could for me and I always appreciated it."

Jacob weakly raised his hand and grabbed Toby's arm, "Toby, I'm sorry... people in black came to my home... they tortured me, asking about you and... your girlfriend. One, an older man... I knew him."

"I know." Toby said through a clenched jaw. "I met them today."

"I told them, I couldn't resist... I tried..." Jacob said as he closed his eyes, "but I just wasn't strong enough. It was just like with your father."

Toby's eyes perked up, "My father, what about him?"

"He had enchanter's powers. He first discovered them when we were in college. They weren't much, but I've never seen anyone else who had them... The same people... that man in black robes came and took him away. We never saw him again..."

Toby looked over his uncle's wounds frantically, "Uncle Jake... I have healing powers. I can save you."

Before Jacob could respond, Toby rubbed his hands together, drawing in as much energy as he could. Once he was ready, Toby placed his hands on Jacobs's wounds and forced the energy into them. He focused hard and pushed more and more energy into the wound, but it felt like something was pushing back. The wounds would not accept the energy.

Lia'na noticed a mark on Jacob's arm similar to the ones in the pictures that the police had shown them, "Toby, it's no good. Alistair used dark magic to curse his body. No magic can save him now…"

Toby shook his head, "No, shut up! I can save him. I just have to focus harder!"

Toby pushed harder and forced even more energy into Jacob in an attempt to heal his wounds. Jacob began to wince in pain as Toby continued to push, "Toby, stop, it hurts too much."

"Uncle… I have to try…"

His uncle smiled at him, "You already did. It's okay, I had a feeling this was going to be it."

"But uncle…"

"Enough Toby, I've lived a good life. There is nothing you can do now… let's not waste my last moments."

Lia'na stepped forward and spoke, "I'm sorry Toby, but he's right. Alistair has done too much damage."

Toby didn't want to give up. Everything inside of him said to keep fighting, but the look in his uncle's eyes convinced him to stop.

"Uncle Jake... the man who attacked you told me something today." Toby said hesitantly.

Jacob lay back gently, "What did he say?"

"He told me that dad went mad with power. He said that dad left us and sacrificed everything, including his own being to become more powerful."

Jacob hesitantly nodded, "It's true, he sought power and knew he couldn't find it with you and your mother. That bastard made it easy for your father to decide and threatened to kill you all if he didn't follow... As for going mad, I don't know. We never heard from him again after that."

"I see… don't worry about it uncle, I'll make them pay!"

"Do it if you can, but don't spend your life going after revenge. Trust me, you'll just lose everything."

The sight was nearly gone from Jacob's eyes, so he fought to sit up a little more to keep himself from fading, "Now… speaking of which, who is your friend there?"

Toby turned and gestured for Lia'na to come forward, "Uncle Jake, this is Lia'na... the girl I told you about."

Lia'na hid her hurt hand behind her back and walked up to the bed, "Hello sir."

"You… you're an elf?" Jacob said in disbelief. "Toby never told me... I haven't seen one of your kind in years."

Lia'na bit her lower lip, "Yes… I am, sorry."

"Don't be sorry, I dated an elf when I was about your age. Are you part of the White Water Clan?"

"I was, but I left the forest."

"Well that's where she was from. I met her when we were in college."

"I never knew about this." Toby said. "What happened to her?"

Jacob closed his eyes, "We were happy for a while. She loved me, but she was so sad during our last year togethr. Then the day came when they discovered the vaccination for the Ulium. Her sadness seemed to disappear overnight."

Now even Lia'na was interested, "So what happened?"

Jacob's eyes began to water as he continued, "She started receiving letters from her clan and went home more often. I never knew what was in the letters, but as time went on, she started spending less and less time with me.

Eventually, she left me saying that she had a duty to her people. I found out later that she had a daughter with one of her own kind, and was struck down with the Ulium a few years later. I wish I'd been there for the end, I loved her, and she loved me. Had circumstances been different… She was the only woman I ever truly loved."

Jacob looked up at Lia'na as his vision finally faded, "It's funny, you look just like her."

Toby watched as his uncle began breathing heavily but more slowly. Tears formed in his eyes as his uncle fought to get words out, "Don't worry about me, I'm going to go be with your father… maybe… hopefully Aliata is waiting for me too."

Lia'na's eyes widened and she covered her mouth with her hand after hearing that name, "Aliata sir?"

"She was… so beautiful." Jacob replied as he put a hand on Toby's shoulder. "Goodbye my boy… Live better than I did."

Toby looked back at Lia'na, "Could you give us a little while? Maybe go see if Gishan and Giselle are hungry."

"I'll take care of it. Take your time ta arshana."

Toby stayed in the room until the end. Each time it seemed like Jacob had finally passed, he forced another breath out. It was as though he was refusing to let go of life. Hours went by as he sat next to his uncle watching the blips on the EKG slow to a halt.

The moment that they stopped, Toby buried his face in the mattress his uncle was laying on as the doctor came in, "No…"

The doctor looked at the EKG and attempted some stimuli to see if he was still alive. When Jacob's body didn't respond, the doctor began writing on his pad, "Note time of death 6:35pm."

He then turned to Toby, "I understand this is a tough time for you, we have a grief counselor standing by if you need it."

"No thanks."

He was completely numb and didn't know what to do. He got up and walked past the doctor without another word. Having nowhere to go, he wandered out to the hallway and just stood there staring at a painting on the adjacent wall. It took him a while, but he managed to find the waiting area and sat down.

Unable to deal with this flood of emotions, Toby buried his face in his hands, "Why…"

A voice appeared in front of him, "There's no answer that will take away your pain, and there never will be, ta arshana."

Toby looked up to see Lia'na watching him sympathetically. Her large hazel eyes were full of sadness, but this time it was not for herself, "Ta soel iene ul ni."

"What?"

"My heart grieves for you. Te arshana ni."

"I thought you were going to see Gishan and Giselle."

"I did, but then I got called in to have my hand stitched up. I've been treated and should be all set. It hurts, but they said that it should pass… Do you want me to leave too?"

"No." Toby said, fighting through his tears. "I'm already the most alone I've ever been. Sending you away will just make things worse."

Lia'na quickly sat down next to her love and put her arms around him, gently squeezing. His tears came slowly as he continuously tried to fight them back. It was painfully obvious that he was losing that fight.

As Lia'na saw his emotional state begin to break down, she let out a comforting sigh and squeezed more. "You are not alone. You have your friends, and you have me… and you always will, as long as you want me."

Toby leaned into Lia'na, hiding his eyes, "Thank you…"

Lia'na looked at her hand with the single bandage over it, "Is there anything at all that I can do for you? Anything..."

Toby closed his eyes, "Send Gishan and Giselle home. I don't like having people waiting around for me when I have no idea how long they'll have to wait. They've done their part. Give them my key and tell them they can have the other bedroom at my place if they want. We'll get a cab in a while. I don't want to keep them waiting all night."

Lia'na got up as Toby moved his head off her shoulder, "Okay, but promise me that you'll stay put?"

Toby nodded as she turned around and headed for the waiting room, "I'll be right back, I promise."

Giselle and Gishan were sitting in the lobby waiting to hear from Toby, but they both stood up when they saw Lia'na. Gishan's eyes were full of concern, "So?"

Lia'na lowered her tear-filled eyes and shook her head. Gishan exhaled deeply and rubbed his forehead with his left hand, "God…"

Giselle put her arm around Gishan as she looked at Lia'na's hand, "With everything going on, it seems like everyone's neglected to ask. How are you doing?"

"I'm worried about Toby. They stitched my hand up and gave me some pain killers. It still hurts a little, but my hand is fine."

"Can I see him?" Gishan asked.

"No. Toby asked me to let you know that you both should go home. He said you can use the condo's second bedroom if you want, but he's not really up for seeing anyone. He really appreciated you both sticking around for all of this."

"It's what I do, Toby's family to me. Are you guys going to be all right getting home?"

"Yeah, we'll catch a cab home. Don't worry."

No words could change what had just happened and nothing Gishan could think of was going to fix anything. Gishan felt helpless and hated the idea of just leaving Toby there, even if it was with his girlfriend, but he had little choice. "Well I guess there is nothing else we can do here. Come on, Giselle, we'll head home."

"Do you want to keys to the condo?" Lia'na asked.

"Nah, we're good. I think we'll just head home, it's not that late."

As Giselle grabbed her bag, Gishan gave Lia'na a very serious look, "Don't let him out of your site. He needs you right now."

"I know, don't worry. I'll take good care of him."

"Make sure you do." Gishan replied as he turned away with Giselle.

Lia'na shook her head with as much of a smile as she could muster, "Dwarves…"

Once they were gone, she quickly disappeared back through the ER doors and rushed to Toby, who was sitting in the small waiting area with his face in his hands. Lia'na could hear him muttering something under his breath, but couldn't quite make out what it was.

Seeing him like that filled her heart with sorrow and tears began to pass down her cheeks. She sat next to Toby and rubbed his back, "I'm so sorry Toby."

Lia'na watched as he slowly raised his head from his tear-soaked hands and rested it on her chest. She put her arm around him and squeezed. Hearing him fight back tears caused even more to fall from her eyes. She held on to Toby as tightly as she could. He heard her quiver and looked up, "Are you okay?"

"Yes… I'm sorry, I should be stronger than this for you. Instead I'm a blubbering mess."

"It's not your fault. You've been really wonderful so far throughout this. I don't know what I'd be doing right now if you weren't here."

Lia'na smiled as his words warmed her heart, "Right now, there isn't anywhere else I'd rather be."

Toby couldn't stand it anymore. He hated crying and feeling his body clench like it had. Jacob would not want him feeling like this. He pulled his head off of Lia'na's chest and sat up. After a couple of deep breaths, Toby started calming down. It was just in time as a department nurse came over to speak to him, "Mr. Arrigan?"

"Yeah that's me."

"I'm sorry to bother you when you've no doubt got a lot on your plate sir, but I'm afraid I have some urgent questions for you."

Toby took another deep breath to calm himself down while Lia'na continued to rub his back, "Go ahead."

The nurse looked over her sheet and adjusted her glasses, "Do you have any specific religious or personal reasons that Jacob's burial would need to take place in the next few days?"

"None that I'm aware of. Why do you ask?"

The nurse turned and looked at her department, "As you can imagine with everything that's been going on today, we're really backlogged. We have several patients that still need to be seen urgently. We're trying to prioritize and expedite the cases for those families that need their loved ones released to them, but given the back-up and the grievous nature of your uncle's death, we really don't want to release him until a full autopsy can be performed."

"Coming through!" An EMT yelled from the other side of the room.

The nurse quickly stepped out of the way as a group took a badly burned patient into a nearby room. The nurse shook her head and turned back to Toby, "As you can see, it may be a while. Say a couple of days to a week."

Toby nodded, "That's fine, just let me know when you're done."

"Yes sir, of course."

"Do you need me for anything else?"

"No, I think that's it. We have your number. We'll call you if anything comes up."

"Thank you."

"Sorry again for your loss. We'll be in touch."

The nurse quickly disappeared in the crowd of healthcare workers trying to make order out of a seemingly endless flow of patients. As Toby took Lia'na by her good hand and led her out the door. After fighting back tears, he turned to face her, "Lia'na…"

She felt his pull and looked up at him, "Hmm?"

"Why did you look so disturbed when my uncle mentioned dating an elf?"

Lia'na exhaled heavily, "Your uncle said that he dated a member of the White Water Clan named Aliata…"

"Yeah he did, so?"

She spoke slowly as she answered, "That was my mother's name."

Toby looked at her in shock, "You're kidding?"

"No… and I never knew she had a human lover."

Lia'na looked at her wounded hand, "It has me freaked out. Were we meant to meet? Is that why we picked each other out of the crowd?"

"Are you saying that fate has a predetermined plan for us?"

"Maybe. I don't have a clue."

At that moment, Toby started connecting the dots, "Wait a minute… My dad and uncle went to college together around the same time. They were only a year apart."

"Yeah, so?"

"So... Your mother met my uncle when he was in college. Which is around the same time my father discovered he was an enchanter."

Lia'na placed her right hand over her chest, where her medallion once rested, "And my mother would have been wearing that medallion, which would have triggered your father's powers."

She clenched her eyes closed, realizing what that meant, "So now history is repeating itself... and if it wasn't for me and my family, you probably would have lived a normal life with your mother and father."

Her eyes welled up with tears that even her clenched eyelids couldn't hide, "Toby, I'm so sorry..."

"What? That's not the conclusion I was going for. Lia'na, I don't blame you or your family. No one could have known this would happen. Alistair is the one who destroyed my family."

Lia'na shook her head, "But we're the ones who brought him down on you."

Toby disagreed, "You don't know that. For all we know, he was just waiting for the right time to come after us."

Lia'na's heart was filled with doubt about Toby's words, but she was comforted by the fact that he didn't blame her. She still felt guilty, but Toby had enough to deal with and her problems could wait until his were dealt with, "I guess you're right. I shouldn't be going on about this anyway; you already have enough to deal with."

"Don't worry about it. You've been wonderful, thank you."

Lia'na smiled sympathetically as they walked out of the hospital.

XIX

Toby called a cab and got home around 8pm. He wasn't in the mood to talk and instead just headed into the bedroom to lie down. Lia'na followed him and flicked on the TV, "Do you want me to make you something to eat?"

"No. I don't feel good."

"I don't blame you, but if you change your mind, let me know. You've been through enough today."

Toby didn't respond and just turned on his side. Lia'na flicked through the channels wanting to see if there was any new information about the attack. She didn't have to look far. Pretty much every channel that was still functional had reporters on practically screaming about the incredible events of the day.

Lia'na frowned, "They already considering this a terrorist attack."

"Can you blame them?"

"I suppose not..."

It took her a while to sift through all of the reports until finally Lia'na settled on Fox Boston. She lay down next to Toby and wrapped her arms around him as she watched the report. The anchor did her best to keep her composure as she spoke, "We're going now live to Newbury Street with our reporter on the ground there. –Jen, what can you tell us?"

The reporter waited a few moments before responding, as though there were a communications lag, "Mike, a few hours ago, this was a scene of total chaos. A massive explosion rocked the neighborhood and the buildings behind me, as you can see are still trying to put out the fires."

Lia'na's eyes narrowed as the report went on, "This is interesting, I don't see any mention of what caused it or who was involved. I guess we weren't seen?"

"It looks like it, I guess. Maybe Alistair prevented it somehow…"

Lia'na continued to watch the report until she felt Toby's body quiver around her. He fought hard to keep it in, but Lia'na knew that he was in pain. It was becoming more and more intense. *We really can't get a break, can we?*

She dropped the remote, pulled up behind him, and squeezed his back tightly, "Toby, I'm with you. Do you hear me? I'm not going anywhere and te arshana ni."

Toby fought out words as he struggled to calm down again, "Is this how you felt when you came here? I'm really alone now… the last of my family…"

"You don't have any other family?"

"No."

"Ta arshana, even so you're not alone. I'm here for you. Whatever you need, all you have to do is ask. I know it's tough, and what happened really sucks, but you won't be the last Arrigan forever. Someday you'll rebuild your family, you know you will. You'll have children, they'll have children, and your family will go on."

"Or will I become more like my father?" Toby asked, sitting up. "He sought power above all, and looked what happened."

A flash of fear entered Lia'na's eyes as she got on her knees and rubbed Toby's back, "Toby, you are not him. He made his choices, but they don't have to be the same ones you make."

"What if I am?"

"What do you mean?" Lia'na asked.

"What if I am like him? I was tempted by Alistair's offer."

"Toby, I understand you want to see your father again, but is it really worth the price? Alistair doesn't just want to restore the Lux Mundi, he's planning on taking over the world. I seriously doubt he cares how many have to die in order for him to do it."

"Would the whole world being united be such a bad thing? He did have a point about the world we live in."

"Maybe... but a free world is never a perfect one and trust me, I see the problems of the world every day. I see how evil people can be, but then I meet people like you and see how good they can be. Giving all the power over to one corruptible person is not the answer. Taking away freedom of will isn't going to solve anything, no matter how well-intentioned you may be."

"Are you so sure?"

Lia'na smiled as she knew she had him cornered, "Would I be here sleeping with you if I didn't have free will? Or would I be living in fear for my life from an abusive husband? You are better than your father. I know this is hard for you, but don't make the same mistakes he did."

Toby emptied his lungs almost completely as he exhaled. "You're right of course... but I don't know if I can do this. How can I be expected to kill my own father?"

"If you don't, then the power of the Lux Mundi will run amuck and everything your people have built over thousands of years will be lost... you know this."

"Yeah I guess I do..."

"No matter what happens, Toby, te arshana ni. In the end, whatever the right choice may be, I know that you'll make it."

"I hope you're right... I'm not so sure I know what the right choices are anymore."

Lia'na closed her eyes and kissed up his shoulder to his neck until her lips reached his ear, "Whatever choices you've had to make in the time I've known you, they've always been for the right reasons. I know you'll always do what you know is right, and whatever decision you make, I will be by your side, supporting you."

Toby said nothing else and just drifted off to sleep. Lia'na pressed her head against his back as his breathing slowed back to normal, comforted by the warmth of her skin. The sound of his heart slowly began to lull her off to sleep as well. Before she lost consciousness, she kissed Toby's back, "Te arshana ni."

*

The next few days consisted of Toby attempting to make sense out of what happened and prepare for the fight ahead. He continusouly read the Magnifica as though it were an obsession, stopping only to eat.

Despite not wanting to, he was forced to get put the book down and deal with the world. Lia'na was true to her word and took care of Toby as best she could, which was a good thing because Gishan called regularly to check up on him.

As the days passed, things started to get back to normal. Toby was eating again and Lia'na had her boyfriend back. He was holding on, but Lia'na had spent enough time with him to know that he was still on the edge of a knife.

It didn't help that, despite her hand healing and the time for her stitches to come out rapidly approaching, it would sting for no reason. Sometimes it got so bad that the pain meds she was given didn't help.

During those times, agony took over and she partially wished that she had the strength to cut her hand off. Not wanting to worry Toby with this, she put on a strong face as best she could, and if it got too bad, she'd retreat to the roof for some alone time. Despite the constant distractions, she was also still acclimating to her new surroundings and the fact that she'd never see her family again.

One day Toby noticed her wince and retreat upstairs. He waited a few minutes before quietly following her up to the roof. When he opened the outer door, he saw her on her knees near the edge, squeezing her wrist tightly. He moved closer, knelt down behind her, and placed his arms around her, "Are you okay?"

She rubbed his arm and leaned back with a sigh, "My hand just stings a little. I'm sure I'm okay, it's probably just healing pains. Once the stitches come out, that should go away."

"Do you need anything?"

"No I'm fine. Besides, last I checked right now, I'm taking care of you. Trust me, I'm okay."

She didn't want to say it, but finally the day that Lia'na dreaded arrived. Toby's cellphone rang, and the hospital's number showed up on the phone. He quickly answered it, "Hello?"

"Hello, Mr. Tobias Arrigan?"

"Yes?"

"This is Pam over at the Brigham, I was calling to let you know that we are ready to release your uncle's body. There are some papers that need to be signed. I know you must be going through a lot, but we're going to need you to come in and sign the release forms."

"All right, I'll be in later today."

"Great, just be sure to have a photo ID with you when you come."

"All right, thanks."

Lia'na could see him fighting back tears again as he hung up the phone. All the hard work they had done, all the nights they had stayed up, and all the suffering he had done, was about to start again.

"Are you okay, ta arshana?"

Toby took in a deep breath and cleared his throat, "I don't even know who to invite to the funeral. For the most part it was just me and him. I don't think he had anyone else."

"I'll go, apparently he made my mother very happy. I'm sure Gishan will too. You should have his obituary put in the paper. You never know who might show up, maybe some coworkers or something?"

"Maybe… Look, I'm not really up for driving, I'm going to grab a bus and get this over with."

"I'm going with you."

"Are you sure? You look like you're in pain."

"I'm not leaving you alone.

*

They arrived at the hospital about forty minutes later. Toby went to the main reception desk and waited in line to speak to the secretary. He kept his eyes on Lia'na the entire time. She was leaning from side to side, looking sick. She looked paler than usual, but he couldn't figure out why; she was awake, alert, and energetic. He made up his mind that if she got any worse, they were going to head over to the ER again.

Before he could think anymore into it, a voice in front of him called out, "Next."

Toby walked up to the counter, "Uh yeah hi, my name is Toby Arrigan. I was told to come fill out some paperwork to have my uncle's body released."

The secretary stared at her computer monitor for a few moments and then typed the name Arrigan into her online record search. It took a moment for the system to process, but the name eventually came up on the screen, "Ah yes, Mr. Arrigan, sorry for your loss. One moment please."

Lia'na suddenly exhaled deeply and fell to the side. Toby reached out in time to catch her, "Lia'na are you all right?"

"I don't feel well…"

"Someone help!" Toby called out to the hospital staff.

The secretary stood up and came around the table to help her to a chair. When the nearby nurses saw what was happening, they flocked over to the reception desk and guided Lia'na to a nearby stretcher. She was immediately taken to an empty room in the ER. The nurse manager spoke to Toby while the rest of her team took care of Lia'na, "What happened?"

"I don't know, her hand was pretty badly cut, but that was days ago, it was treated here, and she said she was doing okay."

"And what's your relationship to her?"

"She's my girlfriend. She lives with me."

The nurse looked surprised, "Hmm... okay. Well does she have any family or next of kin we should know about?"

"No. Not anymore."

"No one?"

"No." Toby said adamantly. "Her clan banished her and told her never to return after she violated their laws. Be my guest and try to call them, but you'll be wasting your time."

"All right, well according to the information from her last visit, you are listed as her emergency contact. That's good enough for me, so once we've got her on the monitor, we'll bring you in."

*

Toby stood in the waiting area for what seemed like an eternity. He feared the worst for his love while at the same time still trying to come to terms with his newfound orphan status. The only way he kept himself sane was by putting his uncle completely out of his head. It was an impossible task, but he did the best that he could.

Finally the nurse manager came back, "Toby?"

He turned quickly and approached her, "What, what is it?"

"She's exhibiting signs of infection. We're taking her blood samples to the lab. I'm afraid that for now you can't see her, we're putting her under quarantine in the ICU."

That was new. He'd been to the hospital with peopel who'd had infection before and they were never treated like this, "What... Why?"

"Given the endangered nature of her species, and that there may or may not be other elves in the hospital, standard procedure dictates that we must treat every case as though it were an infectious disease."

"So what am I supposed to do in the meantime?" Toby asked.

"For now, you'll just have to wait. Once we've cleared her, we'll send her back to the floor. Do you have a cell phone?"

Toby nodded and gave her the number. The nurse took it down and looked up, "All right, I'll give you a call as soon as we know anything. Don't worry, she's in good hands."

"Okay..."

As the nurse turned and left, Toby walked quickly out of the ER and sat down in the lobby for a few minutes. Having nothing else to do, Toby turned on his phone and called Gishan. The phone rang a few times before he picked up, "What's up man?"

"Gishan, we're back at the hospital." He replied. "It's Lia'na..."

"What happened?"

"I don't know... She just collapsed."

There was a rustling sound on Gishan's end as though he were struggling to get up, "All right, we're on our way."

"You don't have to come all the way down here. I just thought I'd give you an update."

"Hey, we're family. I know what she means to you, and I like her too. She's not bad... for an elf."

"Fine, see you in a bit."

Toby hung up the phone and sat down with his face in his hands. This was too much. Was fate now going to take her away from him too? All around him, the noises of people coming and going passed by his ears, but it was all white noise and he was indifferent to it.

One couple passed by with relief in their voice. Toby looked up to see an older man wheeling his wife out of the hospital. He couldn't quite hear their conversation, but he'd sworn he heard the man say something about her not having cancer.

Toby began to wonder about the manner in which he and Lia'na would walk out of there. Would it be together or alone? Would it be with good news or bad? Toby's mind tormented him as more questions and possibilities entered his head. Would she even walk out at all?

Gishan and Giselle showed up about twenty minutes later. Gishan's eyes darted around the ER until he saw Toby, "Hey man!"

They couple sat on either side of Toby before he even had a chance to look up. Giselle quickly surveyed the room as she spoke, "How's she doing?"

"She's in quarantine. She's apparently very sick…"

"Not good… I knew something didn't seem right. Could this have anything to do with that medallion she destroyed? You saw what happened."

Toby couldn't get the thought of her alone in the hospital bed out of his mind. He got up and began walking, "I'm sorry, I can't do this. I need to go… somewhere. I'll be back in a little bit… I'm really sorry… I need to be alone. I know you guys just got here, but I'm driving myself crazy."

Giselle reached after him, "Toby?"

"No." Gishan said, grabbing her hand. "Let him go, I know him. When he's like this, he needs his space."

Giselle looked at him, "You sure? Kind of weird that he would run off on us."

"He'll be back, what's important is that I'm here when he comes back, you know? That's how our family works. Besides, you and I have a few things to discuss. Particularly how having sex with me was a part of your investigation!"

Giselle rolled her eyes and braced herself for a heated debate.

XX

Toby wandered through the hospital public areas looking for refuge somewhere, anywhere. He thanked his lucky stars that the hallways were almost deserted. The afternoon soon gave way to the evening with still no word on Lia'na.

Toby didn't know what to do. He was still a mess from dealing with his uncle's death and now the girl that he loved was trapped in quarantine. He feared what he was almost positive she had. It loomed over him like a dark specter, continuously tormenting him. His heart was frozen in his chest and he couldn't breathe.

Ready to drop, Toby lurched through the nearest door. Perhaps it was by divine providence or sheer coincidence that Toby ended up in the chapel. The lights were on, but no one was there.

Both physically and emotionally drained, Toby dropped to his knees, rested his hands on the floor next to him as he sat back and looked up at the candles positioned on either side of a small wooden table at the end of the isle. The front of the chapel looked like a blue magic eye painting, but he ignored it.

Toby didn't want to just pray, he wanted to be heard. After taking a few deep breaths, he leaned forward and focused on the thoughts of Lia'na and of her smiling face. He also focused on his fond memories of Uncle Jake coming to his baseball games as a child, and his time with Gishan.

When Toby looked up again, his eyes were glowing white. His spirit touched the other side and he began to speak with an echo in his voice, "I know I don't do this very often... but I need help. An evil man wants me dead, he's killed my only family, and now the woman I love may also be dying. All this is over an object you supposedly gave us as a gift. Why would you give us something that could do so much evil if it was you?"

Toby was ready to start yelling when the candles on either side of the small table flared up. They became brighter with each passing moment until Toby was blinded. No amount of magic could protect him from this level of energy, "What's going on, what is this?"

"You want answers, you shall receive them." A calm voice replied.

As the lights faded, Toby found himself in the presence of two women dressed in white robes. Four red wings protruded from their backs. Physically, they looked to be the exact opposite of one another; one had long curly brown hair, while the other had shorter blonde hair. They stepped forward as the blonde one spoke, "Hello Toby."

"What... What are you?"

The other creature stepped forward, "We're beings from another realm. We watch over a planet that is identical to this one in almost every way."

Toby's eyes narrowed, "So what... like Earth in another dimension?"

"As far as your mind can comprehend, yes that is correct. We are creatures known as angels. I'm Roselyn, and this is my friend Ariel."

"Tobias. Now what is going on here?"

The angels looked at each other before Ariel spoke up, "We heard you... we're here to help."

Toby nodded, "I'm listening."

"The diamond you know as the Lux Mundi didn't come to Earth by accident. Some years ago two rogue angels named Lucifer and Michael made a wager that God's creation couldn't be given unlimited power without being corrupted. Michael took the bet saying the opposite. Since God would not allow his children to be used in such a ruthless experiment, Lucifer travelled to a distant reality and placed the diamond in space where it would eventually fall to Earth. He managed to do this without God knowing, and as such God could do nothing to stop it."

"So we've become play things?" Toby asked in an angry voice. "Is that it? We're the throw away world so you can keep your world safe."

Roselyn nodded, "Yes… I'm afraid so, but know that Michael and Lucifer acted outside of God's mandate. Lucifer has been banished from our world and Michael is dead."

"Well that's good." Toby responded. "Now are you going to clean up your mess?"

"Show some respect." Ariel demanded. "We didn't do this. We're as responsible for what they did as you are responsible for the actions of that monstrosity Alistair."

Roselyn touched her arm, "Ariel calm down. Don't forget, he has good reason to be mad. –Toby, there is nothing we can do. Angels can't go anywhere near the Lux Mundi, Lucifer made sure of that. Our powers are repelled by it."

"So what then," Toby asked, "you want me to destroy it?"

Ariel nodded, "The only way to save your world is to do so."

Toby's face stiffened and he was tempted to tear the angel's head off, "My father's soul is trapped inside the Lux Mundi!"

"We know. His soul is what is holding it together, but he was deceived."

"What do you mean?"

"The one you know as Alistair used him to rebuild the diamond." Roselyn said. "As long as it remains intact, your father is trapped."

Toby looked away, "Can I save him?"

"No." Ariel replied. "I'm sorry, there is no way to bring him back. His body is dead and now his soul suffers in isolation. All you can do now is set him free to join us in the heavens."

Toby's heart sank. This wasn't what he wanted to hear. Though he had never known his father, if even the slightest chance of saving him existed, Toby wanted to take it. Defeated, Toby sucked in a slow breath, "How do I destroy it then?"

"Lucifer was such a wicked creature… It appears the only way to completely destroy it is with the blood of the creature known as the elf. Even that would only shatter it."

"I know all this. The elves paid the ultimate price to rid us of it. What your Lucifer did is nothing short of genocide! There are less than a thousand elves left!"

"We know, but we can't undo his actions. If you wish to destroy the Lux Mundi forever, you need to get it off the planet."

"I doubt even Alistair has the power to launch an object into space."

"No, probably not..." Ariel agreed as she placed her hand on Toby's forehead, "but now you can."

Toby felt his spirit jump. He felt stronger than ever before, like he could pick the chapel up off of its foundation and put it back down, "What did you do to me?"

"The powers you were given after encountering the shard have now been… enhanced with some of my power. Use my angelic energy, only when you need it, and you can rid this world of the Lux Mundi. This is the only help I can provide."

"Thank you, but why are you helping me now? Why do you care?"

"Though from different dimensions, our worlds are intertwined. If something happens to one, it affects all others as well. If war happens here, events will unfold to cause it there as well… if your world ends, so will that one. We may not able to change what happened, but we do want this mess cleaned up. I am truly sorry for your father and all others who have been wrongfully caught up in this, but if you save this world, others will be spared as well."

Toby didn't care about other worlds. He barely cared about his own at this point. All he wanted was to save the people he cared about, but if saving the world meant saving them, what choice did he have? "How do I find it… where could it be, and more importantly, how do I help Lia'na?"

The two angels looked at each other for a moment. Finally Roselyn turned back to him, "Alistair's has hidden himself from view. Apparently being alive for thousands of years helped him enhance his powers."

"How is it possible for someone to live that long?" Toby asked.

"The diamond has unusual powers. Each shard has different properties. One of them has granted him this long existence."

"Well that's great..." Toby said as he felt his blood heat up. "What about my girlfriend Lia'na? She's sick and I have an aching feeling I know why. How do I help her? There has to be a way!"

"There is a way," Ariel replied, "but it's not for us to tell you. If we interfere any further, it will draw too much attention."

"So?"

"If the wrong people are drawn to us, we'll have to take back what you've been given and you'll be on your own. There may come a time when you have to choose between your powers, your friends, the one you love, and possibly even your own life. When that time comes, your choices will determine who survives. You are now the stone that divided the stream of time."

Toby sighed, "You really aren't helping me much. Are you telling me that in the end I may have to sacrifice being an enchanter to save people and destroy the Lux Mundi?"

"We're not allowed to say." Roselyn admitted. "Use what we have given you for good, and you will win the day. That is all we can tell you."

The lights in the room flickered and the angels disappeared. Toby was alone once again, but with a renewed sense of purpose. He was about to head back to the ER when his phone went off in his pocket. He quickly fished it out and looked at the screen.

According to the phone, three hours had apparently passed and it was now 5pm. He didn't recognize the phone number calling, but assumed it was the hospital. He picked up to hear the nurse manager speaking in a rather curt voice, "Toby?"

"Yes?"

"I've been trying to get in touch with you for the past twenty minutes. Lia'na is out of quarantine and is asking for you."

"I'll be right there!" Toby replied as he turned around and ran out of the chapel.

He raced down the hall as fast as he could, passed through the double doors into the ER waiting area, blew past Giselle and Gishan who were still arguing over why she slept with him, and into the atrium. The floor was tiled with what looked like black granite. Pine wood paneling lined the walls with various images of the hospital, promoting its care. The entrance was a large atrium with a staircase off to the right, leading up to bridge with a sign at the end labeled "pike." Undernieth the bridge was a hallway, leading to the patient areas.

Toby had no idea where to go, so he turned left and headed over to the reception desk. The uniformed security guard looked up at him and smiled, "Can I help you?"

Toby nodded, "I'm looking for the room where Lia'na was taken. She was just let out of the ICU. Her name is spelled L, I, A, apostrophe, N, A."

The guard looked down at his computer, "Last name?"

"She doesn't have a last name. She's an elf."

The guard quickly typed the name into his computer to try to locate Lia'na. *Come on... how many people could possibly have that name!*

"And you are?"

"Tobias Arrigan. I'm her emergency contact."

"Do you have some I.D?"

Toby pulled it out of his pocket and showed the guard his license, "Here you go."

It took him a few minutes, but finally a name popped up on his screen, "I got her. She's on the 5th floor of the Connor's Center. Security over there should be able to get you in."

With that, he pointed towards the hallway beneath the bridge. Toby nodded and darted off in that direction. "Thank you very much!"

He ran around the corner and nearly hit a padded chair as he continued running. The plants on his left blew by as he got to the staircase and turned right. He kept running until he got to another security desk, positioned right next to the elevators. The security guard here was an dark-skinned woman who looked at him with surprise, "Can I... help you?"

Toby was out of breath, but managed to force out who he was looking for, "Lia'na... 5th floor."

The woman smiled, "Take a moment and breath."

As Toby's lungs caught up with him, he was able to speak more clearly, "I'm here to see Lia'na. I'm her boyfriend, she's on the 5th floor."

The security guard gave him an odd look as she dialed the number. The phone rang for a moment before the guard spoke, "Yeah I've got a visitor for Lia'na?"

"..."

"Yes, his name is Toby."

Toby watched her as she listened to the nurse. Finally she spoke again, "Okay, I understand... yup."

As she hung up the phone, she looked at Toby, "Do you have anyone else with you?"

"Two friends waiting in the lobby, but that's it."

"Sorry, only one person can go up. Lia'na specifically requested a Toby Arrigan, I assume that's you?"

Toby nodded as he ripped the wallet from his pocket and showed the guard his ID. The guard looked at it and nodded, "All right, elevator 2. You're looking for room 522."

"Thank you." Toby replied as he moved towards the elevators.

The second one slid open and Toby went inside. As he pushed the button to take him to the second floor, it made a chirping sound. The door closed and the elevator began to move.

Within moments, the doors opened again and Toby found himself on the 5th floor. He didn't even bother stopping at reception and instead headed directly to Lia'na's room.

The hallways were wood paneled with red and gray carpet on the floor. Patients' rooms lined the exterior side of the corridor with a break room and other utility doors on the opposite side. After examining the numbers, Toby quickly found Lia'na's room.

Lia'na was hooked up to an IV, but she refused to lie down. When Toby saw her, she jumped out of bed, wanting to run to him, but the IV kept her from moving more than a few steps and her robe hadn't been tied properly. Instead of exposing herself to anyone passing by, she decided to let Toby come to her.

Toby pushed through the door and grabbed her. She wrapped her arms around him and held on tight, "Ta arshana, don't you dare leave me here again, you hear me? I hate hospitals."

"Never again."

He took a minute to catch his breath and help Lia'na back into bed, "Did they tell you why they put you in quarantine?"

"They've told me nothing. They said it was strictly precautionary. Though, I don't know if I believe them. They took blood samples and removed the stitches from my hand. They put some sort of liquid skin on it instead and rewrapped it. So apparently my hand is on the mend, but still no one has told me anything about why I'm feeling weird."

"I'm sure we'll find out soon enough. In the meantime, why don't we see what's on TV?"

Lia'na grabbed the wired remote next to her bed and turned on the TV. She flipped through the channels until she got to the news. A report came on about the restoration work going on in Boston to attempt to get the city up and running after the mysterious explosions.

Lia'na sighed as she lay back in the hospital bed, "How are you doing? Did you sign the papers for your uncle?"

"I'm holding it together I guess. I almost fell apart when they took you away from me and no, I didn't sign the papers."

"Ta arshana, I'm so sorry…"

"It's not your fault, I was busy… oh by the way, Gishan and Giselle are here. I called them."

"It was nice of them to show up."

At that moment, the doctors came in. Lia'na looked up as the leading one with the clipboard spoke, "How are we doing?"

Lia'na smiled, "I'm okay now, I don't understand what happened, but I'm feeling better."

"That's good." The doctor replied. "Have you done anything different from your normal routine lately; injected yourself with something or had sexual relations with another elf?"

"No. Why?"

The doctor looked at the test results, "We believe that your illness may have been caused by a fever brought on by infection. We've given you antibiotics to deal with the cut and more fluids."

"Why would she have an infection?" Toby asked.

The doctor sighed, "It's the reason we put you into quarantine. We may have other elves here and its standard procedure when an Elven patient exhibits certain conditions."

"What conditions?" Lia'na insisted.

The doctor clearly didn't want to give her an answer and it was making her nervous, "It would appear that our initial tests show that you have contracted an unusual strand of the Ulium plague. This is the first case we've seen in years."

Toby nearly fell out of his chair, "What?"

"We don't know how it happened," the doctor replied, "but your blood tested positive."

"But you have treatments for that, don't you?" Toby asked desperately. "You can fix this, you can kill it."

"No," the doctor said softly, "unfortunately we can't. Our treatment regimen is more of a vaccine against the disease. It would prevent infants from getting it and keep it from spreading in older subjects, but it would not kill. We tried everything we know to stop the disease from spreading, but this is a mutated strain that seems to be immune to our agents."

Lia'na's eyes filled with tears, "What does this mean for me?"

After going over his notes, the doctor looked back at Lia'na, "Preservation of the Elven species is of pretty high importance to the U.S. Government. They've given us considerable grant money to study the disease. We've taken samples of your blood, and we'll see what they have for new procedures to try. In the meantime, we'll give you pain medicine and continue the treatments we know."

Toby looked into his eyes, "What's the worst case scenario here, doctor? What are we talking about?"

The doctor took a final deep breath as he looked at them both, "Best case scenario, you live out your life the way the rest of your species does, however you need to be prepared. This is a mutated strain... At the rate the Ulium is spreading... you may have as little as a few months to a year to live."

"But my people lived with the disease for years," Lia'na cried out, "and I'm up to date on my inoculations!"

"That's true," replied the doctor, "but the strand of the disease you carry is far more aggressive. The inoculations appear to be ineffective."

Lia'na put her face in her hands and began crying, "No…"

"I'm sorry to be the bearer of this news. Rest assured we'll do everything we can for you."

Toby got up and held on to her as she cried, "What's the game plan doctor?"

One of the other doctors spoke up, "For now, we're sending you home. It's probably better if you're in a more comfortable environment. You'll need to rest as much as you can though."

Toby's eyes narrowed, "You're letting a patient with a communicable disease out the door, just like that?"

The lead doctor nodded, "Well the disease is only communicable through genetics, blood, or intercourse with another elf. Other than the Ulium she's in perfect health. So as long as she doesn't do anything with another member of her own kind, she'll be fine."

"No worries of that…" Lia'na replied through her sobbing.

"I'm sorry," The doctor replied, "I wish I had better news…"

Toby nodded, "Me too."

The doctor placed a sheet of paper down on the table, "Here are your discharge papers. I'll have the nurse come in and take out that IV, and we'll be in touch in a day or two with a game plan."

"Thank you doctor." Toby replied as he cradled Lia'na in his arms.

Her tears will never dry now, Toby thought to himself.

The nurse came in promptly to remove the IV, placed a Band-Aid on her arm, and redressed the bandage on her hand, "You'll want to make an appointment with your primary care ASAP for a follow up."

Lia'na nodded as she wiped her eyes, "Thank you."

The nurse smiled and tossed the needle and bandages into the biohazard box before leaving the room. Once she was gone, Lia'na melted into Toby's arms, "Ta Diesu, piele, no. Not like this, piele, spare me!"

Toby thought back to the events of today and became angry, "You knew…"

Lia'na looked up at him, "What?"

"Didn't you? Slicing your hand open like that to destroy the shard, you knew you'd be infected!"

Lia'na was caught off guard by his words, "Toby I… what do you think, I have some sort of martyr complex or a death wish? Do you really think I want to die? My people have lived with the Ulium for thousands of years. I knew I might be infected, but I didn't think this would happen. I thought I'd be safe because I'd been inoculated. If I hadn't done what I did, Alistair would have my shard now. I couldn't let that happen."

"You don't know that. We could have found another way."

Lia'na didn't want to fight with Toby. She was having enough trouble holding herself together and his words finally broke her down. Tears streamed down her cheeks, "Toby I understand that you're dealing with a lot between your uncle dying, Alistair, and me being ill, but I just got handed a death sentence! Piele don't be mad at me, I need you right now!"

Toby's heart ached, realizing he'd gone too far. He grabbed her and held her close, "I'm sorry, you're right."

"Ta arshana, I want to go home. Piele take me home. I want to get away from all of this and just relax for a while."

"I'll take you anywhere you want to go. Say the word and we're there."

"Just take me home. The only place I want to be right now is with you."

"All right, let's get out of here then."

Toby quickly grabbed Lia'na's handbag while she changed back into her clothes. Toby grabbed the paper and headed for the door to their room, "Ready?"

"I was ready hours ago..."

Toby took Lia'na by the hand and led her out of the Connor's Center, back to the ER. She grabbed on to his arm with both hands as they walked, "Ta arshana, your uncle."

Toby sucked down another breath, trying to keep himself stable for Lia'na, "I'm more worried about you right now."

They entered the hospital ER through the glass doors and walked into the waiting area. Gishan and Giselle saw them and jumped out of their seats. Gishan smiled, "Lia'na, they let you out?"

Lia'na nodded, "There's nothing they can do at this point."

Gishan studied Toby's expression and turned back to Lia'na, "It's the Ulium isn't it? Destroying that shard came at a price."

"Yeah and apparently it's a mutated version of the disease. They don't know how to cure it."

Gishan bit his tongue, careful not to ask any questions that might cause a meltdown. His bluntness was famous, but now really wasn't the time for it, "Toby, what about your uncle, did you get everything squared away with his body, or are you still waiting to hear?"

Toby shook his head, "That's the reason we were here in the first place. I was going to take care of the paperwork when she just collapsed."

"Do you want to take care of it now?" Lia'na asked.

"It can wait."

A look of concern came over her face, "Are you sure?"

"He's dead, nothing is going to change that or make it better. You on the other hand, are not dead."

Hopefully... Toby thought to himself as the air of helplessness continued to loom over him.

XXI

No one really said anything on their way back to Toby's condo. They were either too afraid or too uncomfortable to ask questions. Toby held on to Lia'na's good hand tightly as he watched the city pass by and the lights begin to fade.

Gishan was running his engine as hard as he cold to get them back. He was partially afraid something might happen to Lia'na, but was also extremely uncomfortable with the current situation.

A sense of relief poured over the group as they pulled into Toby's building. As they hopped out of the jeep, Gishan was the first to speak up, "Well it is getting late... It's going to be a long trip home."

Toby shrugged, "You don't have to leave, you know? I have a spare bedroom if you guys want to hang out until tomorrow?"

Gishan and Giselle looked at each other for a few minutes and then back at Toby. It was almost like they were having a psychic conversation, trying to decide what they wanted to do.

"Are you sure?" Giselle asked. "I mean, you know Gishan pretty well, but we just met and having a stranger around the apartment..."

"You're no stranger." Lia'na interrupted. "In my book, you earned your stripes."

Toby nodded, "You're more than welcome to stay. Any friend of Gishan is a friend of mine."

The two of them looked back at the jeep one more time and then at Toby. They thought about it for a moment before Gishan smiled, "Well I'd rather not make such a long trip tonight. All right, you've got us for the night. Hope you're happy!"

Toby did the best he could to laugh, "Come on you guys. Let's go upstairs."

The group headed up to Toby's condo and settled in for the night. Toby handed Gishan the TV remote, "Put on whatever you want. The movie channels are usually pretty good."

He then turned to Lia'na as they sat down on the couch. Lia'na leaned back against the wall, "Toby, I'm spent. I need to lie down."

"Okay, let's get you into bed."

Lia'na turned to see Gishan and Giselle looking at her with worried expressions. Giselle spoke up, "Are you okay, do you need any help?"

"No, I appreciate it, though." Lia'na replied. "I'm just in a little pain. I'm sorry I'm not going to be good company tonight."

"Don't even worry about it. You've had a long day. I hope you feel better."

"So do I...lienes."

Toby guided her gently to the bedroom and helped her undress. She had a hard time with her hand being bandaged, but she managed to get out of her clothes before grabbing Toby's Red Sox jersey and throwing it on over her underwear. She then gently lay back and got comfortable under the blankets.

Toby grabbed her medicine and placed it on the table right next to her. He was about to untie his shoes when Lia'na grabbed his wrist, "Toby..."

He looked over at her, "What's wrong?"

"Kiss me."

Toby sat up from dealing with his shoes and leaned down over her. The two embraced in a soft kiss that neither one wanted to break. When their lips did part, Toby looked into her eyes, "What was that about?"

"So much has happened over the last few days," she said, fighting back tears, "it all felt like a bad dream that wouldn't end. I just wanted to know that I was still alive."

Toby placed his hand against her cheek, "You are not dying on me. Do you understand? There is a cure for this, I know there is. Whatever it takes, I will find a way to save you."

"Save me again? That'll be 3-0, I need to start playing catch up."

Lia'na closed her eyes and chuckled, "Well if anyone can do it, it'll be my knight... I'm so tired right now. I'm going to get some sleep. You go out and spend some time with your friends."

"Are you sure? I'd really rather stay here."

"I'm just going to sleep, ta arshana. There's nothing else you need to do for me right now. Go be with your friends. Just keep the door open a crack so I can call if I need help."

"Okay... under protest... I'll be outside if you need me."

"Te arshana ni." Lia'na said softly as she drifted off to sleep.

Toby stood up and headed for the door, "I love you too."

He stepped out into the hallway and carefully closed the door so that it was just opened a crack. When he then turned and looked at Gishan and Giselle, the two of them were cuddled up together watching some late night comedy show.

Toby was in no mood for anything light hearted. Instead, he bypassed the living room and headed for the stairwell to the roof. He closed the door behind him as a blast of cool air hit his face. The setting sun was beautiful.

Toby watched as clouds painted with a red and purple hue passed by. In the distance, the lights of Boston were still going strong. He stood for a moment watching the world pass in front of his eyes.

To Toby, everything that he saw in front of him was meaningless. It was just the everyday hustle and bustle of several thousand people. He knew that if Alistair got his way, that would all be over in a matter of moments.

Toby leaned forward thinking of his Uncle and of Lia'na. So far he had failed to protect two of the people that mattered to him the most. *Some knight you turned out to be,* he said to himself. *The closest thing you ever had to a father is dead, and your love is suffering a slow death.*

Toby slammed his fist on the railing, "No, I can't let it happen..."

He looked up into the evening sky towards the remains of the sun on the horizon before turning away from the city. His face turned to the other side of the building as though something were telling him to face north, "No one else I care about is going to die."

He charged over to the railing facing north, "Do you hear me Alistair? No more! You took Uncle Jacob from me, you won't take Lia'na! I'm coming for you!"

"He probably heard you." A voice chimed in from behind. "I have a feeling that he's having you watched as we speak."

Toby turned around quickly to see Giselle standing behind him, "Gishan fall asleep?"

"Out like a light, on the couch."

"He always was a lightweight when it came to staying out late. So have you too settled out your differences?"

"Not really, but we're working on it. I think he finally believes me that sleeping with him and forming a relationship wasn't part of my job."

"Well you have that at least. You can't expect to drop a bombshell on a guy and expect him to be instantly okay with it."

"No you can't. In fact, he took it much better than I thought he would."

Toby turned back to staring at the hills, "Can I ask you something?"

"Sure."

Toby looked down to see a few people walking out the back door to their cars. He sighed and looked back up, "What's the U.S. Government's stake in all this?"

Giselle walked over to Toby and stood next to him. With her jacket off, Toby could clearly see the gun holster on her hip as she walked, "The FBI has been investigating Alistair for years."

"You mean you've known about him?"

"Yeah, we discovered some unusual paperwork surrounding him. It's quite extensive; false birth and death records, as well as the continuous laundering of the money that belongs to him. According to his paperwork, he is the latest descendant in a long line of people with the same name."

Toby leaned on the railing, "Well that just sounds like something you'd see in a mafia movie. Not really unheard of is it?"

"No it's not," Giselle admitted, "but each father dies as soon as the son turns 18. The death records are fuzzy, there is never a funeral, and every member of the family is cremated and has their ashes spread at an undisclosed location. This can all be explained away as a series of suspicious coincidences, which is what I thought when I was first assigned to the case, but looking at all the evidence together... it was really something."

But what does this have to do with the Lux Mundi, why is the U.S. Government so concerned with it?"

Giselle turned and faced the opposite direction, leaning her back against the railing, "Can I trust you?"

"Sure."

"No, can I trust you? Seriously..."

"Yes... of course you can."

Giselle lowered her eyes and looked at the ground, "I must be out of my mind... I mean, I just met you. Still... these are fairly odd circumstances... All right, what I'm about to tell you is classified. I will lose my job and probably go to jail for telling you this if you repeat it."

Toby turned to the side so he was facing her while still leaning on the railing, "Okay, you have my attention."

Giselle sighed, knowing the next words out of her mouth could end her career. "An archeologist working for one of our R&D programs has long theorized that the Lux Mundi still existed. He's pushed for years for money to fund an expedition to Mt. Vesuvius, but since this was an international affair, the FBI refused him."

"John Tyran?"

Giselle's eyes perked up in surprise, "Oh you've heard of him?"

"Yeah when we first heard about the attack on the *Luca Ricci,* his name was everywhere."

"Makes sense."

"Did he find it?"

"Yeah…"

"Great… So now we've got an all-powerful diamond missing and a renegade who seems to have discovered some kind of fountain of youth. Why would the U.S. Government let this happen?"

"At first we had no interest in it. It wasn't on our soil, it wasn't our problem, but when we found out what Alistair was doing, we began to put a plan into action to try to prevent it. Alistair wanted to fund John Tyran's dig. He reported it to us and I started looking into it. That's when we came across the Fillis de Lux. When I realized what was going on, I petitioned the FBI directors to put finding the Lux Mundi's remains at the highest priority. It wasn't an easy sell, but they eventually saw the light. So our first step was to ask the Italian government for permission."

"I take it that was the hard part?"

"It took a lot of arm twisting. The U.S. had to make considerable concessions to the Italian government to allow us to remove anything from their soil. Once that was done, the dig site on Mt. Vesuvius was temporarily declared US soil and we let our man do his work. Unfortunately, he was spot on as to the location of the Lux Mundi. The remains were found not too far from the Pompeii site. We quickly got them out of Italy aboard the first available ship we could legally cease and outfit. You know the rest..."

"Not quite. What happened to the man who found the diamond?"

Giselle frowned, "He's dead. When Alistair found out that he had been double crossed, he came after our man. Nothing we did to protect him worked. Alistair has an uncanny ability to always be one step ahead of us. Guess that's how it goes when you live that long."

"Well you've explained a lot, but there is one major question that is still unanswered; what does the US Government want with the Lux Mundi?"

"To study it and keep it safe. It's a major archeological find with extremely dangerous implications. Who knows what secrets it may contain?"

"I can't let that happen." Toby replied adamantly. "Lia'na is right. It has to be destroyed. There is too much power behind the diamond for anyone to control."

Giselle stood up straight and looked directly into Toby's eyes, "You know something we don't, don't you?"

Toby focused his thoughts and energy into making his hand glow as it did before he attacked Alistair, "All I know is that the U.S. Government is now messing with powers that it can't possibly understand. Hell, I don't think I understand it. What I can say is that since the diamond resurfaced, powers I shouldn't have are now at my disposal. I don't want to think about what else may have happened as a result of taking the Lux Mundi from its resting place. All I know is that Lia'na is sick, and my father is trapped inside that terrible thing. It's not meant for this world. If we don't destroy it, then it's only a matter of time before something bad happens."

"Well that's where our missions cross paths."

Toby was about to say something, when Giselle raised her hand, "However, at the moment, our goals are both the same. You want to stop Alistair and find a way to save Lia'na, and so do I. Alistair's lived and remained unchecked for way too long... and from what little I've been able to talk to Lia'na, she seems like a really sweet girl. I don't want to see her die any more than you do."

"Fair enough," Toby agreed, "I just have one last thing I need to know..."

"Please."

"How old are you? You look like you're our age, but you're an FBI agent?"

"I'm 24. I studied international law and criminal justice at John Hopkins University. The FBI recruited me pretty quickly upon graduation and I've been working for them ever since. As to why... well... I love my country, and I want to protect it."

"Good answer."

Giselle saw that Toby had heavy eyes and needed to lie down. She put her hand on his shoulder, "You've been through more in one day than anyone should ever have to deal with. You must be exhausted. Why don't you go get some rest?"

"Yeah... I think I need it..."

Toby turned and walked back down stairs, "Have a good night."

"You too." She called after him.

Toby left the door to the roof opened slightly for whenever Giselle decided she wanted to come back in and walked into the bedroom. He shut the bedroom door behind, and sat down on the bed. After pulling off his shoes and pants, he got under the blankets. Lia'na was fast asleep on the other side of the bed, and wasn't roused by him getting in.

Once Toby was settled, he turned on his side and pressed himself against her. He could feel her skin, but something was different this time; she was cold as ice.

Toby saw her move and knew she that was still breathing, but her body shouldn't be that cold. He quickly covered her over with another blanket and wrapped himself around her to try to get her temperature up.

After a few minutes of holding her tightly, she began to feel warmer. Toby released his grip and gently cuddled her as he began to fall asleep.

Out in the living room, Toby could hear the sound of a door closing and people stirring. Giselle had come back in from the roof and had woken Gishan up. A moment later, he heard movement in the second bedroom and guessed that they were now getting ready to get some actual sleep.

About time.

*

Toby didn't sleep long. His dream world had been corrupted by images of war and destruction. What made it worse was that the focal point seemed to be a table in the middle of the chaos. It was little more than a stone slab which appeared to be covered in blood.

As Toby's mind examined it, a body appeared in front of him. It was stretched out and lifeless as though it had just been sacrificed. Toby was certain that it was Elven, and that it was infected with the Ulium. The body was hazy at first, but as it slowly solidified, confirming his worst fear. The familiar presence of the elf-girl he loved took form.

Toby's eyes shot open as he broke out of the nightmare and looked around. He was back in his room, breathing heavily and covered in sweat. Everything was peaceful, but something wasn't right. As he turned to lie back down, he noticed that Lia'na was gone and the door to their bedroom was wide open.

Toby quickly looked at his cell phone. It was only 10:30pm so he knew that they hadn't been asleep very long. He threw on some pants and ran to the door. His eyes darted around the apartment frantically looking for any sign of Lia'na. Where could she have gone?

A feeling of relief came over him when he saw that the doorway to the roof had been left open slightly. This was out of character for Lia'na as she never stayed up on the roof when it got dark.

Toby pushed the door open and climbed the stairs to the patio. He made his way out onto the roof as the cool air soothed his sweat-covered skin. He was wide awake now and alert as he made his way into the night air.

To his surprise, Lia'na wasn't in her normal spot staring off into New Hampshire. Instead she was looking at Boston, still alive with activity. He slowly began to walk towards her, doing the best he could to postpone interrupting her peace.

As he got closer, Lia'na's ears perked up slightly, signalling that she knew he was there. She smiled slightly without turning around as she spoke, "It's really amazing being up here. Even at night, the city is bustling with activity. I feel like I'm on top of the world, looking down on it from afar. Maybe it's time I stopped looking down on it and started living in it."

Toby stood behind her and placed his hands on her shoulders. She sighed as she felt his warm skin, "Ah ta arshana, I hope I didn't worry you when you realized that I wasn't there."

"Admittedly, it gave me a little shock. We may be being watched... both by Alistair and possibly members of your clan. What are you doing up here so late?"

"I don't know. I can't explain it, but I felt drawn here."

"Are you okay?"

Lia'na didn't reply at first, she just kept taking deep breaths of air. Toby was beginning to worry as she remained silent. He tried again, "Lia'na?"

It took her a few uncomfortable moments, but she finally spoke, "Toby, I know we've talked about this, time and again, but I know you had some time with your mother. What do you remember about her?"

Toby stared blankly into the distance at nothing in particular. He took a moment to piece together what memories he had of his mother before speaking, "I remember long brown hair, blue eyes, and a wide smile. I remember she always gave me whatever I wanted, and what I needed the most. She was always cheerful but…"

Lia'na turned to face Toby, "What?"

"It always seemed like something was eating away at her on the inside. I think it may have been the cause of her death."

"A broken heart because of your father?"

"Maybe."

Lia'na's eyes slowly moved down until she was focused on the ground, "You're lucky you had that time. I didn't know my mother. She was a stranger to me. I never even had a picture of her. Then your uncle tells me that I look exactly like her..."

"It couldn't have been easy."

"No, but for him to recognize her in me... I don't know, at least it gives me some idea. I also remember Masarabi telling me about my mother. She always told me how how lively and energetic she could be."

"Sounds like you."

"You think? But then I remembered… a lullaby that Masarabi used to sing to me. She told me that it was my mother's favorite and that she used to sing it to help me sleep. As far back as I can remember, whenever I was hurt or sad, Masarabi would sing it to me. I hadn't thought about that in years."

"Any song I would know?"

"Unlikely, it's an old Elven song."

"I remember, when I got a little older, I used to sing it myself." She continued. "It always made Masarabi smile when I did."

A surprised look came over Toby's face, "I didn't know you could sing."

"I haven't in a long time. Masarabi taught me how, but I don't even know how good I am."

Lia'na slowly turned to face Toby and looked up at him, "May I sing for you?"

"Yeah, I'd like to hear it."

Lia'na cleared her throat and took a few deep breaths. She paced in a circle a few times before coming to a stop a few feet away from Toby. Then she turned to face him and began to sing,

"Tieme e' vivi
Veniti tymae comre
Rixa e' comrene
Nira oculoi produ te planin
Ut nira ta ara"

Toby sat in a nearby lawn chair that had been left on the roof and rested his chin in his palm as he listened in awe to her singing. Her voice was so enchanting that Toby thought she could have been a mythological muse. It wasn't deep like an opera singer, but she had a similar range and a lot of power.

"Simili soel,
Simili interoi,

Nira ta ara
Ni et complet requien
Simili ta imag
Nira arshana e' serenum
Nihil exu yuel
Ta arshana, ta imag"

Lia'na's voice resonated throughout the entire building. In Toby's condo, Giselle and Gishan were awakened by the sound of her singing through an open window. Gishan looked around as the music continued, "What's going on?"

"Shhh!" Giselle replied with a hand in front of Gishan's lips. "I want to listen. It's beautiful."

In the parking lot, four friends were just stopping off from a bar crawl. They had locked up their car and were making their way inside when they heard Lia'na's voice. It was as though time froze. The four of them stopped walking and stood in silence as the mysterious voice continued,

"Simili soel,
Simili interoi,
Nira ta ara
Ni et complet requien
Simili ta imag
Nira arshana e' serenum
Nihil exu yuel
Ta arshana, ta imag"

Lia'na's voice trailed off after the last word. Even after she stopped singing, Toby was mystified as he stared into her eyes. They appeared to glow in the starlight. It took him a moment to come back to reality as Lia'na stood there, but when he did, he looked at her in amazement, "Lia'na, that... that was beautiful!"

"Lien ni. I'm glad I got to share that with you."

"I hope you'll be able to share a lot more."

Lia'na lowered her eyes again as she spoke, "I don't know that I will be…"

"Don't!" Toby interrupted with a stern voice. "You're not dying on me. There is a way to save you, I know there is."

"You sound almost positive. Do you know something I don't?"

"I can't explain it. It's almost like something I heard about in a dream. I know it sounds crazy, but it may come down to me having to make a very tough choice."

"A choice between what?"

"I don't know… but it's not important. I'm not going to let you die. You hear me?"

"You really won't let it happen, will you?"

"I don't care what it takes. I will cure you."

A sense of relief came over Lia'na. She saw the look in his eyes and truly believed him, "Then I'm not worried."

"Good." Toby replied as he took her hand and beckoned her back to the door, "Come on, it's been a long day, let's get some sleep."

"Okay."

XXII

"Toby, Lia'na, you guys better come see this!"

The two of them were jolted awake by Gishan's gruff voice coming from the living room. Toby rubbed his eyes as he rolled out of bed. Lia'na sat up and turned to Toby, "Enoi mae."

Toby yawned and stretched his arms out, "How are you feeling?"

"A lot better, physically. The pain is almost gone and I don't feel so worn out."

"Good, now let's go see what's going on with Gishan."

The two of them walked out of the bedroom to see their dwarven friend staring out the window. Toby glared at him, "Gishan what's so important that you start waking everyone up like..."

Suddenly, Toby saw what he was looking at. There were large clouds of smoke coming up out of Boston. In the air, Toby could see weird creatures flying between the buildings.

Toby turned to grab the TV remote as Lia'na stepped up to the window, "Let's see if there is anything on the news about this."

While Toby flicked through the channels, Lia'na looked out the window at the flying beasts, "Ai iesau..."

Gishan turned to her, "What is it?"

"They're dragons!"

"Dragons?" Giselle cut in, walking up behind them. "What are we in Disney World now...?"

Then she saw a massive winged lizard pass by the window closest to her, and screamed, "What's going on?"

The moment Toby turned the TV, an on-sight reporter appeared on the screen. Toby turned the volume up and listened in. A reporter on the ground, with a frightened look on his face, was going into great detail about what was happening on the streets of Boston. The scene behind him was total chaos as he spoke, "It appears that creatures most people believed to be little more than myths actually exist. In the last hour alone we've seen dragons, what look like trolls or ogres... or maybe both, I can't really tell. We've also seen these giant one-eyed monsters on the rampage."

The reporter was nearly knocked over by someone running. He regained his composure in enough time for a bunch of little creatures that looked like tiny people to appear on the screen, "Whoa, nice camera buddy!"

"Come on guys, let's get on TV!"

"I'm taking this guy's microphone!"

"Hey, mom, look at me! Ha ha!"

The reporter cried out, "No, get back, no!"

The TV went blank for a moment, and then went to the emergency broadcast screen. Lia'na shook her head, "Brownies..."

Giselle turned and headed for the bedroom, pulling a black phone out of her pocket. Toby couldn't believe it, "All these years… the elves were right. People hated them for what they did, but they saved us all and brought order to a chaotic world."

Lia'na leaned against Toby's arm, "I understand why humans didn't care for us, after my ancestors shattered the Alliance, but we did it for the right reasons."

"I know that, but even if they didn't, I still thought the blame you bore was unfair. Making someone pay for the crimes of their parents is just wrong."

"Parents!" Gishan said as his head perked up. "I've got to see if my mother is okay!"

He ripped out his phone and quickly tapped on his mother's contact info. Almost immediately, an automated voice came up, "All circuits are currently busy, please try your call again later."

"Fuck!" Gishan yelled out in a panic.

"I'm sure she's fine." Lia'na said in a comforting tone. "Hopefully she's somewhere safe."

"If there is such a place," Giselle chimed in as she came back into the room, "I just got off the squawk box with the head office. It looks like this attack is happening all over New England. Each city is having problems. Here in Boston, they're already declaring a state of emergency and calling in the National Guard."

At that moment, two jet fighters flying low passed over the complex. Giselle shook her head, "F-16s... looks like they've deployed the air force to try to deal with these dragons."

Toby watched them until they disappeared, "Do you think they have any chance?"

"Hard to say, they're good fighters, but I've never seen a dragon before. I have no idea how powerful they are."

Gishan couldn't stand it anymore, "I need to go home. I need to make sure my mother is okay."

Giselle nodded, "I'll go with you."

"Give us a minute to get dressed." Toby said. "We're coming too."

Toby and Lia'na quickly went back to the bedroom and threw on clean clothes. They were only gone a few minutes, but Gishan was already on edge. He stood at the door as they came back into the room, "Okay, let's go."

They opened the door and proceeded down the stairs. Other doors were broken and there was shattered glass everywhere. Outside, the group was shocked to see a saber tooth tiger fighting with a centaur. Toby hoped that the beasts wouldn't see them as they exited.

The tiger jumped on its prey and grabbed it by the neck. The centaur roared in pain as it punched viciously at the tiger's stomach. The tiger eventually let go, but it was only dazed. It backed away and geared up for another attack. The centaur raised its fists, attempting to keep its more vulnerable areas defended.

The group quietly made their way out into the chaos and headed towards Gishan's jeep. Gishan turned back and looked at Giselle, "Thank God it's still there."

Gishan had spoken too soon as a large shadow passed over his head. The group looked up to see a massive dragon bearing down on them. The beast roared and unleashed a blast of flame from its mouth.

All four of them dove out of the way and just narrowly missed getting burnt to a crisp. Gishan's car was not so lucky. The moment it was hit by the flame, it exploded. Gishan looked up at his new baby, "Damn it, no!"

Toby scrambled to his feet and helped Lia'na up. He stood next to her for a moment, trying to figure out what to do, when a sudden noise behind him that sounded like something impacting against a steal door, made him jump. He turned back to the garage unit that came with his condo. The faint thud came again and again.

Lia'na looked at Toby, "It almost sounds like someone wants out."

"Who would be in there?" Toby asked. "That's just my father's motorcycle."

"Yes… Your father's bike…"

Toby ran back and opened the garage. He nearly screamed as his bike came rolling out on its own. It circled around and stopped right in front of him before revving its engine as it sat idle.

Toby scratched his head, "Um… what's going on?"

The bike jerked forward a little and revved its engine again. Lia'na smiled, "I think it wants you to get on."

The bike made a sound that resembled purring and turned its headlight to face Lia'na. Toby shook his head, "Um... yeah I don't think so."

Lia'na giggled, "Just give it a chance. It was your father's after all."

As it revved its engine again, Toby gave up and slowly got on, "Dad, if this bike kills me, I'm going to haunt your grave!"

The moment Toby sat down and put his hands on the bars, the bike roared and sped off with Toby on its back, screaming. Gishan watched him go, "What's going on? What is he doing?"

As the bike began to pick up speed, two dragons flew by overhead. One of them closed in and spat a ball of fire at Toby. The bike jerked to the side and narrowly dodged it.

Toby held on tight as it maneuvered, "Good boy… girl… bike?"

The second dragon attacked with a beam of flame, shooting down the street like napalm. Again the bike jerked out of the way. Toby knew that they would get incinerated if they kept this up, but at least the dragons were no longer threatening his friends. He still had to wonder what had happened to those F-16s that were supposed to be dealing with this.

As a third attack came down, Toby leaned forward, "This is not good, if we stay out here much longer, we'll be fried!"

As though responding to him, came to a screeching halt, spun around, and began driving in the other direction. This threw the dragons off for a few moments, giving Toby some distance, but he knew that it wasn't going to last. He had to do something.

As the dragons gave chase, Toby closed his eyes and focused everything he had on his friends. His heart raced as the power flowed through his veins. There had to be some way to bring the dragons down.

The feeling spread throughout his body as his fists started glowing white. Toby raised his hands off the handlebars, over his head, and quickly slammed them back down. The bike roared in response.

Whatever Toby did appeared to work. The tires on his bike turned from black to white and began to glow brightly. Miraculously, the front tire began to rise off the road. A second later, the back one did the same and the bike went airborne. Toby jerked back in his seat, causing the bike to shoot upward.

As Toby found himself heading for the clouds, he realized that he needed turn around. If he didn't do something soon, the dragons were going to catch him. At that moment, the bike turned around on its own. Toby's eyes narrowed as the bike did exactly what he wanted, but now he was heading directly at the dragons.

More than anything at that point, Toby wanted the bike the break right. As though responding to his thoughts, it did just that. *Mental commands,* Toby thought to himself, *that's how I control this thing?*

Toby now knew what he had to do. The dragons passed by and tried to give chase. The bike turned 180 degrees and dropped below the dragons. As it passed underneath them, Toby unleashed a beam of light directly at the dragon's chest.

Blood spewed out of the dragon and it roared in pain. Unable to stay in the air, the dragon fell to the ground and died. The ground shook as the mighty beast hit the road.

Toby smiled as the bike came around behind the second dragon and stood on the foot pedals. He then stretched his hands out and unleashed a massive white blast that vaporized it.

The group cheered as both dragons were destroyed. Lia'na watched in awe as the bike did a barrel roll and came in for a landing. She smiled when she saw the look of euphoria on his face. *Well done ta arshana, your powers are gaining strength.*

The bike spun around and came to a stop right in front of them. Toby's friends ran to his side. At that moment, a stabbing sensation entered Lia'na's stomach. She leaned forward and cried out in pain.

"Lia'na, what's happening?" Toby asked as he got off the bike and ran to her

Gishan grabbed her arm to keep her from falling. He touched her cold skin and looked at Toby, "We need to get her inside, now."

As the group made their way up the stairs, the motorcycle parked itself back in the garage. Inside, Giselle straightened up the pillows on the couch. Gishan and Toby helped Lia'na lay down once she was done.

Toby sat down on the edge of the sofa while Giselle looked on in horror, "Lia'na what's going on, what's happening?"

"It's Alistair... he's rebuilding the diamond."

"How do you know?"

"... my shard... it connected me to it."

Her eyes winced in pain, "Toby, my hand... it hurts... bad."

Toby quickly removed the bandages covering her cut and gasped at what he saw. Red lines, resembling veins, were appearing all over her skin and slowly spreading up her arm. Toby's heart began to race as he watched, "What's going on, what is this?"

"It's the Ulium." Giselle replied. "I've seen what it looks like in the mid stages. These lines appear on the skin and spread all over body of its victim. There is no way to prevent it."

"What's going to happen?" Toby asked, fearing the answer he knew was coming.

"It works similar to any other virus and begins attacking her body. The Ulium attacks blood cells indiscriminately and slowly thins the blood. The body can usually fight it off for a little while, but as time goes on, the blood cells, platelets, and everything else gets reduced nearly to nothing. Once that happens, the body starts weakening and shutting down."

Gishan held her arm and looked the markings over, "But she was just infected a week ago. How can all this already be happening?"

"The virus is a mutated version." Lia'na replied. "Which means the cures won't work."

Gishan backed away, "My God…"

Lia'na's body suddenly convulsed and she let out a painful scream. Toby stood up and turned to Giselle, "Do you see what I mean now? The Lux Mundi is too dangerous to be preserved."

Giselle took a step back, "I… I have my orders."

"Orders…" Gishan scoffed. "Girl, I know you well enough now to know that the rules and directives never meant much to you. You always did what you wanted. That's what made me notice you in the first place; you do what you think is right regardless of what other people say. Why hide behind rules now?"

Lia'na looked up at her pleadingly, "Piele, help us Giselle. You know Alistair better than we do. We need you."

"I…" Giselle lowered her eyes and turned her back to them.

Gishan shook his head as Toby grabbed a warm cloth and dabbed Lia'na's forehead and arms. The red lines slowed their advance as they reached her chest. Lia'na breathed more normally and began to sit up, "… I'm okay now."

Toby helped her as she balanced herself, "Are you sure?"

"Yeah, the pain is more manageable now."

Toby brushed her hair back and ran his fingers along the pointed end of her ear. Lia'na closed her eyes and leaned into him, "Lien ni."

Giselle stood off to the side, not looking at anyone. She was clearly deep in thought, trying to work out her own sense of ethics. After what seemed like deep contemplation, Giselle broke her silence, "We believe Alistair's base is in a cave near the summit of Mount Jefferson. We don't know what he's doing there, but I'm fairly certain that I was able to locate the exact location via satilite."

She handed Toby her phone, "I've plotted it for you on the FBI's satellite GPS. Take it, destroy the diamond, and kill Alistair, and save the world."

Toby took the phone and looked at it closely, "What... the Great Gulf?"

"Oh great..." Gishan chimed in while rolling his eyes. "He couldn't have chosen a more difficult place to get to, could he?"

Toby nodded, "There isn't really a way to get there by car..."

"So what are we going to do?" Lia'na asked.

"We'll need to figure out a way in, but no one is going anywhere today. Lia'na is still too weak, and we need to figure out a plan. That area is too naturally fortified for us to just waltz in."

At first, Giselle didn't say anything. She knew that helping her new friends was going to cost her the position she worked hard for, but it was the right thing to do. That had never been more obvious, "Toby is right, we can't just run in there, guns blazing."

"So what do we do?" Gishan asked.

Lia'na stood up as she looked out the window. The smoke in Boston had died down and several choppers could be seen in the sky. It looked as though the military was attempting to fortify the area.

Toby was about to speak up when a picture came back on the TV and a new reporter with a relieved look on his face stood in front of a cleanup crew as he delivered the update, "So it appears that the National Guard has successfully beaten back the horde of monsters. The few that are left are being rounded up for study. For now, people are ordered to remain inside until the situation is resolved. City officials are trying to figure out where this horde came from, but they have no leads yet, as such no evacuation order has been issues and people are being urged to shelter in place. We have no reports yet of how many casualties or how extensive the damage is, but rest assured that we will bring you those reports as soon as they come in."

Giselle scoffed, "That's a lie. They know where to look."

As far as Toby and his friends were concerned, the National Guard had simply won round one. If Alistair became any more powerful, he would create a force that would soon overwhelm even the best military. It was a haunting notion.

Lia'na sucked in a deep breath as she spoke, "Alistair has lived for thousands of years. He's a dark enchanter, and his powers are unlike anything written about in the Magnifica. Toby is the only one with any hope of beating him."

Those words hit Toby the hardest. It was true; he and he alone would have to challenge Alistair. He couldn't ask his friends or the one he loved to join him. They were really all he had left. He wanted to make sure that he had someone to come back to when this was all over, considering he could come back. "Well we still need to figure out a way to actually get to the cave. It's surrounded by mountains."

"I know that area... There are no roads leading to the caves." Lia'na added. "This could be difficult."

The group had spent the entire day trying to plan a way up to the Mountains. During most of this time, Giselle remained silent, still conflicted. It was an interesting conundrum that had defeated many agents in the past and now fell to her. There was now a fine line between doing her job and doing what was right. It was a decision she had hoped that she would never have to make. Still, she was confident that she'd made the right one, despite the cost.

The rest of the group also had thoughts running through their minds that were difficult to put aside for later. For Gishan, not being able to make sure his mother was okay loomed over him like a dark shadow. It was slowly starting to consume him.

For Lia'na, she had no one waiting for her to return from whatever facing Alistair might bring. Her thoughts did periodically focus on the White Water Clan, but she knew them, they'd vanish into the trees if an enemy attacked. She was more worried about Toby. He would now have to face Alistair and there was little she could do other than offer words of confidence.

Toby had it the worst, in addition to the looming specter of having to face down Alistair, he also knew that time was running out for Lia'na. The disease was slowly spreading and had covered roughly half of her body. The red lines had not stopped spreading and were now moving down to her hips. There had to be a cure, and if anyone knew of, he was certain that it would be Alistair.

As the day turned to night, everyone began to get tired. Toby decided it was time to call it quits for the evening,

"All right, so tomorrow we'll see if we can find anything that's still drivable. We'll pack some hiking gear and follow the GPS signal to the cave."

"It's going to be a long trip." Gishan admitted. "Perhaps Lia'na should stay behind."

"What?" Lia'na said in a surprised tone.

"You're sick. You should take it easy and rest. Let us deal with this."

Lia'na shook her head as she stood up, "Absolutely not, I have as much of a stake in this as any of you. Whether you like it or not, I'm going too."

Toby remained silent. He understood both side of the argument, but didn't know who's side to take, "Giselle, what do you think?"

Giselle thought for a moment before breaking her silence, "I gave you the information I have. You need to develop a plan and be ready. If you're going to try to destroy the diamond, I wouldn't count on much help from the government. That's not their mission."

"That's fine," Toby replied, "we weren't really counting on any help."

Giselle fell silent again and returned to her own little world of moral ambiguity. Gishan tried to comfort her, but didn't know what to say. Instead he focused on the group, "Guys, I hate to put a damper on this… but what about once we get to the cave? Who knows what's in there or what to expect."

"That's true." Toby replied. "I'll be he's probably trying to rebuild his forces there as well. We'll need to slip in carefully."

"Wait," Lia'na cut in, "there is something I don't get… If the government knows where he is and knows what he's doing, why don't they just send in the military?"

"It's not that easy." Giselle replied. "For one, I don't know who has information about Alistair and who doesn't at this point. I was placed under orders from the higher ups to keep this quiet. No one even bothered to investigate the location I found. Telling you was a direct violation of that. We've sent small teams in before, and they have disappeared without a trace, but you can bet that since we've been attacked, the military will be converging on the area pretty quickly."

Toby nodded, "Exactly, so we need to beat them to it. We'll need to leave early tomorrow morning. The more time we waste, the more time the government has to get there first."

XXIII

As the group turned in for the night, Lia'na and Toby sat up in their bed, contemplating what tomorrow would bring. Toby ran his hand up her arm as she looked away. A disgusted look appeared on her face, "Don't…"

"What? What's wrong?"

"Look at me Toby, I'm practically a leper. These red marks are everywhere now."

"You're not a leper. Stop talking like that. I didn't start dating you because I thought you were hot... well... okay not just because you're hot, I did it because I got to know you and I enjoy spending time with you."

Finally Lia'na leaned into Toby, "Lien ni, ta arshana…"

"I never get tired of you mixing Elvish in with your English."

"Some words hold greater meaning when they're spoken in a person's primary language."

The red marks appeared to form under her skin and didn't affect its smoothness. Lia'na pushed into him weakly, "Hold me, Toby, this may be our last night."

"No way, we've got plenty more nights ahead."

It was a lie and Toby knew it, even if they did succeed, there was no guarantee that they'd find a cure. Lia'na might wind up dying a slow and painful death a few months down the road. So what were his choices; bring her and risk her dying, or leave her and hope to get a cure from Alistair?

Lia'na lay back and began to dose off. "Toby, can I ask you something…"

"Sure," Toby replied as he relaxed, "what's up?"

"Do you want to..."

"What?"

Lia'na paused for a moment as though part of her dreaded getting a response. "Remember what I told you about elven mating traditions?"

"Yeah... had I won, I would have gained betrothal rights... but I didn't."

"You didn't win the fight... but in chosing to fight, you won my heart, and because you took me in, elven tradition dictates that my betrothal rights now fall to you."

"How does that work?"

"It's supposed to be a way to further punish an exile. So basically when an elf is alone and destitute, if someone takes them in, that exile is then subservient to the person who cares for them."

"So they'll opt to remain destitute."

"Essentially..."

"So... what now?"

Lia'na smiled warmly, "That's what I want to talk to you about. You have the option to either bind me to you, or set me free from my obligation to you. I was just curious... what would you want to do?"

Toby found himself caught off-guard by the question, "I... I mean... um... wow."

A hurt look came over Lia'na's face, but Toby cut her off before she could speak, "I'm not against the idea. Honestly, part of me really doesn't want to free you because... well it's kind of nice to have Elven law recognize our relationship. I still planned on freeing you if someday you didn't want to be with me."

Lia'na pushed herself up on her elbows so their lips touched. When she pulled back, her eyes lightened up, "Don't free me."

Toby's jaw dropped open, "What?"

"Relax. I'm not asking for a marriage proposal. Think of it as more of what your people would consider a promise ring. You know, that it might be in the cards for us someday?"

"What are you asking me to do?"

"If we win the day, will you honor-bind me to you?"

Toby thought about it for a moment before responding, "I hadn't really expected this... but..."

He looked into Lia'na's beautiful eyes as his brain tried to make up its mind. They still hadn't been together for that long, but he did love her, and in the time they had been together, they literally spent more time together than apart.

Toby's mind finally jolted back to reality, he loved her, she loved him, and he really didn't want to be parted from her, "Yes."

Lia'na's smiled widened, "Really?"

"Lia'na, I love you. I just want you to be happy."

Lia'na lay back down and closed her eyes with a content look on her face, "Lien ni."

"Don't thank me yet. This is all contingent on you surviving, and I don't think you know what you're getting into!"

Lia'na's eyes opened sharply, "Of course, I agree, and I don't care. Te arshana ni, that's all I care about."

Toby lay down and cradled her. It was at that moment that he felt her twinge. Her muscles felt like they were tensed and she was stiff. He looked her over carefully, "Lia'na, are you all right?"

"I'm in a little pain, but it's manageable."

Toby lifted himself up and leaned on his shoulder, "Why are your muscles tensed?"

At that moment, she lost control, allowing her body to momentarily tremble before she tensed up again.. Toby's eyes narrowed, "You're trying to hide that you're trembling."

Lia'na quickly turned over and buried herself in Toby's arms. Her entire body was now shaking, "Fine, yes, you caught me. I'm frightened okay? I don't want anything to happen to you, or Gishan, or even Giselle, but I don't want to die either. I was so stupid, I should have destroyed the shard the moment I found out what it was, but it was all I had from my family."

"Lia'na, you're not going to die. I understand why you hung on to that diamond."

"But you were mad at me. You thought it was dumb of me to destroy the shard."

"The way you did it, yes."

"You couldn't hold out against Alistair forever. You weren't ready to face him. Had we lost, he would have killed us and the Lux Mundi would be able to return to full power."

"All right, enough! There is no point arguing about the past. Decisions were made that may or may not have been the right ones, but there's nothing we can do about that, so there is no reason to fuss about them."

Lia'na let out a deep sigh before nodding and turning back over, "You're right of course… You always seem to be."

Toby placed his hand on her shoulder and gently squeezed. The moment Lia'na felt the pressure, she placed her own hand on top of his and held it there, "Te arshana ni…"

"Say it in English."

"Huh?"

"Just this once, I want to hear you say it in English."

Lia'na turned back over, pushed him on his back, and rested her head on his chest, "I love you."

"Te arshana ni."

Lia'na rolled her eyes as she slowly began to fall asleep, "You are too much."

*

An hour passed as Lia'na slowly fell asleep. Toby faked being tired, but couldn't actually sleep. He spent another hour staring at the ceiling and then back at Lia'na. Images of the fight tomorrow passed through his mind. Each time, he saw Lia'na struggling. He saw her hurt and suffering, and couldn't stand it.

Toby pressed his eyes closed and tried to force the images out of his head, but no matter how much he tried to picture the best case scenario, he was unable to. Once he finally got his eyes closed, he saw Lia'na lying on an altar covered in her own blood. The image jolted him back awake. He turned to see her sleeping on her side with her back to him. *It's no good,* he thought to himself, *I can't do this...*

Toby quietly rolled out of bed, put his pants back on, and threw on his heavy leather jacket. It was the middle of summer, but he was going to need it where he was going.

As he was about to leave, he noticed the Magnifica sitting on the table. Something told him he might need it, so he picked it up and flipped through the pages briefly. Though he wasn't sure, he thought he saw it shine with green sparkles for just a second.

Toby slipped the book into his jacket pocket and headed for the door. He took one last look at Lia'na. Her skin was now almost completely covered with the Ulium. Her neck, face, and parts of her back were still clear, but that was it. Her hair draped down so he couldn't see her face. Only a part of her long ear poked through the strands.

Toby felt a tear drop down his cheek, "Goodbye..."

He slipped out of the bedroom, down the hallway, and out the front door. Thanking his good luck that no one had noticed, he hit the ground running over to his garage. The sound of the heavy metal door rolling up made the motorcycle react. It flashed its headlight as Toby walked it, "We've got something we need to do."

The bike's motor purred in response.

"I hope you're ready, I can't guarantee we'll be coming back from this one."

The bike's motor revved again, signaling it was ready.

"All right, let's get going."

He hopped on the bike and road it slowly out of the garage. Toby looked back up at his condo, "Goodbye guys..."

The bike quickly picked up speed and disappeared into the night. As Toby sped away, he missed seeing the black specter hiding near his condo. Despite his best efforts to sneak away, his departure had not gone unseen. The creature smiled as the last lights from Toby's bike vanished in the distance.

XXIV

Toby rode on through the night. The only thing breaking through the blackness in front of him was the street lamps on I-95 heading north. It was an uneventful trip and the only cars he passed were large semis going the other way.

It didn't take him long before a white sign on the side of the road saying 'Welcome to New Hampshire' appeared. Toby remembered back to the last time that he'd traveled this way and began wishing he could go back in time, but as powerful as he was, that was one thing he couldn't do.

Another sign passed by for the Hampton Beach exit. Toby remembered what it was like going there. From early in the morning until late at night, there was always something to do. If everything worked out, he wanted to take Lia'na there. He had a feeling that she'd like it.

At long last, his exit finally came up. He pulled off of the highway on to exit 4, heading for Route 16. A toll booth stood at the end of the ramp. Toby stopped and received a ticket from the mechanical dispenser. He shoved it in his pocket and moved on.

As Toby entered Route 16, he said goodbye to civilization as the trees and mountains appeared ahead of him. His bike pulled up to another toll booth. Toby handed the ticket and the cash to the worker who looked him over for a moment, "Sweet ride."

"Thanks."

He then gunned the engine and sped away, headed further north. By then, Toby had already been on the road for an hour. He pulled over to make sure that he was heading the right way per Giselle's GPS. Once he had his bearings, the bike picked up speed again.

The sun began to rise as he turned onto Pinkham Notch Road. Toby looked at his watch in amazement. *My God, it's really 5am already?*

The bike's engine roared as it raced off down the deserted highway. He began to slow down when he reached a white sign that stated 'Mount Washington Auto Road.'

At this point, the sun had just cleared the horizon. Toby could see an open field and several small buildings ahead. He rode on past a large complex that looked like a ski lodge and beyond that, his last turn.

Toby's bike stopped before the turn. He looked up to see multiple dragons flying over the mountains. There was no way that he was going to be able to get past them unscathed. "At least I know I'm in the right place."

He revved the engine and prepared for action. Before he could move any further, a large black chopper appeared overhead and a familiar voice echoed from a built in speaker, "Mr. Tobias Arrigan, stay right where you are."

"The fuck?"

The motorcycle pulled over to the side near where the chopper was coming down. Toby looked down at it and yelled, "Hey, no, come on! Damn it!"

The chopper touched down and an irate looking pair jumped out. Gishan was furious, "Let me at him! I'm going to kick his ass! Leave us behind, will ya?"

Giselle nodded, "What's the big idea you two running off like this… wait... Toby... where is Lia'na?"

"What do you mean," Toby asked, "I left her at the apartment."

"She wasn't there when we woke up." Gishan replied. "We thought she was with you!"

A horrible feeling came over Toby as he looked towards the mountain, "No…"

"What?" Giselle asked. "Where is she?"

Toby closed his eyes and breathed heavily, "Don't ask me how I know… but they have her…"

"Alistair?"

Toby looked away without answering as Giselle looked up at the mountains, "Oh this is not good. If he has her, that's going to complicate things..."

"She's bait." Gishan added. "He did seem very interested in you Toby."

Toby clenched his jaw, "If he wants me, he's got me. I'm going in… I don't know how I'm going to get around those dragons but… This just became a rescue mission."

"Leave that to me," Giselle said smiling, "I've taken care of it."

Suddenly, three F/A-18E super hornets passed overhead. Toby watched them fly by in formation, "What the…"

"After we discovered you were gone, I called my bosses at the pentagon and convinced them to move up the strike. You weren't going to get through without help." Giselle replied. "The fighters are here to clear a path. Our commandos will be along later, so you have a small window to get in there."

Gishan nodded, "Yeah you might want to watch yourself on the way in Toby. There are a lot of baddies on the ground. I don't know if this chopper can get us in there."

Toby was too busy being worried about Lia'na, "Leave that one to me!"

Giselle nodded, "I'll see if there's a safe place near the landing zone where we can set down. We'll be right behind you, I promise. You have your cell?"

"Yes," Toby replied, "I'll stay in touch."

"You better, you're not doing this alone."

Toby nodded, "All right let's go. The more time we waste out here, the worse things probably are for Lia'na. We can't let her suffer in there."

The bike's engine purred as Toby looked over at the fighter jets moving in on the dragons. They flew in perfect formation as they neared their targets.

In the air, the lead fighter signaled, "Bakers 2 and 3, follow my lead and stay in tight."

The three fighters moved in on the large group of dragons flying over the gulf. Once they were in range, Baker 1 pushed the safety off of his trigger and pushed the red button underneath, "Baker 1, fox 1!"

The other two pilots responded in kind;

"Baker 2, fox 1."

"Baker 3, fox 1."

The fighters unleashed their payloads on the group of dragons. Three missiles escaped from under the wings of the fighters and flew towards their targets. They impacted on flying beasts and instantly exploded, knocking two dragons out of the sky. The rest of the group turned and headed after the fighters.

Baker 1 watched as the dragons began to charge, "Bakers 2 and 3, break off, and go evasive. See if you can't take some of them with you."

From the ground, Toby saw the sky battle unfold, "Looks like they've got the dragons' attention. That's our cue."

Toby placed his hand over the odometer on the chasse of his bike and closed his eyes, "Let's do this…"

The bike began to vibrate under him in response. The tires faded to white and began to glow. Gishan and Giselle backed away and got aboard the chopper. Giselle turned to the pilot, "Follow that bike."

The pilot looked at her oddly for a moment, "Ma'am?"

"Just trust me, you'll see."

"That's not a part of my mission, ma'am."

Giselle gave him an angry look, "Now listen you. Unless you want another attack on our cities, you'll follow my orders! That boy there is going to need our help, now follow him!"

The pilot sighed and pushed a few buttons as he prepared for takeoff. *The commander is going to have my ass for this...* he thought as the chopper took off.

Toby's bike revved its engine twice more as Toby leaned into it, "Here we go."

The tires on the bike screeched as they started spinning. Dust and small rocks kicked up as it finally jetted forward. The bike picked up speed and began to lift off of the pavement.

Toby watched as the ground got smaller and smaller underneath him. He quickly turned his attention back to flying to the cave. Before leaning forward again, he checked the GPS locator one more time and hit the gas to gain more speed.

Toby soon found himself flying through the thick of the dragon pack. Explosions erupted all around him like anti air flak. The jet fighters were doing the best they could to draw the dragons off so their people could slip in.

It looked like Toby was about to break through when three of the dragons broke off and came after him. One flew overhead, nearly hitting Toby as he ducked and veered downward. He focused all of his emotions into his hands and unleashed a ray of light on it.

Blood poured from the mighty beast as it roared mournfully and fell to its death. The second dragon came up from behind Toby and shot a stream of flame out of its mouth.

The bike broke left and tried to double back, but the dragon wasn't giving up. Toby tried firing light beams at it, but he couldn't get a clean shot. The dragon was slowly closing in.

Suddenly the third and final dragon attempted to hit Toby head on. Startled, Toby pulled back on the handle bars, causing the bike to pull up. He couldn't quite get high enough and his bike's tires impacted on the back of the dragon.

To his surprise, the tires reacted by glowing even more before they cut through the beast's plated skin. Toby looked back to see blood pouring out of the massive gash that he created and the dragon falling limply from the sky.

There was little time to celebrate as the third dragon was still bearing down on him. Toby fired three more shots and did a nose dive, but nothing seemed to work. He closed his eyes, ready for the end, when he heard machine gun fire in the distance.

Toby looked behind him to see the chopper firing everything it had at the dragon. Within moments, the third dragon also lost stability and fell to the ground. Inside the chopper, Gishan and Giselle cheered as the dragon fell out of the sky.

Gishan nodded, "One more down."

Toby turned back and focused on piloting his bike. He passed over another patch of trees, circled around Mount Washington at impressive speeds, and brought his bike down where the map showed the cave to be. In the woods he could see large creatures roaming around like the ones he'd seen in the city.

Not wanting to get caught, Toby held his bike high enough to keep from being seen until he found the entrance. The cave was in a stony clearing where, strangely enough, there were no monsters present. He slowly brought the bike down until it hit the ground. The tires screeched as they once again had traction.

Toby stopped his bike right at the entrance and pulled out his cell phone. Luckily, there was still one bar of reception. He quickly punched in Gishan's number. The phone rang for a moment before Gishan picked up, "We see you Toby."

"Be careful," Toby replied, "this is way too easy. It's got to be a trap."

Gishan paused for a moment, "We'll be down in a moment. We're going to check out the area. If you don't want to wait, go ahead in, we'll meet you inside."

"All right, see you in there."

XXV

Toby parked his bike behind the stone formation at the entrance of the cave. The bike revved its engine one last time before it powered down. Toby put his right hand on the odometer, "Thanks for everything, old friend. I'll see you when all of this over... I hope. For now, keep quiet."

The cave stood about ten feet high from floor to ceiling and was so dark that he could not see more than a few feet in. Toby took in a deep breath and stepped inside. He was almost immediately engulfed in darkness.

Unable to see, Toby flicked his wrist causing it to light up. His hand illuminated enough of the cave to continue going forward. Stalactites and stalagmites were everywhere, water could be heard dripping in the distance, and the entire place reeked like a moldy cloth that had been left damp for too long.

Toby covered his nose as he continued moving forward. The cave's path was long and winding, and it was too dangerous to move too quickly. As he rounded the nearby corner, he came to a large room that looked like it had been man-made. The walls were smooth and lined with torches.

The room was almost completely empty and looked like it had been abandoned in a hurry. At the far back of the chamber stood an altar, which sat atop a staircase that had been carved out of the cave.

Toby almost screamed when he saw Lia'na lying on top of it, wearing a white dress. She appeared to be either drugged or unconscious. She wasn't moving and didn't respond to his voice. Toby's heart froze and he became filled with rage. If she was dead, the world would soon know his pain.

A sudden sound behind Toby made him jump. He turned around with his hands glowing, ready to strike. "Easy there buddy," a familiar voice said through the darkness, "kill us and it'll be you alone in there."

Gishan and Giselle appeared out of the tunnel. Toby nodded, "Thank God it didn't take you guys too long to catch up."

Toby turned back and pointed at the altar, "Look…"

Giselle's eyes widened, "Lia'na!"

"She looks incredibly pale… but I can't see any injuries." Gishan replied. "Except for the Ulium… has it spread since last night?"

Toby nodded, "Yeah, it looks like it… that's not good. I don't know how much longer she has."

He couldn't wait any longer, "I'm going in."

Gishan grabbed his arm before he could charge in, "Whoa, hold on buddy. Not without help."

"What did you have in mind?

At that moment, Giselle pulled a pair of MP5 submachine guns out of her back pack, "A little old-fashioned insurance. Let's not fall into a trap."

She handed one to Gishan and then pulled out her Glock sidearm and handed it to Toby, "This gun has been with me since training. It's literally never been out of my sight. I want it back."

Toby nodded as he took the gun from her and slid it into his pocket, "I doubt I'll need it, but thanks."

Gishan nodded, "All right, let's do this."

The three of them charged into the room. Toby proceeded into the chamber with Giselle and Gishan flanking him close to the walls. To their relief, there was no one in the room. All appeared to be quiet.

Gishan moved cautiously as he stepped closer to the altar. A squeaking sound near his feet startled him. He whirled around without thinking and opened fire on the entrance to the room.

Gishan had never held an automatic carbine before and didn't know how to control it. The gun sprayed more bullets then he had originally intended. Giselle ran up next to him and grabbed the gun, "Good job, lover! If they didn't know we were here before, they do now!"

She snatched the gun from his hands, "I think that's enough fun for you…"

Toby ignored them and quickly ran up the staircase. He reached the altar and quickly untied Lia'na's arms. Her wrists were red, no doubt from struggling against the rope, but weren't cut.

The moment she was freed, he called to her, "Lia'na, wake up, come on, we've got to get moving!"

No response.

Toby frantically untied the rest of her restraints and quickly checked her for a pulse. Feeling her skin as he pressed his finger against the back of her wrist, he began to worry, "She's ice cold…"

Giselle quickly walked up behind him, "Is she alive?"

"I don't know." Toby replied as he gently pressed on her neck and wrist and started to panic. "Giselle, I can't find a pulse!"

Giselle dropped to one knee and leaned in over Lia'na's head so her right ear was an inch away from Lia'na's mouth and nose, "She's breathing. I can hear it."

Toby's sense of relief was fleeting. Giselle stepped back and shook her head, "Just barely though. She's not going to survive long like this."

As Toby continued to searching for more signs of life, he couldn't help but feel like Lia'na was somehow being held there. It was as though an unseen force was keeping her bound to that area.

As Toby's eyes blinked, her appearance became momentarily obscured, as though he were looking at her through flame. He continued blinking and focused his mind. The obscurity appeared again, enveloping her like a cocoon.

Gishan kept his back turned with his fists at the ready in case anything came at them, "What's happening to her?"

Toby shook his head, "I can't explain it, but I think she's been cursed. It's like some spell is holding her in this state, slowly sucking the life out of her."

"But why?"

Giselle looked at the position she'd been left in, "It looks like some kind of sacrificial ritual"

"That doesn't make any sense." Toby replied. "Elf blood and life energy doesn't strengthen the diamond. If this is a ritual, it would only weaken the Lux Mundi."

"Alistair isn't known for his humanity. Maybe he just wanted her to suffer?"

"It doesn't matter." Toby said, dismissing the theory. "She'll die if we don't do something."

Gishan looked over the altar a few times, "What can we do?"

Toby let out a sigh and knelt on the altar next to her, "There may be something I can do. I'm going to try to break Alistair's hold on her."

"Are you sure that's a good idea?" Gishan asked with a worried look. "How do we know Alistair hasn't set up some kind of trap? Breaking his hold could kill her."

"She'll die if I don't do it." Toby replied in a frantic tone. "Her body is ice and she's barely breathing."

Giselle nodded, "I agree. We don't have any other choice, we have to risk it. –Toby, do whatever you have to."

Toby balled his fists and clenched them hard at his side. His eyes closed as he focused his thoughts. He shut out his fears and focused. His mind recreated the altar and placed Lia'na's body on it. He then pictured the cocoon over her.

In his thoughts, Toby began to create cracks in the cocoon using beams of light. Once he had sufficiently compromised it, he raised his fists above his head and brought them down hard on Lia'na's body. He clenched his teeth and drew in as much strength as he could.

Giselle gasped as it looked like Toby was about to hit Lia'na, but his fists stopped a mere inch over her body as though they had impacted on something. There was a blast of cold wind and what looked like particles of clear goo went flying through the air away from her.

Toby knew that he wasn't finished yet. In his mind, he pictured the lungs inside of Lia'na's chest. He reached into them with his thoughts and filled them with air. The lungs slowly expanded like balloons and quickly contracted.

Lia'na gasped as she took a deep breath and let it out again, but she made no other movements. Toby opened his eyes and quickly placed them back on her wrist and neck.

After a few moments, Toby could feel a pulse. A sense of relief came over his face as her body began to warm up. Seconds went by as the color returned to her skin and her eyes opened, "Ta arshana…"

Lia'na's features slowly began to animate and she started moving. He rubbed her hand, trying to warm her up, "How do you feel?"

"Weak." She replied, struggling to right herself. "I think I was drugged. I didn't even have a chance to fight back. I'm sorry Toby."

"You did nothing wrong. We're dealing with powerful beings. It wasn't your fault."

She slowly sat up and looked at her hands. The Ulium was darkening and continuing to spread, "It's taking me Toby. I don't know how much time I have left."

"You have to fight! Fight and fight hard, we don't have much further to go."

Lia'na slowly sat up, "You're right… we still have a job to do."

She carefully placed her bare feet on the ground and tried to stand. Her legs were weak and quivering. The moment she put weight on them, her knees buckled under her.

Toby grabbed her by the waste to keep her from falling, "This isn't good…"

Giselle also knelt down to try to help, "The Ulium is making her weak. We need to hurry."

"I'm fine." Lia'na replied. "Please trust me, I can hold my own."

Lia'na took a few minutes before forcing her legs to hold her up. She balanced herself and took a couple of steps, "Okay, let's go."

"Are you sure?" Toby asked.

"Trust me, piele. I'm fine."

"All right," Toby replied, not at all convinced, "let's move on. We need to get to the diamond."

"Good, let's go."

The group gave each other worried looks as Lia'na fought hard to keep herself steady. Behind the altar was another small hallway that was lit with torches. The floor was adorned with a beautiful red rug that had gold tassels along the edges. The walls were draped in purple tapestries and ancient weapons mounted on display stands.

Gishan eyed some of the décor as they walked by, "Wow, this is incredible, it's like a timeline of war."

He passed by the first collection and pointed, "Look, these are weapons from the Alliance time period, and look over here… ancient Roman spears and shields."

When they passed by a wall with a hammer and an axe on it, Gishan couldn't take his eyes off of them, "Now those are something…"

Lia'na shook her head with an evil smile, "A dwarf picking out the axe and hammer over all other weapons, talk about reinforcing stereotypes."

"Oh funny!"

Lia'na chuckled weakly, "Consider it payback for all the sharpy comments."

"Touché," Toby chimed in, "she got you Gishan!"

"Yeah, yeah," Gishan replied, "okay, I'll give you that one."

The group proceeded deeper into the cave. The further they went, the more modern the weapons on the wall became. Next in line were swords from the early middle ages which then gave way to arquebuses and flintlocks. After those came repeating rifles and bolt actions with bayonets attached.

Toby eyed a rather impressive shrine in the next display, "Wow… this guy had a serious crush on the Nazis."

A scowl appeared on Lia'na's lips as she spoke, "I could believe that… In addition to trying to create a master race of humans, the Nazis wanted everything they viewed either as a threat or inferior wiped out. Jews, gypsies… elves that came out of hiding, we were all a threat to their plans."

"Mad men for sure."

They quickly moved on to the next image which wasn't much better. On this wall was a tribute to Joseph Stalin, and then came Chairmen Mao, Ho Chi Minh, and Ayatollah Khomeini, all the way down to Osama Bin Laden.

Finally, they arrived at the biggest shrine which was seated at the end of the hallway. It was a massive mural that looked like something Michelangelo would have done. The difference was that it was much darker and perverted. A very familiar likeness of Alistair was in the forefront of the painting standing over a pile of corpses.

"Man oh man, this guy is seriously in love with himself." Gishan said in a sickened voice.

"If not himself, he's certainly in love with his plans." Lia'na replied darkly. "Look at the corpses at his feet, those are all elves."

Toby looked down at Alistair's feet and studied the mutilated corpses. Sure enough they all had pointed ears. It was a disgusting display and Toby didn't even want to imagine what it must have been like to paint all of this.

Giselle carefully studied the impressive collection as they moved, "These weapons look authentic. Where do you suppose he got them all?"

"He's been alive for thousands of years." Toby replied. "He's probably collected them from various battlefields over time."

Toby had finally had his fill of looking at these grotesque shrines of corruption, "Let's move on, we've got a lot to do."

Lia'na nodded as the group moved through the next doorway into a massive amphitheater. It was carved out of black stone and just as beautifully decorated as the previous chamber, but here the carvings and designs were ancient dwarven.

There were symbols everywhere in a form of Elvish that Lia'na recognized from the Magnifica. Just as in the room before, the walls were adorned with ancient Alliance weapons, including metal bows, swords, and shields.

At the back of the room stood a ten foot tall orange diamond that had cracks all throughout it. The cracks divided it into sections and showed where the elves of old had shattered it. Toby did notice a small chip was missing near the top, presumably the shard that Lia'na had been wearing around her neck.

As they moved closer, Lia'na cried out and collapsed on the ground, "Toby, help!"

Toby grabbed her and pulled her back, "What's wrong?"

Lia'na looked at him as the red lines began approaching the edges of her face, "It hurts... I can't get any close to the Lux Mundi. My skin felt like it was on fire."

Toby pulled her further back and laid her down on the opposite side of the room. Once he had positioned her so that she was reasonably comfortable, he pulled the Magnifica out of his jacket and handed it to her, "Here, this is yours by right. Hang on to it for safe keeping."

Lia'na took the book and nodded. She leaned in and kissed him on the cheek, "Good luck."

Gishan and Giselle knelt down next to her. Toby placed his hand on Lia'na's cheek and turned to Gishan, "Stay with her, I'm going to finish this."

Gishan nodded, "She's in good hands buddy. Go for it!"

Toby turned around and slowly walked towards the giant diamond. His eyes fixated on it as though he were hypnotized. He only managed to take five steps towards the giant stone before a black cloud appeared in front of him, blocking his path. "Your powers have gained strength, Tobias," a thundering voice echoed through the room, "but you are not strong enough yet."

"Alistair…"

The dark cloud faded away, revealing two men in black robes standing between him and the Lux Mundi. Alistair lowered the hood of his robe and smiled, "It's good to see you, my boy. I have been waiting for you. I trust you have had ample time to consider my offer?"

"I have..." Toby replied, "and I've decided that I'm not going to help you destroy this world."

"So you're just going to let your father die then?"

"He's already dead. He has been since he left me and my mother!"

"So you'd leave him to his fate... he'd be so disappointed. You're not like him at all."

"That's not a bad thing." Lia'na forced out. "Toby is a good person, much too good to fall for your lies! He's not like his father at all."

Toby turned back to see Lia'na sitting up with a piercing look in her eyes. The skin on her face was now completely covered by the Ulium and her breathing became labored. The red lines ran across her nose, around her cheeks, and across her forehead, but there was still a detectable level of strenght in her.

The second cloaked figure reacted to Lia'na by stepping forward, "That's enough out of you, whore!"

Alistair raised his hand for the man to step back, but it was too late. Toby recognized the voice and clenched his jaw, "I don't believe it... Aritem?"

The second hooded figure pulled back his robes, revealing the man Toby had fought to earn Lia'na's freedom, "It's been a while, thief."

"Not nearly long enough." Toby snorted. "First hitting defenseless women, and now aiding a madman in his dreams for world domination. You have fallen far."

Lia'na pulled herself back further towards the wall, "Aritem, why? You know what that diamond did to our people. You know what bringing it back means! Look at me! Do you think you won't suffer the same fate?"

"I am positive..." Aritem replied.

"Enough," Toby shouted, "I don't care about your reasons, and I don't care about power."

Toby turned and looked Alistair in the eye , "I couldn't care less about them."

Alistair laughed, "But you seem to care for that sickly elf? Why, she'll be dead in a few hours anyway."

Toby turned and looked at Aritem, "You cared for her once, so much so that you were willing to do anything to marry her. Now you're just going to watch her die?"

"She rejected me for a human." Aritem replied. "Besides, I have an understanding with the enchanter who cursed the Lux Mundi with the Ulium... the true master who controls it."

Toby stepped back in shock, "Alistair... you... you're responsible for the Ulium?"

"Correct," Alistair replied, "I couldn't allow the Lux Mundi to be destroyed, so I placed defenses around it. Those elves passed through them one by one. When I realized that the diamond was about to be destroyed, I enchanted it with a particularly nasty curse."

Tears fell down Lia'na's cheeks, "So to protect your powers, you killed off most of my people?"

"Not that I owe a sharpy any explanation," Alistair replied, "but I tried to warm them not to proceed with their plan. They went in knowing full well what the Ulium would do to them if they destroyed the diamond. They chose to take that upon themselves anyway."

"What you've done is nothing short of genocide!"

"Maybe," Alistair replied, "but my hand was forced. Still, it did pretty much eliminate the biggest threat to the Lux Mundi. Now there are too few of them and they are too scattered to stop me now."

"But your plan failed," Giselle spoke up, "the Ulium was cured. The remaining elves were saved and are beginning to regain their numbers."

"Ah the FBI agent who has been a consistent thorn in my side," Alistair said in a half annoyed tone, "I've wanted to meet you for a long time. To answer your question, their petty little cure has solved nothing. It's simply postponed the illness. A generation or two will live on without the disease, but it is still in their blood, mutating. Eventually, it'll be strong enough to overpower this new treatment."

Giselle stood up with her MP5 and pointed it at Alistair, intent on shooting him. Before she could pull the trigger, the barrel of the gun blew up in her face, knocking her backwards. She was unharmed, but the guns were completely destroyed.

Alistair shook his head, "You people... No matter how much times change, you're still completely dependent on a few pieces of metal..."

A loud cry cut Alistair off as everyone turned to look at Lia'na. The Ulium was spreading even faster now. The red lines on her face and arms grew darker, her breathing accelerated and became labored, and she began to tremble. She felt her chest seize and began coughing.

Giselle ran her hand over Lia'na's forehead, feeling the severity of her fever. She was about to try to move her, when she noticed that the elf's hands were covered in blood from her lungs. "Oh God. –Toby, she's burning up. Whatever you're going to do, do it now!"

Toby turned his attention back to Alistair and thrust his hands down to his side. They flared up, causing a pair of plasma bolts to appear in each palm, "You're in my way..."

Alistair began to laugh, "Are you going to kill me? The arrogance! I have lived for tens of thousands of years. I have more history in my memory than the Library of Congress and the Library of Alexandria combined. Are you are going to put an end to all of that, all over that one insignificant elf? You'll risk your own life for the mere hours she has left? One flick of my wrist, and I could cut that down to minutes."

"You killed my uncle... you cost me my family... don't you let her die! Don't you dare let her die!"

"What, save that elf? Are you jesting? I would sooner grind the Lux Mundi to dust then save one, especially a female. No, I won't allow them to rebuild their race so they can threaten me again."

Toby thrust his hands forward, sending his plasma bolts at Alistair. The ancient enchanter simply put up his hand, blocking the attack, "You can't beat me, Tobias. Even if you were powerful enough, it would take you longer than she has."

"All right Alistair..." Toby said darkly. "I'll make a deal with you."

"A deal?" Alistair asked in surprise. "All right, I'm always open to an equitable solution. I'll entertain an offer."

"No!" Lia'na cried out, knowing what was coming next.

"My powers, for her life," he said in a near whisper, "heal her, and my powers are yours."

Lia'na struggled, but couldn't get to her feet, "Toby no, you can't do that!"

Alistair smiled, "You definitely have at least some of your father in you, honorable to the last. That you would be willing to give up everything to save someone else, it's just like him. He made the same deal to prevent me from killing your mother."

Toby clenched his jaw harder, "Enough talking, take the deal or leave it!"

At that moment, Lia'na felt the Magnifica began to tremble in her hands. She quickly opened it to the page that was sparkling. *What is this...?*

The smile disappeared from Alistair's face and was replaced by an apologetic look, "Such nobility... unfortunately it's wasted here. The Ulium was a dark conjure, sealed with spirit energy. Those are permanent; once they've been cast, they can't be uncast.... but perhaps if we work together, we can discover a solution..."

"Toby, he's lying!" Lia'na suddenly called out. "It says here that a dark conjure can be undone, but only if the caster is killed. Once he's dead, the damage that the Ulium has done should undo itself!"

Alistair looked down at the dying elf in shock, "The Magnifica... So it still exists. How has it come to your possession?"

Toby shook his head as he took another menacing step towards Alistair, "That doesn't matter now. Answers won't be of any benefit to someone who is about to die!"

"So this is what it comes down to then..." Alistair said as his lips curved into a sinister grin, "Very good, I had partially hoped it would go this way. It's been years since I had a good fight, you better not disappoint me!"

Toby and Alistair unleashed their energy on each other. Lia'na watched in fear as Toby's beam of light connected with Alistair's beam of darkness. Both seemed to struggle to maintain their power.

After a brief standoff, Alistair broke his beam and used his powers to pick up nearby rocks and swirl them around himself. The rocks took the form of a giant creature that towered over Toby. The massive titan slammed the ground, creating a large crater in the floor. Aritem jumped back, protecting the diamond.

Toby focused his energy, drew all of the moisture out of the cave, and focused it forward. A wave crashed over the stone giant and encased it in a massive sphere of swirling water, corroding away the stone.

Alistair found himself unable to breathe as the stone armor was slowly corroded away. Once it was gone, Alistair waved his hand, causing the sphere to explode. The water blinded Toby for a moment as Alistair conjured his next enchantment. He knelt down and touched the ground. An army of diamondback rattlesnakes appeared in front of him and slithered towards Toby, ready to strike.

This was a little out of Toby's element; he hadn't even tried conjuring anything like a living creature before. He didn't even know that it was possible. Acting quickly, he cleared his thoughts and tried to decide what could counter this, but what could he summon that would stand a chance against an army of volatile rattlesnakes?

Then Toby remembered a lesson from one of his environmental science classes and thought back to a video talking about survival in the wild. He now had his answer. The young enchanter focused his mind and closed his eyes, not even sure that his plan would work.

A soft digging sound in front of the snakes broke the silence. Small mounds appeared and out popped eight mongooses. They attacked the rattlesnakes with incredible speed, grabbing the reptiles by their heads and shaking them to death.

As the snakes stopped struggling, the mongooses pulled them back into the holes they had created and disappeared. Toby smiled, "What else you got?"

Alistair was clearly impressed by Toby's skill as he considered his position, "I see you have made good use of the Magnifica. It's clearly enhanced your powers. I'll be sure to put it to good use once you're dead."

Alistair twirled his arms in an odd pattern. Out of the wall came another stone giant that quickly rearranged its appearance and turned into a Minotaur. Toby stepped back in fear as this massive beast came forward and charged at him.

Toby was able to dodge out of the way, but he wasn't quick enough to completely clear out of the beast's path. The Minotaur's arm clipped his leg, causing Toby to fall to the ground in extreme pain. He tried to get back to his feet, but his leg wouldn't hold him.

Debris fell from the ceiling as the Minotaur crashed into the wall. It turned around and geared up for another charge, Toby closed his eyes and focused as hard as he could. His thoughts dwelled on his strongest connections. He thought about that night with Lia'na, the years he spent with his friends and his mother's love.

An odd creature with an eagle's head, wings, a lion's body, and a dragon's tail appeared in front of him. Gishan and Giselle both looked at the creature oddly. Gishan stood over Lia'na to make sure she didn't get hurt by all of the falling debris caused by the Minotaur, "What the hell is that thing?"

Alistair's eyes widened as he stepped back, feeling a twinge of fear for the first time in thousands of years, "It can't be... That's a griffon! How is this possible? They're supposed to be a myth. I've never known an enchanter powerful enough to summon one!"

The griffon stood between its master and the Minotaur, and let out a blood curdling roar. The Minotaur was unshaken by this and attempted another charge. As it ran forward, the griffon jumped on its back and scratched viciously.

The Minotaur let out a mournful cry and fell to the ground. There was a loud thud as both creatures struck the cave floor. Everyone momentarily lost their footing as a result.

The impact caused more debris to fall from the ceiling. One large rock struck Alistair's arm, slicing it open. Intense pain shot through him, but he didn't cry out. Instead he cradled his bad arm and ignored the pain.

The griffon lunged forward and grabbed the Minotaur by the neck and began to shake it. The griffon jerked its head to the side, causing a loud crack and the Minotaur's lifeless head hit the ground. The griffon circled its prey for a moment before turning around and heading back to its master. It gave a nod of approval as it stood before its master.

Toby finally got to his feet by leaning against the nearby wall and scratched the back of the griffon's neck. It purred appreciatively as Toby pet it. After a brief moment of rest, Toby nodded and whispered into its ear, "Thank you..."

The griffon stepped back and lowered its head as it disappeared. Toby turned and looked at Alistair. They were both tiring, and breathing heavily.

Alistair smiled and spoke between gasps of air, "You've become more powerful than I ever thought possible for someone so young. Clearly, I underestimated you. You didn't disappoint me, Toby, I'll give you that. It's too bad that this now has to end."

Alistair once again thrust his arms forward and unleashed a massive beam of darkness against Toby. The young enchanter saw it coming, but he was too weak to counter it. His injury wasn't anything bad, but he was still dazed.

Instead of a beam, Toby summoned a shield of light to protect himself from the blast and hoped that Alistair would tire out. This didn't happen however, and Toby's shield was slowly getting overpowered. Gishan saw this and tried to run to his friend's side, but Giselle grabbed him, "No!"

"Let go," Gishan screamed, "Alistair's going to kill him!"

"Don't you think I know that? I want to help him too, but Alistair could kill us with a single thought. There is nothing we can do to help Toby now, this is his fight."

Gishan struggled under her grip, but his stubby dwarven arms and legs were just not enough to force her off of his back. All he could do was sit by and watch as Toby's shield collapsed little by little.

Aritem smiled. He was sure that the man who stole his betrothed was about to die. A loud thundering noise behind him ruined his revelry and made him turn to see what was going on. To his horror, the Lux Mundi began to change color. Instead of orange, the diamond was now glowing bright red.

Aritem screamed to Alistair, "Master, look!"

Alistair's eyes went wide as he saw the diamond, "You? Stay out of this!"

As the diamond's color turned, the power in Alistair's blast died down. Little by little it began to vanish as the Lux Mundi glowed brightly. Alistair looked at his hands, "This can't be... how do you still have that kind of power?"

He thrust them forward again, but nothing happened. His magic would no longer obey his commands. Toby took in a deep breath. He had no idea what was going on, but it was in his favor, "It's over Alistair. You've lived too long."

Alistair sneered, "Do you realize what you're doing? If you kill me and you destroy the Lux Mundi, then your powers will vanish as well! Are you really willing to give all of that up for the brief lifetime you will have with that elf? You could live forever!"

"I'd take a few minutes with her over a thousand of them watching you destroy the world. You're finished!"

Alistair crossed his arms and closed his eyes, "Fool..."

Toby thrust his hands forward repeatedly, causing small bolts of energy to leave his body. Each bolt impacted on Alistair, creating an explosion of smoke. Alistair made effort to defend himself and did not scream.

One after another, Toby hurled long bolts of light at his opponent. Alistair's world began to go black as his spirit fled its broken body when a bolt hit him in the chest. He looked down at his injury and fell backwards. As his body hit the ground, it immediately turned to dust.

Toby once again collapsed under his own weight. Aritem looked at Alistair's remains in anger. All of his hopes were dashed, "Master... no..."

He then turned and glared at Toby, "You... you took everything from me! It's all gone thanks to you!"

Toby fought through the pain and returned Aritem's gaze, "At least your people will survive now. Don't you care about that at all?"

"I would have found a way to save them once Alistair had served his purpose. I would have made them strong again."

"You would have had to defeat him first. If you thought your plan had any chance, you're a bigger fool than I thought."

Aritem pulled a knife and charged at Toby, "I'll kill you for this!"

Toby was too tired to try to fight back and he could not get away or even raise his arms. Instead he watched Aritem come at him. There was nothing that he could do.

Aritem made on long dash at Toby and brought the knife up over his head, ready to deliver a deathblow, "I'll kill you, and then I'll finish off your little whore!"

There was a sudden faint screeching sound as an arrow appeared in Aritem's chest. The arrow was thick, dark wood with a red tail. He dropped the knife and wheezed. A second one struck him in his left shoulder. He staggered backwards as he looked up to see where the arrows had come from.

Lia'na was standing on the other side of the room, holding one of the ancient bows and a quiver full of arrows. There was no longer any sign of the Ulium on her skin.

Toby looked at her with a smile, "Lia'na... you're okay!"

Aritem clenched his jaw as he staggered backwards, "You..."

She grabbed another arrow, grasped it between her middle and right fingers, and drew it back along the bow, "Go to hell Aritem, maybe a demon will find you a fitting mate!"

She released her hold on the arrow and let it strike Aritem in the forehead. The shock sent him flying backwards on to the Lux Mundi. Blood began to drip out of his wounds down onto the diamond. Everyone watched as the red color in the diamond faded to black.

Toby breathed a sigh of relief, "It's over..."

Lia'na dropped the bow and ran over to Toby, "Ta arshana, you did it!"

Toby looked up at her and ran his hands over her skin which had returned to its original color, completely free of the Ulium, "Lia'na... I love you."

Toby slowly stood up, and before Lia'na could say anything, he took her hand, "As your traditions demand, I have won the day, and hereby claim the betrothal rights granted to me under Elven law."

Lia'na smiled and nodded, "Te complicai cine' nira masan. I recognize your claim, and accept being bound to you, on my honor."

As they approached, Gishan shook his head, "Honor binding himself to that elf, and only after what, six months?"

Giselle shrugged, "Sometimes when you know, you just know. Besides, I've studied Elven law. A betrothal in the Elven tradition doesn't mean the same thing to humans. It's not even an engagement."

"I just hope he knows that."

Giselle rolled her eyes, "Oh will you shut up and stop spoiling the moment. They've earned this several times over."

Toby and Lia'na held each other tightly and embraced in a warm kiss. Gishan and Giselle turned their backs until the young couple was finished. When they finally released each other, Gishan smirked, "So an elf using a bow and arrows huh? Yeah, that's not being stereotypical at all."

Lia'na smiled, "Touché, Gishan."

At that moment, the Lux Mundi flickered white and then back to black. It did it again and again as the group looked on. Toby's eyes narrowed, "What do you suppose that means?"

Lia'na closed her eyes as the flickering sped up. Toby looked at her and noticed that she was smiling, "What is it?"

"Someone wants to talk to you. Go, touch the diamond and have a few last words before we leave."

Toby sighed and turned to the Lux Mundi. The flickering and flashes of light slowed as he walked up and stood in front of the diamond. He held his breath for a moment as his hands came up in front of his face. Slowly, he touched the smooth surface of diamond.

As Toby's fingers pressed against it, his eyes closed and mild warmth came over his body. There was a bright flash and suddenly his felt like he was speeding down the highway on his motorcycle.

Toby opened his eyes and found himself standing at Revere Beach, only it wasn't Revere beach at all. The buildings and layout were clearly Revere, but the sand looked like ground up bits of gold and silver, the water was sapphire blue and almost completely transparent, and the waves crashing on the shore made no sound. Though it was clearly night, the moon lit up the seen so that it was almost as bright as day.

Toby was fairly certain that he was nowhere near home anymore. The stars were wrong, the physics of environment were wrong, everything was wrong. He looked around briefly before an odd looking entity appeared behind him. At first it was only a blur, but it slowly began taking the shape of a human.

Before Toby knew what was happening, he was staring at a man who looked much like himself, except older and less cleanly shaven. The unknown man gave Toby a half smile, "Hello boy, do you know who I am?"

"I… think so, Dad?"

The man nodded, "It's been a long time son. I haven't seen you since you were a baby… since the day I left you and your mother."

Toby had trouble looking him in the eye. He remained silent as his father spoke, "But if you're here now, then that means that you defeated Alistair."

"I did…"

Toby's father sat down in the sand as he spoke, "I knew eventually Alistair would have to pay the piper."

"Why didn't you? Why go along with his plans?"

His father looked up at him sympathetically, "I had no choice. It was either I hand over my powers to Alistair or he would have killed you."

"What about after that? You befriended him, you helped him repair the diamond, and you made a mess out of everything! Uncle Jake was killed and my girlfriend could have died while we were cleaning up after you."

"I know boy… I messed up. I guess after so many years away from you and your mother, I just lost myself."

There was a brief silence when neither of them spoke. Toby had something he'd wanted to say for a long time, but had trouble spitting it out. He finally forced it, knowing his time was limited, "Dad… I… I hate you."

"I know, boy. I guess I should have expected that. I wasn't there for you and instead went off on my own mad quest for power."

He looked up at his son, who was standing over him with his arms crossed and eyes closed. Toby appeared deeply saddened by his words, but his father knew that they had to be said. There was no point in trying to justify it, so his father didn't bother, "I know I don't have any right to ask, but can you sit down with me for a little while? I'd like to hear about your life."

Toby was about to tell him off, but he knew that this was the only chance he'd get to spend any time with his old man. He wasn't sure he wanted to, but for his father's sake, he sat down next to him on the soft sand.

"Did your mother ever remarry?"

"No, she died when I was three. Uncle Jacob raised me."

The man clearly didn't know that the woman he loved was dead, "I always thought I'd find a way out of here to see her again, but I guess now that you're here, I'll be able to do so."

Refusing to let it get to him, Toby's father put it on the back burner to deal with later as his time with his son was limited, "So, do you still have my old bike? I asked your mother to make sure that you got it."

"Yes. I spent two years restoring it. You should see it."

"Wish I could, I miss feeling the wind on my face and the sound of the engine. She was a fine bike."

"She is that, although I just recently found out about her special abilities."

His father laughed, "Yeah it comes out when it wants to. Honestly I wasn't sure it would respond to you, but I'm glad it did. I remember how it used to scare your mother."

He looked at his son with a curious gaze, "So what about you, a girlfriend huh?"

"Yeah, her name's Lia'na."

"Pretty name. What's she like?"

"Well... she's an elf."

"That so? Your uncle was really enamored with an elf-girl back in the day. This was back before elves were granted asylum and given equal rights, so it was even more scandalous. She was very cute though."

"That was Lia'na's mother. Uncle Jake said Lia'na looks just like her."

"You're kidding?"

"No."

"Of all the odd coincidences... That is pretty funny. She must be pretty."

"She's beautiful."

"Smart and fun?"

"Yup."

"Does she like you?"

"I think so." Toby replied sarcastically.

"Good. As long as you have someone who cares about you, it's the most important thing. Treat her well Toby. You never know how much time you'll have with her."

"That was a hard-learned lesson."

"Yeah... Yeah I guess it was."

The two of them sat quietly for a little while watching stars shoot by as the water rolled up silently on the beach. The horizon was a beautiful blue and purple. Toby wished more than anything that he could show it to Lia'na though he knew it wasn't possible, "Dad..."

"Yes son?"

Toby didn't want to say anything because he didn't know how his father would react, "You know I have to destroy the Lux Mundi... right?"

"Yes, I know. I always knew this day would come. It's too dangerous to be left unchecked."

"What's going to happen to you?"

"I'll move on." His father replied. "It's about time too."

"You'll die, you mean."

"I died long ago. Part of me went the day I left you and your mother. The rest went when I merged with the Lux Mundi. My spirit has been trapped here ever since. Believe me, you'll be doing me a favor."

Toby looked down at the sand around his legs without saying anything. His father looked over, "So what's your plan then, elf's blood?"

"No. First off, too many elf lives have been lost. I wouldn't do that. Plus that doesn't destroy the Lux Mundi, it just shatters it. That's not good enough."

"Well then you need to destroy it in a way that no one would be able to rebuild it. How are you planning on doing that?"

"The sun." Toby replied. "I'm going to launch what's left of the diamond into the sun. It's the only way to be sure that its evil is gone forever."

"It sounds like you thought of everything. Son, we don't have much time. Do it, save the world, save Lia'na... save yourself."

"I will, I'll set you free, I promise."

They both stood up and shook hands, looking at each other closely. "Toby... I'm not really one for goodbyes... I just want you to know... I'm very proud of you. You succeeded where I failed, and now you are going to finish what those who came before you started."

"Thanks... Dad." Toby replied.

As they shook hands, neither one wanted to let go. Eventually, Toby's father pulled him into a hug. It only lasted a moment, but Toby's father managed to get out one last thought before he vanished, "I love ya, boy."

"I know dad... I know."

XXVI

Toby began walking back the way he came until the beautiful scenery began to fade. As seconds passed, Toby found himself back in the cave, surrounded by his friends. As he pulled his hand away from the diamond, Lia'na looked into his eyes, "Did you see him?"

"Yeah, my father is in there."

"Really?" Gishan asked. "Can we get him out?"

"No, there is no way. His body no longer exists" Toby replied.

"He gave himself to the Lux Mundi, and there is no going back after that…" Lia'na said sympathetically. "I'm sorry ta arshana. I wish there was something we could do."

"No, he made his decisions, and now it's time for me to make mine... I'm going to set him free."

Giselle took a step forward smiled as she spoke, "Do whatever you have to do. We're all with you on this one."

At that moment, they heard a loud cracking sound overhead and a small amount of sand and debris crashed down nearby. Another piece followed, and another soon after that.

Gishan backed up a little, "The cave is coming down…"

Lia'na nodded, "With the combined power of Alistair and the Lux Mundi gone, there is nothing holding it together. We don't have long."

"All of you get out." Toby said firmly. "This is something I have to do alone. Get out of here, save yourselves."

"Absolutely not. I'm not going anywhere."

Lia'na turned to Gishan and Giselle, "But you two need to leave, now!"

"Not a chance." Gishan insisted.

"Piele. Toby fought so hard for all of us. I'm staying because it is my right under Elven law, but the rest of you need to leave now. Don't let everything Toby did for us go to waste, piele get out of here."

Giselle looked her in the eye, "Are you sure?"

"Yes." Toby insisted before Lia'na could speak. "Please go and take Lia'na too!"

Giselle nodded as she grabbed Gishan. She tried to grab Lia'na as well, but Lia'na saw her hand coming and slapped it away, "No!"

"Lia'na, listen to me..." Toby tried to say.

"No you listen Toby," she interrupted, "you did so much for me, so now I'm going to see this through to the end. Te arshana ni and I'm not leaving!"

Toby sighed and nodded at Giselle to leave. Giselle pulled hard on Gishan. He tried to fight back, but Giselle was too strong, "Let go of me, I'm not going anywhere!"

Giselle pulled even harder, "You don't have a choice. The cave is coming down around us!"

"I don't care. Toby is like a brother to me, I'm not leaving him here."

Gishan struggled against Giselle as best he could, but Giselle managed to get him out of the room. Eventually, Gishan fought back even harder and managed to free himself. He was determined to help Toby in any way he could.

The rumbling got louder and louder and the cave began to shake. Gishan tried to run back to his friend, but the room shook so hard that the hallway began to collapse. Large boulders fell in Gishan's path. For a moment, Giselle and Gishan were blinded by darkness.

Eventually they were able to see through the dust and debris to see a large boulder blocking the doorway, "No!" Gishan cried out. "We've got to clear out this debris."

Giselle shook her head, "It's too heavy. There is nothing we can do."

"But they're trapped! They'll never be able to get out now!"

"I have a feeling they knew that."

"Don't talk like that." Gishan shouted. "They didn't intend to get trapped. They're not suicidal!"

"No, but I think they knew that something like this was going to happen. So they made us leave."

Giselle grabbed his arm once again and tugged, "Come on, there is nothing more we can do here."

The rumbling got louder around them as the cave began to shake. Gishan did the best he could to keep up with Giselle as they ran, "I don't feel right about this, it's not cool just leaving them behind."

"I know. I agree with you, but it's what they wanted."

"It's not right…"

"No, but there is nothing we can do about it, come on."

Giselle led a broken Gishan out of the cave. Once outside, they didn't get far before running into a group of commandos brandishing assault rifles. They were dressed in all black with utility belts and defensive gear. Their commander perked up as he saw them coming, "Identify yourself!"

His features were completely covered by goggles and a helmet, but he appeared to be an older man. Giselle stopped in her tracks and waved her ID, "Easy boys, Federal Agent Giselle Cortez."

"Agent Cortez, we were told to keep an eye out for you. Were you able to take out Alistair?"

"No, my friends killed him."

"Friends? What happened in there? One minute we're engaging hostile creatures out of mythology, the next minute they vanish and we're left alone here in the woods."

"Long story." Giselle replied. "I don't have time to tell it, just know that we need to get clear."

**

Meanwhile, inside the cave, Toby could see the room collapsing around them. He wasn't sure how they were going to get out now, but he knew that he wasn't ready to die yet. There had to be a way out.

Toby gave Lia'na an angry look, "Damn it, why didn't you go with them? I don't want you here when everything collapses!"

"You honor bound me to you. Did you forget what that means? I'm not going to dishonor myself by leaving your side when things get tough."

She turned and looked at the diamond, "Come on. Let's end this before it's too late."

"You know what this means, right? I have to send the diamond into the sun. It's the only way to destroy it. Once I'm done, there will be no more magic, no more enchantments, or anything. I won't be an enchanter anymore."

"Are you going to be okay with that?"

"Yeah. I just wanted you to know..."

"What, did you think I stuck with you because you were the last enchanter?" Lia'na asked as she smiled deviously. "If we make it out of here alive, I'll show you some of the most powerful magic you've ever seen."

"Deal!"

He placed his hand on the diamond and focused his mind, "Goodbye, Dad..."

As Toby's fingertips touched the diamond, his whole body began to glow. His eyes turned white and shined brightly as he focused. The energy flowed around him, creating a shell that prevented boulders from falling on them. A familiar face appeared at his side, "Thank you, son."

"Dad, what are you doing here?"

"Don't mind me. Just focus, you're almost there, just one more push…"

Lia'na felt the intense spirit energy around him and slowly walked forward. Toby turned to face her with his left hand still on the diamond. As she stared into his eyes, she placed her own hand on the diamond and stepped closer to Toby, close enough to kiss him.

As their bodies connected, her entire being began to glow the same way his did. Their eyes closed as the Lux Mundi began to vibrate. Lia'na pressed herself against Toby even tighter as she felt the power around them getting more intense, "No matter what happens here Toby, I'm with you… always… Te arshana ni."

"I love you too."

The cave continued to shake violently around them as the magic was stripped from the walls, leaving nothing to hold the temple together. Huge blocks began fall, but they didn't even notice. They held each other close as the energy absorbed them both in a magnificent explosion of light.

Outside the cave, getting as far away as they could, the group of commandos heard a loud rumbling from the moutain. They looked back to see dust and debris come spewing out of the cave as it collapsed.

"Look!" One of the soldiers yelled, pointing to Mount Jefferson's summit.

A massive white beam shot straight up out of the top of the mountain and into the sky. The beam was followed by a thundering boom that caused the ground to shake. Gishan ignored the beam as it penetrated the clouds. His eyes remained fixed on the cave, "Come on, Toby... come on buddy..."

The strength of the beam intensified, causing the whole mountain to shake. Within seconds, the cave completely collapsed. Gishan cried out as all hope of his friends getting out safely vanished, "No!"

He tried to run to the cave, but one of the commandos jumped on him, "Sir, we can't let you go down there, with all that debris falling, it's too dangerous. You'll be killed in a second."

"I have to go." Gishan replied as he struggled under the commando's grip. "My friends are down there!"

The commando looked over at Giselle with a worried expression. Giselle had tears in her eyes as she shook her head, "Not anymore, I think. No one could have survived that."

**

On the reservation in Milan, New Hampshire, Masarabi sensed the explosion of power nearby and ran outside. She looked up to see a massive white beam in the distance breach the clouds and disappear into the sky. It appeared as though whatever it was, was heading for the sun.

A content smile formed on the elder's lips, "Finally..."

**

In the Great Gulf, Giselle took a deep breath and turned around as the beam of light slowly died down, "At least they destroyed it."

"Destroyed it?" The commando leader exclaimed as he stripped off his helmet, revealing graying hair and an accusing look, "Agent Cortez, you wouldn't be referring to the Lux Mundi would you? Our orders were clear; you were to preserve it at all costs so we could then come in and confiscate it."

"Well it's gone." Giselle replied without a hint of worry or care in her voice. "Good riddance. It's better this way."

"Are you aware that you have now disobeyed a direct order from the Pentagon, and your boss?"

"Maybe, but sometimes doing the right thing is far more important than doing what is expected of me. My conscience is clear."

She knelt down next to Gishan, who still had tears in his eyes over the loss of his friends, "Come on, lover. Let's get out of here."

Gishan looked up at her and nodded. It took him a moment to get back to his feet, but once he was up, he leaned into Giselle as they slowly walked away. The commando leader called after them, "Agent Cortez, I'm still talking to you! You do know that I have to report this to the Pentagon. There will be hell to pay, and you may even face charges."

Giselle turned back and glared at him as she pulled her ID and badge out of her pocket and threw it on the ground in front of him, "Then consider this my resignation. If you want to take me in, you can find me in Natick later. Give the Pentagon my regards."

"I should take you in now."

"You can try, but I won't come quietly, and you'll most likely have to shoot me. That'll be a lot of messy paperwork in addition to what you already have. I'm leaving. If you want to stop me, you're certainly welcomed to try."

The commandos lowered their weapons as Gishan and Giselle made their way out to the clearing. Their leader knelt down and picked up Giselle's badge and wiped it off. When he finally looked up, the couple was gone.

XXVII

Gishan and Giselle made their way back to Massachusetts. Gishan insisted on going directly to Natick to make sure that his mother was okay. They hopped a bus that took them to Boston's South Station and then took a cab the rest of the way.

As the cab pulled off of Route 9 and travelled down Speen Street, a slight look of relief came over Gishan. The fighting hadn't quite reached Natick and there wasn't a lot of damage. They turned into the driveway of Gishan's mother's house and got out of the car.

As Giselle paid the driver, Gishan was startled when he heard a shrieking voice coming at him, "Gishan, my son! Thank God you're okay!"

Gishan looked up to see that his mother was alive and well. Tears of relief began to form in his eyes, but he quickly wiped them away before anyone saw them. His mother looked up at Giselle and smiled, "Giselle, good to see you honey, are you okay?"

"Yeah, I'm okay, a little shaken up, but okay."

His mother turned back to face her son, "Where the heck were you? What happened? How is your friend Toby doing?"

Gishan lowered his eyes, "We've got a lot to talk about, Mom."

*

Gishan and Giselle spent the next week at his mother's house. They told his mother everything. It was a lot for her to take in; Toby dating an elf, the boy who was like a son to her giving up his life to save everyone, and the fact that his son had been caught up in a mythological struggle to save the world. It was an unreal adventure.

Gishan and Giselle arranged a brief funeral for Toby's uncle, Jacob. As far as Gishan and his mother were concerned, Toby and Jacob had always been family to them, so they were more than happy to take care of it. Throughout the small ceremony, Gishan wondered how and if they would do the same thing for Toby at some point.

*

The following Saturday, Gishan sat down for his second helping of breakfast with Giselle. The FBI never did come to collect her, but instead offered a pardon for doing the right thing in the face of disobeying orders. Even with the pardon in hand, Giselle wasn't sure that she wanted to return to her job. Still, she was keeping an open mind none the less.

Gishan flipped three pancakes on to his plate and sat down to eat when he heard the roar of an engine outside. A confused look flashed over his face, "That sound... no it can't be."

Two more blasts of an un-muffled engine being revved echoed through his house, causing Gishan to drop his fork, "It can't be, I'd know that engine anywhere!"

He nearly knocked the table over while struggling to get to the door. Giselle looked at him oddly, "What is it, lover?"

Gishan struggled back to his feet as the engine's roar began to fade away, "There is only one bike out there that sounds that loud!"

"What?"

She knew what he was trying to say, but didn't really believe that it was possible. It had to be something else. Gishan threw open the door and ran outside.

His excitement made him miss the box sitting on the doorstep, causing him to trip and fall on the lawn. He shot up in enough time to see a blue and white Harley speeding off into the distance. Gishan began jumping up and down, waving his arms, and called out, "Toby, Toby, get your ass back here, you son of a bitch!"

Giselle picked up the box that Gishan had tripped over and opened it. Inside, something was covered by a piece of paper. She unfolded paper to reveal a note inside. It was poorly written and barely legible;

Dear Giselle,

I promised to return this to you, I am a man of my word. Don't give up on your dreams and be good to Gishan!

-Toby

Giselle put a hand to her face and gasped. Under the paper sat her Glock 30 pistol. Gishan pounded the ground swearing profusely as Giselle walked up next to him, "It was Toby... look."

She handed him the letter as the bike disappeared around the next bend. Gishan looked over the paper, ready to start crying, "Those crazy stupid sons of..."

Giselle looked down the road, "Nice work, you too. Thank you..."

As the bike rounded the corner, Toby smiled, "Did you see him?"

Lia'na nodded as she leaned back against the hand bar, "Oh yeah, he came out just as we turned. He looked pissed."

Toby revved the engine as the bike blasted down Route 9, "I knew he would be, that'll have him talking for a while."

At that moment, the bike's tires turned white and began to float off the road. As they climbed higher into the clouds, a strong feeling of exhilaration came over Lia'na, "Woo hoo!"

The sky was a beautiful blue and there wasn't a cloud to be seen as they flew high above Route 9. "What about us, ta arshana? What are we going to do now?"

Toby though about it for a moment, "There are tons of other ancient wonders out there for us to find, plenty of adventures too and..."

Toby paused as he held up the Magnifica and handed it to Lia'na, "There is more than one way to be magical."

Lia'na closed her eyes as the wind passed through her hair. They were high off the ground now, but Lia'na didn't care. She had been cured of the Ulium, and the man she loved was right there with her. The breeze smelled sweet as she filled her lungs with the clean air, "I can't wait. I'm ready to get my new life started."

"Eventually. For now though, you and I need to have some fun."

"Oh yeah? What did you have in mind?"

Toby's grin widened, "How does Hawaii sound?"

"It sounds great. Anywhere with you would be paradise."

As Toby revved the engine again, the bike's tires glowed even brighter. Instantly the bike picked up speed and rocketed towards the horizon like a comet.

"Ariel, what on Earth are you doing, that's not the end!"

"I think that's enough for now."

"But..."

"Patience Roselyn, they have other adventures ahead of them, but for now, we have our own world to worry about. Come, let's go home."

James Harrington:

James Harrington was born and raised in Boston, Massachusetts. He holds a Bachelor's in History, but also studied religion and how it related to his chosen subject matter. It was from those studies that Divinity was born.

James has written several essays and short stories, but had never gotten a full-length novel published until his big breakthrough with *Magnifica, The Last Enchanter*. Following its success, two more titles were added to the *Magnifica* series.

James currently lives in Massachusetts with his wife and son.

For more info on James and his books, please visit his Facebook page:

The Creative Works of James Harrington.

https://www.facebook.com/JamesHarringtonsMagnifica

Or his Blog page:

http://jamesharringtoncreativeworks.wordpress.com/

Check out James' other novels:

Magnifica: Tears of the Fallen
Magnifica: Gravestalker
Divinity
Damnation
Soul Siphon: Book 1 of the Vengeance Doctrine

www.ingramcontent.com/pod-product-compliance
Lightning Source LLC
Chambersburg PA
CBHW031438240626
47154CB00001B/320